P9-CIS-001

1%

The
Bawdy Basket

Also by Edward Marston

In the Nicholas Bracewell Series

In the Domesday Book Series

The
Bawdy Basket

Edward Marston

ST. MARTIN'S MINOTAUR
 NEW YORK

www.minotaurbooks.com

ISBN 0-312-28501-9

First Edition: August 2002

10   9   8   7   6   5   4   3   2   1

This one is for Judith.

These bawdy baskets be also women, and go with baskets and cap-cases on their arms, wherein they have laces, pins, needles, white inkle and round silk girdles of all colours. . . . And as they walk by the way, they often gain some money with their instrument by such as they suddenly meet withal. The upright men have good acquaintance with these, and will help and relieve them when they want. Thus they trade their lives in lewd loathsome lechery.

—Thomas Harman, *A Caveat for Common Cursitors* (1566)

The
Bawdy Basket

[PROLOGUE]

*A*s he stumbled out of the tavern into the darkness, the man was too drunk to know where he was going and too tired to get himself there. He used a wall to support himself as he tottered along. When the man reached a corner, a stranger offered a helping hand.

"Steady, my friend," he said. "Lean on me."

"Thank you, good sir."

"Where do you dwell?"

"In Turnmill Street," replied the man. "Will you take me there?"

"Gladly, my friend."

Taking his weight, the stranger led him through a maze of streets until they came to an alley that was little more than a narrow slit between the houses. The man swayed uneasily and peered into the gloom.

"Is this my home?" he asked.

"It is where you will lay your head this night."

"Thank you for your kindness. What is your name, good sir?"

"It matters not," said the stranger, easing him forward into the alley and pulling a dagger from its sheath. "Remember me by this."

He pushed him facedown on the ground. Stunned by the fall, the man hardly felt the blade of the weapon as it was thrust expertly into his back and through his heart. The stranger admired his handiwork with a smile.

"Two birds," he murmured.

[CHAPTER ONE]

A plague on this weather!" growled Laurence Firethorn, sinking down on a bench. "It will be the death of me, Nick."

Nicholas Bracewell waited until the next scene in the play was firmly under way before he glanced up from the prompt book. They were in the tiring house at the Queen's Head, the site of their inn yard theater, during a performance in front of a packed audience. Nicholas could see that Firethorn was in some distress. His eyes were dull, his breathing heavy, his sturdy frame slack from exhaustion. Playing the title role in *Hannibal* on a hot summer's afternoon was proving to be a sustained ordeal. The famous Carthaginian general had just led his army across the frozen Alps, urging them on through a blizzard that existed only in the imagination. While Firethorn and his soldiers pretended to shiver onstage, the sun beat down mercilessly and mocked their snow-covered blank verse. Clad in body armor and helmet, Firethorn felt as if he were being baked alive.

"Who *chose* this damnable play?" he complained.

"You did," said Nicholas with a quiet smile.

"I must have been mad. August calls for rustic comedies, where we can feast and frolic. Not for martial tragedies that require me to fight a battle every five minutes and roar down the walls of the enemy's fortresses."

"All goes well," noted Nicholas, keeping one eye on the performance.

"Not with me," said Firethorn, removing his helmet to wipe the perspiration from his brow with a forearm. "Look at me, Nick! I'm being roasted like a pig on a spit. Sweat comes gushing out of me from every pore. My face is a burning waterfall; my armpits are stagnant pools. There's a steaming swamp between my thighs and my pizzle lies in the middle of it like a dead lily. God's tits! How can I duel with Scipio when I've no strength to lift a sword?"

"Owen feels the heat, just as much as you."

"Which of us will expire from it first?"

"Stand by for your entrance."

"Already?" groaned Firethorn.

Nicholas raised a hand. "Wait but a moment."

"Shame on you, Nick! You're a cruel Nebuchadnezzar, sending me back into the fiery furnace." Hannibal put the gleaming helmet on again. "I'm supposed to commit suicide at the *end* of the play, not every time I step out into that flaming cauldron."

"Enter!" said Nicholas, lowering his hand.

Accompanied by four soldiers, Firethorn went storming back onstage to stamp his authority on one more scene. A small miracle occurred. Close to fatigue only a second before, the actor-manager drew on hidden reserves of energy to berate his troops and to instil fresh confidence in them for the conflict that lay ahead. Firethorn strutted with all his usual arrogance, his voice stronger than ever. The audience responded to his entry with a buzz of expectation. Everyone crammed into the galleries, or standing shoulder to shoulder in the pit, knew that they were in the presence of the finest actor in London. In the part of Hannibal, he had a role that allowed him to display all his gifts, and he did so with magisterial control. Whatever his discomfort, Firethorn did not let the spectators get the tiniest glimpse of it. Proud, fearless, and peremptory, he looked completely at ease in his armor, ignoring the mischievous rivulets that ran beneath it all over his body.

Nicholas Bracewell paid scant attention to Hannibal. He could rely on Firethorn to surge powerfully on, regardless of the weather. The actor had performed during howling gales, sudden downpours, and even a swirling snowstorm in the past. He would not be defeated by the hot embrace of summer. Where he led, others followed. In the guise of Scipio, the ebullient Welsh actor Owen Elias was also suffering, but nobody would have guessed it from his appearance. Nor did Barnaby Gill, the acknowledged clown of the company, seem troubled in any way, capering nimbly around the stage in one of his celebrated jigs as he lightened the heavy drama with comic interludes. Edmund Hoode, too, the company's actor-playwright, appeared to be in his element. Westfield's Men blossomed in the sun. When they came onstage, they actually seemed to be enjoying the sweltering heat.

There was a single exception, and it was he whom Nicholas studied with concern. Francis Quilter was faltering badly. In the important role of Hannibal's military advisor, he stumbled over lines and forgot crucial moves. At one point, he almost blundered into the mighty general. Nicholas had great sympathy for the young actor. He knew that Quilter was not upset merely by the scorching weather. The latter was distracted by private grief as well. Something had been gnawing away at him for weeks, and he could no longer contain it. His performance suffered as a consequence.

Laurence Firethorn had no compassion for the actor. He expected sterling support from his company. When he came offstage again, he was in a towering rage.

"Did you hear that idiot, Nick?" he cried, dripping with perspiration. "Did you see what he almost did out there?"

"Frank is in difficulties," said Nicholas tolerantly. "Bear with him."

"I'll do more than that if he bumps into me again. I swear that I'll run the rogue through with my sword. He's a walking liability. What ails the fellow?"

"He has something on his mind."

"He should have *Hannibal* on his mind, for that is the play we perform today. Does he expect to be *paid* for this afternoon's mistakes? Even that dolt, George Dart, has given a better account of himself. Heavens!" he exclaimed. "Frank Quilter is supposed to be my chief advisor in these wars. I'd sooner take counsel from a one-eyed baboon. The creature would be sure to remember more of his lines than Frank."

"Be patient with him," urged Nicholas.

"My patience has run dry."

"He'll rally yet."

"If he values his life, he will."

"Frank is a talented actor."

"Then where has his talent fled?"

It was a rhetorical question, because Firethorn had to enter the fray once more, and Nicholas had to give other members of the company their cues. The play rolled on with gathering force. Acutely aware of his earlier failures, Quilter made an effort to atone for them. His lines were spoken with more confidence, his movements became more controlled, and his general deportment was more appropriate to his role. Instead of garnering unintended laughs, he now earned the respect of the audience. Of more significance to him was the fact that he also retrieved a grudging approval from Firethorn. Instead of staring into eyes that blazed with accusation, Quilter saw a faint gleam of gratitude. Firethorn was impressed by the way that his colleague had markedly improved his performance. The errors vanished. As the tragedy moved into its final act, Quilter was showing his true mettle as an actor.

Nicholas watched it all from his position behind the scenes. He did not envy the actors. Discomfited by the heat himself, he could imagine how much worse it was for the others as they stepped out into the bright sunlight. There was an additional problem for them. Nicholas caught only the faintest whiff of it, but the company would have to endure the full impact. Pressed closely upon each other in the pit, hundreds of sweat-sodden, unwashed bodies gave off a fearsome stink, intensified by the bad breath of the standees and mingling with the odor of fresh manure that came from the stables. Seated in his familiar position in the gallery, Lord Westfield, the troupe's patron, was holding a pomander to his nostrils, and many of the spectators in the upper levels were sniffing nosegays or pomanders to ward off the stench from below.

Only a performance of the highest quality could make the audience forget the torrid conditions, and Westfield's Men provided it. With a revitalized Frank Quilter at his best, the play moved into its closing scenes with cumulative power. Firethorn was supreme. Having watched his military triumphs being overturned by the enemy, he felt that suicide was the only way to make a dignified exit. His final speech was truly harrowing. As the erstwhile conqueror collapsed in a heap on the ground, there was a collective sigh of pain, sorrow, and regret. It was some time before applause rang out to fill the inn yard.

All discomfort was now forgotten. Actors who had sagged in the stifling heat positively bounded back onstage to bask in the ovation. Laurence Firethorn led his troupe out with eager strides, holding a position center stage and bowing in turn to different sections of the audience. His face was now one big, broad, gracious, endearing smile. High above him, surrounded by his effete entourage, Lord Westfield discarded his pomander long enough to clap his gloved hands enthusiastically together. *Hannibal* was among his favorite plays, and he was delighted with the way in which the company that bore his name had acquitted itself. As the noisome reek rose up from the pit, he resorted to slapping his thigh with one hand while the other held the pomander in place. Heat and stink notwithstanding, it had been a remarkable performance.

Francis Quilter was relieved that it was finally over. He was a tall, slim, wiry, sharp-featured man in his twenties, with a handsome face that lent itself to comedy or tragedy with equal facility. Having discharged his duty, he was preoccupied with more serious concerns. While the others beamed and grinned at the cheering spectators, he remained detached and expressionless. He knew that he had let his fellows down badly in the earlier part of the play but hoped that he had done enough to make amends. A confrontation with Firethorn was inevitable, and there would be criticism from other quarters, as well. Barnaby Gill, in particular, would voice his displeasure at Quilter's shortcomings. So would the forthright Owen Elias. A testing time lay ahead for the young actor. The sole support would come from Nicholas Bracewell. The book holder was Quilter's one real friend in the company, the only person in whom he had confided his grim secret. With Nicholas at his side, he felt, he could face anything, even the wrath of an enraged Laurence Firethorn.

Nicholas, meanwhile, resolved to protect his friend. When the actors quit the stage at the end of their curtain call, he took Quilter aside to whisper some advice.

"Keep clear of Master Firethorn," he said.

"Is he angry with me, Nick?"

"Furious."

"He has every right to be. I was abysmal."

"You were distracted, Frank. That is all."

"I was completely lost at the start," admitted Quilter. "I gabbled the first lines that came into my head."

Nicholas gave a kind smile. "Fortunately, some of them were correct."

"Most of them were not. Master Firethorn's eyes were ablaze."

"You vexed him in the extreme."

"I thought he was going to strike me."

The whole company was crowding into the tiring house. Complaining about the heat, most of them tore off their costumes and sat down on the rough wooden benches that were arranged around the walls. Firethorn was the last to leave the stage, preening himself in front of his public before departing with a final wave. When he swept into the tiring house, his mood changed. He glared around the room.

"Where is that traitor?" he demanded.

"Here it comes," murmured Quilter, bracing himself for the onslaught.

"Where is that tongue-tied lunatic who dared to take part in my council of war? I should have killed him in the Alps and left his rotting body to feed the birds!"

"I am the clown in the company," protested Gill, waving a peevish hand, "and I was robbed of my just reward. I blame you, Laurence. You let that gibbering imbecile, Francis Quilter, run amok so wildly with his lines that he provoked more laughter than I. I'll not stand for it, do you hear?"

"Be quiet, Barnaby!"

"Not until you censure an appalling performance."

"If you wish," retorted Firethorn sharply. "You gave an appalling performance, Barnaby, and it's earned my severest censure."

"I was at my peak!" yelled Gill over the mocking jeers of the others.

"Then I would hate to see you at your worst."

"Francis should bear the brunt of your admonition—not me."

"I agree with you there, Barnaby," said Owen Elias. "I know that Frank is new to the company, but he should know the difference between an exit and an entrance by now. If I'd not pushed him off when I did, he would have been party to a debate in the Roman camp. Try to remember whose side you are on, Frank."

"I crave your pardon, Owen," said Quilter.

"We'll need more than an apology," resumed Firethorn, determined to upbraid the actor in front of his fellows. "To begin with, we need an explanation. How could an actor in whom we have placed such faith betray us so completely?"

Nicholas moved in quickly. "Before we hear his answer," he said politely, "I have some news to report. It concerns the day's takings."

"Nothing is amiss, I hope?" asked Firethorn anxiously.

"Not with regards to the money itself. The gatherers did brisk business. *Hannibal* has made a tidy profit for us this afternoon. Our efforts were richly rewarded." There was a murmur of approval from everyone. "No," he went on seriously, "the problem, I fear, is related to the landlord."

Firethorn snorted. "That death's-head! Marwood is an eternal problem."

"He is due to collect the rent from us today."

"Then pay him off and keep his hideous visage away from me."

"That will not be possible, I fear."

"Why? The varlet is not trying to raise his charges again, is he?"

"He's in no position to do so."

"Then why even bother me with the hated name of Alexander Marwood?"

"Because I bring sad tidings." Nicholas paused to make sure that everyone was listening. "The landlord is so ill that he has taken to his bed." A spontaneous cheer went up. "The rent is to be paid instead to his wife."

"Marwood, ill?" said Firethorn, rocking with laughter. "This is wonderful news, Nick. Why did you keep it from us, man? By heaven, I'll ride to church this very afternoon and pray for the continuance of his malady!"

"I'll gladly kneel beside you, Laurence," said Elias, grinning happily. "If that miserable devil is abed, we can venture into the taproom with pleasure for once."

"Am I authorized to pay Mistress Marwood?" asked Nicholas.

"Yes," replied Firethorn. "Give the money to that old gorgon and have done with it. Tell her that, if her husband has the grace to die of his disease, we'll gladly open a subscription for his coffin. And I'll be the first to dance on it."

The remark unleashed general hilarity. Alexander Marwood, the gloomy landlord of the Queen's Head, was their sworn enemy, a man who loathed the presence of actors on his premises, yet who welcomed the regular income that they brought in. At the best of times, Westfield's Men had an uneasy relationship with him and his flint-hearted wife, Sybil. If either of them were laid low by sickness, no tears would be shed in their behalf in the company. It would be seen as a welcome gift to the actors.

"This calls for a celebration!" announced Elias. "Come, lads! Let's drink to our deliverance. We've sweated enough for one day. It is time to slake our thirst."

There was immediate agreement. Everyone hurriedly changed out of costume so that they could troop off to the taproom. Nicholas took care to keep Firethorn talking so that the actor-manager's ire was deflected from Quilter. When their discussion came to an end, the room was almost deserted. By the time that Firethorn remembered the sins of his military advisor, the miscreant had slipped quietly away.

"This is your doing, Nick," decided Firethorn.

"What is?"

"This ruse to distract me so that Frank Quilter could sneak off."

"The news about the landlord's illness was important."

"That's why you saved it until now, you cunning rogue. You used it as a cloak to throw over the misdemeanors of a bad actor."

"A good actor, on a bad day," corrected Nicholas.

"I'll hear no excuses."

"Nor will I offer any. I'll simply say that Frank has learned his lesson and is duly contrite. It will never happen again. I give you my word on that."

"I want to hear the promise from his own mouth."

"You will, have no fear."

Firethorn unclipped his breastplate and tossed it aside. After wiping his face with a piece of cloth, he stared at Nicholas through narrowed lids. The anger had now gone from his voice. It was replaced by curiosity. He scratched his beard ruminatively.

"You like Frank Quilter, do you not?"

"I like him as a friend and admire him as an actor."

"There was little to admire in his performance today."

"I disagree," said Nicholas. "He may have gone astray at times, but he was very conscious of his waywardness. When he found his bearings, he sailed through the rest of the play without a single mistake. Reproach him for his faults, if you must, but give him credit for pulling himself together."

"Can the fellow be trusted, Nick?"

"Without a doubt."

"Are you sure?"

"I'd stake my life on it."

"Look to the man's history," warned Firethorn. "Before he came to us, he was a sharer with Banbury's Men, our deadly rivals. I thought that he joined us to belong to a superior company, but this afternoon's disgrace made me consider a darker motive."

"And what might that be?"

"He was planted on us with deliberation by Giles Randolph."

"Never!"

"Instead of yielding up one of their best actors, Banbury's Men were putting an enemy in our midst to wreck our best endeavors."

"That's unjust!" returned Nicholas with vehemence.

"Is it?"

"Frank Quilter is proud to be a member of Westfield's Men. It's the fulfillment of a dream. He would not willingly inflict damage on us for the world."

"Then what was he doing this afternoon?"

"His mind strayed to other things."

"What other things?"

"It's not for me to say."

"*What* other things?" repeated Firethorn, stepping in closer. "Come, Nick. I must know. I have responsibility for what happens out there on the stage. If I am to risk letting Frank play with us again, I need to understand the man and be aware of his concerns. Out with it! What caused his mind to stray?"

Nicholas glanced around the room. It was now completely empty. He could not go on shielding his friend indefinitely from Firethorn's chastisement. The best way to help Frank Quilter was to tell the truth.

Hands on his hips, Firethorn would clearly settle for nothing less. He raised a challenging eyebrow. "Well, Nick?"

"I must first swear you to secrecy. Frank does not want it noised abroad."

"I'll be as close as the grave."

"Then thus it stands," said Nicholas quietly. "Frank is sorely troubled by a problem in his family, and it preys on his mind."

Firethorn was scornful. "We all have problems in our families," he said harshly. "Look at me, for example. My wife hounds me from breakfast until bedtime, my children tax me with their incessant demands, and my servants irritate me with their stupidity. I tell you, Nick, in all honesty, there are days on which I regret that I ever surrendered my freedom and married. Here at the Queen's Head, I'm a bachelor still. Whenever I step upon that stage, I repudiate the very existence of a wife and children." Striking a pose, he made a grand gesture with his arm. "An actor should have no family."

"Frank has no choice in the matter."

"When he takes part in a play, his family should disappear."

"A disappearance is the source of his grief."

"Tell him to pattern himself on me."

"His troubles are not related to a wife and children."

"Then they are mild by comparison," boasted Firethorn. "Marriage is the high road to suffering. It's nothing but a case of wedding, bedding, and woe. What, then, irks Frank Quilter, a single man? Has his mother been robbed of her purse? Does he have a sister who has unwisely parted with her maidenhood?" His sarcasm deepened. "Or is it some more distant family catastrophe? A second cousin who has mislaid his hat, perhaps? A nephew with a speck of dust in his eye?"

"Something far worse than all these together."

"Then tell me—as long as you expect no sympathy."

"I ask for nothing but understanding," said Nicholas calmly. "The reason that Frank Quilter faltered out there this afternoon is quite simple. His father will be executed at Smithfield next week."

Francis Quilter was in a quandary. Wanting to escape to the privacy of his lodging, he felt obliged to stay at the Queen's Head in order to make peace with his fellows. If he stole away, he feared, he would only set up resentment among the others, yet if he joined them in their celebrations, he was sure to be the target for ridicule and tart comment. There was no easy way out. Having enjoyed the privileges of being a member of the company, he had to pay the penalties that were sometimes involved. Accordingly, Quilter gritted his teeth and entered the taproom. A flurry of gibes greeted his appearance.

"Look!" said Owen Elias, pointing a finger at him. "Wonder of wonders! Frank has entered through the correct door for once."

"I'll warrant that he won't remember the correct lines," observed Barnaby Gill.

"He won't even remember the title of the play."

"Or the name of the playwright," sighed Edmund Hoode. "When I wrote the tragedy of *Hannibal*, I thought I was its sole creator. This afternoon, I learned that I had a coauthor, for Frank invented new speeches every time he opened his mouth."

"What will you call the piece now, Edmund?" teased Elias with an arm around Hoode's shoulder. *"Hannibal and Quilter?"*

"Quilter and Hannibal," decided Gill. "For the former conquered the latter."

"Not with intent," said Quilter with an apologetic shrug.

"You mean that you could have ruined the play even *more?*"

"I offer a thousand pardons to you all."

Gill was dismissive. "It will take more than that to buy me off."

"My price is lower," said Elias, downing his ale in one monstrous gulp. "Fill up my tankard, Frank, and we are friends again."

"Gladly!" agreed Quilter.

"You do not need to spend your way into my good graces," said Hoode. "Though you stumbled through the first half of the play, you trotted through the rest with the grace of an Arab stallion. The final scene has never been played with more poignancy, even though I've taken your role myself on more than one occasion. Welcome to the company, Frank! We are glad to have you."

"Yes," added Elias with an affectionate chuckle. "There's no shame in what you did. None of us is perfect. We all have poor days upon the boards."

"Speak for yourself," said Gill with disdain.

"All of us except Barnaby," joked the Welshman.

"Consistency is the mark of true art."

"Is that why you have nothing *but* poor days?"

Gill's apoplectic reply was lost beneath the guffaws of his fellows. While they praised his comic skills onstage, they detested his self-glorification whenever he left it. Gill was far too arrogant and condescending. Firethorn and Elias were the only two members of the company who were able to pierce his pomposity with a verbal rapier thrust. Such moments were savored by the others. A servingman was called, and fresh ale was ordered by Quilter for his friends. The taproom was now full. Hot weather was good for business. Spectators who had sweated in the sunshine were zealous customers; their numbers swelled by the arrival of the actors. The atmosphere was convivial, the noise increasingly deafening. Quilter squeezed into a place on the oak settle between Hoode and James Ingram, one of the younger sharers. He felt accepted again. He was one of them. His mind was still preoccupied with the fate of his father, but he was grateful that he had elected to join the other actors. They were his family now.

Edmund Hoode did not linger. After finishing his drink, he made his apologies and rose to leave. Elias tried to persuade him to stay.

"Toast your success, Edmund," he urged. "*Hannibal* was a triumph."

"Thanks to my fellows," said Hoode modestly. "Plays are nothing but words on a blank page. Only actors can breathe life into them."

"You are an actor yourself, remember. You took your part."

"And I was happy with the result, Owen. But now, I must leave you."

"When the carousing has not yet begun?" asked Ingram.

"Yes, James. I have an appointment elsewhere."

"An assignation, more like," said Elias, nudging his companion. "Who is she, Edmund? Only a beautiful woman could tear you away from us. What is the divine creature called?"

Hoode smiled. "Thalia," he confessed.

"A bewitching name for a mistress."

"She occupies my brain rather than my bed, Owen," explained the playwright. "Thalia is the muse of comedy and idyllic poetry. It is to her that I fly."

Brushing aside their entreaties to stay, Hoode made his way to the door.

"Is Edmund at work on a new play?" wondered Quilter.

"Yes," replied Ingram. "He is contracted to write a number of new pieces for us each year, as well as to keep old material in repair. Truly, he is a marvel. No author in London is as prolific. Words seem to flow effortlessly from his pen."

"It's one of the reason I sought to join Westfield's Men. Your stock of plays outshines all others. Banbury's Men had no Edmund Hoode to supply fresh work of such a high standard."

Gill flicked a supercilious hand. "It has no Barnaby Gill, either."

"Then fortune has favored them," said Elias waspishly.

"I suspect that this latest play of Edmund's is something of note," said Ingram. "He has been working on it for weeks and has shunned our fellowship many times."

"What can it be that it absorbs him so completely?" wondered Quilter.

Elias looked up. "Here's the very man to tell us," he said, seeing Nicholas Bracewell pushing through the crowd. "Come, Nick. There's room on the settle for you, and George can sit on my knee."

George Dart recoiled at the suggestion, even though it was made in fun. As the smallest, youngest, and least experienced member of Westfield's Men, the assistant stagekeeper had become its familiar whipping boy. He was a willing laborer. While the actors were relaxing in the taproom, Dart had been busy. Under Nicholas's supervision, he had helped to put away the costumes and properties, and clear the stage of its scenic devices before dismantling it. The oak boards on which Hannibal had trod were put away with the barrels that had supported them. Trotting at the heels of his master, Dart had accompanied Nicholas when he paid the rent to Sybil Marwood and inquired after her husband's health. Only now could the two of them join their fellows in the taproom.

Nicholas took the place vacated by Hoode, and Dart found a corner of a bench on which he could perch. Drink was ordered for the newcomers. After the usual badinage, Elias returned to his theme.

"What is this new play that Edmund is writing for us?"

"He will not tell us, Owen," said Nicholas.

"Is it comedy, tragedy, or history?"

"A mixture of all three, from what I can gather."

"He said that Thalia was his inspiration," recalled Quilter.

"Then the drama will tilt more towards comedy."

"Has he given you no hint of its content, Nick?" asked Elias.

"None whatsoever, Owen."

"Does he have a title?"

"Of course," said Nicholas, "but he has kept it from us."

"Laurence must surely know what piece he has commissioned."

"All that Edmund will say is that it is to be his masterpiece."

"*Hannibal* could lay claim to that description," said Quilter with admiration.

Elias cackled. "Not when *you* are in the cast, Frank!"

The taunt produced more mirth. Even the hapless George Dart joined in the laughter. Nicholas was the only person to give Quilter a look of sympathy. He was pleased to see that the actor had joined the others in the taproom, knowing that he would encounter a degree of hostility. It showed that Francis Quilter had courage. He endured the latest sniggers with a philosophical smile. Attention shifted to Dart.

"Frank was not the only person at fault," said Elias, switching his gaze to the diminutive figure. "You remembered the few lines you had, George, but you were so clumsy on the stage today. You knocked over a stool, kicked over the campfire, and dropped the sword during the execution of the prisoners."

"He committed a graver sin than that," insisted Gill.

Dart was trembling. "Did I?"

"Yes, you stood between me and the audience during my jig. You obscured their view of my dancing. That was unforgivable."

"George soon corrected his error," said Nicholas defensively.

"It should never have occurred in the first place."

"Nor should the jig," goaded Elias. "It has no place in a drama of that nature."

Gill was outraged. "My dances are appropriate in *any* play."

"Not when they delay the action, Barnaby."

"They serve to heighten the suspense."

"Tragedy needs no prancing Fool to diminish its power."

"I diminish nothing, Owen. I strengthen the force of a drama."

"Yes," agreed Dart, relieved that the conversation had moved away from him. "Master Gill prances so well. It is a delight to see him."

"Thank you, George," said Gill, partially mollified.

"I am sorry if I hindered you in any way."

Elias patted his knee. "No apology is needed, George. If you obscured Barnaby's antics from the audience, you did them all a favor."

Gill rose to his feet. "That's an unpardonable slur on my genius!"

"Our only genius carries the name of Laurence Firethorn."

"A floundering apprentice beside me," said Gill, and then he flounced off.

"How easy it is to ruffle his fine feathers!" said Elias.

Hauling himself up, the Welshman sauntered off to relieve himself. James Ingram chatted to George Dart, reassuring him that his mistakes that afternoon had been only minor ones and advising him to ignore complaints from Elias and Gill. Nicholas was free to have a confidential word with Quilter.

"How do you feel now, Frank?" he asked.

"As tormented as ever."

"You were a Trojan to get through the performance today."

"A useless one, however," said Quilter sadly. "But where is Master Firethorn? I expected him to come charging in here like an angry bull to toss me on his horns."

"You've been spared that."

"How?"

"I told him something of your troubles. Don't worry," he went on quickly, seeing the alarm in Quilter's face. "He can be trusted to say nothing. Master Firethorn deserved to hear the truth. It took all the fury out of him."

"That's some relief, at least."

"It was wrong to keep it all to yourself, Frank. We share our problems here."

"I was too ashamed to share the tidings."

"Why? You told me that your father is innocent."

"No question of it, Nick."

"Then he goes to his death unjustly."

"And long before his time," said Quilter, wincing at the thought. "Father is still in his prime. It's cruel to cut a man down like that." He glanced at the others. "But you speak aright. It was folly to keep it secret from my fellows. They'll know the horrid truth soon enough."

Nicholas put a consoling hand on his arm. Ingram asked the book holder about the plays to be performed in the coming week, and all four of them began to discuss their relative merits. Elias rejoined them to add his pertinent comments. Quilter took a full part in the debate. Enthusing about plays helped to take his mind off his father's predicament. Nicholas was glad to see the frown vanish from Quilter's face at last. The actor was an intelligent critic with a persuasive manner. He was caught up in the discussion until *The Loyal Subject* was mentioned.

"I do not know the piece," he said.

"It is a wondrous drama," announced Dart, eyes widening. "One of the best that Master Hoode has ever written. We performed it at Court. Her Majesty thought that *The Loyal Subject* was magnificent."

"Every Queen relies on loyal subjects," remarked Ingram.

"What is so special about the play, George?" asked Quilter.

"It is so exciting," said Dart. "It ends with the most thrilling execution."

Elias grinned. "Why? Is Barnaby Gill beheaded? I'd pay to see that blessing."

"So would I," added Ingram.

"The death was so frightening," said Dart, "that I could not bear to look."

"Then you have never seen a real execution, George," said Elias. "You have never stood at Tyburn or Smithfield, as I have. It is an education. The best way to gauge a man's true character is to see how he bears himself at the hour of his death. Take the execution of Anne Brewen and John Parker, for instance."

"Need we dwell on such things, Owen?" said Nicholas.

"I merely wish to show George what he missed."

"And was glad to do so," said Dart.

"Anne Brewen and John Parker were lovers who plotted to murder her husband. John Brewen was a goldsmith, a blameless man whose only crime was to love his wife too much. With the help of her lover, his wife poisoned him, and he died in agony. It was only right that the murderers did likewise. Do you know how they died, George?"

Dart shook his head. "I'm not sure that I want to."

"Anne Brewen was burned to death while John Parker was hanged before her eyes. I was in the crowd when it happened," said Elias, unaware of the effect he was having on Quilter. "They were evil killers and deserved their fate. Everyone cheered to the echo when the villains went to their deaths. They were made to *suffer*."

Dart gulped, Ingram turned away in disgust, and Nicholas flashed a look of disapproval at Owen Elias. But the most dramatic response came from Quilter. As he started to retch aloud, he held a hand over his mouth and then leapt up from his seat to dash out of the taproom at full speed. The Welshman was taken aback.

"What did I say?" he wondered.

Edmund Hoode hurried through the crowded streets with his mind racing. Others might think that his plays jumped full-grown onto the page, but he knew the truth of the matter. Each new drama made huge demands on him. Days of concentration were needed before he could even force himself to pick up his goose quill; then weeks of hard, unremitting work ensued, during which he invariably lost faith in the project in hand and fell back on extensive revision of the text. Additional changes would be necessary when Laurence Firethorn read the new play, and Hoode always sought the opinion of Nicholas Bracewell, as well. Only when the piece had its premiere at the Queen's Head could he start to relax, like an exhausted mother who has given birth after an interminable labor. To someone like Hoode, the creative act was a painful and debilitating experience.

What made *The Duke of Verona* so special was that it was attended by none of the usual problems. There had been no doubts, no un-certainties, no descent into black pessimism. The physical effort of writing had not left him with his habitual pallor and bloodshot eyes. Instead of approaching each session at his table with trepidation, he could not wait to get back to work. *The Duke of Verona* filled him with an elation he had not known since he secured his first commission from Westfield's Men. It was a comedy with dark undertones and moments of wild farce. Hoode brought such enthusiasm to the play that it seemed to write itself. He was in the grip of an obsession. It made for difficulties with his fellows because he was always rushing away from them after a performance, but he knew that they would forgive him when they saw the masterpiece that he would shortly deliver. The end justified the means. Edmund Hoode would go to any lengths to finish *The Duke of Verona*.

As he strolled along, he was rehearsing the next scene in his mind, inventing speeches that would roll off the tongue, and which combined poetry with meaning in the most effective way. So preoccupied was he with the dialogue between the Duke and his intended bride that he did not realize he was being followed at a discreet distance by a well-dressed youth. When he got to his lodgings, Hoode did not toss even a casual glance over his shoulder. He simply went straight into the house, clattered up the stairs, and let himself into his room. *The Duke of Verona* awaited him, scattered across the table on dozens of sheets of parchment: patient, welcoming, and inspiring. Hoode did not hesitate. Lowering himself onto his stool, he took up his pen and sharpened it with a knife before dipping it into the inkhorn. The first bold words of the new scene dropped onto the page.

"Master Hoode!"

He did not even hear his landlady's voice outside the door.

"I have a letter for you, sir!" she called.

When there was no response, she knocked on the door before opening it.

"Excuse this interruption, Master Hoode," she said.

It was only when her shadow fell across his table that he became aware of her presence. Because she was a pleasant and amenable woman, Hoode enjoyed a warm relationship with his landlady. Understanding the nature of his work, she knew that he hated to be disturbed. He was angry that she had done so, all the more since the creative impulse was at its most urgent. Before he could scold her, however, she thrust the letter into his hands and backed away.

"The young man said that it was very important, sir," she explained, "or I would not have dared to come into your room like this."

"Young man?" he said.

"He called a moment ago. You must have heard him knock."

"I heard nothing."

"But he pounded so hard on my front door."

"When I am writing a play, I would not hear the report of a cannon. I thought that you appreciated that. Isolation is vital for a dramatist," he said pointedly. "I place myself beyond knocks on the door and missives that claim to be important."

"Of course, Master Hoode," she said penitently. "Forgive me, sir, I beg you."

Backing out of the room, she closed the door behind her as silently as she could. He was sorry that he had had to chide her, but *The Duke of Verona* had prior claims. Tossing the letter aside, he bent over his table once more, intending to resume at the point where he had stopped. But the spell had been broken. Instead of streaming from his pen, words came out haltingly. They lacked fluency and bite. Soaring poetry was now reduced to dull prose. Witty repartee was replaced by stale humor.

Hoode was too kind a man to blame it solely on his landlady. She had done only what the messenger had requested, and the letter might, after all, be important. As long as it lay unopened, it would be an irritating distraction, something that lay at the back of his mind to impede his creative endeavor. Once read, it could be cast aside. Hoode picked it up, glanced at the seal, and then inhaled the bewitching aroma of perfume that rose from the letter. When he opened it, he found himself looking at neat calligraphy. The contents were startling. His eyes widened in surprise as he read the missive. It brought him to the verge of a blush. A beatific smile settled on his face. When he read it through for the second time, his heart began to beat audibly. Hoode let out an involuntary laugh. The third reading was slower and more indulgent, giving him time to relish the honeyed phrases.

He reached for his pen, but it was not to continue work on the play. He was drafting a reply to the letter. *The Duke of Verona* was completely forgotten now.

[CHAPTER TWO]

Anne Hendrik knew him well enough to be able to gauge his moods with some precision. When he fell silent for long periods, she sensed that Nicholas Bracewell was nursing a private sorrow. If he broke that silence with inconsequential chatter, she realized that he was grieving on behalf of someone else. She had learned from experience not to probe for details. Nicholas would yield them up only when he was ready to do so. Over a frugal breakfast at her house in Bankside, he talked intermittently about the weather, the rising cost of crossing the Thames by boat, and the approach of Bartholomew Fair. She decided that he was introducing trivial subjects as a prelude to more serious conversation. Anne bided her time. The attractive widow of a Dutch hatmaker, she now ran the business, in the adjoining premises, that Jacob Hendrik had started when he first came to London as an exile. In the early days, she had taken in a lodger to defray her expenses and found, in Nicholas Bracewell, the soundest investment she had ever made. Their friendship had matured into something as close as marriage without any of the legal complications or drawbacks associated with holy matrimony. Mutual love and understanding made for a deep but unspoken commitment.

Nicholas finished his meal and pushed his platter away. He sought words to explain his behavior in recent days. Anne waited patiently.

"I feel that I owe you an apology," he said at length.

"Why?"

"My manner has been somewhat abstracted."

"So has mine, Nick," she said pleasantly. "I have been so immersed in my work of late that I have been less attentive to you. If an apology is called for, it should surely come from me."

"No, Anne. Mine is the graver fault."

"I doubt that."

"Hear me out," he asked, reaching across the table to take her hand. "Something has been troubling me, but I have been unable to confide in you because I was sworn to secrecy. The events of this afternoon absolve me of that oath."

"This afternoon? Westfield's Men perform *Mirth and Madness*, do they not?"

"Indeed, they do—but I will not be at the Queen's Head to help them."

Anne was astonished. "Where *will* you be?"

"At a more tragic performance. No mirth of any kind is involved, though there is a degree of judicial madness. I'll be at Smithfield to witness a public execution."

"An execution? What could possibly take you there?"

"Loyalty to a friend. I go but to lend support to poor Frank Quilter."

"But he should be acting onstage in Gracechurch Street."

"Not when his father plays the title role in Smithfield."

She was horrified. "His father is to be *executed*? For what crime?"

"That of murder," he replied solemnly, "though Frank is convinced of his innocence. He believes that his father has been falsely accused. Having heard the evidence, I am inclined to take the same view."

"Who was the victim?"

"A man called Vincent Webbe. He and Frank's father, Gerard Quilter, were old and bitter enemies, it seems. At a chance encounter, their tempers got the better of their common sense, and a brawl resulted. Gerard Quilter confesses as much. What he denies is that he killed Vincent Webbe during that brawl. His defense is simple. The victim was stabbed to death, yet Gerard Quilter carried no weapon about him."

"How, then, was he convicted?"

"On the word of two men who claim to have witnessed the brawl."

"Did they *see* Master Quilter wield a dagger?"

"So they avouch."

"What manner of man is Frank's father?"

"I've never met him, Anne," admitted Nicholas, "but if he is anything like his son, I take him to be honest and industrious. Gerard Quilter was a mercer in the city before he retired to the country. That argues wealth and position. Why throw it all away with the thrust of a dagger?"

"Yet he does concede that he took part in the brawl?"

"Only to protect himself. It was Vincent Webbe who struck first."

Anne now understood. Nicholas took the responsibilities of friendship seriously, and there was a double obligation in this case. Frank Quilter and he were fellows in the same company, bound together by professional ties. In helping the young actor through the ordeal of the execution, Nicholas was providing the moral support that he would have offered to any member of Westfield's Men.

"How will they cope without you, Nick?' she asked.

"Indifferently, I hope," he said with a grin, "for then they will know my true worth." His face clouded. "But it's no time for levity. The company will manage because they have done so before. Necessity is a wise teacher. Laurence Firethorn was not happy to release either of us. He did so only because *Mirth and Madness* is a play we have staged so often that it is proof against any disaster—even with George Dart holding the book in my stead."

"George Dart? I spy danger there."

"Give the lad his due, Anne. It is only when he ventures onstage that George is a menace. Behind the scenes, he is keen and conscientious. He'll not let us down."

"What of Frank Quilter?"

"Ask me when this afternoon's trial is over."

"Would it not be better for him to avoid the distress by staying away?"

"I suggested that," said Nicholas, "but he felt that it would be a betrayal of his father. Frank believes that there ought to be one person in the crowd who is aware of the condemned man's innocence."

"Two, if you include yourself."

"I do, Anne. I am not merely aiding a friend at a time of crisis. My thoughts are with Westfield's Men. Frank Quilter is a brilliant young actor. We need his talent to shine for us, and it will not do that if he is fretting about his father. That's my embassy," he explained. "To take him back to the company in the right state of mind. It's a most difficult assignment, and I'm not sure that I shall succeed."

She squeezed his hand. "If anyone can succeed, Nick, you can."

"Thank you. Am I forgiven, then?"

"There is nothing to forgive."

"I hate to keep secrets from you."

"You were forced to do so."

He nodded. "I fear that I was. I only confided in Laurence Firethorn to save Frank from his rebuke. This business has haunted Frank and sullied his work onstage."

"That is hardly surprising."

"What concerns me is how the rest of the company will respond."

"Are they aware of the situation?"

"All of London is aware of it today. It can be hidden no more."

"Westfield's Men will surely rally behind Frank."

"I hope so, Anne," he said, pulling his hand gently away, "but I have my doubts. Frank and I may believe in the innocence of his father, but will the others? All they will see is an actor whose father has faced the disgrace of a public execution. Some of that disgrace will rub off on Frank himself. He may come in for harsh treatment."

As they gathered for rehearsal at the Queen's Head in Gracechurch Street that morning, it was the sole topic of conversation. Everyone knew about the execution of Gerard Quilter, and all of them had an opinion. Barnaby Gill's was unequivocal.

"I say that he should be banned from the company!" he argued.

"Do not be so hasty," said Laurence Firethorn.

"We must not have a criminal in our ranks."

"Frank is no criminal. It's Gerard Quilter who goes to his death this day."

"Like father, like son."

"That's unfair."

"Is it, Laurence?" asked Gill, jabbing a finger at him. "It's what everyone else in the company feels. Frank Quilter is tainted. His father's crime is of so heinous a nature that Frank will never outlive it."

"Only if the man *is* guilty of the murder."

"Why else should they hang him?"

"Frank contends that his father is innocent."

"Pah!" sneered Gill. "What son will ever admit that his father is a ruthless killer? The fact remains that the man was arrested, charged, and convicted in a court of law! He must now pay the ultimate penalty, and I, for one," said Gill with emphasis, "will shed no tears for the villain."

"Do you have no sympathy for Frank?" asked Owen Elias.

"Not a jot!"

"Well, I do, Barnaby, and with good cause. When I talked about an execution in Frank's hearing the other day, I had no notion of this afternoon's event. No wonder he fled from the taproom in disgust." The Welshman shook his head sadly. "It was cruel of me to dwell on such details in front of him. My only excuse is that I did not know the truth at the time."

"None of us did, Owen," said Gill. "Except Nicholas, of course. He has been privy to the information from the start and should be sharply reprimanded for keeping it to himself."

"But he did not," confessed Firethorn. "He confided in me."

Gill was astonished. "You *knew*, Laurence?"

"Only a few days ago."

"Yet you said nothing to the rest of us?"

"I was asked to remain silent."

"To what end?" demanded Gill. "The news should have been divulged to us. By delaying it, all you did was to increase the force of the blow. The company is in a state of shock to learn that it has a killer in its midst."

"The son of a putative killer."

"He must bear the sins of his father."

"Not if the man is falsely accused."

"The law does not make mistakes."

"I hate to say it," added Elias, "but I agree with Barnaby for once. From all accounts, the evidence against the prisoner was clear and decisive. Two witnesses saw him stab the victim repeatedly. Gerard Quilter deserves to die."

"And his son deserves to be expelled," said Gill.

"I would not go that far, Barnaby."

"No more would I," said Firethorn. "Whatever the rights and wrongs of the case, Frank Quilter is a valuable member of the company. I wish to keep him with us."

Gill was adamant. "Impossible!"

"Give him the benefit of the doubt."

"He'll corrupt the whole lot of us."

"Enough of such wild talk!" snapped Firethorn.

"It's not wild, Laurence," said Elias with a sigh. "What Barnaby says is what most of our fellows think. Actors are superstitious by nature, as you well know. They will feel uneasy at the idea of playing alongside a man with Frank's pedigree."

"As an actor, his pedigree is almost faultless."

"We judge him first as a man."

"Owen speaks well," said Gill. "Put a rotten apple in the barrel, and the rest will soon decay. There's no remedy for it, Laurence. Frank must go forthwith."

Firethorn stiffened. "That's a decision that only I will make."

"It has already been made by the company."

"I fear that it has," admitted Elias. "There's a lot of bad feeling against Frank Quilter. I do not share it myself, but I would be a liar if I denied that it was there."

Firethorn scratched his beard. Accustomed to dominating his company, he hated to be thrown on the defensive, especially when it was Barnaby Gill who was gaining a temporary advantage over him. When he had first learned of the execution, he had been shaken by the intelligence, afraid of the consequences of keeping Quilter in the company. What reassured him was the ardor with which Nicholas Bracewell had proclaimed the innocence of the condemned man. He was tempted to accept that Gerard Quilter might, after all, be the victim of rough justice. Having taken soundings from the other actors, however, he was beginning to revise that opinion. Disapproval of Frank Quilter was widespread and vocal. Even the more compassionate members of the troupe, like Owen Elias and James Ingram, believed in the guilt of the prisoner. Unable to make up his mind or to subdue Gill in open debate, Firethorn did what he always did in such circumstances. He summoned his book holder.

"Nick, dear heart!" he called. "A word in your ear!"

"It is Nicholas who should have whispered a word in *our* ear," complained Gill.

"He had his reasons," said Elias.

Nicholas strolled across to the three men. They were standing in the innyard while their makeshift stage was being erected. Unable to attend during the performance itself, the book holder was there for the morning rehearsal to shepherd George Dart through the intricacies of his role as a substitute. When he saw the expressions on their faces, Nicholas knew what his fellows had been talking about.

"Tell them what you told me, Nick," encouraged Firethorn.

Gill was petulant. "We've heard enough already, and it comes far too late."

"The company is restive," said Elias gently. "We need guidance."

"Then do not look for it from Nicholas," said Gill with a dismissive gesture. "He is but a hired man. The decision must be left to the sharers."

"What decision?" asked Nicholas.

"The eviction of Frank Quilter from Westfield's Men."

"But there's no question of that. Frank is contracted to the company. You cannot rescind a legal document in a fit of pique."

Gill was insulted. "This is no fit of pique, I promise you."

"Nor is it a considered judgment, Barnaby," said Firethorn.

"I speak on behalf of the majority."

"Then you speak in ignorance," said Nicholas civilly. "If you knew the full facts of the case, you would not be so ungenerous. Nor would you show such disloyalty to one of your own. Frank Quilter has been a great asset to Westfield's Men. We are fortunate to number him in our company."

"He was no great asset to us in *Hannibal*," said Gill spitefully.

"True enough," conceded Firethorn.

"Frank was sorely troubled," Nicholas reminded them. "Who would not be with something as grievous as this hanging over him?"

"Had he forewarned us, Nick," said Elias, "we might have understood his plight."

"Yes," insisted Gill. "And thrown him out before he did even more damage."

"That will never happen," said Nicholas levelly.

"It will, if I have my way. Most of the sharers are of the same mind."

Nicholas was hurt. "I cannot believe *you* side with them, Owen."

"I do not," affirmed Elias. "I deplore what his father did, Nick, but I would not oust Frank on that account. If we were all responsible for our father's mistakes, none of us would escape whipping."

"Murder is more than a mistake!" protested Gill.

"Granted," said Nicholas. "But I've yet to hear convincing evidence of Gerard Quilter's guilt. From what I know of him, he is simply not capable of murder."

Firethorn was resigned. "Guilty or not, he faces execution this afternoon."

"And we suffer the consequences," said Gill, "as long as his son remains."

"He must remain," Nicholas contended. Turning to Firethorn, he saw the doubt in the latter's face. "You support Frank to the hilt, surely?"

"I would like to, Nick," said Firethorn quietly, "but, in truth, I find it difficult to do so. And I do not want a revolt on my hands. I can lead only where others will follow. When all is said and done, the company is greater than any individual actor."

"Westfield's Men have a reputation for helping each other."

"Not when someone commits such a crime," said Gill.

"Frank's only crime is to be the son of Gerard Quilter."

"That is enough, more than enough."

"No," replied Nicholas, looking to Firethorn once more. "Do you set yourselves up as judge and jury, yet give Frank no chance to defend himself?"

"We'll hear him out, naturally," said Firethorn.

Elias gave a nod. "It's the least that we could do."

"Of course," said Gill with exaggerated sweetness. "We'll give him a fair hearing first, then we'll kick him out of the company for good."

"What of his contract?" asked Nicholas.

"This afternoon's events revoke it completely."

"I do not agree with you there, Barnaby," said Firethorn ruefully. "Broken contracts are meat and drink to lawyers. The last thing we must do is to invite litigation. Much as I hate to say this, Nick," he went on, turning to the book holder, "the best way forward may be to persuade Frank to withdraw from the troupe of his own free will. Would you undertake that task?"

"No," said Nicholas firmly.

"We demand it of you!" cried Gill.

"My answer remains the same."

"Nick knows that he would be wasting his time," reasoned Elias. "Frank Quilter has his pride. He'll not slink away from the company with his tail between his legs. The only way to get rid of him is to dismiss him summarily."

"Then that is what we must do," said Gill. "Do you not see that, Laurence?"

Firethorn shifted his feet. Circumstances had conspired to put him in the most awkward position. It was ironic. Westfield's Men had been enjoying an unprecedented success. Fine weather had brought in large audiences on a daily basis. Their repertoire was wide and received with acclaim. The advent of Frank Quilter had both strengthened them and weakened their hated rivals. Edmund Hoode was on the verge of delivering what he believed to be his finest drama. Topping it all was the news that Alexander Marwood, the melancholy landlord, was confined to his bed. Westfield's Men had never known such good fortune. Yet, at the very moment of triumph, their equilibrium was threatened. The actions of someone outside the company had shaken them to the core. As long as one particular actor remained, Firethorn's beloved troupe was at risk. Nicholas Bracewell was a dear and respected friend of his, but Firethorn had to disappoint him for once. He took a deep breath.

"I see no future for Frank Quilter in the company," he announced.

Gill beamed. "Common sense wins the day at last!"

"I'd be sorry to part with Frank on this account," said Elias.

"So would I," declared Nicholas, "but the decision lies not with me. On one issue, however, I do have a deciding voice, and that is with regard to my own future. Dispatch Frank Quilter, if you must," he said, straightening his shoulders, "but bear this in mind. If *he* goes, you will need to replace me, as well."

She was there. Edmund Hoode sensed it the moment that he stepped out onstage. The anonymous lady who had written to him in praise of his work was somewhere up in the galleries. Whenever he could, he let his gaze scan the faces above him, trying to find that special countenance that looked down on him with such favor. It was not only Hoode's plays that had been hailed by his correspondent. She had lauded his performances as an actor, as well. When he read between the beautifully written lines of her letter, he saw that she was really enamored of him. Without even meeting the lady, Hoode had made a conquest. Satisfying to any man, it was especially exciting for him because he so rarely aroused such uncompromising love in a woman. The moon-faced dramatist with receding hair was a veteran of doomed romances. Desire on his part was always urgent yet seldom fulfilled. Unrequited love was his usual suit. It was almost as if he sought out unattainable ladies in order to be punished by their rejection. Now, at last, against all the odds, through no effort of his own, someone had picked him out. The elegance of her hand and the scented aroma of her missive spoke highly of the sender. Clearly, she was a person of discernment.

Inspired by the thought that she was watching him, Hoode excelled himself. He entered with sprightly step, delivered his lines with brimming confidence, and brought out every aspect of his character. His performance was all the more striking because of the dross that surrounded it. *Mirth and Madness* was a standard play from their repertoire, a lively comedy that was shot through with moments of high farce. Since the action took place in midsummer, it seemed an ideal choice for a hot afternoon in August, replete, as it was, with songs and dances, and blissfully free from the technical problems associated with *Hannibal.* As a piece of theater, it had never failed them. This time it was different. Word of their unfortunate link with a public execution had upset the company deeply, but the news about Nicholas Bracewell was even more distressing. He was one of the mainstays of Westfield's Men. His resourcefulness had saved them from disaster—even extinction—on more than one occasion. The thought that he might desert the troupe caused fear and panic to spread.

Even the acknowledged star of the company wavered. Laurence Firethorn took the leading role with a distinct lack of enthusiasm. His mind was patently not on the play. Where he could usually reap a whole harvest of laughter, he now barely managed to arouse no more than an occasional giggle. Owen Elias, too, was a shadow of himself, booming away halfheartedly as if he had no real faith in the part that he was taking. Most of the actors were similarly dispirited, moving through the play like sleepwalkers, unable to shake off their apprehensions about their revered book holder. Barnaby Gill, by contrast, was superb. Untroubled by the impending loss of Nicholas Bracewell, he filled the gaps left by the others and seized every opportunity to dazzle. His three comic songs and four hilarious jigs allowed him to monopolize the laughter. Along with Hoode, he injected some zest into the play, and the spectators were duly appreciative. To Firethorn's disgust, it was Gill and Hoode who received most applause when they took their bows.

The clapping was sustained, the cheers loud. Edmund Hoode heard none of it. His eyes were roving the galleries in search of his mystery correspondent. He was certain that she was there because he could feel her gaze upon him like rays of sunlight. His own gaze went swiftly along the rows of smiling faces. Handsome gallants and pretty ladies were there in profusion, but he could not pick her out on the crowded benches. The important thing, he told himself, was that she could see him and she had watched him perform on a day when he was head and shoulders above most of his fellows. For the first time in his life, he had even outshone Laurence Firethorn. Somewhere up there was the lady who made it all possible, the spur to his talent, the beat of his heart. His face glowed with happiness. The impossible had happened. He had fallen in love with someone whom he had never even seen.

As the applause weakened, the actors began to quit the stage. Hoode could not linger. He was about to give up his search and leave when she finally revealed herself. She was seated in the middle of the upper gallery, directly in front of him and with a perfect view of the stage. Rising to her feet, she raised a gloved hand to give him a little wave of congratulation. Hoode trembled involuntarily. She was rather older than he had imagined, and more matronly in appearance, but that did not matter. His admirer was a gorgeous lady with dark hair curling out from beneath her hat and a smile that ignited her whole face. Wearing a dress in the Spanish fashion, she seemed to him the epitome of all that was good in womanhood. He had known younger, daintier, more vivacious ladies in his time, but this one had a quality that they had all lacked. She was his.

[31]

When he backed his way offstage, Hoode was still in a dream. His mind was filled to bursting with the vision of loveliness he had just seen. It was only when he collided with George Dart that he realized he was in the tiring house.

"Steady, Master Hoode!" said Dart in alarm.

"Oh, forgive me, George. My thoughts were elsewhere."

"It was so for most of the company during the play, for their thoughts were neither on mirth nor madness. There were times when I wondered if I was holding the correct book. The actors wandered so."

Dart was immensely proud that he had been chosen as Nicholas Bracewell's deputy. While the others mocked him for his misfortunes onstage, the book holder showed tolerance towards him. He knew that the more responsibility Dart was given behind the scenes, the better he discharged it. Aided by Thomas Skillen, the ancient stage-keeper, who stood at his side ready to box his ears in the event of a mistake, Dart had been remarkably efficient in his new role. He knew *Mirth and Madness* well and had watched Nicholas in action enough times to pick up hints from him. While many others floundered on-stage, Dart held his nerve. It was only when the play was over that he let his anxieties show.

"I never thought to get through the afternoon," he confessed.

"You did well, George."

"Did I?"

"Yes," said Hoode. "You held the tiller with a steady hand."

"It did not feel very steady, Master Hoode."

"Nick Bracewell would have been proud of you."

"There's no higher praise than that." His face puckered with concern. "He is a prince of his craft. Westfield's Men would be lost without him."

"That's why we will never let him go."

"But he's threatened to leave us. Have you not heard the news?"

Hoode came out of his daze. "News?"

"There is a danger that we may lose Nicholas," said Dart, biting his lip. "Many people are calling for Master Quilter to be ousted from the company. If he goes, Nicholas has warned, then we will have lost our book holder, as well."

"Nick Bracewell said *that*?"

Hoode was dumbfounded. He had heard the rumors earlier in the day but had been far too preoccupied take them in. If someone as lowly as George Dart could report the ultimatum, then it must have a basis in truth. Hoode shuddered. Nicholas Bracewell was much more to him than a crucial member of the company. He was a close friend of the playwright's, more reliable than Laurence Firethorn and far less critical than Owen Elias. The one person to whom Hoode could turn in the emergencies that seemed to litter his life was the book holder.

Nicholas was also the only man in whom he confided details of his private life, and since that had taken such a delightful turn, he needed someone to listen to the tale of his good fortune. Hoode would sooner surrender a limb than lose the companionship of Nicholas Bracewell. The consequences for Westfield's Men were unthinkable. The playwright resolved to raise the matter instantly with Laurence Firethorn, who was sitting gloomily on a bench, contemplating the defects of his performance that afternoon. Hoode walked towards him. Before he could reach the actor-manager, however, he was intercepted by a shamefaced James Ingram.

"You came to our rescue out there, Edmund," he said.

"Did I?"

"We gave a poor account of ourselves this afternoon. But for you and Barnaby, *Mirth and Madness* could more properly have been called *Misery and Badness*. We betrayed the play by being too full of self-affairs. Thank you for helping to save our reputation. You were heroic."

"I gave of my best, James, that is all."

"It was more than the rest of us managed to do."

"I felt inspired today."

"We were too jaded to follow your example."

Patting him on the shoulder, Ingram moved away. His place was immediately taken by a servant who worked at the Queen's Head. The lad blinked at Hoode for a moment and then handed him a letter.

"I was asked to deliver this, sir," he said.

"By whom?" The question became irrelevant when Hoode glanced at the handwriting. It was from her. "Thank you, thank you," he mumbled.

While the boy ran off, Hoode retreated to a corner of the room so that he could read the letter. It contained only one sentence, but it was enough to make his head spin. He almost swooned with delight. The first missive had been unsigned, but this one had the tantalizing initial of *A*. He speculated on what her name might be. Adele? Araminta? Alice? Arabella? Anne? Audrey? Antonia? Unable to select the correct name, he decided that *A* must stand for *angel,* for that is what he felt she was, descending from heaven to bring him unexpected joy. The letter was a gift from God. All else fled from his mind. When the firm hand of Laurence Firethorn fell on his shoulder, he hardly felt it.

"We owe you a debt of gratitude, Edmund," said Firethorn. "Thank you."

Hoode looked at him. "For what?"

"The services you rendered the company this afternoon."

"Barnaby was the real savior."

"He did no more than he always does," said Firethorn irritably. "Prancing and pulling faces is the height of his art. But you lifted yourself to a higher plane, Edmund. None of us could rival you."

Ordinarily, Hoode would have lapped up the congratulations. They rarely came from such a source. A vain man, Firethorn spent more time in boasting about his own theatrical triumphs than in praising the work of others. He believed that simply by allowing other actors to appear beside him onstage, he was conferring tacit approval on them. They deserved no more encouragement. To admit that someone actually gave a superior performance to his was a unique concession. Yet Hoode was unable to enjoy it. He was still caught up in the mood of exhilaration. Hoode would listen to praise from only one source. Her letter was warm in his hand.

"Will you stay to celebrate with us in the taproom, Edmund?"

"No, Laurence," he replied. "I must away."

"That's dedication indeed! I'll not try to keep you from it," said Firethorn. "Once it is finished, the whole company will be the beneficiaries. Then they will understand why you've scurried off alone each day." He nudged Hoode. "How goes it?"

"Very well."

"Are you pleased with the results?"

"Extremely pleased."

"When do we get to view this masterpiece?"

"I've not had that privilege myself yet, Laurence."

Firethorn gaped. "But you have been slaving at it for several weeks now."

"Have I?"

"You know that you have, Edmund. You have devoted every waking hour to it. Though we missed your company, we admired your sense of purpose. So," he said, whispering into Hoode's ear. "Where is it?"

"What?"

"The work of art you are rushing off to finish. The new play, man, the new play!"

Hoode stared at him with blank incomprehension.

"Play?" he said at length. "What play?"

Entertainment of a different kind was on offer at Smithfield that afternoon, and it drew a more ghoulish audience. Spectators at the city's playhouses had gone to be moved by counterfeit deaths and fake horrors. Those who congregated at Smithfield wanted no deceit. They came in search of the real thing. Nicholas Bracewell and Francis Quilter were part of a milling crowd. Renowned for centuries for its horse-market, the grassy acres that "Smoothfield," as it had been called, comprised were redolent with a grim history. It had been a place of public execution for over four hundred years. Countless villains had been put to death before the eyes of the commonalty. Most were hanged from the gallows that stood between the horse-pool and the wells, but, in the reign of Henry VIII, Tyburn became the regular site for executions. Smithfield, however, was not wholly discarded. At the command of Mary Tudor, over two hundred martyrs were burned at the stake there, and it continued to be used on certain occasions. Gerard Quilter was unfortunate enough to be singled out for one of those occasions.

Nicholas was there in a supportive capacity. His presence was vital. Quilter was so tense and queasy that he seemed about to keel over at any moment. Both men tried to shut their ears to the foul language and gruesome anticipation they could hear all around them. When his friend rocked slightly, Nicholas steadied him with a hand.

"You did not need to put yourself through this, Frank," he said.

"My ordeal is nothing beside that of my father."

"Remember him as he was, not as you will see him today."

"He will expect me to be here, Nick."

"Yet he will never observe you in this crowd."

"Father will *know*," asserted Quilter. "If there were ten times this number here, he would be keenly aware of my absence. I'll not let him down in his hour of need." He forced a smile of gratitude. "I know what it cost you to be here with me today, Nick. It's a favor I'll not easily forget."

"It was the least I could do, Frank."

"Nobody else in the company volunteered to take on the office."

"Westfield's Men had a play to stage."

"So did you."

"Your need was greater."

"The others did not think so."

"There was a lot of sympathy for you, Frank."

"But much more resentment, I'll warrant. Is it not so? I bear the name of a brutal killer, that is what they believe. They'll want no part of Frank Quilter after this. And who can blame them? In their eyes, I'm stained with the blood of the victim."

"Only because they do not know the truth."

"How can we persuade them?"

Nicholas's reply was lost beneath a roar of approval as the crowd welcomed the condemned prisoners. Gerard Quilter would not die alone. Flanked by armed riders, two carts were pulled along by sweating horses through the mass of people. Cruel jeers and vile taunts filled the air. Arms pinioned, Gerard Quilter was in the first of the carts, standing up with the hangman's assistant beside him. Nicholas saw the family likeness at once. The father had the son's handsome face and dignified bearing. Even in his dire distress, Gerard Quilter contrived to keep his back straight and his chin up. He was coping with the grisly situation by drawing on his faith, praying to God to help him through the ordeal that lay ahead and asking that his reputation would one day be vindicated. That was his only source of comfort. Frank, his only son, would be there to witness his humiliation. His father was ashamed to be seen by him in such a condition. All that he could hope was that his son was so revolted by the hideous spectacle that he would not rest until the family name was cleansed.

Nicholas was impressed by the way that Gerard Quilter held himself. There was no hint of dignity in the following cart. Jane Gullet, a snarling virago, was hurling abuse at the crowd and ducking to avoid the ripe fruit that was thrown at her from all sides. Convicted of witchcraft, she was sentenced to burn for using her black arts against her husband, an old man who had died, it was alleged, as a result of a spell put upon him. The poison she put in his food was the more likely cause of his death, but the crowd would not be deprived of their witch. What they saw was no rebellious wife. Instead, they viewed a venomous hag with a vicious tongue from which a stream of imprecations flowed. The only fit place for her was among the flames. Had Gerard Quilter been hanged alone, he would have been taken to the gallows at Tyburn. Since he shared the day of execution with Jane Gullet, it was decided to dispatch both of them at the same venue. It was an added humiliation for him. As a condemned murderer, Quilter was attracting enough opprobrium. Partnered with the feral old woman, he looked as if he was her confederate, an accessory to the poisoning of her husband and a willing participant in the evils of witchcraft.

As the carts trundled towards the gallows, some of the spectators were not satisfied with flinging taunts or tossing missiles. One man clambered up beside the prisoner in the first cart and tried to belabor him. Nicholas had to restrain Quilter from trying to go to his father's assistance. It was, in any case, a futile urge. Quilter could never have barged through the press. Besides, his father's attacker was quickly overpowered and hustled away. Quilter was shaking with anger.

"Why do they goad him so?" he asked. "Is he not suffering enough?"

"Turn your head away," advised Nicholas.

"From my own father? I would not do that even if they tear him to pieces with their bare hands. I want to see everything, Nick. Each remembered detail will fire my need for vengeance."

"Against whom?"

A second question went unanswered as a fresh roar went up. Hauled from her cart, Jane Gullet was dragged towards a pile of faggots and tied to the post that stood in the middle of them. As the crowd spat and yelled, she replied with curses and dark laughter. On the gallows nearby was a more controlled spectacle. Helped up the steps by the hangman's assistant, Gerard Quilter was met by a chaplain who asked him to repent his crime. Nicholas did not hear the reply in the tumult, but he guessed its nature by the way that the prisoner bore himself. There was no admission of guilt, no sense of final capitulation. Head held high, Gerard Quilter was a visible symbol of the innocence that he professed. His son was duly proud of him.

Nicholas did not watch the burning or the hanging. Public executions were anathema to him. They brought back unhappy memories of his time at sea, sailing with Drake on his circumnavigation of the world. Nameless cruelties had been inflicted during the voyage. Nicholas recalled only too well the occasions when he was forced to witness executions aboard the *Golden Hind*. Even if men were guilty of terrible crimes, he took no pleasure in the sight of their deaths. When a man was innocent—as he believed Gerard Quilter to be—he could not bear to look. Alone in the crowd, he averted his eyes. Others watched avidly, cheering as the noose was put around one prisoner's neck and whipping themselves into a frenzy when the faggots were lighted beneath the other.

Francis Quilter was on the verge of collapse. There were two tiny consolations for him. The hangman knew his trade. When the trap was opened and the body plunged, the prisoner's neck was broken instantly. There was no lingering death. Gerard Quilter had been spared any additional agony. Divine intervention seemed to be responsible for the second consolation. A gust of wind came out of nowhere to fan the flames of the fire and to send the smoke so thickly across the gallows that it obscured the hanged man. Jane Gullet became the focus for attention, howling in anguish and defying the crowd to the last. Only when she was consumed by the flames did the collective hysteria start to abate.

Taking his friend by the arm, Nicholas led him away.

"You have seen enough, Frank," he said.

"They're no better than animals," muttered Quilter, gazing around. "What sort of people enjoy such horrors? And why must they be made public?"

"The authorities believe that they are setting an example. Each victim who goes to his grave in such an appalling way stands as a warning to others."

"But why hang my father when they are burning a witch?"

"It was a heartless decision."

"He did not belong in the company of that repulsive creature."

"Neither of them deserved the hatred and ridicule they provoked."

"Father was innocent, Nick!" urged Quilter, bunching a fist to strike the palm of his other hand. "What we saw today was nothing short of judicial murder."

They fell silent and walked swiftly away. Pleased with the entertainment, the crowd was now dispersing with grim satisfaction. Nicholas hoped that his friend did not hear some of the bloodthirsty comments that came from the lips of other spectators. One woman complained bitterly that the hanging had been over too quickly, and that they had been cheated of the victim's frantic twitches as he choked to death. As soon as they got clear of Smithfield and its denizens, Nicholas guided his friend towards a tavern. When his companion bought him a tankard of ale, Quilter took a long sip before speaking.

"This must be avenged, Nick," he said firmly.

"If your father did not kill Vincent Webbe, then someone else did. The only way to clear the family name is to find the real murderer."

"It will be my mission in life."

"Where will you start?"

"With the two men who bore false witness against my father."

"Count on me if you need help, Frank."

Quilter was touched. "You have gone well beyond the bounds of friendship, as it is," he said. "It would be unfair of me to burden you any further."

"A shared load would be lighter for both of us."

"No, Nick. Your first obligation is to Westfield's Men. They will have missed you badly this afternoon. And why? Because you chose to bear me company on the worst day of my life." He gave a weary smile. "Laurence Firethorn would not spare you again."

"He is not my keeper," said Nicholas.

Quilter became wistful. "Until today, he was my idol, the actor whom I admire most in the world and on whom I try to pattern myself. Not anymore, alas," he sighed. "How eager will he be to have me beside him after *this*?"

"You have a contract with the company, Frank."

"I have violated its terms already by missing a performance. And because I am the son of Gerard Quilter, I have probably endangered the whole document. You were at the rehearsal this morning, Nick," he said. "What was the general feeling?"

"There was much uncertainty," replied Nicholas tactfully.

"Do not hide the truth to spare my feelings. I can imagine the harsh words that were spoken against me by some. They want me out, do they not?"

"One or two, perhaps."

"What of Laurence Firethorn?"

Nicholas shrugged. "He feels the pressure from the others."

"In other words, he is against me, as well. Then my cause is truly doomed."

"No, Frank."

"I would hate to lose my place among Westfield's Men."

"Nor shall you," said Nicholas.

"I've brought shame to the company, or so it will be seen. I'll be an outcast. What is to stop them from expelling me?"

"The fear that they will lose more than a good actor."

"What do you mean?"

"If you are forced to leave," said Nicholas, "then I have refused to stay."

Quilter was dismayed. "But you are the very essence of Westfield's Men."

"I hope that others share that view."

"No, Nick. I cannot allow this. It's too great a sacrifice. I'll fight to hold my place in the company and will go reluctantly, if I fail. But your own future must never be conditional on mine. If I'm to drown, I'll not take you down with me."

"It may not come to that, Frank. Hot words were spoken at the Queen's Head this morning. When tempers have cooled, our fellows may talk with more sense. They should certainly learn to show more loyalty to one of their number."

"You've enough loyalty for all of them."

"I believe in you, Frank—and in your father's innocence."

"How can we convince the others?"

"By doing as you say. Vindicate his reputation, and Westfield's Men will be only too keen to woo us back into their ranks."

"No," said Quilter, shaking his head. "I'll not be the cause of your departure, Nick. Whatever happens, you must stay. I need one friend in the company."

Nicholas pondered. "Then there may be a middle way," he said at length.

"Betwixt what?"

"Retention and expulsion. After the events at Smithfield this afternoon, a black cloud hangs over the company. I'd be misleading you if I said that you would be welcomed back into the fold. Try to hold them to the contract," he went on, "and they might still find a way to eject you. But if you sue for leave of absence, you will be free to conduct your investigation and Westfield's Men will be spared much embarrassment. Will this content you?"

"It will," said Quilter eagerly. "That way, both parties are satisfied."

"Let me put it to Laurence Firethorn."

"Do not forget to mention the prime benefit. Harp on that, Nick."

"On what?"

"Westfield's Men will not only be getting rid of me at a time when I might cause them some unease," said Quilter. "They will also have Nicholas Bracewell back at the helm. It will be the finest bargain they ever struck."

[CHAPTER THREE]

Margery Firethorn was a motherly woman of generous proportions, with wide hips, a thickening waist, and a surging bosom. As befitted the wife of a famous actor, she had a decidedly theatrical air herself and, in the heat of argument, could match her husband for sheer power, strutting and ranting to such effect that she might have been treading the boards at the Queen's Head before a large audience. In point of fact, Laurence Firethorn was the sole spectator of her towering rages, stirring performances that he would not inflict on any man, however much he hated him, and which, in the interests of domestic harmony, he did his best to avoid at all costs.

Still handsome, and with an appetite for pleasure equal to his own, Margery was a loyal, long-suffering wife who ran their home in Shoreditch with bustling efficiency, brought up their children in a Christian manner, nurtured the company's apprentices, and coped with the multiple problems of sharing her life with the wayward genius who led Westfield's Men. Those unwise enough to cross Margery felt the lacerating sharpness of her tongue, but there was one person who invariably brought out her softer side. When he called at the house that evening, she wrapped him in a warm embrace.

"Nicholas!" she said with delight. "What brings you to Old Street?"

"The pleasure of seeing you, Margery," he said gallantly.

"Fetch yourself in. Laurence did not tell me that you were expected."

"I called in hope of a private word with him."

"Then your arrival is timely. He has just returned home."

Closing the door behind her, she led Nicholas Bracewell into the parlor with a girlish giggle of delight. Firethorn was in parental mood for once, balancing a son on each knee while one of them read a passage from the Bible. When he saw his visitor, he ruffled the boys' hair, told them that their reading was improving, and then sent both lads on their way. Margery followed them into the kitchen to get some refreshments. Firethorn waved Nicholas to a chair and then sat on the edge of his own.

"Thank heaven!" he said. "I need you mightily, Nick."

"How did the play fare this afternoon?"

"It was a disgrace. Owen Elias blundered around the stage, James Ingram forgot more lines than he remembered, and I was worse than the pair of them put together. The rest of the company was woefully slothful. I tell you, Nick," he continued, rolling his eyes, "I was ashamed to put such a half-baked dish before an audience. The only person who distinguished himself was Edmund Hoode."

"What of George Dart?"

"A poor substitute for Nicholas Bracewell, but the lad worked well."

"I knew that he would."

"*Mirth and Madness* was a foolish choice," said Firethorn, sitting back in his chair. "No man can play comedy with a heavy heart."

"It sounds as if Edmund contrived to do so."

"We'll come to him in a moment, Nick. First, tell me your news."

"It was as frightful as you would expect," said Nicholas. "I hope I do not have to see such pitiful sights again, or hear such obscene taunts from a crowd."

"We were the ones deserving of obscene taunts today."

"They would have been mild beside the scorn and derision at Smithfield."

Nicholas gave him a brief account of the executions, omitting some of the more gory aspects and playing down the effect on him and on

Francis Quilter. Stroking his beard with the backs of his fingers, Firethorn listened attentively. When his visitor had finished, his host heaved a deep sigh.

"You and Frank were not the only ones to witness an execution today," he confessed. "Our audience was present at one, as well. *Mirth and Madness* was butchered to death by Westfield's Men. I'll warrant that you can guess why."

"Unease about Frank's position in the company?"

"That was only a minor cause, Nick. This afternoon's disaster arose mainly from another source. It concerns the future of our book holder." A pleading note came into his voice. "You surely cannot mean to leave us."

"I stand by my word. If Frank is evicted, I go with him."

"But where would the company be without Nicholas Bracewell?"

Margery came sailing in from the kitchen with a tray that bore two cups of Canary wine and some honey cakes. She arrived in time to catch her husband's last remark, and it put an expression of disbelief on her face.

"Westfield's Men without Nicholas?" she cried. "That would be like the River Thames without water—empty and meaningless. What's all this talk of losing Nicholas?"

"A mere jest, my love," said Firethorn, patting her affectionately on the rump. "It was in bad taste, and I withdraw it forthwith."

"I should hope so, Laurence," she warned, putting the tray on the table. "When you find a jewel among men, you do not throw him heedlessly away. Hold on to your book holder with both hands, do you hear? By heavens!" she exclaimed, face reddening with indignation. "The very notion makes every part about me quiver. I'll not stand for it. Let me be blunt, Laurence. Lose Nicholas and you lose my love. It is as simple as that."

She handed them a cup of wine each and then pressed a honey cake upon Nicholas while studiously ignoring her husband. Tossing her head to indicate her displeasure, she swept out of the room. Firethorn took a long sip of wine.

"You see my dilemma, Nick," he asked. "If you desert us, the marital bed will turn to ice. Can you not see what harm you will bring to this house?"

"Not of my own choosing."

"What Margery says is what the rest of the company believe. Except for Barnaby, of course," he added, "but his voice will always dissent. You are our guardian angel. When they heard that you might be leaving us, our fellows were stricken with remorse. The results were on display this afternoon at the Queen's Head."

"How does the company feel about Frank Quilter?"

Firethorn paused. "Uncertainly."

"Would they welcome him back?"

"Not without reservations," admitted the actor.

"Then my own place with Westfield's Men is in jeopardy."

"Do not be so rash, Nick! Would you turn your back so easily on our years of fellowship and achievement? Think of all we have been through, all that we have accomplished together."

"I do think about it," said Nicholas quietly. "I weighed it carefully in the balance. Truly, it would break my heart to leave the company, but I could not stay if it turned on one of its number at a time when his condition is so piteous. All I ask for Frank is simple justice. It was denied his father, but it must not be held back from him."

"I agree, I agree."

"Yet you declared that there was no place for him in Westfield's Men."

"You misheard me, Nick," said Firethorn, renouncing his earlier decision. "What I was trying to do was to protect Frank from further ignominy."

"By taking his occupation away from him?"

"No, by removing him from the public gaze. Murder has strong lungs. At present, it is bellowing the name of Quilter throughout London. Some of those raucous knaves you saw at Smithfield will seek their amusement at the Queen's Head tomorrow. They will be part of our audience. What will happen if they discover that Gerard Quilter's son is in the company?" He drank more wine. "They will turn their abuse on him, and we will all suffer as a result."

"That is not what you were saying this morning," observed Nicholas.

"It is what I am saying *now*."

"Then you still mean to expel Frank?"

"No, dear heart. I'd stop well short of that. The plan I'd commend to the others is that we simply rest him for a while, until his name no longer excites unruly elements. When the tumult dies down," he said with a persuasive smile, "we invite him back to grace our stage. This was my intent all along."

"Then it accords with my own suggestion," said Nicholas, grateful that Firethorn had been forced to change his mind. "Frank is resolved to clear his father's name. Give him leave of absence to do so by releasing him from his contract, and, when he returns, the family name will be a source of pride once more."

"And you'll stay with us?"

"All the gunpowder in London would not shift me."

"Wonderful!" said Firethorn, slapping his thigh.

"But I'll hear no disparagement of Frank Quilter," Nicholas cautioned. "Those who traduce him behind his back will have to answer to me."

Firethorn rose quickly from his seat. "They'll feel my wrath first, Nick," he promised, grabbing a honey cake to slip into his mouth before washing it down with the remainder of the wine. "I'll ban the very mention of his name."

"There is no need for that."

"Great minds think alike. I knew that we could make common cause."

Nicholas sampled his own wine before nibbling at the honey cake. He was pleased with the compromise that had been reached, especially as it had required little advocacy on his part. Margery's intervention had been crucial. She had applied the kind of pressure that her husband was powerless to resist. Nicholas was glad that he had confronted the actor in his own home rather than in the crowded taproom at the Queen's Head. He recalled an earlier remark made by his host.

"You made mention of Edmund a while ago."

"Why, so I did."

"And you say that he alone burgeoned on the stage?"

"He put the rest of us to shame, Nick," said Firethorn. "Edmund was burning with zeal during the performance today. He was happier than I have ever seen him. I thought at first his elation sprang from the progress he was making on his new play."

"And it was not?"

"Alas, no. When I asked him about the piece, he looked at me as if he did not understand what I was talking about. His mind was miles away."

"Oh, dear!" sighed Nicholas. "That can only mean one thing."

Firethorn grimaced. "Who is the poor creature *this* time?"

Avice Radley was a comely woman in her late twenties with a buxom figure and a face of quiet loveliness. Still in the dress she wore to the play, she sat on a high-backed chair in the parlor of the house and composed herself for what she believed would be a significant encounter in her life. When the front door was opened to admit the visitor, she heard the sound of voices, and then footsteps echoed across the oak boards. There was a knock on the door before her maidservant entered. After ushering Edmund Hoode into the room, the girl withdrew as swiftly as she had been ordered. Avice Radley smiled. There was a long silence while the two of them appraised each other. Hoode was transfixed, staring at his admirer with mingled awe and hope. The vision he had glimpsed in the upper gallery at the Queen's Head now took on corporeal shape and additional luster. His nostrils detected the perfume that had enchanted him when it arose from her first letter. Hoode was enraptured.

For her part, Avice Radley was in no way disappointed. The dramatist whose plays she had watched and whose acting she had applauded could never be described as handsome, but his features were so pleasant and his manner so willing that his outward defects became invisible. After receipt of her invitation, Hoode had repaired to his lodging to put on his finest doublet and hose. Remembering that he had not yet doffed his hat, he whisked it off with a flourish and gave a low bow. She smiled again.

"Thank you for coming, Master Hoode," she said.

"Nothing would have kept me away, dear lady."

"Nothing?"

"Apart from sudden death."

"No wife, no mistress, perhaps?" she probed. "No family obligations?"

"I live quite alone."

"Then what sustains you?"

"My work," he said. "But even that is put aside for you, dear lady."

"Good."

She indicated a chair, and he lowered himself on to it, putting his hat on the table.

"I feel at a disadvantage," he said nervously. "While you know much about me, I have precious little information about you beyond the fact that you hold a pen with the most graceful hand and write words that could charm a bird out of a tree."

She laughed. "Are birds able to read, then?"

"This one is," he said, a hand on his breast. "When your first letter came, I dashed off a reply before I realized that I knew neither your name nor your address." He glanced around the room. "One of those omissions has now been repaired."

"Not exactly, sir. I only keep this house in the city for those few occasions when I visit London. My principal dwelling is in Hertfordshire, near St. Albans."

"You own two houses, then?"

"Both inherited from my late husband."

"I see."

Hoode's guess had been confirmed. As soon as he came into the room, he sensed that she was a widow. She was far too attractive not to have married, yet was so patently full of Christian goodness that adultery would never even have been a remote option, let alone a temptation. Also, when he scrutinized her face, he saw traces of sadness around the eyes and mouth. Evidently, she was a woman who had known grief.

"I am sorry to learn of his death," he said softly.

"It was a bitter blow. He was the kindest man in the world, Master Hoode, but none of us can choose the time when we are called. I mourned him for two years," she confided. "Now it is time to live my own life again."

"I would be honored to be part of it, dear lady."

"Then first, know my name."

"The letter *A* must stand for *angel,* must it not?"

"You flatter me, Master Hoode."

"Not as much as you flatter me, I assure you."

"My name is Avice Radley, so another mystery is solved."

"That leaves only the greatest mystery of all, Mistress Radley," he said. "Why should someone like you take an interest in a humble author like myself?"

"There is nothing humble about your work, sir, I assure you. It is the glory of the stage. And so were you this afternoon," she went on. "You made the other actors look like buffoons beside you. When we quit the inn yard, it was your name that was on the lips of the audience. I was thrilled that I might chance to meet you."

"It was so with me."

"You are a magician with words, Master Hoode."

"Then we are two of a kind," he said with a disarming smile, "for your letters entranced me. I have never met anyone who could conjure up such sweet phrases and delightful conceits."

"It is good to hear that we have something in common already."

"And much else besides, I venture to hope."

"I share that wish, Master Hoode."

"Be so bold as to call me Edmund, for I feel that we have stepped over the barrier that separates acquaintance from friendship."

"Very well, Edmund. That contents me."

He waited for a similar concession on her side, but it did not come. Avice Radley was too conventional to allow ready access to her Christian name so early in a friendship. He admired her for that. It was a right that he would have to earn. Hoode sat there and luxuriated in her presence. The opulence of the house and the quality of her apparel suggested a considerable degree of wealth. Her voice was an indication of her character. Soft and melodious, it spoke of intelligence, tolerance, and decency. Avice Radley was obviously not one of the many rich, widowed, promiscuous women who haunted the playhouses regularly in search of random lovers. She was highly selective, and her choice had fallen on him. Her poise faltered for a second.

"I am in uncharted territory, Edmund," she confessed.

"How so?"

"I have never done anything like this before."

"I suspected as much."

"Was my invitation too impulsive and unseemly?"

"Far from it, Mistress Radley," he said, raising a palm. "I, too, am somewhat adrift here. This is a situation in which I do not find myself every day."

"Merely once a week, then?" she teased.

He became impassioned. "No, dear lady. Someone like you will come along only once in a lifetime!" He checked himself and offered an apologetic smile. "Forgive me. I am a trifle overwhelmed at my good fortune."

"But you hardly know me, Edmund."

"I know enough to see that you are an answer to a prayer."

She was touched by his rejoinder. It restored her aplomb. She studied him for a long time, remembering the pleasure he had given her in various ways on the stage at the Queen's Head. What surprised her most was his remarkable modesty. He had none of the vanity and ostentation that went hand in glove with his chosen profession. Edmund Hoode was a man entirely without airs and graces.

"You carry your talent so lightly, Edmund."

"It is not a heavy burden."

"Burden?" she repeated. "Do you see it as a load that you must bear?"

"Sometimes, Mistress Radley."

"Yet you said earlier that you live for your work."

"Only because I have to honor my contract."

"Do you not *enjoy* writing plays?"

"It is too vexing a business to permit enjoyment," he said. "Sweat and suffering are my constant companions when I sit at my table. Scenes have to be beaten out of my brain like horseshoes upon an anvil. Uncertainty ever sits on my shoulder. The only play I have worked on with any semblance of pleasure is the latest one."

"And what is that called?"

He needed a moment to remember the title. *"The Duke of Verona."*

"Does it bring you a sense of fulfillment?" she asked.

"I thought it did, Mistress Radley. Now, I have my doubts."

"What of your work as a player?"

"That is always secondary. There is a certain satisfaction in the applause that we receive, but I am conscious that the spectators are rarely acclaiming me. I can never rival the magnificence of a Laurence Firethorn or the inspired clowning of Barnaby Gill or even the skills of a lesser mortal like Owen Elias."

"You outshone all three of them in *Mirth and Madness.*"

"That was due to their weakness on the day rather than to any superior strength on my part. Besides," he acknowledged, "I did not eclipse Barnaby. He was in fine form this afternoon and reminded the audience that we were playing a comedy."

"I saw nobody on stage but you, Edmund."

"Then I am glad I was worthy of your indulgence."

She looked at him quizzically. "Writing plays can be onerous, then?"

"Onerous and unrewarding."

"And you do not take yourself too seriously as an actor?"

"It would be dishonest to do so."

"Wherein, then, does the pleasure lie?"

"In the fellowship of Westfield's Men."

"Is it enough to make you forget the pain of composition?"

"Most of the time, Mistress Radley."

"And on other occasions?" she pressed.

"I am close to despair," he said, pursing his lips. "When a play of mine does not work on stage, or when a performance I give carries no conviction, I wonder what I am doing in the company. I feel as if I am a species of trickster."

"That is not what I see, Edmund. You are the soul of honesty."

"Thank you."

"Are you not happy with Westfield's Men?"

"Life in the theater is never without its torments."

"Does that mean that you would consider renouncing it?"

He shrugged. "How, then, would I feed and clothe myself?"

"By doing what you *really* want to do," she urged. "By responding to the impulses within your breast. Tell me, Edmund. If you could choose to spend the rest of your life doing one thing, what would it be?"

"That is an easy question."

"Tell me your answer."

"I would write sonnets."

"Sonnets?"

"In praise of you, Mistress Radley."

She was deeply moved. Bringing a hand to her mouth, she looked at him with even more intensity. Hoode thought he saw the hint of a tear in her eye. At a stroke, their relationship became markedly closer.

"I think it is time that you called me Avice," she said.

Nicholas Bracewell did not waste any time. When he left Shoreditch, he walked swiftly back to the city and called on Francis Quilter at his lodging in Silver Street. The latter was relieved to hear that he had been granted temporary leave of absence from the company while he pursued his investigation. Though he still had obligations of his own to Westfield's Men, Nicholas pledged his help. They began their inquiries at once. It was the testimony of two witnesses that had brought about Gerard Quilter's downfall. His son had managed to find the address of one of the men, a merchant name Bevis Millburne. On their way to the house, Nicholas asked for more detail about the case.

"Why did your father hate this Vincent Webbe so?" he asked.

"Because the rogue betrayed him."

"In what way?"

"They were partners at one time, Nick," explained Quilter, "and my father grew to like and trust Master Webbe. The trust was badly misplaced. He discovered that his partner was guilty of embezzlement. Vincent Webbe denied it hotly, but there could be no doubt of his villainy."

"Was his crime prosecuted?"

"Alas, no. My father was too softhearted to pursue the business. Out of kindness to the man's wife and family, he drew back from that step. I think it was a mistake to let the malefactor escape scot-free. He should have been sent to prison for what he did."

"Vincent Webbe should have been grateful to your father."

"Any other man would have been," agreed Quilter, "but he never forgave my father for finding him out. The dissolution of their partnership left him in severe straits. While my father prospered, Master Webbe's fortunes declined rapidly."

"He had only himself to blame for that, Frank."

"That was not how he viewed it. He preferred to blame my father."

"The enmity was clearly very strong between the two."

[52]

"And it seemed to grow with time," said Quilter. "It was one of the reasons that my father retired early. While he stayed in London, there was always the fear of a chance meeting with his partner. I was there on one occasion when their paths did cross. It was not a pleasant event, Nick."

"What happened?"

"Master Webbe had taken drink. No sooner did he set eyes on my father than he began to rant and roar, accusing him of ruining his life and throwing his family into destitution. My father was a mild man, but even he was provoked. Had I not pulled him away, I fear that he might have exchanged blows with the man."

"But the provocation was all on Master Webbe's side?"

"His language was revolting, Nick."

"Was he armed?"

"Only with a vicious tongue."

"What of your father?"

"He never walks abroad with a weapon."

"How long did this feud between them last?" asked Nicholas.

"Three years or more."

"And your father took care to avoid his erstwhile partner?"

"Every possible care."

They turned a corner and lengthened their stride. It took them some time to reach Cornhill, but they had so much to discuss on the way that it seemed like only a matter of seconds before they reached the abode of Bevis Millburne. The house had an impressive façade. Its owner was clearly a man of wealth. When they knocked on the front door, it was opened by a servant in neat attire. He told them that his master was not at home. They offered to return later, but he assured them that it might be several hours before his master came back as he was at supper with friends. Nicholas managed to wheedle out of him the name of the tavern where Millburne had gone. Leaving the grand house, the friends turned their steps towards the Golden Fleece, a place frequented by the gentry and known for its excellent food and high prices. As it came into sight, Nicholas turned to his companion.

"Wait outside for me, Frank," he suggested.

"Why?"

"Because your face might be recognized in there. Your father was seen at his worst today, but the family resemblance was still unmistakable. I would not have you go in there to stir up abuse and ridicule."

"I'll endure anything in my father's behalf."

"Then do so by adding discretion to your boldness," advised Nicholas. "Why should a man like Bevis Millburne desert his house and family to sup with friends on this particular day? Could it be that he is celebrating the gruesome event that we witnessed at Smithfield?" As Quilter started, he put a hand on his arm. "You are rightly aroused, but you'll achieve nothing with anger. Let me go in alone to sound the man out. He'll not suspect me of having any link with your family."

"Lure him out so that I may question him, as well."

"No, Frank."

"I'll beat the truth out of the knave!"

"Threats accomplish far less than subtler interrogation."

With great reluctance, Quilter accepted his friend's counsel. Nicholas stationed him on the other side of the street before crossing to enter the Golden Fleece. It was a large, low, well-appointed establishment filled with a mixed aroma of ale, tobacco, roasted meat, fresh herbs, and delicate perfume. The atmosphere was boisterous. Gallants and their ladies supped at the various tables. Larger parties were catered to in private rooms. Nicholas bought a tankard of ale and fell into conversation with the landlord, an amiable man of middle years with a florid complexion.

"You're a stranger to the Golden Fleece, I think, sir," he remarked.

"I did dine here once before," claimed Nicholas, "on the recommendation of a friend. He spoke highly of your venison, and he was not deceiving me."

"I am glad that we did not disappoint you."

"I had hoped to see him here this evening. He was headed this way."

"What is his name, sir?"

"Millburne, my friend. Master Bevis Millburne."

"Then you've come to the right place," said the landlord jovially. "He sups with companions in the next room. Sir Eliard Slaney, among them. They are in high spirits today. Shall I tell him that you are here?"

Nicholas shook his head. "I prefer to surprise him."

The landlord soon moved off to serve other customers. Sidling across to the adjoining room, Nicholas peeped in. Guests occupied the four tables, eating their food, downing their wine, and indulging in loud banter. Unable to pick his man out, Nicholas lurked and listened to scraps of conversation from the various tables. Eventually, he heard the name of Bevis mentioned in the far corner. It belonged to a sleek, portly man in his forties with a large wart on his left cheek that vibrated visibly whenever he laughed. Millburne had three companions. Two were somewhat younger and, judging by their deferential manner, might be employed by Millburne. The fourth man was older and had an air of distinction about him. Nicholas decided that it must be the aforementioned Sir Eliard Slancy, a wiry individual with watchful eyes set into a face the color of parchment. Wearing immaculate apparel, he had a whole array of expensive rings on both hands.

Nicholas summoned one of the servingmen, asked him to deliver a message, and then slipped him a coin. He withdrew to the next room and waited. Bevis Millburne eventually waddled out, eyes blinking with curiosity. Nicholas closed on him.

"Master Millburne?" he inquired.

"Are you the fellow who asked to speak with me?"

"I am, sir, merely to congratulate you."

"On what?"

"Your performance in court, Master Millburne. I was there when that villain, Gerard Quilter, was tried. Your evidence helped to send the fiend to his death."

"I did what any honest man would have done," boasted the other.

"You and Master Paramore, both," said Nicholas.

"Yes, Cyril did his part in court. But what's your interest, sir?"

"I was at the execution today and saw the condemned man hanged for his crime. Though, I must admit, I was surprised to go to Smithfield for such a pleasure when the gallows stand at Tyburn. Why not there?"

Millburne chuckled. "Being hanged beside a witch inflicted greater shame on the fellow. It could not have been arranged better. I thought it a most satisfying affair."

"You were at Smithfield yourself, then?"

"I would not have missed the spectacle for the world."

"Is that what you are celebrating now?"

"What is it to you?" asked Millburne, growing suspicious. "Who are you, and why do you drag me away from my friends?"

Nicholas held up both hands in a calming gesture. "I simply wished to thank you, Master Millburne," he said with a bland smile. "You helped justice to take its course. But I am sorry to have taken you away from your celebration. I'll let you get back to Master Paramore and the others."

"Cyril Paramore is not here."

"Not here to enjoy your day of triumph?"

"His ship does not return from France until tomorrow," he said, staring intently at Nicholas. "Look, why all these questions? You have not even given me a name. What's your purpose in coming here like this? Who *are* you, fellow?"

"A grateful friend," said Nicholas, backing away.

And before he could be detained, he slipped quickly out the front door of the tavern. Quilter was waiting impatiently for him across the road. He came forward.

"Was he there, Nick?"

"As large as life."

"Did you speak with him?"

"Briefly," said Nicholas. "I left before I aroused his suspicion too much."

"What did you learn?"

"What I expected, Frank. He was celebrating this afternoon's event with friends."

"Was that lying knave, Cyril Paramore, among them?"

"No, we will talk to him tomorrow."

Quilter's hopes rose. "You know where he lives?"

"No," admitted Nicholas, "but I am certain where he will be. And we'll be there to meet him. My conversation with Master Millburne was short but highly instructive. I take him to be just the sort of unprincipled rogue you suspect. We may judge his accomplice to-morrow."

"When?"

"When he disembarks from his ship. He is returning from France."

"Is there nothing we can do meanwhile, Nick?"

"Try to get a good night's sleep."

"There'll be no rest for me tonight," said Quilter. "My thoughts will be with my father. I doubt if I shall ever sleep soundly again until we clear his name."

"We have made a start, Frank."

"Why break off now? One of the men who sent him to the gallows is filling his belly at the Golden Fleece. He is glorying in my father's death. I'll not allow it. Let's drag the villain into the street and cudgel a confession out of him."

"No," said Nicholas, restraining him with an arm. "Once your identity is known, my own disguise is weakened. We must move privily to gather evidence, Frank. Show our hand too soon, and we forewarn both Bevis Millburne and Cyril Paramore."

Quilter was rancorous. "*They* are the ones who deserve to be hanged."

"Then let's find the rope that will do the office. But we must be cunning in our search. Master Millburne is a person of standing. He has important friends. One of them sups with him this evening."

"What's the fellow's name?"

"Sir Eliard Slaney." Quilter snorted with contempt. "You know the man, I see."

"Only through my father's eyes, Nick."

"And what did they see?"

"One of the meanest rascals in the whole of London."

Owen Elias was strolling jauntily along Cheapside when he spotted his friend coming towards him. He waved cheerily, but there was no acknowledgement. Head down, eyes dreamily searching the ground, Edmund Hoode was oblivious of all around him. His face was ignited by a smile, his body animated by a deep inner joy. If the Welshman had not blocked his passage as he tried to go by, Hoode would have gone straight past. He came out of his reverie.

"Owen!" he exclaimed. "Well met, old friend."

"Well met, indeed!" replied the other. "Thank heaven you are accosted by me and not by some lurking thief. Keep your wits about you, man. You are such a ready target when you amble along like that. A blind man with one arm could have robbed you, and you'd have been none the wiser."

"Nobody could deprive me of my most precious gift."

"That does not mean you should toss your purse away so idly."

"Money is only money, Owen."

"Therein lies its attraction. It buys food, drink, and the company of fair ladies."

"Some ladies spurn the notion of payment."

"Well, I have never met such a creature, Edmund," said the other cynically. "Women are all one to me. You may hire their bodies for a night or, if you marry them, you will have to pay in perpetuity. That is why I spread my charm amongst those already wed. A mistress who gives herself for love needs far less expenditure when she has a husband to buy to her command. Choose a married woman for sport, Edmund. Your purse will profit."

"It is far better to be chosen than to choose, Owen."

"On that point, we do agree. Though there is some deceit involved," conceded Elias. "When I pursue a woman, I always convince her that it was her idea and that she set the trap for me. It's the shortest way to happiness."

"I have found my own route there."

Elias laughed. "How many times have we heard that vain boast?"

"Do not mock me, Owen."

"Then do not set yourself up for mockery. The only women you ever find were put on this earth to break your heart. Your whole life is one long, desperate, lovesick sigh. But enough of that," said Elias, turning to a more serious matter. "Have you seen Nick since this afternoon?"

"No, why should I see him?"

"Because he is the best friend you have. Do you know a better reason?"

Hoode simpered. "I have been otherwise engaged this evening."

"Did you spare no thought for Nick and Frank Quilter?" he prodded the other man in the chest. "Shame on you, Edmund! I can see from your face that you gave neither of them a moment's consideration."

"Why should I?"

"Because they went through an ordeal today. So did our audience, of course," he added, "because we gave them poor fare on stage this afternoon. Nick and Frank were part of a different audience. They watched a public execution at Smithfield."

"Did they?" asked Hoode, as if hearing about it for the first time.

"You *know* they did, Edmund."

"I vaguely recall something to that effect."

"The company was buzzing with the news."

"My thoughts were some way distant, Owen. Why did Nick and Frank desert us in order to watch an execution? Their place was at the Queen's Head with us."

"Would *you* have been there if your father was being hanged?"

Hoode was startled. "Nick's father was the condemned man?"

"No, you idiot!" shouted Elias. "It was Gerard Quilter who went to his death today on a charge of murder. Have you not been listening to your fellows? They spent the whole rehearsal calling for Frank's removal from the company. Barnaby thinks we will be in bad odor with our audiences if we let the son of a killer remain in Westfield's Men. I am unsure. I have been having second thoughts on the matter."

"Why?"

"Frank alleges that his father was an innocent man. Nick supports his cry."

"He was hanged unjustly, then?"

"Who knows?" said Elias. "The fact remains that the two of them went through a terrible ordeal at Smithfield this afternoon. Whatever the rights and wrongs of the case, my heart goes out to both of them."

"So does mine," agreed Hoode. "What a hideous predicament to be in."

"It lands us in a quandary. Do we keep Frank or spurn him altogether?"

"I've no opinion on the subject."

"You must have, Edmund. It's the duty of every sharer."

"I'll be guided by Laurence."

"I fancy that Nick Bracewell will be the better guide. I'll side with him."

"That might be the wiser course."

Hoode was obviously shocked to be reminded about the execution, but Elias did not get the impression that it engaged his interest at any profound level. The playwright was still partly diverted by other concerns. Elias believed that he could guess what they were. His voice became a confidential whisper.

"How does your new play prosper, Edmund?"

"Slowly. Very slowly."

"They say that it may be your masterpiece."

"I entertained that delusion myself at one time."

"Your faith in the piece has slackened, then?"

"It has all but disappeared, Owen."

"You always say that when a new play nears completion."

"I can summon up no interest in the paltry work."

"That, too, is a familiar cry," said Elias with a grin. "This bodes well. When you begin to lose heart, it means the piece is far better than you expected. I hope there is a part worthy of my talents, Edmund. What is the piece called?"

"No matter."

"But I wish to know. You have kept it from us too long already. Come, Edmund, this play has been your mistress for well over a month now. You've fled from us day after day in order to take your pleasure from her loins. Give me some hint of what lies in store for us," he begged. "Tell me the title."

Hoode was only half-listening. His mind had already strayed back to the meeting he had just enjoyed with Avice Radley. It had not merely changed his opinion of himself, but it had altered his whole perspective on his work, as well. The play on which he had expended so much patient labor held none of its former appeal for him. Indeed, the whole notion of working with a theater company seemed rather frivolous now. The truth had to be faced. He had alighted on something infinitely better.

"The title, man!" repeated Elias. "What is the title of your masterpiece."

As the beautiful face of Avice Radley arose before him, Hoode beamed.

"*The Queen of My Heart,*" he said.

* * *

It was late when he arrived back. Nicholas Bracewell had spent hours with his friend as he tried to still the demons that plagued Quilter. It was a forlorn exercise. While he had managed to bend him to reason, Nicholas could not lift him out of despair or wipe away the memories of a testing afternoon. After arranging to meet Quilter early the next day, Nicholas set off for Bankside. The long walk gave him ample time to reflect on the events of the day and the details of the case. Gathering evidence to vindicate Gerard Quilter would be no simple task. His brief encounter with Bevis Millburne had taught him enough about the man to provoke his suspicion, yet there was a big problem. Millburne was no practiced liar hauled off the streets and paid to incriminate someone else in a court of law. He was a wealthy merchant, a responsible citizen whose voice would be respected. It was unlikely that any bribe could make such a man perjure himself. What motive, then, had driven him to accuse Gerard Quilter of murder?

Cyril Paramore, too, he suspected, would be a man of means who was beyond the reach of a bribe. Why had he borne witness against the prisoner? Were he and Millburne friends of the dead man, driven by lust for revenge? Or were they sworn enemies of Gerard Quilter himself, only too willing to implicate him in a murder he did not commit? It was baffling. What did weigh heavily with Nicholas was the fact that Millburne had attended the execution and then celebrated the event at the Golden Fleece. Witnesses in murder trials were not usually impelled by such feelings. Once they had given their evidence, they let the law takes its course. Bevis Millburne, however, had gained obvious satisfaction from the hanging of Gerard Quilter. It was not only a perverse joy that he was exhibiting. During his exchange with the man, Nicholas thought he noticed a sense of relief, as if a danger had been passed.

He was still asking questions of himself as he crossed London Bridge, but answers proved elusive. Nicholas plunged into the teeming streets of Bankside. Uneasy by day, the area was hazardous at night, filled, as it was, with taverns, brothels, gaming houses, and tenements that attracted all manner of low-life. Drunken revelers lurched out of inns, prostitutes blatantly tried to lure clients, thieves and pickpockets were constantly on the alert for fresh prey, and brawls were common sights. Nicholas's broad shoulders and brisk gait deterred all attackers. Even in the half-dark, few men were brave enough to tackle such a sturdy fellow. He walked with impunity past petty villains and roaring drunkards. Bankside held no fears for him. It was his home.

Anne Hendrik had waited up for him. She had a light supper in readiness.

"Welcome back!" she said, kissing him on the cheek.

"It is good to see the end of this day, Anne."

"Was it so distressing?"

"My distress lay in the sight of another's, Anne," he said. "Today was nothing but a torture chamber for Frank Quilter. I thought he would never survive it."

"Did he hold up?"

"Bravely."

"No small thanks to you, I dare venture."

"There was little I could do beyond bearing him company."

Nicholas sat at the table and picked at the supper she had prepared for him. He told her little about the execution itself, suppressing its viler aspects completely. Anne was pleased to hear about his visit to Laurence Firethorn.

"You have bought Frank some time, then?"

"Yes, Anne," he said. "He has time to recover and time to conduct his search."

"For what?"

"The real killer of Vincent Webbe."

"Is there no question of his father's guilt?"

"None at all. Gerard Quilter went to his death like a wronged man, not like a skulking criminal. Frank talked so fondly of his father. He was a kind man, a gentle soul who avoided violence of any kind."

"How, then, did he become embroiled in a fight?"

"That is one of the many things we have to find out, Anne. We have picked up the trail already. This evening, I accosted one of the witnesses from the trial."

She was fascinated by his account of the visit to the Golden Fleece. Knowing him to be such a sound judge of character, she took his estimate of Bevis Millburne at face value. Anne was revolted at the idea that anyone could attend a public execution for pleasure before rushing off to sup in style at a tavern.

"What sort of man would do such a thing, Nick?" she asked.

"It wounded Frank to the quick."

"I am not surprised," she said. "You mentioned that Master Millburne shared a table with three other people. Was the other witness, Master Paramore, among them?"

"No, Anne. But, then, he is out of the country at present. That was something I gleaned from Bevis Millburne. Whom the two younger men at his table were, I have no idea, but I did hear the name of his other companion."

"And who was that?"

"Sir Eliard Slaney."

"The moneylender?"

He was surprised. "You've *heard* of him?"

"Yes, Nick."

"So had Frank Quilter," he said, "though nothing good about the fellow had come to his ears. By all accounts, Sir Eliard Slaney is a thorough scoundrel. What do you know of the fellow, Anne?"

"Only what his wife has told me."

"His wife?"

"Yes," she said. "Lady Slaney is a client of mine. As it happens, I am making a hat for her at this very moment. She is one of our best customers."

[CHAPTER FOUR]

A long and grueling night had left Francis Quilter pale and drawn. Plagued by memories of his father's execution and spurred on by thoughts of revenge, he had been unable to steal even a moment's sleep. Instead, he tossed restlessly on his bed or paced up and down the narrow room. His brain was in such turmoil that it threatened to burst his skull apart. When he could no longer bear the pain, he quit his lodging and hurried to the parish church, spending an hour on his knees in humble supplication. It took its toll on him. By the time he met Nicholas Bracewell, early the next morning, he bore little resemblance to the handsome actor who attracted so much female admiration whenever he appeared onstage with Westfield's Men. His friend did not recognize him at first. Nicholas peered more closely at him.

"Is it you, Frank?" he asked.

"Good morrow, Nick."

"A better day for me than for you, it seems. What ails you?"

"Grief has dressed me in its ghostly garb."

"Then we must find some means to allay that grief."

"A hopeless task, unless you bring my father back to me."

"His reputation can at least be restored."

They met in Thames Street, close to the busy wharf where vessels returned as they sailed up the estuary from the English Channel.

Quilter was early, but Nicholas had nevertheless been there some time before him.

"We might have enjoyed an hour or two more in bed, Frank," he said.

"There's no enjoyment of sleep for me."

"I've made inquiry. No ship is due from France until late afternoon at least. It will be several hours before Cyril Paramore sets foot on dry land again."

"I'll be waiting for him," vowed Quilter.

"Try to rest beforehand."

"No rest for me until this business is concluded."

"You will need to show patience," warned Nicholas. "It will take time."

"However long it takes, I'll not falter."

"I make the like commitment."

"Thank you, Nick," said Quilter, embracing him. "You are a true friend. I fear that I leaned too heavily on your kindness yesterday. It must have been near midnight when you finally got back to Bankside."

"One day was indeed about to slip into another."

"Anne will blame me for keeping you out so late."

"There was no word of reproach from Anne," said Nicholas fondly. "She was waiting up for me last night. Anne is a willing convert to your cause. She appreciates the anguish you have been through and wishes to lend her own help."

"Sympathy is welcome from any source, but I cannot see how Anne can help."

"That is because you have met her only as my friend. You have not seen her manage her business affairs in the adjoining house. She employs four hatmakers and a bright apprentice. Her late husband would be proud of the way she has made his enterprise grow."

"How does this advantage me, Nick?"

"Anne is able to reach places denied to us."

"Places?"

"The home of Sir Eliard Slaney, for instance."

Quilter was astonished. "Anne is an acquaintance of his?"

"No," said Nicholas, "but she knows his wife, Rebecca, very well. Lady Slaney is a woman of discernment. She'll not buy a hat from anyone but Anne Hendrik. Now do you see how she may render some assistance?"

"I begin to, Nick."

"When I saw Master Millburne last night, he and Sir Eliard Slaney seemed to be the closest of friends. Why was Sir Eliard present at such a celebration?"

"To gloat over the death of my father."

"Why so? What did the moneylender have against him? Was there a falling out between the two men? Did you father have any dealings with Sir Eliard Slaney?"

"None, to my knowledge. But he always spat out the man's name with disgust."

"Anne may be able to find out why."

"I would not have her put herself in danger on my account."

"From what I hear," said Nicholas, "she will have little difficulty in securing answers to her questions. Lady Slaney never ceases to prattle about her husband and his wealth. She takes every opportunity to boast of her good fortune."

"What sort of hats does Anne make for her?"

"Ones that catch the eye, Frank. No expense is spared to achieve ostentation. It seems that Lady Slaney has a vanity that would rival that of Barnaby Gill."

Quilter smiled wearily. "Barnaby's attire certainly demands attention."

"He likes to be noticed."

"Lady Slaney and he are birds of a feather."

"Not quite, I think. Barnaby Gill has no parallel."

"Forget him for the moment," said Quilter. "My interest is in Anne's customer. This is a stroke of fortune, Nick. Any information we can gain about Sir Eliard, or about his friendship with Bevis Millburne, will be valuable. I beg of you to thank Anne most sincerely on my bchalf."

"I have already done so."

"Good. But what does the day hold for you?"

"First, I'll share a breakfast with a certain Frank Quilter."

"No, Nick. I'll not stir from here until Cyril Paramore's ship docks."

"You cannot wait on an empty stomach," insisted Nicholas.

"Come, there are ordinaries aplenty in Thames Street. We'll choose one that is but a stone's throw away."

"Well, if you wish," said Quilter with reluctant acquiescence. "But I'll want to be back here at my post before long."

"So you shall, I promise you. I must away to the Queen's Head."

"What play do you stage this afternoon?"

"Love's Sacrifice."

"The work of Edmund Hoode, is it not?"

"None other, Frank. The title is one that pertains closely to its author."

"In what way?"

"When you know Edmund better, you will understand. No man has made sacrifices to love so often and so recklessly. He still bears the scars. My fear is that another sacrifice is in the wind." He put an arm on Quilter's shoulder. "Let's away."

"What's this about another sacrifice?"

"The signs are all too evident."

"I thought that Edmund was absorbed with his new play."

"So did we all," said Nicholas, "but his behavior tells another tale. I'll talk to you about Edmund while we eat. He is truly a martyr to Cupid."

"Oh, treason of the blood! This news will kill us all!"

Laurence Firethorn was so furious that the veins stood out on his forehead like whipcord and his cheeks turned a fiery red. It seemed as if flames would shoot out from his nostrils at any minute. Stamping a foot, he waved both arms wildly in the air.

"This is rank lunacy, Edmund!" he yelled.

"It is a considered decision," replied Hoode.

"I see no consideration of me, or of the company, or of our patron. All that I see is an act of gross betrayal. Where is your sense of loyalty, man?"

"It lies exhausted."

"I'll not believe what I am hearing!"

"You hear the plain truth, Laurence."

"Then it is not Edmund Hoode that speaks to me," said Firethorn. "It is some sprite, some devil, some cunning counterfeit, sent here in his place to vex and torment us. You may look like the fellow we know and revere, but you do not sound like him."

Hoode smiled serenely. "I am in love," he announced.

"Heaven preserve us! Now you *do* sound like Edmund."

They were at the Queen's Head, and Firethorn's voice was booming around the innyard, disturbing the horses in the stables, waking any travelers still abed in the hostelry, and keeping other members of the company at bay. When their manager was in a temper, sharers and hired men alike tried to stay well out of his way. Barnaby Gill had no such trepidation. Attired with his usual flamboyance, he rode into the yard, and he saw what appeared to be the familiar sight of Firethorn in full flow as he upbraided Hoode for some minor solecism. He dismounted, handed the reins to George Dart, and strode across to the two men without realizing the gravity of the situation. Doffing his hat, Gill gave them a mocking bow.

"Good morrow, gentleman," he said. "At each other's throats so soon?"

Firethorn glowered. "It is all I can do to hold back from slitting Edmund's."

"Are you still jealous because he outshone you in *Mirth and Madness*?"

"No, Barnaby. I was the first to acknowledge his superiority in the play. But, having helped to save us on one day, he threatens us with extinction on the next."

"You exaggerate, Laurence," said Hoode.

"Let Barnaby be the judge of that," retorted Firethorn, turning to the newcomer. "Edmund has been slaving for weeks at his new play and was so enamored of it that he pronounced it the finest piece he had ever written. It is all but finished, Barnaby, yet he has put down his pen and resolved never to take it up again in our name."

"But he must," said Gill sharply. "Edmund has a contract with us."

"Contracts can be revoked," argued Hoode.

"I'll hear no talk of revocation," growled Firethorn. "By heavens, Edmund, you'll finish that accursed play if I have to stand over you with a sword and dagger."

"I'll not be moved, Laurence."

"Can you be serious?" demanded Gill, seeing the implications.

"The decision has already been made, Barnaby."

"Without even consulting your fellows?"

"It was the only way."

"Are you saying that you'll never write a play for us again?"

"That yoke has finally been lifted from my shoulders."

Gill blenched. "But your work—along with my own, of course—is one of the crowning glories of Westfield's Men."

"You waste your breath in praising him, Barnaby," said Firethorn. "I've told him a dozen times how much we rely on his genius, and he shrugs the compliment off as if it were without meaning."

"It is now, Laurence," said Hoode. "I need no compliments from you."

"You cannot simply walk out on the company."

"I understand that, and I will honor some of my obligations. It would be wrong to do otherwise. Count on me to take my role in *Love's Sacrifice* this afternoon, and in every play we stage from now until the end of next month. That will give you time to seek a replacement for Edmund Hoode."

"There *is* no replacement for you!" howled Firethorn.

"I agree," said Gill. "Lose you, and we lose the best of our drama."

Hoode was magnanimous. "I bequeath you all my plays."

"We need you to write new ones, Edmund. Novelty is ever in request. As one piece drops out of fashion, we must have fresh material at hand."

"London is full of eager playwrights."

"Eager for success, perhaps," said Firethorn, "yet lacking the talent to achieve it. We've plenty of authors who can write one, even two plays of merit, but there it stops. No dramatist has your scope and endurance, Edmund. Will you take it from us?"

"Forever."

"But *why?*" asked Gill in dismay.

Firethorn was sour. "Can't you guess, Barnaby?"

"Surely not a mere *woman?*"

"Oh, no," replied Hoode proudly. "She is much more than that."

"You would put a female before the future of the company?" said Gill with utter disgust. "I abhor the whole gender. I cannot understand why any man should let a woman near him. To squander an occupation at the request of one of those undeserving creatures beggars belief. You are bewitched, Edmund."

"I am, I am, Barnaby. And happily so."

"Then you'd do well to remember what happens to witches."

"Well spoken," said Firethorn, taking over once more. "Barnaby gives us a timely reminder. Yesterday, at Smithfield, a foul witch was burned at the stake. Had the decision been in my hands, Edmund, this sorceress of yours would have burned beside her."

"She is no sorceress," said Hoode. "She has ethereal qualities."

"Well, they are not in demand among Westfield's Men."

"I am sorry to leave you, Laurence, but I go to a better life."

"How can you say that when you are taking a leap into the unknown?"

"I take it without the slightest hesitation."

"For whom?" asked Gill. "Does this enchantress have a name?"

"She does, Barnaby. She is Mistress Avice Radley."

"How long has this foolish romance simmered? A fortnight? A month? A year?"

"Two days."

"Two days!" echoed Gill in disbelief.

"The most wonderful two days of my life."

"And the worst of ours, it seems," added Firethorn. "Would you really turn your back on us for the sake of a woman you have known but two days? Merciful heaven! You could not even learn to fondle her paps properly in so short a time, let alone get to know the rest of her body with requisite thoroughness. It takes at least a decade to understand a woman's true character. I learn new things about Margery every day."

"Yet you married her without the slightest fear."

Firethorn's face darkened. "Fear came soon afterwards, I assure you."

"That will not be the case with me."

"Stop him, Laurence," cried Gill, puce with anger. "He must not be allowed to break his contract like this, especially for some simpering dame with a pretty face. Does she know the havoc she is creating? My whole career is at stake here. I rely on Edmund to tailor roles to my particular needs. I'll not have him whisked away from me."

"No more will I," asserted Firethorn. "However many lawyers it takes, we'll hold you to your contract. Be warned, Edmund. Defy us, and we'll take you to court."

"Proceed, then, if you must," said Hoode.

"You'll not only lose the case, you'll also be faced with a crippling fine that you cannot afford to pay." He wagged a finger in Hoode's face. "Do you wish to invite financial ruin?"

"That will not occur," said Hoode blithely. "Avice is a wealthy woman. She has promised to meet any costs that are incurred. Regardless of your protests, we mean to be together soon."

"Sharing a cell in Bedlam," sneered Gill.

"Tasting a love and freedom I have never known, Barnaby. Scoff, if you will," he went on as both men sniggered, "but I am resolved. Avice, too, is resolute. If it is the only way to secure Edmund Hoode, she is prepared to buy the Queen's Head outright." He grinned inanely at them. "Now, do you see what a paragon among women I have found?"

Bartholomew Fair was an annual event, held on the broad acres of Smithfield and mixing commerce with entertainment so skillfully that visitors came flocking from far afield. It had been founded almost five hundred years earlier by Rahere, jester to King Henry I. The story went that Rahere had been taken ill during a pilgrimage to Rome, reflected on the errors of his ways, and became determined to amend his character. Accordingly, he founded a priory and hospice dedicated to St. Bartholomew. The fair that was held for three days from the eve of St. Bartholomew's Day, late in August, was the greatest cloth fair in England. Even when he became prior, the reformed jester, Rahere, still acted as Lord of the Fair and frequently performed his juggling tricks for the amusement of the crowd. The influence of the Church over the event had long since declined, but the spirit of Rahere survived. Jugglers, dancers, clowns, acrobats, puppeteers, wrestlers, strong men, freaks, and performing bears were just as much a part of the fair as the hundreds of stall holders who came to sell their wares.

Though there were still two days to go, some of the participants had already started to converge on London, and a number of booths were being erected. Among the early arrivals was Moll Comfrey, a pert young peddler whose large basket was filled to the brim with pins, needles, combs, brushes, assorted trinkets, and rolls of material of every kind and color. Hanging from the basket were sundry ballads, and pinned to her skirt were dozens of other bits of material that could be used to patch clothing. Her frail appearance belied her robust health. Moll walked long distances between fairs and markets, in all weathers, and carried her heavy basket with practiced ease. Her occupation had given her a strength and tenacity that were not visible. What people saw on first acquaintance was a pretty girl of no more than seventeen or eighteen years with fair curls poking out from beneath her bonnet. There was an air of battered innocence about her that made her stand out in a crowd.

Moll was talking to one of the stall holders when a voice rang out behind her.

"Is that you, Moll?" asked the man.

"Lightfoot!" she exclaimed with a laugh as she turned to see the figure who was somersaulting towards her over the grass. He came to a halt in front of her and gave her a kiss on the cheek. "I was hoping to find you here today."

"We've found each other."

"You look wondrous well."

"I keep myself in fine fettle," he said. "Watch!"

Lightfoot did a series of cartwheels that took him in a complete circle. When he bounced upright again, he was standing directly in front of his friend. The acrobat was a cheerful man in his late twenties, slim, short, and lithe. Gaudily dressed in a red doublet that sprouted a small forest of blue and yellow ribbons, he wore bright green hose that showed off the neat proportions of his legs. During his energetic display, his pink cap with its white feather somehow stayed on his head. Lightfoot had an ugly face that became instantly more appealing when he smiled.

"Look!" he said, pointing to the carts that were trundling towards them. "Three more booths to be set up. Half the fair will be up before tomorrow morning. When did you reach London?"

"Within the hour."

"Thank heaven you did not come yesterday."

"Why?"

"Smithfield was not a happy place to be, Moll."

"Not happy?"

"Public executions were held here. A man and a woman."

"Then I am glad I came no earlier," she said with a shudder. "But I thought they hanged murderers at Tyburn now. I saw three dangling from the gallows when I was last in the city. The sight turned my stomach for days."

"Had you been here yesterday, you'd not have eaten for a week. They burned a witch over there," he said, indicating the spot with an outstretched hand. "You can still see the ash. They tell me that people danced around the blaze for hours."

Moll grimaced. "I wish you'd not told me that, Lightfoot."

"The woman is dead now."

"Yes, but her curse will remain. I felt something strange when I first stepped upon this grass," she said, eyes darting nervously. "It was like a cold wind, yet the day is hot and sunny. I think it was an omen, Lightfoot. That witch has put a spell on the place."

"These are childish thoughts," he said amiably, patting her on the arm. "Bartholomew Fair is at hand. Three days of riot and enjoyment lie ahead. The Devil himself could not spoil our fair, let alone a dead witch."

"I hope that it is so."

"It is so, Moll. Come, let's find a place to eat."

"Yes," she agreed, brightening at once. "I am so glad to see you again."

"Then let me carry your basket for you."

She dropped a mock curtsey. "Thank you, kind sir."

They fell in beside each other and set off. Moll was delighted to meet Lightfoot so soon. He was more than simply a friend. Traveling the highway for a living exposed her to all manner of dangers, and Lightfoot had rescued her on more than one occasion. Whenever she was with him, she felt safe. He was a clever acrobat. Though she had seen his tricks many times, Moll never tired of watching them. Lightfoot had another virtue. He picked up news faster than anyone else she knew. If they arrived at a new fair, he would always have the latest tidings to report.

"What was the woman's name?" she asked. "This witch that they burned."

"Jane Gullet."

"And you say a man died with her?"

"A murderer, hanged for his crime."

"Who was his victim?"

"One Vincent Webbe, stabbed cruelly to death."

"Then the killer deserved to hang," she said. "What was his name?"

"You are so full of questions today, Moll," he said with a laugh.

"Only because I know that you will have the answers."

"It will cost you a kiss to hear the man's name."

"Most men pay for my kisses."

"I pay with information."

She giggled and nodded. "As you wish."

"Then first, my kiss."

"That must wait, Lightfoot. I want a name before you claim your reward."

"So be it. His name was Gerard Quilter."

Moll stopped dead in her tracks. Her face turned white, her eyes widened in fear, and she began to tremble violently. She grabbed him by the arm.

"No!" she protested vehemently. "You are mistook. Whatever it was, it could not have been that name."

"I heard it loud and clear."

"Never!"

"The murderer was Master Gerard Quilter."

"Then there must be two men with the same name. Do you know anything else about him, Lighfoot? Was he old, young, tall or short? Where did he dwell? What occupation did he follow?"

"As to his age and size," he replied, "I can tell you nothing, but I do know that he lived in the country. Before that, Gerard Quilter was a respected mercer here in the city." He grinned hopefully. "I've given you a name, Moll. Where is my kiss?"

But she was in no position to give it to him. After letting out a sigh of distress, she promptly fainted and ended up in a heap on the ground.

Nicholas Bracewell waited until the performance was over before he made his move. Having failed to make any headway themselves, Laurence Firethorn and Barnaby Gill had pleaded with him to speak to their resident playwright in order to persuade him to renounce his decision to leave. Nicholas was as disturbed as they were to hear the news of Edmund Hoode's impending departure, but he did not wish to tackle him until *Love's Sacrifice* was over and his duties as a book holder had been discharged. Before his friend could slip away after the performance, Nicholas took him into the little room where the properties and costumes were stored.

"You distinguished yourself yet again, Edmund," he observed.

"Thank you, Nick. I felt inspired today."

"Your play brought out the best in everyone."

"Nothing I have written is closer to my heart," said Hoode dreamily. "There are lines in the piece that turned out to foretell my own future."

"That is what I wish to touch upon," said Nicholas gently. "There seems to be some doubt about your future with the company."

"No doubt at all, Nick. I am to withdraw."

"When you have the success you gained this afternoon?"

"Applause soon dies away. What is left in its wake?"

"Satisfaction," argued Nicholas, "and the feeling that you have served the play and your fellows as best you may. Since you are the author of the piece, you had a double triumph onstage today. Does it mean nothing to you?"

"It gave me a brief pleasure, I grant you."

"You said that you felt inspired."

"Why, yes," replied Hoode, "but not by a play we've given a dozen times before. Parts of it begin to stale already. What lifted my spirits was the thought that I was acting in front of my redeemer. She was *there*, Nick."

"So I understand."

"And before you utter another syllable, let me warn you that I am deaf to all entreaty. I know that Laurence has set you on to me but to no avail. I am adamant." He tried to move off. "And I must not keep a lady waiting."

"Hold still," said Nicholas, blocking his path. "I'd hoped our friendship earned me more than a minute of your time."

"It does, Nick, it does. You have been a rock to which I have clung many times and I'll not forget that. When I leave Westfield's Men, I mean to keep Nick Bracewell's friendship."

"That depends on the manner in which you depart."

"I go for love—what better reason is there?"

"Set it against the loyalty you owe to the company."

"That is what I have done."

"On the strength of two days' acquaintance with a lady?"

"You sound like Laurence," said Hoode with a chuckle. "That rampant satyr had the gall to lecture me on the folly of falling in love so swiftly when he has done so twice a week at times. We've both seen him pursue a woman within the very hour that they first meet. At least, I cannot lay that charge at Barnaby's feet." He smiled discreetly. "Only a pretty boy with a winsome smile can take his fancy."

"We are talking about you, Edmund, not them. Their private lives do not threaten the future of Westfield's Men. Yours, however, does. All that I ask is that you reflect on your decision before it is too late."

"What blandishments has Laurence told you to offer?"

"None," said Nicholas firmly. "I speak on my own account. It would distress me greatly to lose you as a friend and as a fellow. If you have found true love, I wish you every happiness. No man deserves it more. But must it sever your bonds with us? If you flourish onstage when your beloved is in the audience, why not continue to delight her and the other spectators?"

"Because there is a world elsewhere."

"You once thought Westfield's Men was your whole universe."

"It was," replied Hoode earnestly. "And I leave it with much regret. But I have achieved all that I can within the company. A new life beckons me, with new challenges and fresh delights." He looked sad. "I see that you censure me, Nick."

"You can hardly expect my blessing."

"Wherein lies my crime?"

"You leave us at a time when we most need your talents."

"That argument did not carry much weight for you, as I recall."

"What?" said Nicholas, taken aback.

"It was only yesterday that you threatened to leave the company, as well."

"Circumstances differed, Edmund."

"Did they? I think not. You put loyalty to a friend before your obligations to Westfield's Men. I have done the same, Nick. The only difference is that *my* friend also chances to be my future wife."

"That is an unfair comparison," complained Nicholas.

"Not in my eyes," said Hoode. "Laurence may have thought that you could win me over, but he sent the wrong ambassador. We are too alike. Both of us are ready to quit the company in the cause of a greater commitment. Westfield's Men rely on you just as much as on me, Nick. If treachery is afoot, we are both guilty of it."

Nicholas had no answer. There was a grain of truth in Hoode's argument, and it left him speechless. He stood aside so that the other man could leave. Nicholas was upset that his persuasive tongue had made no impact on his friend. Hoode had made impulsive decisions before, but he could usually be talked out of them. This time, Nicholas sensed, the playwright was beyond the reach of cold reason. He was still brooding on his failure when Laurence Firethorn came bustling in.

"I've just seen Edmund leave," he said. "Did you change his mind?"

"Not entirely," admitted Nicholas.

"But you are our last hope. Did you wrest no concession from him?"

"Edmund would give none."

"Does he still purpose to leave the company?"

Nicholas nodded. "I'll speak to him again. This was not the time or place."

"Where and when better?" asked Firethorn. "Edmund has just given a stirring performance in one of his own plays. He has experienced those unparalleled joys that drew him to the theater in the first place. It should have left him ripe for conversion."

"His mind was set against it, I fear."

"It is not his mind that Mistress Avice Radley works upon, Nick, but his body. Let him fall into her arms again, and Lord Westfield himself could not pull him safely out."

"We'll need to be more subtle in our argument."

"No," decreed Firethorn. "Our survival is at stake. We need to be more brutal."

Francis Quilter hardly moved from his chosen position throughout the day. Having stationed himself close to the river, he watched a whole array of vessels come and go. None hailed from France, and nobody could give him confirmation that the *Speedfast*, the expected ship, would arrive at all that day. Contrary tides might have held it up across the Channel, other problems might have delayed its departure. Quilter grew increasingly frustrated. As afternoon declined towards evening, his spirits were ebbing slowly away. The arrival of Nicholas Bracewell revived him at once.

"What news, Frank?" asked the newcomer.

"I am heartily sick of looking at the Thames. That is all the news I can offer."

"No sign of Master Paramore's ship, then?"

"Not so much as a glimpse," said Quilter. "But I'll not be moved from this spot. I'll sit here all night and all day tomorrow, if need be."

"I hope it will not come to that."

After leaving the Queen's Head, Nicholas had gone back to the river. He was chastened by his interview with Edmund Hoode. It was painful to be reminded that he, too, had threatened to abandon the company, but the fact had to be acknowledged. Now that he was back with Quilter again, he felt the compassion that led him to make the earlier decision. Fortunately, a way had been found to release the actor while retaining the services of the book holder. No such compromise could be used in Hoode's case.

"How did the performance fare?" wondered Quilter.

"It courted excellence, Frank."

"Who took my role?"

"James Ingram, though with slightly less success."

"I doubt that. James is a fine actor."

"Granted," said Nicholas, "but he was trying too hard. Since Edmund was both author and actor in the piece, James was straining every sinew to impress him. He was not alone. Owen Elias and the others followed his example."

"Why should they need to impress Edmund?"

Nicholas told him about the playwright's ultimatum, and one more member of the company was dumbfounded. Though he had not been with them long, Quilter knew how crucial a figure Hoode was to Westfield's Men. It was inconceivable to him that Hoode should even consider leaving. Nicholas discussed the problem at length, grateful for a subject that took Quilter's mind away from his father's fate. As they talked, the sails of a ship were gradually conjured out of the distance. The whole vessel soon appeared, scudding along the water in midstream and forcing them to stop their conversation abruptly. They watched with interest until the *Speedfast* eventually glided towards the wharf. Quilter was eager to race to the water's edge, but Nicholas held him back.

"Stay, Frank," he said. "The ship is not safely moored yet."

"I want to be there when he steps ashore."

"But you do not even know who he is. Cyril Paramore might walk straight past and you, none the wiser. Besides," added Nicholas, "it is important that he does not realize who you are or he'll be frightened away."

"Only because he has something to hide."

"We'll not find it by accosting him boldly."

"How, then, do we proceed, Nick?"

"As before. You stand apart and let me pick him out."

"When you do not recognize his face?"

"We are not the only ones here to greet the vessel," said Nicholas, pointing to the small crowd on the wharf. "I'll lose myself in the press and shout his name aloud as the passengers disembark. That way, he'll declare himself, and I'll approach him."

"Let me go with you."

"Watch and wait, Frank. You can judge the fellow from a distance."

It took skill to bring the *Speedfast* alongside the wharf to moor it securely. Having spent so much time at sea himself, Nicholas took a keen interest in the way that the crew went about their business. They were agile and well drilled, responding swiftly to the shouted commands from their bosun. Passengers lined the bulwarks in readiness, but Nicholas had no idea which one of them would be Cyril Paramore. Recognizing friends and relatives aboard, the crowd on the wharf began to wave and call their welcomes. Nicholas mingled with them and stood behind the tallest man he could find. When the gangplank was lowered, a member of the crew tested it before the passengers were allowed to disembark. The long procession began. Noisy reunions were taking place all around Nicholas. There was only one imminent reunion that caught his attention. It sent him scurrying back to Quilter.

"What's amiss?" asked the actor. "Is he not aboard?"

"I'm certain of it, Frank."

"Then why not accost him?"

"We have someone to do it for us," explained Nicholas. "You see the tall man who is standing apart from the crowd? He has just arrived and can only be here to greet Master Paramore."

"How can you be so sure, Nick?"

"Because his name is Sir Eliard Slaney."

"Sir Eliard Slaney!" repeated Quilter. "Is *that* the villain?"

He looked at the tall, wiry, immaculate figure, who was standing several yards from the wharf with two servants in attendance. Sir Eliard Slaney raised a hand to acknowledge someone aboard and then clicked his fingers to send the two servants running towards the vessel. He followed them at a more leisurely pace. As the passengers filed off the vessel, a short, neat man in dark attire took his turn in the queue, carrying luggage in both hands. The servants relieved him of his cargo the moment he stepped ashore and left him free to embrace Sir Eliard Slaney. The two men were evidently close friends. As they left the wharf together, they were sharing a laugh.

Nicholas took careful note of Cyril Paramore. He had none of Bevis Millburne's facial ugliness and oily complacency. Still in his twenties, he had a pleasant demeanor and a dapper elegance. As a witness in court, Nicholas gauged, he would be convincing.

"What do we do now?" asked Quilter.

"Follow them at a distance," advised Nicholas. "Master Paramore does not live far away or Sir Eliard would have met him in a coach. When we know his address, I can call on Cyril Paramore at a time when he is alone. It would be foolish to approach him while his friend is at his side."

"Friend! Sir Eliard has no friends, only cronies."

"Then we have identified two of them, Frank."

"Yes," said the other through gritted teeth. "Bevis Millburne and Cyril Paramore."

"We know what devilish part they played at your father's trial. All that we have to decide is what role Sir Eliard Slaney took behind the scenes."

"How do we decide that?"

"We must hope that Anne can provide help there," said Nicholas, watching the two figures moving off. "Come, Frank. Let's see where they go."

When she married her husband at the age of seventeen, Rebecca Nettlefold was a slim and attractive young girl with a quiet disposition. In the intervening twenty-five years, her status and her character had changed out of all recognition. Having become Lady Slaney, she was now obese, self-absorbed, and garrulous. In persisting in the choice of dresses that were more suitable for someone much younger, she came close to making herself look ridiculous. She had a particular fondness for ostentatious hats, chasing the latest fashions with a waddling urgency. Anne Hendrik found some of her commissions quite absurd, but she was not there to criticize the taste of her customers. Her task was to design and provide whatever Lady Slaney requested.

When Anne called at the house, Lady Slaney was delighted to see her.

"I did not expect you for days yet," she said.

"Your hats always take precedence, Lady Slaney," said Anne. "And I know that you would prefer to have this one sooner rather than later."

"Quite so, quite so. Set it on the table."

They were in the parlor of a sumptuous house near Bishopsgate. The room was large, rectangular, low ceilinged, and well appointed. Gold plate stood on the gleaming oak court cupboard and on the magnificent Venetian chest of carved walnut with its gilded decoration. Anne always noticed the sheer size of the locks on the chest. Belgian tapestries covered two walls while gilt-framed portraits were displayed on the others. Sir Eliard Slaney was a man who liked to advertise his wealth. His wife's costly, if rather incongruous apparel, was another means of doing so.

"Let me see it," ordered Lady Slaney.

Anne undid the cloth in which she had carefully wrapped the hat and then stood back so that her customer could view the results. Lady Slaney gasped with joy and clapped her hands like a child receiving a present on its birthday. The hat incorporated jewelry that she had coaxed out of her husband. Tall-crowned and brimless, it was made of light blue velvet and was decorated with jewelry around the lower part. The hat was ornamented with high-standing ostrich feathers that were fastened with precious stones. It positively glistened. Lady Slaney reached forward to grab it.

"I must put it on at once," she said.

"Let me help," counseled Anne, taking it from her to place it on her head. "Is it comfortable, Lady Slaney?"

"A perfect fit, my dear. Quick—I must see for myself."

She crossed to the ornate mirror on the far wall and preened herself in front of it, making minor adjustments to the tilt until she was completely satisfied. When she saw the final result, she giggled with pleasure.

"I will turn every head when I wear this abroad," she announced.

"I am glad that you are content," said Anne. "It becomes you, Lady Slaney. You could grace a royal event in that hat."

"That is my intention. My husband has great influence at Court. That's to say," she added with a laugh, "he is owed money by half the nobility. There are many of them who would long ago have been bankrupt if they had not turned to Sir Eliard Slaney for their salvation."

"Your husband is such a shrewd man."

Lady Slaney tittered. "That's why he married me," she said. "But you are right, my dear. He is a species of genius. He makes money without even trying. There is no one to match him for sagacity. Others inherited their titles, but Sir Eliard has had to work for his and deserves the honor." She gave a brittle laugh. "My husband will not rest there. We look to be Lord and Lady Slaney one day."

"And this is all the fruit of usury?" asked Anne.

"That is not a word Sir Eliard likes, my dear. It smacks too much of Jewry, and he has no dealings with those strange people. No, my husband is a man of business, pure and simple. He buys, sells, holds licenses, acts as a surveyor, transacts loans, and generally helps those in financial need."

Anne looked around. "This house is a worthy tribute to his success."

"It is only one of three that we own," boasted Lady Slaney, "and we hope to secure a fourth property near Richmond very soon. And that, mark you, does not include the charming residence we keep on the isle of Jersey."

"Jersey?"

"It is a small paradise, my dear. If I did not hate sailing so much, I'd spend more time on Jersey. Our house is one of the finest on the island. My husband acquired it from Lord Groombridge when the poor man defaulted on a loan. His loss is our gain," she said, peering into the mirror once more. "Sir Eliard expects to take possession of the property in Richmond by the same means."

"Do you *need* so many houses, Lady Slaney?"

"I could never be happy in just one. It would soon begin to stale. By moving from one property to another, we stave off boredom and ensure a regular change of scenery."

"Which house is your favorite?"

Lady Slaney needed no more encouragement. She launched into a description of every place that she and her husband had ever lived in, listing its merits and demerits, noting the improvements that she herself had introduced in each case, and charting the upward progress of their fortunes. She was as indiscreet as she was voluble. Anne learned more from her on this visit than on every previous one. She reserved her most important question until she was about to leave. After receiving payment from her customer, she expressed her thanks and moved towards the door.

"A friend of mine was at Smithfield yesterday," she said casually. "He thought that he saw your husband there. Could that have been so, Lady Slaney? Did Sir Eliard witness the public executions?"

Nicholas Bracewell had difficulty in restraining his friend. The long day's wait had made Francis Quilter restive. When they followed Cyril Paramore to his home, he was ready to challenge the man openly. Nicholas advised against it, repeating the need to gather more evidence covertly before any accusations could be made. What he attached significance to was the presence of Sir Eliard Slaney, a visible link between the two key witnesses at the trial of Gerard Quilter. Leading the disappointed son away, Nicholas walked all the way back to his friend's lodging with him. A most unexpected visitor awaited them. Squatting outside the door of the house with her basket beside her was a peddler. When she saw the two men approach, she leapt nimbly to her feet.

"Master Quilter?" she asked, looking from one to the other.

"I am Frank Quilter," he said. "Who are you?"

"My name is Moll Comfrey, sir, and I beg you to listen to me. It has taken the best part of a day to track you down, and I could never have done it without Lightfoot."

"Lightfoot?"

"A friend, sir."

"What would you have with me?"

"A few words, Master Quilter." She looked at Nicholas. "In private, I hope."

"Say what you have to say in front of Nick," urged Quilter. "I have no secrets from him." Moll bit her lip and hesitated. "Well, girl, speak up?"

"At least, have the grace to invite her in, Frank," said Nicholas, weighing the visitor up. "My guess is that our young friend here has come to London for the fair. She has probably walked some distance to get here."

"That is so, sir," agreed Moll. "Seven miles or more."

"And you have trudged even more in pursuit of Frank, you say. It must be urgent business if you go to so much trouble."

"It is very urgent, sir." She turned to Quilter. "I knew your father."

Nicholas could see that his friend was both embarrassed and alerted by the news. Moll Comfrey was not the sort of person with whom he expected his father to have been acquainted. Her trade was clearly not confined to the sale of the wares in her basket. Young women of her sort congregated at fairs and offered the delights of their bodies in return for payment. Quilter was reluctant to invite such a person into his lodging, but the mention of his father intrigued him.

"What do you know of him?" he asked.

"I know that he was wrongfully hanged at Smithfield yesterday," she replied.

"How?"

"Because he did not commit a murder, sir. Your father was too sweet and loving a man to kill anyone. I'd stake my life on that. Besides, sir, I have proof."

"Proof?" echoed Nicholas.

"Yes, sir. Lightfoot found out when the murder took place."

[84]

"It was at the end of July," said Quilter. "The last day of the month."

"That is what Lightfoot told me, sir, and that is why I know your father is innocent. I'd swear it in a court of law, so I would, sir. I'm an honest girl."

"I'm sure that you are," said Nicholas softly. "But why can you say so confidently that Gerard Quilter was innocent of the crime?"

"Because he was not in London on the day of the murder."

"How do you know?"

She gave a wan smile. "He was with me, sir," she said. "For the whole day."

[CHAPTER FIVE]

It was midevening when Nicholas Bracewell returned to the house in Bankside. Anne welcomed him home and then gave him an account of her visit to Lady Slaney. He was grateful for all the information she had garnered in the course of her visit. The details of Sir Eliard Slaney's domestic life accorded very much with his expectations, and Nicholas had been pleased to get confirmation of the fact that Slaney had been at Smithfield to watch the last minutes of Gerard's Quilter's life. It strengthened the link between him and the two witnesses at the murder trial. Nicholas's own tidings, however, could not wait. Before Anne could relate everything she had heard from the busy lips of Lady Slaney, he began his tale of the fortuitous arrival of Moll Comfrey.

Anne Hendrik was so surprised and amused by what he said that she burst into laughter.

"A bawdy basket!" she exclaimed.

"That is what Frank calls her. He was using thieves' cant."

"And how would you describe this Moll Comfrey?"

"As a girl who struggles to make the best of herself," said Nicholas. "Moll is no common trull. She is too unspoiled to have been at the trade for any length of time, and too decent a girl to sell her favors unless she was in dire distress. If she is the bawdy basket that Frank takes her to be, then she has been forced into it. Necessity feeds on virtue, Anne. I take Moll Comfrey to be the prisoner of necessity."

"Then you take a kinder view than Frank Quilter, by the sound of it."

"He was too shocked to believe what she said at first."

"Shocked?"

"Yes," said Nicholas. "His father was a God-fearing man, virtuous, upright, and respected in the community. He had been a widower for some years but, according to Frank, he would never turn to someone like Moll Comfrey for pleasure."

"Is that what he did?"

"I think not."

"What does the girl say?" asked Anne.

"Simply that she was a friend of Gerard Quilter. She refused to explain the strength or nature of that friendship, except to say that they met from time to time. Moll found him good-hearted and generous. He gave her money, it seems." Anne raised a skeptical eyebrow. "No, Anne," he said defensively. "You are wrong, I am sure. Nothing of that kind occurred between them. I am certain of it. Apart from other indications, he was so much older than she."

"Since when has that held any man back?"

"True."

"If he did not buy her favors," she suggested, "could she possibly have been his child, conceived outside the bounds of marriage?"

"That, too, I considered, only to dismiss the notion when I knew a little more about her. But I could see that the same thought crossed Frank's mind."

"Small wonder he was embarrassed by her arrival."

"He accepted the value of her testimony in the end," said Nicholas. "If her word can be trusted, she puts Gerard Quilter twenty miles away from London the day when Vincent Webbe was stabbed to death."

"What of this brawl the two men are alleged to have had?"

"That must have been on the day before, Anne."

"Then he could not possibly have been the killer," she concluded. "Why did he not call the girl to speak up for him at the trial?"

"I doubt if he had any idea where Moll was. She travels far and wide with her basket of wares. How could he summon her to his aid if she was several counties distant?" he asked. "She came to London to see him. Moll said they had planned to meet again at Bartholomew Fair, but that will never happen now."

Anne became serious. "Can the girl's word be relied upon?"

"I believe so."

"Would Frank agree with you?"

"Moll convinced him in time."

"How?"

"By talking in such detail about his father," explained Nicholas. "There can be no question that she knew him well. Master Quilter was very proud of his son. Though he disliked the notion of Frank being an actor, it did not stop his adoration of him. He talked to Moll about him in the warmest tones. In spite of his reservations, he once saw his son perform with Banbury's Men. That was how Lightfoot tracked Frank down."

"Lightfoot?"

"A tumbler who'll perform at the fair."

Anne smiled. "Bawdy baskets? Tumblers? Who else is in this story?"

"Do not mock Lightfoot," he warned. "He is Moll's best friend. When she heard of Gerard Quilter's execution, it was Lightfoot who supplied the details. But for him, we might never have had this important new evidence."

"How did she get to Frank's lodging?"

"With the help of this tumbler. When Moll told him that Frank was an actor, he went to every theater troupe in the city in search of him. Someone at the Queen's Head said that Frank was a sharer with Westfield's Men." He shrugged his shoulders. "It was as simple as that. Lightfoot found out where he lived and passed on the information to Moll Comfrey."

"This tumbler has great enterprise."

"We all have cause to be thankful to him, Anne. And to the girl."

"Did she come alone?"

"Alone and forlorn. That's what persuaded me of her sincerity."

"How?"

"The way she responded to the man's death," said Nicholas. "She was deeply moved. Their friendship was clearly of great moment to her. What girl would mourn the passing of a mere acquaintance, who paid for her favors now and then? She *loved* him, Anne. That's what disturbed Frank most."

"Most sons would feel uneasy in such a situation. You have vindicated Frank's father in the space of a single day."

"It is not so easy as that, I fear."

"Moll Comfrey's testimony will stand up in court, will it not?"

"If we can find a judge to open the case once more."

"But you must, Nick. In the name of justice."

"Judges and justice do not always go together," he pointed out. "If they did, then Gerard Quilter would not have met such an ignominious death. Our first task was to let Moll Comfrey make a sworn statement in front of a magistrate."

"And did she?"

"Willingly."

"What did the magistrate say?"

"He was not sanguine, Anne," he confessed. "He did not think we could overturn the verdict in a murder trial on the strength of a deposition from an ignorant girl. That was not the way he described her to me in private," he recalled with irritation. "His language was more contemptuous."

"He took her for a bawdy basket, as well, then?" she said.

Nicholas grew angry. "It does not matter what she is or how she makes her living. Moll Comfrey came forward only because she has testimony that will absolve a man she cared for from the charge of murder. It took courage on her part. The girl can neither read nor write, Anne. The magistrate bullied her until she was utterly confused."

"Will she hold up under examination, Nick?"

"I think so. Moll was confused but never browbeaten."

"What happens next?"

"The magistrate promised to look into the matter," said Nicholas with a sigh, "but he warned us that it would take time before any decision was made. The law is quick enough to condemn a man to death, but it moves like a snail when a miscarriage of justice has occurred."

"How did Frank Quilter react to all this?"

"Sadly. He expected too much, too soon."

"Will you need more than Moll Comfrey's word?" she asked.

"Much more, Anne. The magistrate made that clear."

"Not a helpful man, then, it would appear."

"No, said Nicholas. "At times, the fellow was all but obstructive."

"What is his name?"

"Justice Haygarth."

Adam Haygarth rode through the peopled streets at a steady trot. A big, fleshy, round-shouldered man in his fifties, he had gray hair and a wispy gray beard that looked as if it had been blown on to his chin by a strong wind instead of actually growing there. Ordinarily, he moved through London with an air of condescension, looking down in disdain at the citizens he passed from his elevated position as a justice of the peace. This time, however, he put his self-importance aside in the interests of speed. All that he could think about was reaching his destination. When the crowds thinned slightly, he was able to kick his horse into a canter. It was a warm evening, still light. By the time he reached Bishopsgate, there were thick beads of sweat on his face. He dismounted, tethered his horse, and hurried to the front door of the house. After licking his lips nervously, he knocked hard.

Sir Eliard Slaney was at home. A servant conducted the visitor into the parlor, where Sir Eliard was being forced to admire his wife's latest purchase from her milliner. Wearing the new hat, Lady Slaney was parading up and down so that her husband could view her from different angles. When she saw Haygarth, she insisted that he, too, should tell her how remarkable she looked in the hat. With an effort, he duly obliged. Haygarth signaled the importance of his visit with a glance at Slaney, who immediately ushered his wife towards the door.

"The hat is a triumph, Rebecca," he said, easing her out of the room. "But you must excuse me while I talk to Justice Haygarth."

"When shall I wear it in public, Eliard?"

"As soon as you wish, my dear."

He closed the door behind her and gave a world-weary sigh.

"My wife has a strange passion for hats," he explained.

"I have always admired the way that she dresses herself, Sir Eliard."

"That is her only fault, alas. Rebecca demands rather too much admiration. Still," he went on, "I doubt if you came to discuss the skills of her milliner. What means this unexpected visit, Adam? You look as if you have been running."

"Riding hard," said Haygarth.

"You were wont to move more leisurely when you are in the saddle."

"Urgency required speed, Sir Eliard."

"Urgency?"

"I had inquiries to make elsewhere at first," said Haygarth, taking a paper from inside his doublet. "Once they were completed, I came here as fast as I could."

"You sound as if you had good reason."

"The best, Sir Eliard. Disaster is in the air. I thought the problem was solved when Gerard Quilter was hanged yesterday, but it is not to be."

"What do you mean?"

Haygarth offered him the paper. "First, read this. It is a frightening document."

"Nothing frightens me," said Sir Eliard, taking the paper from him to glance at it. His expression changed at once. His eyes bulged in alarm. "Can this be true?"

"The girl gave her statement earlier this evening, Sir Eliard."

"She claims to have been with Master Quilter on the very day he was alleged to have committed the murder. Does this have any substance? If it does," he continued, "then we are all in serious danger."

"That's why I brought you the news posthaste."

"Who is this creature called Moll Comfrey?"

"A bawdy basket, arrived in the city for Bartholomew Fair."

Sir Eliard grinned slyly. "Then we are surely safe," he said, relaxing. "No judge would take the word of some common prostitute against that of worthy fellows like Cyril Paramore and Bevis Millburne."

"The girl has solid support, alas."

"Support?"

"Two men came with her, Sir Eliard. One is Master Quilter's son."

"An actor with Westfield's Men, as I hear."

"And a most determined young fellow," warned Haygarth. "Had the girl come alone, I could have dismissed her story out of hand, but Francis Quilter is not so easily swept aside. His friend is just as resolute."

"Friend?"

"One Nicholas Bracewell, as stubborn a fellow as I've ever met. With two such people at her back, the girl is prepared to take her Bible oath that Gerard Quilter was unjustly convicted of murder."

"A pox on Moll Comfrey!"

"We are all like to catch it from her, Sir Eliard," whined the other. "If the truth can be established in court, all four of us face the wrath of the law. As a justice of the peace, I will be especially humiliated."

"Cease this sniveling, man!" ordered Sir Eliard. "Let me think."

He paced the room and read the statement through once again before slapping it down angrily on the oak table. It took him a full minute to reach his decision. He rounded on Haygarth with such menace that the magistrate took a step backwards.

"Where is this Moll Comfrey now?" he demanded.

"That is what delayed me, Sir Eliard," said Haygarth. "I went to find out where the girl is lodging while she is in London. And I spoke with one or two people who know Moll Comfrey. Among her kind, she is popular and well respected."

"Her popularity has already worn thin with me," said Sir Eliard, curling his lip. "Where does she stay?"

"At Smithfield. She'll sleep in the booth of a pie man and his wife. They are old acquaintances of hers and among the first to arrive today. Smithfield is already half-covered in stalls and booths," he said. "You would not recognize it as the place where public executions took place yesterday."

Sir Eliard was rueful. "Bartholomew Fair does not cover everything so completely as we would have hoped, it seems. If this girl is allowed to give her evidence, a hundred thousand booths will not hide the mischief behind the hanging of Gerard Quilter." He snapped his fingers. "Is the girl at Smithfield now?"

"Yes, Sir Eliard. I glimpsed her as I left."

"And you could point out the place where she will lay her head?"

"The smell would guide me to it, for they are still baking pies there."

Slaney went to the table and picked up the paper again. After reading it through for the third time, he scrunched it up in his hand and tossed it to the floor.

"She must go," he decided.

Moll Comfrey was sitting on the grass as she shared a warm pie with Lightfoot. She was glad to be back at Smithfield again. Newcomers had been arriving throughout evening to pitch their tents and set up their stalls. A sea of colored canvas was slowly engulfing the whole field. Moll felt at home. The sturdy itinerants who traveled around fairs and markets were people she liked and understood. She was part of their fellowship and had made several friends. None was more valued than Lightfoot.

"This is the tastiest supper I've had in a month," he said through a mouthful of meat pie. "Though you might have done even better for yourself, Moll, had you kept your wits about you."

"Done better?" she asked.

"Did you not say that you met Master Quilter?"

"Yes, Lightfoot. He was a true gentleman."

"Then he should have bought a lady a fine supper in gratitude," he argued. "What you took him in exchange was worth far more than the price of a meal."

"I did not go there to *sell* the information."

"That is what I'd have done in your place, Moll. Yes," he added, swallowing the last of his pastry and licking his fingers, "and I'd have expected money as well as food."

"They did offer me money."

"Then why did you not take it, girl?"

"Because I thought they did so to make trial of me," she said. "Master Quilter did not trust me at first, I could see that. Why should he? I am a complete stranger, arriving out of nowhere to claim that I knew his father. He offered me money to see if I was trying to sell worthless tittle-tattle. When I spurned it, he began to listen more carefully to me."

"What of this other man you met?"

"He was kinder to me from the start. His name was Nicholas Bracewell, and he helped to convince his friend that I was telling the truth. They took me to a magistrate, and I told him what I knew. Justice Haygarth turned up his nose at me," she recalled bitterly, "and would have thrown me out as soon as look at me. It was this Nicholas Bracewell who made him take my evidence seriously."

"I hope that it helps, Moll."

"It must," she insisted. "A terrible wrong has to be righted."

"They'll make you stand up in a court of law," he cautioned.

"I'm not afraid of that, Lightfoot. Gerard Quilter was a good friend."

"Did you tell them why?"

She lowered her head. "Some things must forever be kept secret." Moll nibbled at her own piece of pie. "Now you may see why I fainted when you broke the news about the execution to me. It shocked me so deeply. When I came to Bartholomew Fair, I expected to meet him again, yet I find that he was hanged on the very spot where the fair will take place." She shivered involuntarily. "And I've not forgotten Jane Gullet. She was burned for witchcraft here."

"Eat your pie and pay no attention her."

"How can I when her spirit still walks on Smithfield?"

"Think of the spirit of Master Gerard Quilter," he suggested.

"I do, Lightfoot," she said solemnly. "I've thought of nothing else all day. This whole field is now accursed. An innocent man was hanged by the neck, and a witch was burned to a cinder. Can you not smell the menace in the air?"

"All that I can smell are those wonderful pies."

"I'm worried, Lightfoot."

"There is no need," he assured her. "What will happen now?"

"We wait on the word of the magistrate."

"The law will not be rushed."

"That is what Justice Haygarth said. I'm to remain in London until I am called."

"That may take weeks," he said. "How will you live? Where will you stay?"

"Nicholas Bracewell has offered to find me a roof over my head. He works with the theater troupe that performs at the Queen's Head. He has influence there and believes he can secure me a small room."

"Then you are blessed in his friendship, Moll. The Queen's Head is a fine inn. I went there myself. You are rising in the world," he teased. "While you lie in a warm bed there, I will be sleeping under a hedge."

Moll finished her pie. "I've slept under enough hedges myself in the past," she said, "and look to spend a night under many more." Stifling a yawn, she rose to her feet. "I am tired, Lightfoot. It has been a long day, and this business has worn me down. I know it is still early, but I am ready to lay down my head."

"Not before you honor your promise," he said with a grin.

"Promise?"

"I gave you a name, Moll. Where is my kiss in return?"

"That particular name does not merit a kiss."

"A bargain is a bargain," he argued.

"True enough." She got up to kiss him softly on the lips. "There's your reward, Lightfoot," she sighed. "But you'd have had a thousand more kisses if you could have told me that Master Gerard Quilter was still alive."

When he returned to the Queen's Head that evening, Nicholas Bracewell saw that some of Westfield's Men were still there. Their mood was somnolent. Instead of carousing, they sat in a huddle, nursing their ale and sharing their concerns about the company. Before he joined them, Nicholas went across to Sybil Marwood, the landlady, a fearsome woman with a basilisk stare that could quell any affray that broke out on the premises. While she shared her husband's dislike of the troupe, she was far more tolerant of its presence, knowing how much distinction and custom it brought to the inn. Over the years, she had also developed a sneaking fondness for Nicholas, the most polite and presentable member of the troupe. His approach actually managed to crack her face into something resembling a smile.

"Good even, Mistress Marwood," he said.

"You are welcome, sir."

"How does your husband fare?"

"Indifferently well."

"I am sorry to hear that. Is he still abed?"

"He is," she complained, "and likely to remain there for another week at least. I begin to think his illness is deliberate so that all the responsibility of managing the Queen's Head falls on my shoulders. Alexander has left *everything* to me."

"But you do it so well," he flattered. "Far better than your husband."

"Is that so?"

"Everyone in the company has noticed."

"Have they?" she said, softening even more. "I shall tell that to Alexander. It may help to speed his recovery. He believes that custom will dry up without him. He is such a jealous man where the Queen's Head is concerned."

"It is in safe hands with you, Mistress Marwood."

"Thank you, sir."

"I think that you were born to the life."

Her smile broadened. "The approval of Nicholas Bracewell is always a pleasure."

"You have earned it, dear lady," he said. "Convey my regards to your husband."

"I will, I will."

Having cheered the grim landlady, Nicholas crossed to the table where his friends were sitting. All five of them were despondent. Owen Elias looked up at him through glazed eyes. The Welshman had lost all his usual effervescence.

"Have you come to take part in the funeral, Nick?"

"What funeral?" asked Nicholas.

"The one that we are holding for Westfield's Men."

"When the troupe is still alive and in good health?"

"But it is not," replied Elias. "We've lost Frank Quilter from our ranks. You, too, were in danger of leaving. And now we have this message of doom from Edmund."

"All may yet be well, Owen," said Nicholas. "Frank's departure is a temporary loss, and I have resolved to stay with the company. As for Edmund, he is in the grip of an infatuation, and we have seen many of those before."

"Not like this one, Nick," said James Ingram.

"No," added Elias. "Every time a woman smiles at him, Edmund falls in love—but his passion is always unrequited. That is not so here. This creature called Avice Radley is a bird of prey. She hovers above our heads, ready to snatch our playwright in her talons."

"How long will we survive without him?" moaned Ingram.

"It may not come to that, James," said Nicholas.

"Laurence is in despair. He hoped that *you* could talk sense into Edmund's ear. Yet even your attempts were met with failure."

"I'll try again with more cogent argument."

"A dip in the Thames is the only cogent argument for Edmund," said Elias sourly. "Let's throw the wretch from London Bridge. The water may bring him to his senses."

"Violence will not be called for, Owen," said Nicholas. "Once the novelty of this new romance is past, Edmund will listen to reason." He saw someone coming in through the door. "But you must excuse me, friends. I must have private conference with Frank. His troubles make our own seem small."

Nicholas went over to intercept his friend and guide him to a quiet corner of the taproom. It had been Quilter's idea that they should meet at the Queen's Head, but he was having reservations about the decision now. He looked furtive and uneasy, keeping his head down and unwilling even to glance towards the other actors. Conscious that some of them still wanted him discharged from the company, he no longer felt part of it. Nicholas ordered ale for both of them and then told him what Anne Hendrik had learned during her visit to the Slaney household. Quilter pounced on one revelation.

"And so Sir Eliard Slaney *was* at Smithfield yesterday!" he noted.

"Standing beside his friend, Bevis Millburne, no doubt."

"Two yoke devils, exulting in their wickedness."

"We have no proof that Sir Eliard was involved," Nicholas reminded him.

"Then why is he so thick with the two false witnesses who brought about my father's death? He *has* to be in league with them, Nick."

"I agree, but we must establish that fact for certain."

"Anne is our best hope there," said Quilter. "Does she have good reason to visit the house again before long?"

"Happily, yes," said Nicholas. "Lady Slaney was so pleased with her new hat that she wishes to commission another. Anne is to call on her soon to discuss the style she prefers and the material she wishes to choose. I am glad that I went back to Bankside to hear the intelligence she gathered today. It is invaluable."

"I've not been idle since we parted."

"Where have you been?"

"I kept vigil outside Master Paramore's house," explained Quilter. "We did well to follow him when he disembarked. That taught us where the villain lived and in what obvious comfort."

"He is a prosperous man, Frank."

"But wherein does that prosperity lie? That is what I went to find out. You'll recall there was a tavern close to his house."

"The Black Unicorn, was it not?"

"The very same," said Quilter. "I bought a drink and asked the landlord if Cyril Paramore ever dined there. He does so regularly, Nick, and always orders the best of everything. There's more. The landlord told me that he sometimes dines at the Black Unicorn with his employer."

"Employer?"

"Sir Eliard Slaney."

Nicholas nodded. "That explains why Sir Eliard met him off the *Speedfast* today."

"The first thing that Paramore would want to know, I daresay, is what happened at Smithfield while he was absent. Only when my father was dead would he feel safe."

"That safety is now under threat," said Nicholas. "Thanks to Moll Comfrey."

"I wonder if he is aware of that."

"How could he be? Her statement is lodged with Justice Haygarth. The wheels of the law are sluggish, Frank. The magistrate schooled us to be patient. No," he decided, "there is no way that Paramore could have caught wind of Moll's evidence."

"He has caught wind of something, Nick."

"What do you mean?"

"Only this," said Quilter. "I watched his house above an hour from the comfort of the tavern. Then a messenger rode up. What news he brought, I do not know, but it frighted Cyril Paramore mightily. He rushed out of his house and called for a horse from his stable. His wife was alarmed at his sudden departure. I could see it in her face as she stood at the door. When her husband rode off hell-for-leather, she was bewildered."

"I do not blame her," said Nicholas. "When he has been away in

France for a time, she has a right to expect that he would spend his first evening at home with her. It is strange behavior for a husband."

"I could not have followed him on foot."

"Even your young legs would not move that fast."

"And I did not wish to keep you waiting here."

"You did well to discover what you did, Frank."

"There was one thing more, Nick."

"Yes?"

"The landlord at the Black Unicorn told me that Paramore was devoted to his wife, but I saw little devotion in the way he abandoned her on the doorstep. He did not even bid the poor woman farewell."

"The news he received must have been truly grievous," said Nicholas. "Nothing else would make a loving husband act in such a way." He ran a thoughtful hand through his beard. "Where could he have been going?"

While his visitors were on the verge of panic, Sir Eliard Slaney remained icily calm. Bevis Millburne and Cyril Paramore were in great discomfort as they sat in the parlor of Sir Eliard's house. They had still not managed to assimilate the tidings.

"Where did this creature spring from?" demanded Millburne.

"She is in London for the fair," said Sir Eliard. "It was sheer chance that she arrived on the very heels of yesterday's business, though there may be consolation in that."

"Consolation! I see no consolation, Sir Eliard."

"Calm yourself, Bevis."

"How can I when this girl holds a knife at our throats?"

"Bevis is right, Sir Eliard," said Paramore. "Let this bawdy basket give her evidence in court, and we are all done for."

"Therein lies the consolation, Cyril," replied Sir Eliard. "Had the girl appeared *before* the trial, it might not have had such a rewarding outcome for us. Her word might have rescued Quilter from the noose that we so cleverly put around his neck. The pair of you would have been arrested on a charge of perjury."

"Horror!" cried Millburne.

"We only did your bidding, Sir Eliard," argued Paramore.

"Cyril has hit the mark there. The plan was not of our devising."

"You must take the greater share of the blame."

Sir Eliard was scornful. "Be quiet, you craven cowards!" he shouted. "You were quick enough take my money when it was offered. I heard no complaints from you then. This is a time when each of us must keep our nerve, not descend into bickering. I expected Bevis to whimper," he went on, "but I looked for better from you, Cyril."

Paramore squirmed in his chair beneath the withering gaze of his employer.

"You have my apology, Sir Eliard," he muttered.

"What are we going to do?" wailed Millburne.

"Act like men," insisted Sir Eliard, "and not like terrified women. Take hold on yourself, Bevis. If one of us stumbles, he brings the rest of us down."

Sir Eliard went to the table to pour three glasses of wine. When it was handed to him, Millburne took a long sip from his glass. His hands were shaking visibly. Paramore had regained his composure. He had more faith in his host. There had been other storms to weather in the past. They would doubtless survive this new squall. A sip of wine put more confidence into him.

"All that we have to do is to defy this bawdy basket," he said airily. "What value will a judge place on her word when it is ranged against that of respectable citizens like Bevis and myself? Her evidence will be laughed out of court."

"Not if it is supported by others," said Sir Eliard.

"Others?"

"Yes, Cyril. The girl was *seen* with Gerard Quilter on the day in question. According to Adam Haygarth, she can call on two or three who will vouch for the fact. Travelers, like herself. They'll be here for the fair."

Millburne was aghast. "Are we to be brought down by the sweepings of the streets? I'll not endure it, Sir Eliard."

"You will not have to, Bevis."

"We may still brazen it out," said Paramore. "A dozen bawdy baskets and their kind could not discredit our evidence."

"The case must never come to court," urged Millburne. "Buy the creature off."

"That was my first instinct," admitted Sir Eliard, drinking his own wine. "But our helpful magistrate tells me that she is beyond the reach of a bribe. Moll Comfrey did not visit Adam Haygarth's house alone. She went with Francis Quilter."

"The son! Then are we all damned."

"Be silent, Bevis."

"With his support, the girl is a more credible witness."

"We'll not buy Quilter's son off," said Paramore anxiously. "He'll want the family name cleansed of its stain. There's danger here, Sir Eliard."

"Grave danger. We sent an innocent man to his death, and now we'll pay for it."

"He was *not* innocent," retorted Sir Eliard, eyes blazing. "Gerard Quilter had the gall to cross me, and no man does that with impunity. He deserved his fate, and I'm proud that I contrived it. I'd do the same again. Bear that in mind," he warned, looking from one man to the other. "I'll brook no opposition. I did not achieve my position by being kind to my enemies. I simply destroy them. Is that understood?"

"Yes, Sir Eliard," said Paramore meekly.

"Bevis?"

Milburne nodded. "Yes, Sir Eliard," he whispered.

"Do as I tell you, and none of us need fear. One solitary person stands between us and our peace of mind. A bawdy basket called Moll Comfrey." He gave a sneer. "Are we going to let some roadside punk defeat us?"

"No, Sir Eliard," said Paramore.

"Never!" added Millburne.

Sir Eliard gave a cold smile. "Then this is what must be done."

Anne Hendrik was waiting for him when he returned to Bankside that night. Seated at the table in the parlor, she was examining some drawings she had made of new hats. She rose to give him a welcome kiss. Nicholas Bracewell squeezed her affectionately.

"It is good to see a face that bears a smile," he said, "especially when the face happens to be yours, Anne. I saw precious few smiles at the Queen's Head."

"Is the company so distressed about what happened to Gerard Quilter?"

"What issued from it has hardly cheered them. They have lost the services of a fine actor, and opinion is divided as to whether they should have him back. Frank did himself no favors by his surly behavior towards them this evening. He pretended that his fellows were not even there."

"Is that what removed the smiles from their faces?" she asked.

"No, Anne," he said, sitting down. "They hardly noticed that Frank was with me. It's another departure that vexes Westfield's Men. They fear to lose Edmund."

"Edmund Hoode?"

"He has elected to go."

"Surely not, Nick."

"I did not believe it myself at first."

"What possible cause could make him quit the company?"

"Her name is Mistress Avice Radley."

"Ah," she sighed, understanding the situation. "Of course. It had to be a woman's hand who tries to pull him away."

"She may accomplish what a team of horses could not do, Anne, for they would not make him budge an inch from the Queen's Head."

"Who is the lady?"

"A wealthy widow," he said, "with enough money to support them both and sufficient greed, it seems, to want Edmund all to herself. He is besotted with her."

"He is always besotted with some woman or other."

"This one is set quite apart from the others, Anne."

"In what way?"

"No stalking was involved here, no futile pursuit of his prey. Mistress Radley came to him. Edmund says that she descended out of heaven on a white cloud. You can see that he still sees her through the eyes of a poet."

"How long will that last?"

"In perpetuity, he claims."

"His loss would be a bitter blow to the company."

"Crippling, Anne," he agreed. "Laurence Firethorn is tearing out his hair."

"Can he not persuade Edmund to stay?"

"I fear not. No more can I," he admitted, "though not for want of trying. I can usually reason with Edmund, but he would hear none. His decision has been made. He vows that it will not be changed."

"Who made the decision? Edmund or Mistress Radley?"

"He swears the compact is mutual."

"Then Westfield's Man are truly under threat," she concluded, sitting at the table. "To lose an actor like Frank Quilter is handicap enough. To be deprived of the author of your best work will make you weak, indeed. Your rivals will prosper at your expense."

"That is what the company fears. It has touched them all. Even Barnaby Gill has been forced to acknowledge how important Edmund is to our success." His eye twinkled. "You can imagine his derision when he learned that a woman was the cause of it all."

Anne smiled. "At least Barnaby will not be led astray by a wealthy widow."

"He lives for the theater, Anne. So, I believed, did Edmund."

"Is this Mistress Radley such a paragon of virtues that she can lure him away?"

"None of us has met the lady."

"Someone should do so," she advised. "On the company's behalf, I mean. You are the man for that task, Nick. Edmund may be impervious to reason, but his inamorata may not be. Why not approach her direct?"

"That would be unfair to him."

"Seek his permission first."

"He is unlikely to grant it," said Nicholas. "This lady is like no other whom Edmund has met. He is shielding her from us." He grinned. "Laurence Firethorn cannot understand why she did not pick him out instead."

"His vanity knows no bounds." She gathered up the drawings. "But how did you find Frank Quilter this evening? Is he still weighed down with grief?"

"He was heartened by what we learned today."

"So he should be, Nick. This young peddler whom you met has the power to proclaim his father's innocence. Even though her occupation does embarrass Frank."

"Moll Comfrey did not choose her occupation."

"Where is the girl now?"

"She stays at Smithfield in the booth of some friends."

"What happens when the fair breaks up?"

"That is where we encounter trouble," he confessed. "Justice Haygarth insisted that she stay in London until she is called to give her evidence in open court. That may take time. I hope to use my position at the Queen's Head to find her a bed there."

"Would she be safe at an inn like that, Nick?"

"Yes," he replied. "If I was there to keep an eye on her."

"We could both do that, if Moll Comfrey chose to come here instead."

"Here?"

"There's room in the attic for her and her basket," she said. "It is important that she remains in London, you say. Why did you not invite her to Bankside?"

"Without your permission, I did not feel able to do so."

"Well, now you have it."

"Thank you, Anne," he said, getting up to kiss her. "I am most grateful. It is the best solution of all. You will like Moll. She is a charming girl."

"Yet her charms do not seem to work on Frank Quilter."

"He will come to like her in the end. Moll Comfrey is his savior."

Smithfield was still alive as midnight approached. Hundreds of people had now arrived in readiness for the fair. Booths, tents, and stalls had been set up in favored positions. Those who would sell, perform, or otherwise seek payment at Bartholomew Fair were united in common fellowship. Old friends met up to exchange news and gossip. Whole families sat out in the warm night air to speculate on what weather they might expect for the fair and what effect it would have on the crowds. Fires had been lit to cook food, and dozens still sat around them to talk, argue, complain, reminisce, or simply stare into the embers. The lights of the city might be going out, but the sturdier souls at Smithfield needed less sleep. It would be hours before the heavy murmur of conversation died away.

Moll Comfrey was oblivious of it all. While her hosts were still out under the stars, she had long since crept into their booth and found the corner allocated to her. She lay on a piece of sacking on the bare earth, curled up beside her basket. Fatigue had taken her to the booth, but heartache prevented her from falling asleep. Her mind was filled too vividly with shifting images of Gerard Quilter, a man she had come to love as much as anyone in the world. The meeting with his son had been both salutary and upsetting. Francis Quilter looked so much like his father that he revived fond memories of her time with the older man, while simultaneously reminding her of his dreadful fate. The son had the same features, the same voice, the same gestures, and the same way of holding his head at a slight angle. Francis Quilter also had the same integrity, the same fundamental decency and consideration for others that would never allow him to stoop to murder. His father had been the victim of false witnesses. Moll was dedicated to the notion of clearing his name. Her hand tightened around a small gift that the older man had once given her. Its aroma always helped to sweeten her sleep.

When exhaustion finally got the better of her grief, she dozed off, but she did not desert her dearest friend. He followed her into her dream, walking beside a river with her, talking with her, showing his concern and affection, offering her money to help her through any difficult times ahead. Time spent with Gerard Quilter was a haven of peace in an otherwise fraught existence. When they arranged to meet at Bartholomew Fair, she was delighted. The thought that she would soon see him again would steady her through any troubles she might encounter. As they parted beside the river, he kissed her gently on the forehead, pressed some money into her palm, and then vanished from her sight.

He returned to her almost at once, but the scene had changed. Bartholomew Fair was at its height, turning Smithfield into a cauldron of noise and merriment. Lightfoot was doing somersaults, a performing dog was prancing on its back legs, a man was swallowing fire, a champion wrestler was taking on all comers. Enormous crowds were swirling around the booths. Moll was selling her wares when she saw her friend emerging out of the crowd. Quilter gave her a cordial welcome. Buying some ribbons from her, he tied them neatly in her hair. She felt elated and danced around with joy. Then he suddenly disappeared again, and she could not find him. Moll was desolate.

She ran wildly here and there, searching with increasing desperation, until she bumped hard into a gallows and looked up to see Gerard Quilter's body dangling above her.

It brought her awake with a silent cry. Before she could even realize where she was, she saw a figure moving towards her in the gloom. Had her friend come back for her, after all? Had he escaped the cruel death she had seen in her dream? Was he there to take her away from the hardship of her life? Longing to be reunited with Gerard Quilter, she sat up with open arms to beckon him forward. Her wish was granted.

Moll Comfrey soon joined her friend in an untimely grave.

[CHAPTER SIX]

Laurence Firethorn had more reason than any actor in the company to be grateful for the talents of Edmund Hoode. The playwright had furnished him with most of his finest roles. The imperious Pompey the Great and the courageous Henry V were recreated magnificently from life, but the heroes of *The Loyal Subject, Death and Darkness, The Corrupt Bargain,* and a dozen other plays sprang up like vigorous new shoots from Hoode's fertile brain. The dramatist was equally at home with history, comedy, or tragedy, allowing the actor-manager to exhibit the full range of his incomparable abilities. Even when Hoode was merely a coauthor of a piece—as with *The Merry Devils* or *The Insatiate Duke*—his contribution was distinctive. When he thought of the countless old plays by other hands that Hoode had repaired or substantially improved, Firethorn was reminded how valuable a member of Westfield's Men his friend really was. Given his abilities, the playwright was remarkably self-effacing. There were occasions, it was true, when he wrote eye-catching parts specifically for himself to play, but that was a permissible indulgence. In his own way, Firethorn came to see, Edmund Hoode would be an even more terrible loss than Nicholas Bracewell.

A desperate situation called for desperate measures. With that in mind, Firethorn arose even earlier than usual and ate a hasty breakfast before either his children or the apprentices had even been turned out of bed by a clamorous summons from his wife. Margery gave him a kiss before he took his leave.

"Tell him from me that he must never desert Westfield's Men," she said.

"I do not intend to speak to Edmund as yet, my love."

"Then why set off so early for his lodging?"

"To watch and wait," replied Firethorn.

"For what?"

"Guidance."

"You must surely speak with him to get that."

"He will not even know that I am there."

"Then why bother to go?"

"I am acting on instinct."

"How will that help to keep a renegade playwright in the company?"

"You will see, Margery."

"Give him time, and he may come to his senses."

Firethorn was bitter. "We do not *have* time," he said. "The longer we delay, the more firmly this witch will have Edmund under her spell. It must be broken soon."

"How, Laurence?"

"That is what I am going to find out."

"Why not take Nicholas with you?"

"He has tried and failed. Diplomacy has made no ground at all. Rougher methods must be called into play. Nick is not the man to employ them." He embraced her warmly. "I must away, my love."

Margery was puzzled. "Rougher methods?"

"Farewell."

He was soon riding out of Shoreditch at a steady canter, vowing to use whatever means it took to retain Hoode's services for Westfield's Men. Unlike his book holder, he was completely unscrupulous and would devote all his energies to the removal of Avice Radley from the playwright's life. Before he could achieve that end, he needed to know more about the lady who threatened to undermine the stability of the company that he led so proudly. In order to do that, he required unwitting assistance from Hoode. When he entered the city through Bishopsgate, he turned his horse in the direction of his friend's lodging, clattering along thoroughfares that had been baked hard by the hot summer. London was already wide awake, streets crowded, markets teeming with customers, but Hoode would not rise until it was time to leave for the morning's rehearsal at the Queen's Head. Firethorn reached the house, saw that the shutters on his window were still locked and dismounted. He had timed his arrival well. A narrow lane, some thirty yards away, provided an ideal hiding place from which to watch the house.

Edmund Hoode was a creature of habit. Whenever he was in love—a not uncommon situation for someone so full of random affection—he would spend half the night sighing outside his lady's bedchamber and then return in the morning to blow a kiss up to her window on his way to Gracechurch Street. It had happened so many times before that a pattern had been established. All that Firethorn had to do was to follow. It irked him that he had been kept in the dark about Avice Radley. Hoode had divulged nothing about her apart from her name and her determination to rescue him from the squalor of London and the precariousness of his profession so that they could live together in rural bliss. He had been very careful to give no indication of where she lived and, in spite of Nicholas Bracewell's efforts at persuasion, had fled so swiftly after the performance of *Love's Sacrifice* that nobody had been able to see where he went. Firethorn was taking a first important step in the campaign against Avice Radley.

"Know thy enemy," he said to himself. "Track her to her lair."

Firethorn did not have long to wait. Ten minutes after he took up his position, he saw Hoode's face appear at the open window as the shutters were flung back. Smiling happily, the playwright inhaled the fetid air of the city as if it were the scent from a flower garden. He soon descended to the ground floor to let himself out of the house and saunter along the road. Firethorn led his horse by the rein in the wake of his friend. He had no fears that Hoode would turn round to see him. The man had eyes for no one but his beloved, and it was an image of her that floated entrancingly before him. It was clear from the start that he was taking no direct route to the Queen's Head. After snaking his way through a warren of back streets, Hoode came out into a wide road with a ribbon of houses along both sides. Firethorn trailed him until he stopped outside one of the largest dwellings and gazed up.

"Good morning, Avice," said Hoode, blowing a kiss.

His arrival was not unexpected. At the very moment when he made his gesture of affection, shutters opened in the bedchamber at the front of the house and Avice Radley appeared in a long blue gown. Beaming graciously, she waved a greeting to Hoode that made him tremble with ecstasy. It was minutes before he could drag himself away to fulfill his obligations at the Queen's Head. Firethorn did not immediately pursue him. Even after the woman had withdrawn, he stared up at the window in disbelief. Avice Radley had a statuesque beauty that took him quite by surprise. She was a woman of noble mien allied to considerable physical charms. She embodied all the qualities he found most attractive in the female sex, her widowhood suggesting an experience that tempted him even more. Firethorn no longer wondered how Avice Radley had ensnared his playwright. It was an upsurge of envy that now filled his breast.

"Why choose Edmund," he murmured, "when you could be *mine?*"

Nicholas Bracewell was the first to arrive at the Queen's Head. By the time that Thomas Skillen and George Dart rolled into the inn yard, the book holder had inquired after the landlord's health, conversed affably with Sybil Marwood, swept some horse dung from the innyard, wheeled out the barrels on which the stage was to be set, and unlocked the room where they stored their scenery and properties. Westfield's Men performed six days a week, their location within the city making it impossible for them to stage plays on Sunday because of an edict against such a practice. No such legal technicality hindered the two Shoreditch playhouses, the Theatre and the Curtain, nor the popular Rose in Bankside, all three being outside City jurisdiction. While their rivals at the Queen's Head were forced to rest on the Sabbath, they could present their work to large audiences. Few plays had more than occasional consecutive performances at any of the London playhouses. Variety of fare was required, and it was not unusual for Westfield's Men to offer six entirely different dramas in a week. If high standards were to be maintained, daily rehearsals took on special importance.

George Dart was still only half-awake when he trotted up to Nicholas. "What do we play today?" he asked.

"You should know that, George."

"I think it is *Love's Sacrifice.*"

"That was yesterday's offering," said Nicholas.

"Then it must be *Black Antonio.*"

"Not until tomorrow."

"I am sorry," said Dart, rubbing his eyes. "My brain is addled today."

"It is always addled," complained Skillen, cuffing him around the ear. "Get more sleep, lad. I'll not have you confusing one play with another. Today, we rehearse a bright comedy for a bright afternoon. *Cupid's Folly* will be seen here."

Dart grinned. "I like the play. It makes me laugh so."

"Then you'll know what scenery we need," said Nicholas.

"Every last piece."

"Fetch it, George." Dart ran off, and Nicholas turned to the old man. "You are too hard on him, Thomas. A word of praise would not come amiss."

"Let him deserve it first," said Skillen.

"He held the book well in my place, remember. Did you commend him for it?"

Skillen chuckled. "In a way, Nick. I did not box his ears for the whole afternoon. That's the highest praise I can offer to George Dart. To spare him punishment."

The actors were beginning to drift in. Most of them were on foot, but a few, such as Barnaby Gill, wearing one of his most lurid suits, were mounted. Nicholas noted the general lack of enthusiasm among the troupe. Owen Elias was sullen, James Ingram was dejected, and Rowland Carr looked as if he was overcome with a secret sorrow. Even Richard Honeydew, the youngest and most able of the apprentices, a boy whose angelic features were almost invariably touched with a smile, seemed jaded. The person who had caused the pervading gloom was blithely unaware of the effect he was having on the others. Grinning broadly, Edmund Hoode bounded up to scatter greetings to all and sundry. He was met with cold stares and muttered resentment. Nicholas alone gave him a warm welcome.

"Have you had time to reflect on what I said, Edmund?"

"When?" asked Hoode.

"Yesterday. After the performance, we had a brief talk."

"Did we?"

"It made little impact if you cannot even recall it," said Nicholas resignedly, "so my question answers itself. You have not given any thought to my argument."

"I did, Nick, but only to dismiss it once again."

"Can no appeal reach you?"

"Not while I tread in Elysium."

"It is not in your character to be so indifferent to your fellows."

"I am not indifferent," said Hoode, distributing a smile around the others. "I love them all dearly, but I am the happy prisoner of a greater love that has determined my whole future. Share my joy, Nick. Wish me well in my marriage."

"I'll be the first to do so," promised Nicholas. "You will be a dutiful husband. But I am sorry that you have to divorce twenty people in order to wed one. Is there no means by which we may all keep our mutual vows?"

"None, I fear. The die is cast."

"We'll talk further, Edmund."

"To no avail."

Hoode went off to speak to Barnaby Gill, who was even more morose than usual. Nicholas was left to supervise the construction of the stage and the disposition of the scenery for the beginning of *Cupid's Folly*. Nathan Curtis, the carpenter, was standing by in case his skills were needed to make a few repairs. Hugh Wegges, the tireman, was bringing the costumes out. Peter Digby and the other musicians were tuning their instruments in readiness. Every member of Westfield's Men was there except its leader. When he finally made his entrance, Laurence Firethorn was in no mood for delay. Something had put new spirit into him. Cantering into the yard, he reined in his horse, leapt down from the saddle, tossed the reins to George Dart, and glared around at his discontented company.

"Wherefore this Stygian gloom?" he yelled. "Anybody would think that the landlord had recovered from his illness. We've work to do, my friends. Let's about it straight. Come lads," he exhorted. "Strong hearts and honest endeavor are all that's needed here. Show me what you can do."

Firethorn's vitality helped to lift the company out of its melancholy. Nicholas admired the way that he moved among them, soothing, encouraging, and setting a positive example for the others to follow. Smiles reappeared and friendly badinage started once more. Firethorn was leading from the front. When the rehearsal began, he did not hold back in his customary way to save his full power for the audience that afternoon. Showing all his comic gifts, he committed himself totally to the play and released the deeper chords in *Cupid's Folly* as well as its abiding humor. Everyone responded to his call. Barnaby Gill was supreme, dancing and clowning his way through the piece with effortless skill. Owen Elias, too, seemed to have been reborn as an actor, matching Firethorn himself for sheer volume and comic intensity. James Ingram's was another inspired performance, and the apprentices brought a new sharpness to the female characters. Instead of dominating the play, Edmund Hoode was all but rendered invisible by the display around him. It was almost as if the company were getting its revenge on its disloyal playwright, consigning him to insignificance in a play whose title was an appropriate comment on his latest romance.

At the end of the rehearsal, the company dispersed in search of refreshment. Firethorn waited until Hoode had departed before he drifted across to Nicholas. The actor-manager grinned broadly and stroked his beard.

"Our troubles may be over, Nick," he said.

"You can convince Edmund to stay with us?"

"I prefer to work on the lady herself."

"Mistress Radley?"

"She holds our lovesick author in thrall. Persuade her, and we free Edmund."

"Tread with care," advised Nicholas.

"This romance throws us all into jeopardy. I'll nip it in the bud."

"That may prove a hard task."

"Trust me, Nick," said Firethorn confidently. "I have a plan."

Without elaborating on his scheme, Firethorn went off to join the others for a light meal before the performance that afternoon. Nicholas was mystified, wondering what had transformed the actor-manager's mood. After giving some last orders to Skillen and Dart, he moved off to take a short break himself. Before he could enter the inn, however, he was confronted by a curious figure in colorful attire. The newcomer's face was lined with grief. Over his arm, he was carrying a large basket, filled to the brim with wares that Nicholas felt he recognized.

"They told me I would find Nicholas Bracewell here," said the man.

"He stands before you."

"Thank heaven, sir! My name is Lightfoot."

"Ah, yes," said Nicholas, smiling at the tumbler. "You are Moll Comfrey's friend. I thought that might be her basket that you carry."

"It is all she had to leave."

"Leave? She has surely not quit London?"

"London, and every other place besides, sir," said Lightfoot. "Poor Moll is dead."

"Dead?" cried Nicholas in alarm.

"She was murdered as she lay. Some villain squeezed every last breath out of her. And the worst of it is," he went on, tears forming in his eyes, "we were sitting no more than five yards away."

"We?"

"Ned Pellow, the pie man, and his wife. All three of us were outside the booth, talking happily until well after midnight. When we took to our beds, Ned looked in on Moll and saw her sleeping soundly, as he thought. She was very tired last night and laid her head down early." Lightfoot brushed a tear from his cheek. "It was only when they tried to wake her this morning that they learned she had been killed."

"How could they be sure it was a case of murder?"

"By the marks upon her, sir. Moll had bruises on her neck, her arms, and her shoulders, as if she had been held down while some fiend smothered her. The blanket that did the foul deed lay beside her. It did not belong to Ned Pellow." He bit his lip to hold back his anguish. "If only she had cried out. We could have gone to her aid."

Nicholas was shocked by the news, not merely because the witness who might have cleared Gerard Quilter's name had been summarily removed. He had liked Moll Comfrey. His acquaintance with her had been fleeting, but he had seen enough to note her honesty, her courage, and her uncomplaining acceptance of her lot. She was a remarkable young woman and far too healthy to have died a natural death. It was horrifying to think that her life could be snuffed out so easily, like a candle. He was bound to wonder if her murder was linked to the evidence she had been brave enough to give.

"What action has been taken, Lightfoot?" he asked.

"Constables were summoned," replied the tumbler. "They took statements from us all then had the body removed to the mortuary. I could not bear to look on her as the cart took Moll away. She was such a dear friend to me, sir."

"Yes, I know. Moll told us how much you had helped her."

"I've never met anyone who asked for so little out of life."

"Have you taken these sad tidings to Master Quilter?"

"No, sir."

"Why not? You know where he lodges. This affects him more than me."

"That is why I went first to his house," explained Lightfoot, "but he was not there, and his landlady had no idea of his whereabouts. Then I remembered what Moll had said about Nicholas Bracewell."

"Oh?"

"She felt that you trusted her, sir. You spoke up for her before the magistrate. What really touched her was that you offered to find her a room where she might stay."

"I would gladly have done so."

Lightfoot held up the basket. "That's why I brought it to you, sir."

"I've no need for a basket."

"It's what was inside that you should see." Putting the basket on the ground, he rummaged among its contents. "I found it quite by accident when I looked to see if any of Moll's wares had been stolen. It was tucked away at the bottom."

"What was, Lightfoot?"

"This, sir."

He extracted a letter and handed it over. Nicholas glanced at the name and address on the front of the missive. He was puzzled.

"Did you not think to deliver it to the man whose name it bears?" he asked.

Lightfoot was shamefaced. "If I'd been able to read it, I might have done."

"The letter is addressed to a lawyer, here in London."

"A lawyer," echoed the tumbler. "Moll had no dealings with such men. It was all she could do to scrape a bare living. Nobody in her trade could afford a lawyer. One thing is certain, sir," he added. "Moll did not write that letter herself. The open road is all the schooling we've had. Reading and writing are not for the likes of us."

Nicholas was decisive. "I'll see it delivered to the right hands," he promised, "and I'll inform Master Quilter of the tragedy that has occurred. I'll want to visit Smithfield myself to see where the crime actually happened. Will you be there, Lightfoot?"

"Yes, sir. Look for me at Ned Pellow's booth. I'll not be far away."

"Good. We may need your help."

"You can have more than that," vowed Lightfoot, straightening his shoulders. "I'll not leave the city until we've caught the killer. I owe it to Moll to find the rogue. Count on me for whatever you need, sir. Lightfoot is yours."

"Thank you. I'll bear that in mind."

"Moll saw this coming. That's the tragedy of it, sir. When we got to Smithfield, she smelled the stink of calamity in the air. Moll said the place was cursed," he went on, picking up the basket again. "Her friend had been hanged there, and a witch had been burned nearby. To my eternal shame," he admitted. "I didn't believe her, sir. Moll was right. There *was* a curse, and she has become its victim."

Frank Quilter's zeal was undiminished. Having spent most of the morning keeping Bevis Millburne's house under surveillance, he had, seeing nothing of value, transferred his attentions to the home of Cyril Paramore, the other man whose testimony had helped to send his father to the gallows. Quilter was not sure what he could expect to find out, but he stayed at his post regardless. His vigil was eventually rewarded. As he watched from his vantage point in the Black Unicorn, he saw a plump, red-faced man arrive on horseback. From the description that Nicholas Bracewell had given him of the merchant, he guessed that it was Millburne. What interested him was that Paramore opened the front door himself in order to greet his friend. The younger man was far more relaxed than when Quilter had last seen him, dashing away from his home. As they went into the house, both of them were smiling broadly. Convinced that they were confederates in the plot to incriminate his father, Quilter was tempted to rush across the road to confront the men. Discretion held him back. Then he caught sight of another horseman and hurried out of the tavern in surprise.

Relieved to have tracked his friend down, Nicholas Bracewell dismounted.

"I hoped that I might find you here, Frank," he said.

"Why are you riding Laurence Firethorn's horse?"

"I told him of my urgency. He lent the animal to me to make sure that I returned in time for the afternoon's performance. This meeting must be brief."

"What has happened, Nick?" asked Quilter. "I see great sadness in your face."

"Lightfoot came looking for me at the Queen's Head."

"Moll's friend? Did he bring news of her?"

"The worst kind, Frank," said Nicholas, swallowing hard. "The poor girl is dead."

Quilter was rocked. "Dead? This cannot be."

"There's greater woe still. Moll Comfrey was murdered."

Nicholas passed on the details that he had been given by Lightfoot, impressing on him that the tumbler was eager to join in any pursuit of the killer. Quilter was too shaken to reply at first, sensing that all hope of exonerating his father had gone. Despair gave way to remorse as he thought about the defenseless young girl who had been smothered to death. He scolded himself for being so contemptuous of her at first when all that she was doing was to try to aid his cause. It now appeared that she might have died in the name of that cause. Quilter was overcome with a sudden fury.

"They are behind this, Nick," he insisted, pointing a finger at the house opposite. "Cyril Paramore and Bevis Millburne. They are there together even now, basking in their wickedness. Let's drag them into the street and tear out their black hearts."

"No, Frank," said Nicholas, "that is not the way. Supposition is not proof."

"Who else would have a reason to kill Moll Comfrey?"

"I cannot say, but I'll not rush to judgment. How could they possibly know of the girl's existence, still less of her friendship with your father?"

"They are guilty. I feel it in my bones."

"Once again, I counsel patience. I somehow doubt that they are the culprits. But if they are indeed behind the crime, we'll find the evidence that will unmask them. Until then, we must work unseen and not give ourselves away."

"They have the blood of two victims on their hands now."

"We need to find out why," Nicholas reminded him, taking the letter out from inside his buff jerkin. "But there's something else before I withdraw. This was found in Moll Comfrey's basket. Lightfoot thought to deliver it to your lodging, but you were not there. That's why he sought me out." He handed the letter over. "It is addressed to a lawyer named Henry Cleaton and may be of importance. I wanted you to see it first."

Quilter glanced down. "My father's hand. I'd know it anywhere."

"Is the name familiar?"

"Very familiar, Nick. Henry Cleaton handled father's affairs. Thank you for this," he said, holding up the letter. "I'll see it delivered at once."

"I'll want to know what transpires," said Nicholas, putting a foot in the stirrup. "Let's meet as soon as the performance is over." He hauled himself into the saddle. "I am sorry to be the bearer of such dreadful tidings. Moll Comfrey did not deserve this."

"Nor did she deserve my harsh words," confessed Quilter. "I should have shown her more courtesy. I bitterly regret the way that I treated her, Nick."

"Then make amends by helping to avenge her death. She was a blameless girl whose only desire was to clear your father's name of disgrace. Now, it seems, she may have paid for her readiness to speak out. Leave off your vigil here, Frank," he said. "Master Paramore is not the leader in this business. He and Master Millburne are but accomplices. The man to watch is Sir Eliard Slaney."

When she returned to the house near Bishopsgate that afternoon, Anne Hendrik took her most experienced hatmaker with her. Preben van Loew was a pale, dour, haggard man in his fifties with watery eyes that glistened on either side of a hooked nose. He was laconic by nature, but his employer had not taken him along for the benefit of his conversation. In the first instance, he provided a degree of protection for her on the journey. After crossing the Thames by boat, they had been faced with a long walk up Gracechurch Street, passing the Queen's Head in time to hear roars of delight from the spectators who were watching *Cupid's Folly*. Two other reasons prompted Anne to bring the exiled Dutchman with her. While she might design the new hat for Lady Slaney, it was Preben van Loew who would actually make it since he was particularly skillful at creating ostentatious headgear for the gentry. Apart from anything else, Anne felt that he should be there to receive his share of the praise for Lady Slaney's most recent purchase. But the main reason for requesting his company was so that he might provide cover for her, a shield behind which she could hide while plying Lady Slaney with the questions she had been asked to put.

They were admitted to the house and conducted to the parlor. It was not long before Lady Slaney surged into the room with a welcoming titter, wearing a jeweled gown in the Spanish fashion and looking as if she were about to entertain royalty rather than give orders to her milliner. When she was introduced to the Dutchman, in his sober black garb, she gave a gasp of pleasure.

"So *you* are the genius who makes my hats!" she cried.

"I do as I am bidden, Lady Slaney," he said modestly.

Anne was more forthright. "Preben ever hides his light under a bushel," she said. "I am fortunate to have him in my employ. When my late husband lured him to England, he told me that Preben van Loew was the finest hatmaker in Holland."

"Their loss is my gain," said Lady Slaney.

"Both us are always at your disposal."

"What have you brought to show me?"

"Some early drawings that should accord with your wishes, Lady Slaney."

Preben van Loew was too overawed by the sumptuous surroundings to do more than stand meekly in the background as Anne laid out the drawings on the table. Lady Slaney clucked over them like a hen whose first chick has just hatched. When she had selected the design she preferred, she suggested minor improvements to which Anne readily agreed. Privately, her companion thought that the chosen hat was even more ludicrous than the one he had just completed for her, but his personal opinion was hidden behind the impassive face. Whenever called upon for approval, he simply nodded his assent. It was half an hour before Lady Slaney had finished adding her refinements to the hat she had selected from the designs. Anne took careful note of every instruction.

"Everyone admired the hat you brought yesterday," said Lady Slaney bountifully.

Anne smiled. "I hope that Sir Eliard shared in the admiration."

"He would not dare to play the apostate," said the other with a tinkling laugh. "He knows how much value I set on appearance, and the right hat is such a vital element in the picture." She clapped her hands. "What a thought! I'll have another portrait painted of me, and this time, when I sit for the artist, I'll wear my new hat. I'll speak to my husband about it this very afternoon."

"Which new hat?" asked Anne. "The one I delivered yesterday or the one that you have just commissioned us to make for you?"

"Whichever flatters me the most."

"It is you who flatter us, Lady Slaney. We are deeply aware of the favor you bestow on us when you wear one of our hats in public. To have one seen at Court would indeed be a privilege for us."

"My husband will arrange that in due course."

"Sir Eliard seems able to arrange almost everything."

"It is the reason I chose him, my dear," said Lady Slaney with a giggle. "He likes to think that he proposed to me, of course, but it was I who drew him carefully on. Oh!" she exclaimed, glancing coyly at the Dutchman and putting a hand to her mouth. "Do I give away female secrets in front of a man? That was indiscreet of me. And I am sure that it was not the case when he proposed to his own wife."

"Preben is not married, Lady Slaney," said Anne, noting the blush that tinged his cheeks. "But how did you and Sir Eliard first meet?"

"That is an interesting story."

Lady Slaney told it as if she had rehearsed it many times, concentrating on her own role in the domestic saga yet confiding a great deal of information about her husband in the process. Anne memorized it in silence. It was only when the other woman came to the end of her tale that Anne had to prompt her.

"You never told me *why* Sir Eliard went to Smithfield the other day."

"It was to watch a public execution."

"I know, Lady Slaney," said Anne, choosing her words with care, "but it seems unlike your husband to take pleasure from such an event. Judging from what you say of him, he is a fastidious man who would be offended by the spectacle. Only some personal interest could draw him to witness it, surely?"

"I believe that he knew the wretch who was hanged for murder," said Lady Slaney offhandedly. "A man by the name of Gerard Quilter."

"He knew him?"

"Yes, my dear."

"And did this Gerard Quilter ever visit your house?"

"Not that I remember."

"But you heard his name mentioned?"

"With frequency."

"Was it spoken kindly?"

"No, his character was treated harshly."

"Sir Eliard must have known him well to attend his execution. Is that true?"

Anne Hendrik had asked one question too many. She was so absorbed in her covert interrogation of Lady Slaney that she did not notice the figure who now stood in the doorway. Sir Eliard Slaney was filled with cold anger. Walking into the room, he glared at the visitors with undisguised suspicion. He towered over Anne.

"What are you doing here?" he demanded.

The applause that reverberated around the innyard at the Queen's Head was well deserved. While not scaling the heights of which they were capable, Westfield's Men had given a lively performance of a romp that was a perennial favorite with their audiences. *Cupid's Folly* had entertained and exhilarated for two whole hours. Avice Radley had been as amused as anyone in the galleries. Seated on the cushion she had hired from one of the gatherers, she enjoyed every moment of the play, even though Edmund Hoode was not able to shine quite so brightly as an actor on this occasion. Laurence Firethorn, Barnaby Gill, and Owen Elias were the ruling triumvirate onstage, and there was exceptional support from Richard Honeydew and the other apprentices. Knowing that his beloved was there, Hoode did all he could to match the leading actors, but they overshadowed him with ease.

Avice Radley was mildly disappointed. Though she intended to take him away from the company, she liked to be reminded of just how talented he was as an actor. Hoode's creative skills would soon be put entirely at her disposal, making her as much of a patron as Lord Westfield. The difference was that she would not have to go to the Queen's Head to endure the crush in the gallery, the stink from the commonalty below and the general rowdiness in order to appreciate Hoode's brilliance. He would be hers alone, devoting his pen solely to her and creating a purer and more intense poetry. She would be his muse. Inspired by his wife, he would write and perform in the privacy of their home. It was the ideal recipe, she believed, for connubial delight.

Yet even as she luxuriated in thoughts of their future happiness, her gaze moved away from her captive playwright to the man who led the company with such verve and magnificence. Laurence Firethorn was unquestionably the brightest star in their firmament. He acknowledged the ringing cheers from all quarters of the innyard but he was looking directly at Avice Radley. When their eyes locked, she felt a tremor of surprise. Producing his most charming smile, he dedicated his next bow specifically to her and then waved a hand familiarly in her direction before taking his company from the stage. She was baffled.

"Moll Comfrey was your father's *niece?*" asked Nicholas Bracewell in amazement.

"In a manner of speaking, Nick. She was the child of my uncle, Reginald, born out of wedlock and kept ignorant of her true parentage for many years. Henry Cleaton showed me the letter that my father had written in her behalf."

"Did your uncle support the girl?"

"For a while, it seems," said Francis Quilter, "but he died in poverty a couple of years ago. My uncle was a dissolute man, I fear. He was the ruination of his wife and family. Drink and gambling made him lose what little fortune he had, and he was reduced to borrowing money at exorbitant interest. That was the real discovery in the lawyer's office, Nick," he continued. "When he died, Uncle Reginald was heavily in debt. I've no doubt you'll be able to guess the name of his chief creditor."

"Sir Eliard Slaney, perhaps?"

"The same."

"So *that* is the connection with your father."

"It goes deeper," said Quilter. "According to Master Cleaton, my father did everything that he could to prevent his brother's house from being possessed by Slaney in payment of his loan. They were in and out of court month after month. It was a battle royal. That despicable usurer got the house in the end, but it was a Pyrrhic victory. My father was a doughty litigant. In the course of their legal encounters, he wounded Slaney badly and won a substantial reduction in the amount of money owed."

Nicholas was fascinated. "Your visit to the lawyer has been profitable."

"It was a revelation, Nick. I learned so much about my own family. As you know, my father was very unhappy when I chose to join a theater company. He and I lost touch for some time." He cast his eyes downward. "You can imagine how much I regret that now."

"I can, Frank."

"The talk with Henry Cleaton opened my eyes."

"It also gave us the secret for which we've been searching, Frank."

"Secret?"

"Yes," said Nicholas. "Sir Eliard Slaney's motive for murder. Your father injured him severely in court. He wanted his revenge."

They were walking briskly towards Smithfield. Once his duties at the Queen's Head had been fulfilled, Nicholas had met up with Quilter to hear what had transpired at the lawyer's office. As they headed for the site of Bartholomew Fair, important new facts were beginning to emerge. Nicholas sought clarification.

"Why did your father give the letter to Moll?" he asked.

"Because he had taken on responsibility for her," said Quilter. "Even before his brother had died, he was the one who really cared for the girl. They met very rarely, but he always gave her money when they did so. Uncle Reginald never acknowledged her as his daughter, and my father did not want to distress his wife and family by telling them of Moll's existence. Poor creature!" he sighed. "When my father was hanged, she lost the one person in the world who showed her any parental love."

"It must have been an appalling blow for her."

"She was completely dazed, Nick. That's why she forgot it."

"Forgot what?"

"The letter," explained Quilter. "It was written two years ago. Moll was told that, in the event of my father's death, she was to deliver it to his lawyer. But she put it away in the bottom of her basket and thought no more of it. Because she could not read, the letter had no real meaning for her."

"What did it contain?"

"Provision for her in my father's will. Master Cleaton said that there was a codicil, naming Moll Comfrey as one of the beneficiaries, if and when she presented the letter to the lawyer."

"It's too late for that now," said Nicholas ruefully. "But I'm surprised that Master Cleaton told you nothing of the codicil before."

"He was forbidden to do so, Nick. My father never divulged anything to me about the girl. I suspect that he kept her existence hidden so that I would not think unkindly of Uncle Reginald. He was so protective towards his brother. And, of course," he went on, "there was no reason why I would ever learn the truth about Moll."

"No, Frank. Had your father died by natural means, she could have presented her letter to Master Cleaton and claimed her inheritance. You would have been none the wiser." Nicholas pursed his lips. "The fact that your father was executed as a murderer changed everything."

"That was the other discovery," said Quilter.

"What was?"

"The information I gleaned about the victim."

"Vincent Webbe?"

"Yes, Nick," said Quilter. "I knew that Master Webbe had fallen on hard times, largely because of his own failings. What I had not understood until the lawyer told me was that Vincent Webbe, too, had been a client of Sir Eliard Slaney—just like my uncle."

"Had he borrowed heavily?"

"Too heavily. He'd put his house in pawn."

"That signals desperation."

"He put the blame on my father. Master Webbe was no gentleman. I told you how he accosted us that time. He was so belligerent towards my father. If anyone had used such vile language to me, I would have had difficulty in staying my hand."

Nicholas was thoughtful. "When Vincent Webbe died," he said, "his debts must still have been unpaid. What happened to his property?"

"Sir Eliard Slaney took it into his possession."

They walked on in silence. As they approached Smithfield, Quilter was starting to feel queasy, recalling the dire humiliation he had seen his father endure on their last visit to the place. Nicholas, meanwhile, was trying to sift through the new information that had come to light. It said much for Gerard Quilter that he had not only defended his brother against the extortionate demands of Sir Eliard Slaney, but he had taken responsibility for an illegitimate daughter that his brother had fathered, as well. His conduct throughout had been exemplary. The codicil that Gerard Quilter had added to his will indicated a man of compassion. Nothing he had ever heard about him suggested to Nicholas that he could be capable of murder.

Hundreds of yards away from Bartholomew Fair, they were aware of its presence. Pungent smells of all description were carried on the wind, and a mild tumult could be heard. The vast majority of vendors and entertainers had now arrived, setting up their stalls and erecting their booths so close to each other that there appeared to be a continuous blaze of color across Smithfield. Curious dogs and inquisitive children had come to look around, as did the local prostitutes and pickpockets, taking their bearings so that they could see where best to operate on the following day when huge crowds descended on the fair. When they plunged in among the booths, Nicholas caught a strong whiff of roast pig mingling with that of a dozen other aromas, including the stench of animal dung. Some of the performers were already practicing their tricks, giving the watching children free entertainment. There was no sign of Lightfoot among the tumblers on display.

Nicholas asked for directions to the booth where Ned Pellow's pies were sold. He and Quilter were soon introducing themselves to a big, bearded individual in a leather apron that shone like silver in the sun. Now in his fifties, Pellow was a giant of a man with thick eyebrows curving outwards from a central position above his nose before merging with his beard. His wife, Lucy, was equally large and even more hirsute, her long black hair trailing down her back like the tail of a mare, her craggy features, dark mustache, and bristled chin making her look more like Pellow's younger brother than his chosen bride. However unprepossessing they might look, the pair were warm, friendly, and caring. Both had been deeply fond of Moll Comfrey.

"She was like the daughter we never had," said Pellow. "Lucy will tell you."

"Yes," said his wife in a voice that was little more than a squeak. "Moll was the sweetest girl in the world. It was a pleasure to know her. She always stayed with us when we met up at a fair or a market. Ned used to say it was because she had a taste for our pies, but I like to think it was because she was fond of us."

"I'm sure it was," said Nicholas. "Lightfoot told us how good you were to her."

"Yet we let her down when she really needed us, sir," admitted Pellow, plucking a sizable piece of pie from his beard. "So did Lightfoot. The three of us were sitting out here while that fiend was smothering her inside the booth. If I ever get my hands on the villain," he warned, flexing his muscles, "I'll tear him to pieces."

"And I'll help you, Ned," vowed his wife. "I want my share of his blood."

"You shall have it, Lucy. He took our Moll away."

"What did the constables say?" asked Quilter.

"They promised to look into the crime," replied Pellow bitterly, "but they made it clear that they would not do so with urgency. If a member of the nobility had been murdered in our booth, Smithfield would be crawling with officers of the law. Because she was only a bawdy basket, Moll does not rate any attention."

"She does from us," said Nicholas firmly. "That's why we want to track down the killer. Anything you can tell us will be of value. What mood was Moll in when she went to bed? How did she seem when you peeped in on her? When did you discover that she had been murdered? What steps did you take?" He looked from one to the other. "Take your time. Every detail is important. We'll be patient listeners."

Pellow nodded vigorously. "We'll tell you all we know, sir," he said earnestly. "Moll had kind words to say of Nicholas Bracewell. She sensed you were a friend."

Nicholas smiled, but Quilter shifted his feet uneasily, knowing that he had made a bad impression on the girl at first. Both men waited for Ned Pellow to launch into his speech. Ably supported by his wife, who contributed additions and variations at every stage, he described what had happened from the moment when Moll had returned to the fair after her visit to the magistrate. When they reached the point where the dead body was discovered, man and wife wept copiously. Nicholas warmed to them. They were kind, generous, affectionate people who had adopted Moll Comfrey as their own, offering her free accommodation whenever they met.

"How did the killer enter your booth?" asked Nicholas.

"He cut the canvas with a knife, sir," replied Pellow. "Lucy had to sew the tear up again this morning. I'll show you the place, if you wish."

"Please do."

The pie man first took them to the rear of the booth to point out the gash that had been made in the painted canvas. Nicholas and Quilter were then allowed inside to view the exact spot where Moll had slept. It was separated from the Pellows' own sleeping area by a large flap of canvas. Unbeknown to them, they had slumbered beside a corpse for the whole night. Nicholas examined the blanket that had been used to suffocate her. Made of wool, it was of a quality that set it apart from anything else in the booth. It had belonged to someone with far more money than Ned Pellow and his wife.

"We'll not sleep a wink tonight," confided the pie man.

"No," squeaked his wife. "We'll be thinking about what happened to Moll."

Leaving the booth, they came out into the fresh air. Nicholas looked around. Circumstances had favored the killer. The crowded acres of Smithfield had provided him with the cover he needed to slip into the booth, smother an unprotected girl to death, and make his escape into the darkness. What puzzled him was how the murderer knew where to find Moll Comfrey. He was still assessing the possibilities when Lightfoot emerged from the crowd. The tumbler grinned appreciatively.

"You came, sir," he said. "I knew that you would."

"It is good to see you again, Lightfoot," said Nicholas. "This is Frank Quilter, of whom you have heard so much."

"I am in your debt, Lightfoot" said Quilter, shaking him by the hand. "That letter you gave us was most helpful."

"Did it tell you who might have wanted to kill Moll?" asked Lightfoot.

"Not exactly."

"But it contained many valuable clues," explained Nicholas. "It also showed the great affection that Frank's father had for Moll. He had bequeathed her some money in his will."

"Would that she had been able to collect it!" sighed Pellow.

His wife began to weep. "Moll was robbed of her inheritance."

"Who would *do* such a thing?"

"Did she have any enemies here at the fair?" wondered Nicholas.

"None, sir," said the pie man. "We are all fellows here. It is like belonging to one big family. At fairs like this, we all look out for each other."

"But only someone in your fraternity would know where Moll slept."

"That is what troubled me, sir," said Lightfoot, "and I have spent the afternoon searching for the answer. I think I may have found it."

"Go on," urged Quilter.

"I talked to everyone I could who was here yesterday. Not just those who were within reach of Ned's booth but stall holders on the very fringe of the fair. One of them was Luke Furness."

"The blacksmith?" asked Pellow.

"Yes, Ned. With so many horses being sold here, Luke always does well at Bartholomew Fair. He's a vigilant man who keeps his wits about him."

"What did he tell you?" asked Nicholas.

"That he was accosted by a gentleman yesterday," replied Lightfoot, "asking if he knew anyone by the name of Moll Comfrey. The blacksmith did, of course. Luke Furness has been coming here so often that knows almost all of us. He told the gentleman that Moll could be found at Ned Pellow's booth."

"Did he describe the man?"

"He did, sir. Luke remembered him well. He said the fellow was big and fat with a pale face and hard eyes. He wore dark attire and seemed like a man of distinction. Luke took note of how fine a horse he rode."

"How old would he be, Lightfoot?"

"Older than any of us here."

"Did he, by chance, have a gray beard?"

"Why, yes," said the tumbler. "A small gray beard hardly worthy of the name."

"Thank you, my friend. This intelligence is timely."

"You recognize the man?"

"I think so," said Nicholas. "His name is Justice Haygarth."

[CHAPTER SEVEN]

As he rode along Cheapside at a steady trot, Laurence Firethorn congratulated himself on his deft stage management. When the performance of *Cupid's Folly* was over, he took Edmund Hoode into the taproom and plied him with Canary wine until the playwright was in an amenable mood. Barnaby Gill and Owen Elias had been recruited to lend their help, and they moved in on cue to take over. While they engaged Hoode in conversation, Firethorn slipped quietly away to put his plan into practice. Having given Avice Radley time to return home, he now headed in the same direction. There was a limit to how long his friends could delay her beloved, but Firethorn was confident that his horse would get him there well ahead of Hoode, who would travel on foot. He reached the house and tethered his mount. When a maidservant answered his loud knock on the door, his tone was peremptory.

"Tell your mistress that Laurence Firethorn is without," he declared.

"Yes, sir," she replied, gaping in awe at the actor.

"Hurry, girl. Hurry!"

The command sent her scurrying into the house to gabble the message. It took Avice Radley by surprise, but she was sufficiently curious to invite him in. Escorted into the parlor by the maidservant,

Firethorn gave her the kind of bow that he reserved for his audiences at the Queen's Head. He positively exuded charm.

"Forgive this intrusion, dear lady," he said, "but I could not help observing that you were in the gallery this afternoon to witness our humble efforts."

"There was nothing humble about your performance, Master Firethorn."

"You are very gracious, Mistress Radley. And even though we are, in a sense, strangers to each other, I find that I know you well enough to call on you."

"That depends on why you are here, sir," she said.

"In the first instance, it is for the pleasure of meeting you."

"That pleasure is shared. I have long admired your work at the Queen's Head."

"Then why do you seek to hinder it?"

"I seek nothing of the kind, I assure you."

"It seems so to us, Mistress Radley," he said with an appeasing smile. "But I am sure the damage you are about to inflict is not deliberate. Ignorance of our company leads you unwittingly to hurt us in this way."

"I have no desire to hurt anyone, Master Firethorn."

"That is what I told my fellows. When you understand the true state of affairs, you will, I am certain, change your mind. I can see at a glance that you are a reasonable person." He lowered his voice to a soft purr. "You are also the most delightful and beautiful creature to have graced our inn yard for many years."

"Dispense with this needless flattery," she advised, looking him in the eye. "It will not advantage you in the least. Now, sir, if it is not too much trouble, I would be pleased to hear why you have paid me this unheralded visit. Edmund warned me that you would try to win me over."

He was taken aback. "Warned you?"

"He is very familiar with your methods. That was why Edmund did his best to conceal my address from you. May I ask how you found it?"

"A happy accident."

"For whom?"

"For both of us, I hope."

He smiled again and inclined his head forward in a token bow. Avice Radley fought hard to resist the sheer force of his personality. A man who was able to dominate a large audience at the Queen's Head was almost overwhelming in a more intimate setting. If only to stop him from looming over her, she invited him to sit. Firethorn mistakenly took it as a sign of progress, and he surged on quickly.

"You have followed the fortunes of Westfield's Men?" he asked.

"Very closely, sir."

"Which is your favorite play?"

"The Merchant of Calais."

He inflated his chest. "Because of my performance in the title role?"

"No," she replied, "because it is one of Edmund's finest dramas."

"Nicholas Bracewell had a hand in it," he said peevishly. "It is by no means pure invention by Edmund. The character I play is inspired by Nick's own father."

"So Edmund told me. We have discussed every play he wrote."

"Did he mention his latest work?"

"Yes, he described the plot of *The Duke of Verona* in detail to me."

"That is more than he has done for me," he complained. "You obviously have skills of persuasion far greater than my own. I could tease nothing out of Edmund beyond the fact that the play would be his most rewarding."

"He no longer labors under that illusion, Master Firethorn."

"It is no illusion. I have known him many years and have learned to read him like a book. He is not given to boasting. If Edmund pronounces a play to be his finest, then I trust his judgment implicitly." He sat forward in his chair. "Would you deprive London of Edmund Hoode's masterpiece?"

"The decision is entirely his own."

"Strongly influenced by you, Mistress Radley."

Firethorn was disappointed to have had so little visible impact on her. Beside the balding and unremarkable Hoode, he accounted himself exquisitely handsome, and women usually fell at his feet in submission. It was not simply his striking appearance and glorious voice that they adored. What attracted his female admirers in such profusion was his bubbling energy. Avice Radley seemed strangely impervious to it. The irony was that he was increasingly drawn to her. Arresting when viewed from a distance, she was even more appealing in close proximity.

"I hoped that we might be more closely acquainted," he said with a coaxing smile.

"It would be an honor to be numbered among your friends, sir."

"That is my dearest wish."

He gazed steadily at her with seductive charm, conveying interest, affection, and desire in equal proportions. That look in his eye had presaged a whole series of conquests, but Avice Radley was not about to join their ranks.

"You must visit us in the country," she said politely.

"I would prefer to visit you on your own."

"Edmund told me that you would, Master Firethorn. He knows you better than you know yourself. But it would be quite improper of me to receive attentions from anyone but my husband. Besides," she added, turning the knife gently in the wound, "you are yourself a married man, I hear. Did you swear no vows of fidelity?"

Firethorn was flustered. "My private life is irrelevant," he said with a sweeping gesture. "Put it aside, I pray. I am here on behalf of my company to plead for your assistance. If you have any feeling for Westfield's Men, or any desire for the continuation of the high quality of its work, do not rob us of one of the main reasons for our success. In short, the excellence of Edmund Hoode's plays."

"I am no robber, sir. Edmund's withdrawal is voluntary."

"It is a catastrophe!"

"Only until you find a worthy successor."

"There *is* no worthy successor to Edmund."

"He has many imitators. School one of them."

"We would rather retain the original, Mistress Radley," he argued, "and it lies within your power to grant us that favor. Enthrall him, if you must, tease him, spoil him, pamper him, even marry him, if that is your ambition. But do not build a dam to hold back the torrent of his creative genius."

"I hold nothing back, sir. My intent is to encourage that creative genius. I can think of no better way to invest my wealth than by placing it at his disposal."

"I can," he said, seizing on the remark. "If you seek investment, why not donate the money to the company itself? Lord Westfield is our patron, but he lacks the funds to lavish upon us. We are ever in need of money to buy new costumes, make new properties, train new apprentices, and commission new plays. Put your wealth at *our* disposal," he went on, excited by the notion, "and you would bring *The Duke of Verona* to life, along with many other splendid dramas from the pen of Edmund Hoode."

"There is only one problem with that bold idea, Master Firethorn."

"What is that, dear lady?"

Avice Radley gave him a cold, bright, proprietary smile. "I do not wish to share him," she said flatly. "Edmund is mine alone."

The visit to Bartholomew Fair had been enlightening. Nicholas Bracewell and Francis Quilter left Smithfield in a far more positive frame of mind than on the earlier occasion. The information obtained by Lightfoot gave them what was potentially their most important clue to date. Nicholas was circumspect. Instead of accepting the tumbler's version of events without confirmation, he and Quilter called on the blacksmith in question and heard the evidence from his own lips. Luke Furness was open and honest with them. His memory was sound. As they walked away from his forge, they were even more convinced that the person seeking the whereabouts of Moll Comfrey had indeed been Justice Haygarth.

"No wonder he was so obstructive when we met him," said Quilter.

"I put that down to judicial caution," admitted Nicholas. "Moll had many virtues, but, to a magistrate, she did not look like a reliable witness. Let us remember that, when she first came forward, *you* did not take the girl at her word."

"I confess it freely, Nick."

"She was the victim of her profession."

"At least, we now know who contrived her death."

"Do we?"

"Yes," said Quilter. "It's as plain as the beard on Ned Pellow's face. The villain was that devious magistrate, Justice Haygarth."

"That's by no means certain, Frank."

"Why else would he come in search of Moll?"

"So that he could take a fuller statement from her," suggested Nicholas. "Or in order to establish where she might be for the next few days in case he needed her. You may recall that he did ask her where she lodged. All that Moll would say was that she would be staying with friends."

"And stout friends they were to her," noted Quilter.

"Just like your father."

"The magistrate *must* be involved, Nick. Apart from us, he was the only person aware of the damning evidence that Moll could give in court. He passed on the news to confederates." Quilter became animated, bunching his fists in anger. "Justice Haygarth has betrayed us. It is too great a coincidence that Moll should be killed on the very day that she comes forward as a witness."

"I agree, Frank. But we still rely on conjecture."

"We have linked Sir Eliard Slaney with the two false witnesses," said Quilter. "There's no hint of conjecture there."

"Linking them together was not difficult," Nicholas pointed out, "especially as Cyril Paramore is employed by Sir Eliard. Proving that they were in league to send your father to the gallows will not be so straightforward. And the role of the slippery Justice Haygarth still remains unclear."

"Not to me, Nick. He's another accomplice."

"We would need to be absolutely sure of that before we accuse a magistrate. His position as a justice of the peace is a strong defense in itself. Accuse him, and he would bring an action for slander against us."

"Challenge him about his visit to Smithfield yesterday."

"He would deny it outright. What then, Frank?"

"We have the word of the blacksmith."

"Will it stand up in court against that of a duly appointed magistrate? And even if it did," said Nicholas, "what would we achieve? There is nothing to prevent anyone from visiting Smithfield. We may prove that he was there, but that will not convince anyone that he was contemplating murder."

"Very well, then," rejoined Quilter. "Let us go back to his house. Confront him with the blanket used to smother Moll Comfrey."

Nicholas shook his head. "It would be a waste of time," he decided. "Whoever owned that blanket, it was not Justice Haygarth. You met the man, Frank. He may be a deceitful rogue, but he is no killer. Can you imagine him creeping through Bartholomew Fair at night with intent to commit murder?"

"No, Nick," conceded the other. "He'd lack the nerve."

"So would Bevis Millburne. He's too fat and slovenly for such work. I have my doubts about Master Paramore, as well. He's young and strong enough to do the deed but would be found wanting in other ways. No, Frank," he concluded, "I'd absolve all three of them. All four, since we must include the name of Sir Eliard Slaney. Remember what we saw at the pie man's booth. I think the crime was the work of a hired assassin."

Quilter was scornful. "Sir Eliard pays others to do his dirty work for him."

"What we need is proof that Justice Haygarth has taken his bribes."

"How do we find that?"

"Go back to Master Cleaton," advised Nicholas. "Lawyers pick up all the gossip about magistrates. Ask him what he knows about Justice Haygarth and whether the man is worthy of the position he occupies."

"He disgraces it, Nick."

"Then we must expose him. But only if we have sufficient evidence."

"I'll speak with Henry Cleaton at once."

"Good. I'll make my way to Bankside."

"Shall I join you there?"

"No," said Nicholas. "We'll meet at your lodging. It will give us the privacy we need to trade what intelligence we gather."

"But it is such a long walk from Bankside for you."

"That is why I'll spare my legs. I'll borrow a horse from Anne this evening and ride back over the bridge. I'd not been in the saddle for weeks until today. It is by far the quickest way to get around the city."

"What time shall I expect you?"

"As soon as may be," said Nicholas. "But I must speak to Anne first. She called on Lady Slaney today to discuss the design for a new hat. Anne may have gathered further information for us about Lady Slaney's husband. He is the crucial figure here."

Sir Eliard Slaney found that the easiest route to marital harmony was to indulge the whims of his wife, at whatever cost. It kept Lady Slaney happy and, more important, out of his way. While he provided the money, she supplied the marriage with decoration and respectability. It had always seemed a good bargain until now.

"I'll not hear of it, Eliard!" she protested.

"The decision has already been made, my dear."

"All my hats are made by Preben van Loew."

"His interest in your wardrobe ceases forthwith."

"But why? He is a magician at his trade."

"It is his employer that I distrust," said her husband. "Mistress Hendrik is far too inquisitive. She was here to design a new hat for you, not to ask questions about me."

"You are bound to provoke curiosity, Eliard."

"It was rather more than curiosity."

"Not at all," she insisted. "Anne Hendrik is the most polite of women. She would never pry into our personal affairs. If you must blame anyone, blame me. I love to trumpet your achievements abroad. And why not?" she asked, touching him on the arm. "My husband is a rich and successful man. I am surely entitled to sing his praises."

"That is not what you were doing, Rebecca."

"It was, it was."

"My presence at a public execution is hardly a cause for praise."

The couple were in their bedchamber, a large, low room with carved paneling that gleamed all round them. While her husband worked himself up into a rage, Lady Slaney surveyed the collection of hats set out on an oak table.

"They are my pride and joy," she said fondly.

"They can continue to be so, my dear," he told her. "But they must no longer be purchased from the same milliner."

"Why not, Eliard?"

"Because I say so."

"I would never presume to tell you where to buy *your* hats. Why do you try to take away my freedom of choice?"

"Because it has been abused."

"By whom?"

"The woman who was here earlier, Rebecca," he said vehemently. "How did she even *know* that I went to Smithfield for the execution? What business is it of hers what I do with my time? She was interrogating you. I'll not have this Anne Hendrik in the house again. Do you understand?"

"Then I'll visit her in Bankside."

"No!"

"Why not?"

"Because I forbid it."

"Would you stop me from selecting my milliner?"

"I'll prevent you from ever seeing this one again," he asserted. "London has no shortage of milliners. Find another to make your hats."

"When I already have the best available?" she argued, picking up her most recent purchase. "Look at it. Preben van Loew is a master of his craft."

"Forget that melancholy Dutchman."

"I need his skills to enhance my beauty."

"My word is final," he said with exasperation. "Why do you disobey me?"

"Because I have just cause."

"Rebecca!"

"I do, Eliard," she pleaded. "It is every woman's right to employ the dressmakers and milliners that she finds most congenial. Anne Hendrik has become a friend."

"Only in order to spy on me."

"Why on earth should she want to do that?"

"Never you mind."

"But I do mind, Eliard," she said tenaciously. "I've been a good wife and never once ventured to disagree with you. No husband could have less to complain about. You must admit that. On one thing, however, I must assert my privilege. Humor me, sir," she cooed. "It is little enough to ask, surely?" She held up the hat for inspection. "Have you ever seen a more exquisite piece of work than this?"

Her husband exploded. Grabbing the hat, he flung it against the wall with such force that most of its jeweled accessories were dislodged. Lady Slaney let out a cry of horror and tried to pick up the hat. Firm hands took her by the shoulders and swung her round. Sir Eliard Slaney was in no mood for resistance from her.

"Do as I tell you, Rebecca!"

"Yes, yes," she said between sobs.

"There's more to this than you could understand."

"If you say so, Eliard."

"She dwells in Bankside, you say?"

"That is true."

"Where?" he demanded. "I need to know her address."

Anne Hendrik's account was both interesting and alarming. While he was pleased with the information she had gained, Nicholas was disturbed that she had fallen foul of Sir Eliard Slaney. He blamed himself for putting her in a position of danger.

"It was wrong of me to send you again so soon, Anne."

"I went at Lady Slaney's request."

"And asked questions at mine," he said. "Because of that, you are like to lose your most lucrative source of income."

"I would hardly have retained it much longer if Sir Eliard is the monster you take him to be. He frightened me, Nick," she confessed. "Had I not had Preben with me, I might have endured more than merely his reproach."

He took her in his arms. "Can you forgive me?"

"The fault is as much mine as yours."

"No, Anne."

"It was," she said. "I should have been more careful. But once Lady Slaney begins to talk, it is difficult to make her stop. I sought to take advantage of the fact by feeding her questions. It was foolish of me not to see her husband enter."

"What you found out was well worth the visit."

"Then I am content."

He kissed her on the lips and embraced her warmly to show his concern. They were in the parlor of the house in Bankside. Nicholas had returned from Bartholomew Fair at as brisk a pace as the busy streets and a crowded London Bridge would allow. He was glad that he had made the effort to see Anne. After her unpleasant confrontation with Sir Eliard Slaney, she needed the sort of comfort and re-assurance that Preben van Loew could never offer.

"What of your day, Nick?" she asked.

"It has been filled with surprises."

"I want to hear about each one of them."

"Then I must start with the visit of Lightfoot."

Nicholas told her about the letter that was discovered in Moll Comfrey's basket and what transpired when the missive was delivered to the lawyer. He also gave her a full description of the visit to Smithfield. Her sympathy was immediately aroused.

"Poor Frank!" she said. "It must have been torture for him to return to the very place where his father was executed."

"I could see that the memory haunted him."

"He has been through so much in these past few days."

"Frank will gladly undergo far more in order to vindicate his father."

"I still do not understand why Gerard Quilter was falsely accused."

"It was an act of revenge, Anne," said Nicholas. "Sir Eliard Slaney had many bruising encounters with him in court and never forgave him for the courageous way that Gerard Quilter defended his brother's property."

"But how would he know when to strike?"

"By choosing the moment with care."

"The meeting with Vincent Webbe was a pure accident, surely," she said. "How could Sir Eliard have known that the two men would clash like that?"

"Because he arranged it."

"Arranged it?"

"That's my guess," he said. "You forget my occupation, Anne. I spend my whole working day helping to devise effects onstage. I can discern contrivance when I see it elsewhere. Gerard Quilter lived in the country and visited London only rarely. One of those occasions was the annual banquet at his guild hall. Knowing that he would be there, I suspect that Sir Eliard arranged for Master Webbe to be nearby when Frank's father arrived. That is where their brawl took place, close by the Mercers' Hall in Cheapside. Vincent Webbe provoked the argument."

"Why?"

"He had reasons of his own to hate Gerard Quilter."

"And you believe he was set on?"

"No question but that he was."

Anne was confused. "Then his murder was premeditated?"

"It had to be," he reasoned. "The brawl took place on one day, yet the victim, as we now know, met his death the following night. A definite plan was followed, Anne. Moll Comfrey was the only person who could have absolved Gerard Quilter in court, but he was unable to call her in his defense."

"And the voices of two witnesses sent him to the gallows."

"Two false witnesses, paid and instructed by Sir Eliard Slaney."

"It accords with my experience of the man," she said. "Lady Slaney praises her husband to the skies, but I saw another side of his character today. When he came into that room, there were murder dancing in his eyes. I was terrified, Nick."

"You'll not have to go through that ordeal again."

Anne smiled. "Then I'll be saved from a further agony," she said. "Lady Slaney all but talks my ears off. I may lose her custom, but I'll also be spared that garrulous tongue of hers."

Nicholas embraced her again. He stayed long enough to restore her confidence before making his excuses to leave. Anne readily acceded to his request to borrow the horse from her stable. She stopped him at the door.

"Where will you go?"

"To see what Frank Quilter has learned from the lawyer."

"And then?"

"To the Queen's Head," he said. "I promised to tell Laurence Firethorn what progress we are making. He wants Frank back in harness as soon as possible. The loss of a good actor like Frank is a bitter blow to the company. Though not," he added, "as profound a loss as that of our playwright."

"That shocks me, Nick," she said anxiously. "Edmund Hoode is such a loyal fellow. Can he really mean to desert Westfield's Men in this way?"

"So he affirms. But his plan may yet be thwarted. Laurence Firethorn has a scheme to halt Edmund in his tracks," said Nicholas. "I hope it meets with success."

* * *

Edmund Hoode was horrified at the news. He realized how he had been duped.

"So *that* is why Barnaby and Owen kept me distracted for so long!"

"Yes," said Avice Radley. "He wanted to visit me without impediment."

"What did Laurence say?"

"Exactly what you warned me he would say."

"Did he try to charm you into acquiescence?"

"He tried and failed, Edmund."

"This is unforgivable," he said, stamping a foot. "Laurence had no business to interfere in my private life. How did he even know where to find you?"

"I fancy that he somehow always manages to learn what he wishes to know. When I first heard the knock on my front door, I hoped that it was you. Instead," she went on, "it was Master Firethorn, as bold as brass."

"He should never be left alone with *any* lady, least of all mine."

"I was proof against his wiles."

Hoode beamed. "I never doubted you for a moment, Avice."

"Forewarned was forearmed."

"Every woman in London needs to be warned about Laurence."

Hoode was agitated. When he arrived at Avice Radley's house, his euphoria had vanished as soon as he heard about her earlier visitor. He was vengeful. His resolve was steeled even more. Seated beside her in the parlor, his eyes sparkled with determination.

"In trying to keep me, he has only managed to drive me away more speedily."

"There'll be worse to come, Edmund."

"Worse?"

"I think so," she cautioned. "You know your friend better than I do, but I sense that he is not a man to give up at the first repulse. Master Firethorn will be back before long with another stratagem."

Hoode was defiant. "I'll not let him make trial of your virtue again, Avice."

"He'll use other means next time."

"Not if I order him to stay clear of my beloved."

"Master Firethorn is not inclined to obey orders. He prefers to issue them."

"Too true," he agreed. "You have caught his essence there. Laurence has the habit of command, but I have tired of being told what to do and when to do it. As an actor, he is supreme. As a husband, he is unreliable. As a friend, alas, he can be duplicitous."

"What of the others?"

"They, too, have tried to persuade me to stay."

"Have you been swayed by their arguments?"

"Not an inch, Avice. My only commitment is to you."

"And to your work," she corrected.

"That, too, naturally," he said, "though it will be solely in your service. I can imagine nothing more wonderful than writing sonnets in praise of the woman who has transformed my life. It is strange," he mused, stroking her hand. "A week ago, I would not have believed that anyone could separate me from Westfield's Men. The theater has been my life for so long. It has brought me heady triumphs and dear friends. Yet now I am ready to turn my back on them without a hint of regret."

"There must be some remorse, surely?"

"None whatsoever."

She was pleased. "Are you so completely mine, then?"

"Wholly yours, my love. Before we met," he explained, "I only dwelt on the more pleasant aspects of working with Westfield's Men. They have been my family, Avice. But since I met you, I see the defects of such a life. It is narrow, selfish, and vainglorious. I pretend that I have the freedom to write, but it is a poor sort of liberty. I have to meet Laurence's demands and Barnaby's requests and serve the needs of an audience made up of everyone from mean apprentices to pampered courtiers. When I am at the beck and call of so many competing demands, wherein lies my freedom?"

"Only in your imagination, Edmund."

"I want the privilege of writing what I choose to write."

"Then I am the person who is able to grant it to you."

"I'll be eternally grateful, Avice."

"The gratitude is all mine," she said, squeezing his hand. "I was a grieving widow until I met you. Now, I have the heart and happiness of a young girl."

"I will study to increase that happiness," he promised.

"Will you, Edmund?"

"Put me to the test."

She looked at him shrewdly. "What did you dislike most about your life?"

"Its emptiness."

"Yet you were feted every afternoon at the Queen's Head."

"Applause soon dies away. It has no tangible quality."

"What else will you be glad to leave behind?"

"There are so many things," he said as he pondered. "Uncertainty, for a start. The fear that plague, fire, or Puritan disapproval will drive us from our innyard. Then there is the constant bickering of my fellows, the sheer pain of creation, the rowdiness of our audiences, the shortcomings of the Queen's Head, and the endless arguments with its miserable landlord. And one thing more, Avice."

"Go on."

"The cruelty of my occupation."

"Cruelty?"

"No matter how hard I work," he said gloomily, "no matter how cunningly I spin my webs of words, no matter how many different demands I try to answer, there is always someone to carp and criticize. Perfection is a mirage. I will never write the play that actors and audiences love without reservation. I inhabit a world of approximation. My plots are *almost* sound, my characters are *nearly* convincing, my verse borders on an excellence that I'll never attain when I'm the servant of so many masters."

"And when you come to me?" she asked.

"I'll be a willing slave to one mistress."

She smiled. "I'll expect some mastery from you, as well, Edmund."

"You shall have it in abundance."

"There will be times when *I* may choose to play the slave."

"That is more than I dare wish," he said, grinning broadly. "I love you, Avice. Until you came into my life, I never appreciated what true love really was. We will be overwhelmed with ecstasy."

"When?"

"When we are together."

"I am glad that you mentioned that," she said, moving closer to him. "I have an idea I wish to put to you, Edmund."

* * *

It was midevening before Nicholas Bracewell climbed the stairs at his friend's lodging. Francis Quilter occupied two small attic rooms that were drafty in winter and stuffy during summer months. Low beams obliged visitors to duck at several points. Scant furniture owed little to the carpenter's art. The cheap accommodation was a testimony to Quilter's commitment to his profession. As the son of a wealthy mercer, he could more easily have followed in his father's wake and led a comfortable existence in a large house. Instead, he spurned the luxuries that were his birthright in favor of the more ambiguous joys of the playhouse. Prosperity was an irrelevance to him. The riches that Quilter sought lay hidden in the plays in which he performed. That was where his true wealth was to be found. Yet even those rewards were far from his mind now. Another mission had supplanted his quest for glory on the stage.

"Henry Cleaton was more than helpful," he announced.

"What did the lawyer tell you, Frank?"

"No more than I expected to hear. Justice Haygarth is not held in high regard with the legal profession. He has a reputation for being sly, supercilious, and unnecessarily harsh on offenders."

"Can he be trusted?"

"Not according to Henry Cleaton."

"How can such an unsuitable man become a magistrate?"

"Patronage, Nick."

"It is the bane of our country," said Nicholas. "Those with influential friends will rise while more deserving people are pushed aside. It is shameful. Justice will never be dispensed fairly when it is in the hands of men like Master Haygarth."

"There is a more glaring example than him."

"Is there?"

"Think of the judge who sentenced my father to death," said Quilter. "The higher a man goes in the law, the greater the damage he is able to create. Henry Cleaton was the first to admit it. The judicial system is rife with corruption."

"How much did you tell him, Frank?"

"Enough to whet his appetite."

"Is he of the same mind as we?"

[145]

"Yes, Nick," replied the other, "but he advises care. He is a true lawyer. Caution is ever his cry. Nothing I divulged surprised him in any way. He is ready to believe the very worst of Sir Eliard Slaney."

"So am I now, Frank."

"Why?"

"He had the gall to turn on Anne."

Nicholas told him about the visit to Lady Slaney that she had made that afternoon. Quilter was upset that he had been indirectly responsible for her discomfort at the house.

"Anne should never have gone there on my account," he said. "It only deepens my feeling of guilt, Nick. I must not let my concerns put you or her in danger."

"That is not what happened."

"Yet you say that Sir Eliard turned on her."

"Anne is well able to look after herself," said Nicholas proudly. "Besides, his anger was checked by the presence of his wife and of Preben van Loew. As for the loss of custom that ensued, she sees it as a blessing in disguise."

"It might shortly have been curtailed in any case."

"I hope so, Frank. If we are able to put Sir Eliard and his friends where they belong, Lady Slaney will have no income to pay for her expensive tastes. It is clear that her husband has beguiled her completely. She knows nothing of his villainy."

"The woman has been living in a fool's paradise."

"Not for much longer," said Nicholas. "What you have learned about Justice Haygarth is no more than we suspected, but his name has yet to be linked to Sir Eliard. Is there any means by which we can do that?"

"Henry Cleaton willingly took on that office."

"Good. This lawyer is proving his worth."

"He never doubted that the evidence against my father was false and vindictive," said Quilter. "Yet he was unable to save him. It troubles him like a deep wound. He will do all in his power to assist us."

"So will Lightfoot," recalled Nicholas. "We must not forget him."

"What help can *he* offer?"

"He has already placed Justice Haygarth at the fair for us, and I am sure there is more assistance he can render. Moll Comfrey was a creature of the fair, Frank. That was her universe. Lightfoot is our guide, and we'll not find a more eager man."

"True."

"He loved Moll as a friend. He begs to be of use."

"We need all the support that we can muster."

"Yes," said Nicholas, "and we have gathered plenty already. The tumbler and the lawyer have been staunch allies, and Anne has been in a position to offer particular help. Then there is Laurence Firethorn," he added. "Without his agreement to release you from the company, none of our inquiries would have been possible."

"I'll hope to repay him in due course."

"You will do that best by exonerating your father."

"I know, Nick. What is the next step to be?"

"That must be taken by you and by Lightfoot. I am somewhat preoccupied, Frank. You may be liberated from the company, but I must attend a rehearsal and performance tomorrow. Until late afternoon, I'll not be able to join the hunt."

"Direct us instead."

"Lightfoot will continue his work at Bartholomew Fair," said Nicholas. "It was the blacksmith who spoke with Justice Haygarth, but there may be someone at Smithfield who caught a glimpse of a more sinister visitor at midnight. If there was such a witness, Lightfoot will track him down."

"What of me?"

"Return to your lawyer in the morning, Frank. We do not simply need evidence of a friendship between Sir Eliard Slaney and a corrupt magistrate. There is someone else whom we must scrutinize."

"Who is that, Nick?"

"The person whom we have forgotten," Nicholas reminded him. "Vincent Webbe, the murder victim. We know why Sir Eliard Slaney wanted to wreak his revenge on your father, but he must also have had a strong reason to see Master Webbe killed. What was his motive, and whom did he hire to carry out the murder? Look to Vincent Webbe," he advised. "There may be matter in it."

Opinions at the Queen's Head were still divided with regard to the execution of Gerard Quilter. As they sat around a table in the taproom, Barnaby Gill, Owen Elias, and James Ingram jousted once more. Gill was emphatic.

"Laurence should show leadership for once and ban Frank from the company."

"On what grounds?" asked Elias.

"The name of Quilter brings opprobrium to Westfield's Men."

"So does the name of Barnaby Gill."

Gill bridled. "There is no need to descend to insult."

"Then stop insulting one of your own fellows."

"Barnaby did not mean to do that," said Ingram, trying to calm them down. "He has a high regard for Frank Quilter as an actor, as do we all. Unfortunately, this business has tainted his name. Any ballad-maker will sell you a song about the foul murder of Vincent Webbe. The name of Quilter is on everyone's lips."

"That does not mean we turn our back on Frank," said Elias.

"We have to bow to circumstance, Owen."

"James shows the sense that you lack," said Gill, jabbing a finger at the Welshman. "I took Frank to be an honorable fellow, but I was mistaken. Anyone else in his predicament would have resigned from the company to spare it any damage."

"That is what he has done, Barnaby," said Elias.

"He has merely withdrawn from us and left us short of a good actor. Were he to quit, we would be able to replace him with a new sharer."

"There is some truth in what Barnaby says," decided Ingram.

Elias turned on him. "Will you desert Frank Quilter, as well?"

"A complete rest from the playhouse might be in his best interests."

"What would you have him do, James? Skulk away from London?"

"Most people in his position would prefer the shadows."

"Only if they believed their father to be guilty."

"As he patently was in this case," insisted Gill.

Ingram sighed. "The evidence against him left no room for doubt, Owen."

"It did in Frank's mind," said Elias, "and in Nick Bracewell's. They'll turn the city upside down in the search for the truth."

"I fear that we already know the truth. Gerard Quilter was guilty."

"Meanwhile," said Gill irritably, "we are deprived of an actor who should be replaced and saddled with a book holder whose concentration is elsewhere."

Elias banged the table. "That's a foul calumny!"

"I agree," said Ingram. "Nobody does his work more conscientiously than Nick Bracewell. That was an unjust remark, Barnaby."

"Was it?" retorted Gill. "Then why did he rush off as soon as the performance was over this afternoon? It was to help Frank Quilter in a fruitless search for evidence. How can Nicholas fulfill his obligations when his mind is elsewhere?"

Elias and Ingram joined forces to refute the accusation. They were still defending Nicholas strongly when Laurence Firethorn bore down on them. His arrival brought the argument to a halt. Attention shifted to a more immediate threat to the company.

"Well, Laurence," asked Elias, "did you visit the lady?"

"I did," said Firethorn, forcing a smile, "and I was warmly received."

"In her bedchamber, I hope."

"Our meeting lacked that particular delight, Owen."

"But that was the reason we detained Edmund," said the Welshman. "You swore to us that you could quash this romance in the wink of an eye, if you were but left alone with Mistress Radley for a short while."

Firethorn cleared his throat. "That course of action proved superfluous."

"She rejected him," announced Gill.

"Quite the reverse, Barnaby. It was I who had to fight her off."

"I have never known you resist such advances before."

"Nor I," added Ingram.

Elias was suspicious. "What happened at Mistress Radley's house?"

"The lady began to see reason," replied Firethorn.

"Reason to leave Edmund alone?"

"It fell short of that, Owen. What I convinced her to do was to think about the effect his departure would have on Westfield's Men. In short, I changed her mind."

"It does not sound like it to me, Laurence," said Gill. "You boasted that you could charm the lady into bed and make her forget that Edmund Hoode even existed. I fancy that you have come back empty-handed."

"No, Barnaby!"

"Then what did you actually achieve?" wondered Ingram.

"Time to reflect," said Firethorn.

"On what?"

"On what she is doing. Avice Radley is an intelligent woman. She appreciated the cogency of my argument. It will prevent her from making any rash decisions. That was my achievement, gentlemen," he said, almost believing it himself. "I have bought additional time. Edmund will be ours for longer than we thought. That will give us more opportunity to work on him—and on his beloved."

Gill was derisive. "Is that all you have brought back? A stay of execution?"

"Have faith in my powers of persuasion, Barnaby."

"They are at their best between the sheets of a bed," observed Elias.

Firethorn ordered a drink and tried to move the conversation away from the delicate subject of Avice Radley. The others were plainly disturbed. Hoping for a positive result from his visit to the lady, they sensed that it had only made the situation worse. Gill was especially fearful, predicting the collapse of Westfield's Men.

"Without Edmund, we are all doomed!" he cried.

"I admit that I'd sooner lose you from the company," said Firethorn spitefully.

"But I am its unrivaled clown."

"Comic jigs are more easily replaced than a talented playwright."

"We need both," said Ingram, "so stop baiting Barnaby. He has no equal."

Gill was mollified. "Thank you, James. It is a relief to know that I have one friend in the company."

"Two," said Elias with an affectionate grin. "We have our differences, Barnaby, but I've never seen a clown who could hold a candle to you. Like the rest of us, however, you shine best when Edmund has supplied the opportunity. We must not lose him."

"Nor shall we," insisted Firethorn with false confidence. "Leave him to me."

But they would not relent. They continued to bombard him with questions about his visit to Avice Radley until they had him in open retreat. Firethorn was grateful when relief arrived in the form of Nicholas Bracewell. He embraced the book holder.

"Thank heaven you have come, dear heart!" he said. "I need your help."

"It is yours for the asking," offered Nicholas. "What has happened?"

Gill was malicious. "Laurence has been spurned by a woman at last. He waggled his codpiece at Mistress Radley, and she sent him on his way."

"That is untrue!" howled Firethorn.

Nicholas was worried. "Did you call on the lady?"

"Yes, Nick."

"Was that wise?"

"I thought so at the time. Barnaby and Owen distracted Edmund so that I could pay my respects without interruption." He turned to the others. "And I did put our case with vigor," he insisted.

"You promised to reserve your vigor for her bedchamber," said Elias.

"Was *that* the device?" asked Nicholas with disgust. "I am glad that I had no part in it. What a cruel way to treat Edmund after all he has done for the company. Had you succeeded, you might have blighted this romance, but you would certainly have put Edmund to flight. Could you really expect him to stay with fellows who would descend to such underhand means?"

"He need never have known the truth, Nick," bleated Firethorn. "I hoped to charm the lady in such a way that she would not even agree to see him again."

"Your charms grow weary, Laurence," teased Gill.

Elias chuckled. "You should have sent me."

"No," said Nicholas. "It is not a subject for mockery. Edmund loves the lady. The romance may not suit our purposes, but that is no reason to destroy it utterly. Edmund is our friend and deserves to be treated with more respect."

"Nick speaks well," agreed Ingram. "Your behavior was gross."

"We were forced into it by desperation," said Firethorn.

"It was you who did the forcing, Laurence," noted Gill. "Owen and I were mere accomplices. You were the author of the device."

"It might have worked, it might have worked."

"Plainly, it did not," said Nicholas. "What will the consequences be?"

"Have no qualms on that account," said Firethorn airily. "Where charm failed, reason took a hold. I am convinced that I made Mistress Radley reconsider her actions."

Nicholas was stern. "I hope that you regret yours."

"You should, Lawrence," said Ingram. "They were ill founded."

"We were fools to think you could ever succeed," concluded Gill.

"Enough of my adventures," said Firethorn, trying to wave the topic away with a swing of his arm. "Let's hear what Nick has to say. Edmund will stay with us for at least a month. Frank Quilter has already gone. When may we expect him back, Nick?"

"Never, if the decision were mine," said Gill.

"It is not, Barnaby."

"You and he have brought disgrace upon the company, Laurence."

"Frank is determined to remove all hint of disgrace," said Nicholas, interrupting the row before it could develop. "We are not only certain that his father was innocent of the charge of murder, we have also gathered sufficient evidence to prove it. All that we need is a little more information before we can seek a review of the case."

"Information, Nick?" asked Firethorn. "What sort of information?"

Nicholas did not wish to discuss their investigation in such a public place and was spared the awkwardness of having to do so by the appearance of Edmund Hoode. The playwright burst into the tap-room with uncharacteristic urgency and glared around until he spotted Firethorn. Teeth gritted, he stamped across to the actor-manager.

"I have just come from Mistress Radley's house," he said. "She tells me that you had the audacity to call on her earlier, Laurence."

"Yes," admitted Firethorn. "I just happened to be passing and felt it only a courtesy to introduce myself."

"How did you even know where she dwelt?"

"That is neither here nor there, Edmund."

"Laurence tells us that he prevailed upon your inamorata, Edmund," said Gill, seeing a chance to embarrass Firethorn. "As a result of his persuasion, he assured us, Mistress Radley would make you change your mind."

"And so she did, Barnaby," said Hoode grimly. "I have considered afresh."

"There!" shouted Firethorn in triumph. "I knew that I could bring it off."

"All that you have brought off is our friendship, Laurence. How dare you interfere in this way! I did not think that even you would sink so low. But it *has* forced me to change my mind," Hoode said with emphasis. "When I announced my decision to leave, I offered to remain until the end of next month. In view of your appalling behavior today, Laurence, I will alter my date of departure."

Firethorn was hopeful. "You'll stay much longer?"

"No," affirmed Hoode. "Westfield's Men will lose me at the end of *this* month."

[CHAPTER EIGHT]

When he left the Queen's Head later that evening, Nicholas Bracewell was in a state of considerable disquiet. The ride home on the borrowed horse gave him an opportunity to reflect on Edmund Hoode's impassioned declaration. The playwright had revoked his earlier promise to remain with the company until the end of September. Instead, shocked by the crude attempt to woo Avice Radley away from him, and in defiance of his contractual obligations, he was now planning to leave Westfield's Men in less than a week. The decision had shaken them. Hoode was one of the most placid and undemonstrative of men, not given to rash pronouncements. Nicholas had often heard him moan about the perils of life in the theater, but his friend had never before threatened to bring his career with the troupe to such a premature end. Yet he was patently in earnest. At the end of August, they could no longer call on his services.

Nicholas blamed himself as much as anyone else. Revolted and annoyed by Laurence Firethorn's failed seduction of Avice Radley, he nevertheless took some responsibility for the predicament in which they found themselves. Nicholas had always been much more than simply the book holder with Westfield's Men. A number of other duties fell to him, one of which was to keep an eye on members of the company in order to spot any potential sources of trouble. Since he enjoyed the confidence of his fellows, he was uniquely placed to listen to complaints, offer advice, quell anxieties, subdue any discord, and spread contentment. Problems that actors would never dare raise with Laurence Firethorn were taken to Nicholas Bracewell and, more often than not, solved before the actor-manager even caught wind of them. Edmund Hoode had turned to the book holder a number of times in the past, and the outcome had always been fruitful.

Apparently, those days were over. Nicholas's powers of persuasion had been wholly ineffective. Hoode had ignored the appeal he had made on behalf of the company and, outraged by Firethorn's actions, was walking out on them almost immediately. Having made his announcement at the Queen's Head, the playwright had turned on his heel and stalked off before anyone could stop him. Firethorn, Owen Elias, and James Ingram had been stunned. Because he and Hoode had always been so close, Nicholas felt the pain of being spurned. Westfield's Men were about to lose a gifted author, a talented actor, and a leading sharer, but Nicholas was also forfeiting a friendship that was very dear to him. He felt a sense of profound guilt. In devoting so much attention to Francis Quilter's plight, he had not shown sufficient interest in Hoode's private life. During his many previous romantic entanglements, his friend had invariably confided in him, using Nicholas first as a mirror in which to admire his own happiness and, then, when the romance withered on the vine, as it inevitably did, seeking his companionship for the sympathy and understanding that he needed.

A rift had opened up between them, and Nicholas was bound to put some of the blame on himself. As a result of Firethorn's clumsy and inglorious attempt to steal his lady away from beneath his nose, Hoode had widened that rift even more. Nicholas could not reason with him. In the playwright's eyes, he was no more than part of a world that had to be abandoned once and for all. It was a sad comment on their long friendship. Nicholas hoped that there might yet be some way to retrieve the situation. When word of Hoode's imminent departure spread among the company, they would be devastated. The new play on which he had labored so hard, and in which he had such faith, would never even be finished. Instead of being able to offer Hoode's masterpiece, Westfield's Men would have to fall back on older material, pieces that had been staled by overuse and lacked the appeal of novelty.

So much had changed in such a short time. That was what disturbed Nicholas. At the beginning of the week, fortune seemed to favor them. They presented an exciting play to a packed audience at the Queen's Head and reaped the many benefits of having their difficult landlord struck down by illness. Company spirit was high. Hoode was totally committed to his new work. All seemed well. Crises swiftly ensued. The execution of Gerard Quilter was a black cloud over Westfield's Men, and the sudden infatuation of their playwright was a torrential downpour that would leave them bedraggled. When they next stepped out on stage, the actors would be thoroughly depressed. It was worrying. Nicholas knew that a poor performance on the following afternoon would be accorded little respect by their spectators. If they felt they were getting anything less than their money's worth, they would mock, jeer, protest aloud, and even hurl things at the cast. A dark tragedy like *Black Antonio* would be severely handicapped if the actors spent some of their time dodging apple cores and other missiles. The company's reputation would suffer, and their takings would dwindle. It was a daunting prospect.

Although he did not regret helping Quilter to exonerate his father, Nicholas was the first to admit that it was diverting some of his energies from his work. The sooner that a gross miscarriage of justice was exposed, the sooner he could concentrate more fully on his other duties. What puzzled him was the speed of Hoode's change of direction. Avice Radley had clearly made a tremendous impact on him. If Nicholas had gained anything out of the visit to the Queen's Head, it was an increased respect for the lady. Evidently, she had repelled the attentions of Laurence Firethorn with robustness, and that indicated strength of character. Westfield's Men were now the victims of that strength of character. When she pursued a course of action, she did so with iron determination. To have achieved what she had done in a matter of days, he judged, Avice Radley must indeed be a remarkable woman. Nicholas wondered if he would ever get to meet her.

He had reached the fringes of Bankside before he realized that he was being followed. As he rode his horse at a trot down a narrow lane, he heard another set of hooves clacking over the hard surface behind him. Whenever he turned a corner, the other rider pursued him. The sense of danger that was ever present in a notorious area like Bankside was intensified. Night was falling and shadows were darkening. Thieves were on the prowl. Nicholas kept one hand on the hilt of his dagger. When he urged his horse into a brisker trot, he heard the answering hoofbeats behind him. They seemed to be getting closer, yet, when he looked behind him, there was nobody there. His phantom stalker had vanished. Certain that he was still being trailed, Nicholas pressed on until he reached Anne Hendrik's house. He dismounted to stable the horse and then ambled round to the front of the house. As he paused at the door, he was even more conscious of being under surveillance, yet the street appeared to be completely empty. It was eerie.

Anne was waiting for him. There was a hint of fear in her eyes.

"Is he still there?" she asked.

"Who?"

"The man who was watching."

"I saw nobody," he said.

"Neither did I at first, Nick. But I felt that someone was out there earlier this evening. I peeped out half a dozen times, but there was no one in sight. And then," she went on with a shiver, "I caught a glimpse of him, sitting astride a horse on the corner of Smock Alley, staring at the house. When he saw me, he disappeared down the alley at once. It shook me, Nick. I haven't dared to step outside the front door since."

"What time did you see him, Anne?"

"All of two hours or more ago."

"Can you describe the fellow?"

"Not in any detail," she replied. "I saw him for only an instant. He wore a black cloak and a hat pulled down over his face. I was frightened."

Nicholas gave her a reassuring squeeze before going back to the door. Opening it swiftly, he darted out and looked up and down the street before running diagonally across to Smock Alley. Long and narrow, it knifed along in a straight line between the tenements that stretched on down to the river. The alley was too dark for Nicholas to see anything at all, but he heard the distant clatter of hooves as a horseman sped away. Neither he nor Anne had been mistaken. For some reason, they were being watched. Nicholas could still feel the sense of menace in the air.

Adam Haygarth enjoyed his moment of power on the bench. As he sat in judgment on his fellow men, he became brusque, imperious, and uncompromising. Mercy was never allowed to influence any sentence that he imposed. Those who came before him, and whose guilt was established, could expect the severest treatment. He closed the day's session by sentencing a woman to a term of imprisonment for the crime of stealing bread in order to feed her starving children. Sweeping her heartrending pleas aside, he ordered that she be taken out by force. Haygarth glowed with satisfaction. Having spent so long wishing to become a justice of the peace, he was relishing every second of it now. The Clerk of the Court then handed him a letter that had just been delivered. Its contents soon wiped the complacent smile from Haygarth's face. Calling for his horse, he left court at an undignified speed.

A summons from Sir Eliard Slaney had to be obeyed. Haygarth rode swiftly until he reached the house. He was still panting for breath as he was shown into the parlor by a manservant. Seated at a table, Sir Eliard glanced up at him.

"Why this delay?" he asked sharply.

"The court was in session, Sir Eliard."

"You should have declared an adjournment."

"Is it that serious?"

"It could be," said Sir Eliard, rising to his feet. "We have a problem, it seems."

"Of what nature?"

"I am not certain yet, Adam. That's why I needed to speak to you. Tell me about Nicholas Bracewell."

"Who?"

"Nicholas Bracewell, man!" snapped the other. "One of the people who brought Moll Comfrey to your house to make her statement."

"Ah, yes," said Haygarth, nervously stroking his beard. "I remember him. A sturdy fellow with an intelligence I would not have expected from a man in his occupation. He is the book holder with Westfield's Men and a friend of Francis Quilter. Of the two, Nicholas Bracewell was by far the more capable, with a knowledge of the law exceeding that of Gerard Quilter's son." He gave a shrug. "That is all I can tell you about him, except that he struck me as an obstinate fellow, far too resolute for my liking. Why do you ask about him, Sir Eliard?"

"He lodges with my wife's milliner."

"Is that a reason to take an interest in him?"

"Yes, Adam," said Sir Eliard. "Because the lady in question, one Anne Hendrik, has taken a sudden interest in *me*. She was here only yesterday, interrogating my wife, probing away to find out why I had attended the execution at Smithfield. That is hardly the kind of question a milliner puts to a customer."

Haygarth was anxious. "Someone has set her on."

"Exactly, my friend. We do not need to look far to name him."

"Nicholas Bracewell."

"The inquisitive milliner had the gall to ask my wife how well I knew Gerard Quilter and whether or not the man had ever been to my house."

"Saints preserve us!" cried Haygarth.

"In other words," said Sir Eliard, moving across to him, "Nicholas Bracewell has somehow stumbled on the fact that I am involved in this business. Now, how could he possibly do that, Adam? I hope that you did not let anything slip when you met him."

"No, Sir Eliard!"

"It will go hard with you, if you did."

"Your name was never mentioned, I swear it!"

"I helped to secure you a place on the bench," warned Sir Eliard, "but I can just as easily have you unseated. I thought I could rely on your discretion."

"You can, Sir Eliard," said Haygarth, starting to tremble.

"What did you say when they brought that bawdy basket to you?"

"As little as possible. I simply examined the girl then pointed out that the law moves slowly and that they must not expect a speedy response. My intention was to send them on their way so that I could come here posthaste."

"Were you followed, by any chance?"

"No question of that, Sir Eliard. I waited until they had gone off in the other direction before I even left the house. Besides," he said, "I rode hell-for-leather, and they were only on foot. There is no way that they could have known my destination."

"They have linked my name to the crime somehow."

"Not through me, Sir Eliard, I assure you."

Haygarth was quivering with apprehension, fearing his host's displeasure as much as the consequences of what he had just been told. Sir Eliard studied him with a mixture of curiosity and suspicion. The visitor squirmed under his gaze.

"Very well," decided Sir Eliard. "I accept that you were not responsible for leading Nicholas Bracewell to my door, but somebody was. I wish to know his identity."

"Then look no further than Francis Quilter."

"Quilter?"

"He must have been aware of the enmity between you and his father. Is it not likely that your name was mentioned to Nicholas Bracewell at some stage? That fellow has a quick brain. He'd wish to find out more about you."

"And did so through the agency of his landlady," said Sir Eliard with disgust. "It was the second day in succession that the milliner came in search of information about me. I love my wife dearly, but Rebecca is not the most reticent of women. She is inclined to boast, and that breeds carelessness of discourse."

"How much did she tell this Anne Hendrik?"

"Enough to convince me that the milliner was here with a purpose. I had her house in Bankside watched yesterday," he explained. "And I had Nicholas Bracewell followed home from the Queen's Head, where he spent the evening with his fellows. You can imagine how I felt when I learned that he lived under the same roof as the milliner."

"This is unsettling news, Sir Eliard."

"It shows the importance of discretion."

"I have been as close as the grave."

"Would that my wife had been so, as well! However," said Sir Eliard, pacing the room to relieve his tension, "I interrupted them before anything too ruinous was divulged. Needless to say, my wife has been ordered to dismiss her milliner."

"It is the lodger that we need to worry about, Sir Eliard."

"I agree."

"What is to be done?"

"In the first instance, I have alerted Bevis and Cyril to the situation. They need to be on their guard in case anyone comes asking questions about them. They were the witnesses at the trial. Francis Quilter is bound to turn his attention to them."

"They are staunch men. They'll not let us down."

"Nor must you, Adam," cautioned the other. "I'll not tolerate any sign of weakness. You must stand foursquare with us."

"That goes without saying, Sir Eliard."

"Betray me, and I'll carve the sentence on your heart."

Haygarth shuddered. "You will have no cause to do that."

"Describe him to me."

"Who?"

"Nicholas Bracewell. All that you have told me is that he is sturdy and resolute. What of his age, his height, his coloring, his attire, his bearing?"

"Well," recalled Haygarth, "he'll not see thirty years again, Sir Eliard. He is a tall man, something of your own height, with fair hair and beard. In his own way, I suppose, he is handsome enough. Francis Quilter was in doublet and hose, but Nicholas Bracewell wore a buff jerkin. He bore himself well," he said. "In short, he was a fine, upstanding fellow, more able to control his temper than Master Quilter."

Sir Eliard was thoughtful. "It *has* to be the same man," he decided.

"The same man?"

"Your description tallies with that given to me by Bevis Millburne. On the night of the execution, we celebrated at the Golden Fleece. A stranger arrived to see Bevis and congratulate him on his part in the trial. He left before Bevis could find out his name, but I am certain it must be Nicholas Bracewell. This is upsetting," said Sir Eliard, chewing his lip. "Since he saw Bevis at the Golden Fleece, the chances are that he noticed me, as well. Small wonder that he is poking about in my affairs."

"What are we to do about him, Sir Eliard?"

"I think that you predicted his future accurately, Adam."

"Did I?"

"Yes," said the other with a ghost of a smile. "You said that you were as close as the grave. There's nothing as close as that, is there? Graves seal up everything tidily. Gerard Quilter learned that, and so did Moll Comfrey. I think it may be time for Nicholas Bracewell to make the same discovery."

* * *

Henry Cleaton defied all his expectations. When he was introduced to the lawyer, Nicholas Bracewell expected to find a worthy, studious man in the dull garb of his profession, careful in speech and obsessed with the need for caution. Instead, he was looking at a jovial individual of fifty with a shock of red hair that matched the color of his cheeks, and a stocky frame in a blue doublet. There was a faintly bucolic air about Cleaton. His office was small and cluttered, making its occupant seem even larger. Chuckling to himself, the lawyer cleared piles of documents off a chair and a stool so that his visitors could sit down. He glanced at Nicholas.

"Frank tells me how helpful you have been to him," he said.

"Nick has been a godsend," affirmed Quilter. "Without him, I'd be lost."

"At a time like this, you need a reliable friend."

"I'm happy to lend my assistance," said Nicholas. "I do not know the full details of the case, but I am persuaded that a terrible injustice has taken place."

Cleaton's face clouded. "It is monstrous!" he declared. "Gerard Quilter was the most inoffensive of men. He would not kill a fly, still less a human being. Those who sent him to the gallows committed a heinous crime, and they must answer for it." His manner softened as he appraised Nicholas. "So you are the famous book holder, are you? I have oftentimes been in the gallery at the Queen's Head to watch the company at work. They are always well drilled."

Nicholas was modest. "That is Master Firethorn's doing rather than mine."

"Do not listen to him," said Quilter. "Nick is the true power behind the throne. If a play runs smoothly, it is usually because of his control behind the scenes. That reminds me," he added, turning to his friend. "How did *Black Antonio* fare this afternoon?"

"Very poorly, Frank."

"I am surprised to hear that," said Cleaton. "When I last saw the piece, it was acted with a vigor that set my old heart racing. What was amiss today?"

"The actors' minds were elsewhere," explained Nicholas. "They were slow and lackluster. The audience let them know it. We rallied towards the end but, in truth, it was not an occasion in which we could take pride."

The performance had, in fact, verged on chaos, but Laurence Firethorn had saved the day with his brilliant account of the main character. Alone of the other actors, Edmund Hoode had managed to shine in a supporting role, attesting his excellence on the eve of his departure and reminding everyone of what they would be losing when he went. Nicholas had stayed long enough to see everything cleared away before joining Quilter at the lawyer's office. He warmed to Cleaton on sight. The man had a bristling intelligence.

"Inquiries have been made," said the lawyer, reaching for a document on his table. "I have spent the whole day asking questions and chasing down the answers like a dog after a rabbit. We have made progress, gentlemen."

"Good," said Quilter.

"What have you found out, sir?" asked Nicholas.

Cleaton read from the paper before him. "Firstly, that a certain Adam Haygarth became a justice of the peace as a result of the direct intercession of Sir Eliard Slaney. There's no doubting it. Haygarth is Sir Eliard's creature in every way."

"Then he must have told him about the new evidence that came forward."

"Yes, Nick," said Quilter, "and thereby prompted the murder of Moll Comfrey. The man is beneath contempt. He ran to his master like the cur he is. What hope have we for justice if rogues such as Adam Haygarth administer it?"

"Not everyone in the law is so devoid of honesty," promised Cleaton. "There are still a few of us who believe in the ideals that brought us to the profession. One of those ideals is to root out injustice wherever we find it, and there is no more appalling example of it than here. But there's more," he went on, looking down again. "Haygarth is also a friend of Bevis Millburne, close enough to be invited to his wedding, I am told. And he must be acquainted with Cyril Paramore, too, because the latter works with Sir Eliard at all times."

"In short," said Nicholas, "all four men are confederates."

"So it would appear."

"Your inquiries prove it beyond any contention, Master Cleaton."

"True, sir," replied the lawyer. "I've unearthed several links between the four of them. What I cannot prove as yet, however, is that they were instruments in the death of Frank's father."

"They were!" asserted Quilter.

"I know and I am as eager as you to proclaim it to the world. But the law requires more evidence, Frank. Trial for murder is a most serious business. To overturn a verdict will take much more than we have at our disposal."

"Moll Comfrey was the decisive witness," said Nicholas. "That is why she had to be silenced so abruptly. Sir Eliard Slaney is a ruthless man."

Cleaton gave them a warning nod. "You would do well to remember that. When he becomes aware of what you are doing, your own lives may be at risk."

"That will not stop us," said Quilter boldly.

"No," said Nicholas, "but it does mean that we should be more circumspect, Frank. I was followed home last night, and Anne tells me that someone was watching the house earlier. I spy a connection with Sir Eliard."

"Everything seems to be connected with him somehow," said Cleaton, studying the document in front of him. "The paper trail leads directly to his house in Bishopsgate."

He listed all that he had found out about the relationship between Sir Eliard Slaney and the other three men. Nicholas and Quilter were duly impressed with the amount of information he had gathered in such a short time. There was, however, a significant omission.

"What did you learn about Vincent Webbe?" asked Nicholas.

"Precious little, I fear," replied the lawyer. "My energies were taken up with the inquiries I made in other directions. All that I discovered about Master Webbe is where his widow now lives." He wrinkled his nose. "It is not the most salubrious part of London."

Quilter was positive. "Wherever it is, I'll visit her."

"No, Frank," said Nicholas. "This is work for me. Vincent Webbe hated your father. The name of Quilter will bar the door against you. Let me call on the widow. We'll first to the fair to seek out Lightfoot; then I'll on to speak to the lady. She'll not suspect me. I'll say I was a friend of her husband. Then I'll draw her out. Leave her to me, Frank," he insisted. "I'll find out much more on my own."

* * *

When the visitor gave her name, Avice Radley's surprise turned to incredulity. The last person she expected to come to her house was Margery Firethorn. During the social niceties, they weighed each other up. Margery was struck by the other's handsome features and by her rich attire. By the same token, Avice Radley was impressed by her comely appearance. Margery's crimson gown had actually been donated to the company and been worn by one of the female characters in a number of plays, but it was far more striking on its present owner. A mutual respect was established between the two women at once. Both had great self-possession. As she took her seat, Margery knew that she would have to use reason instead of bluster against her hostess.

"I do not need to tell you what has brought me here," she began. "Edmund Hoode is a good friend of mine, and I would hate to see him abandon the company."

"Save your breath," said Avice politely. "Edmund's future has been decided."

"In so short a time?"

"The moment we met, I knew that I wanted to marry him."

Margery smiled appreciatively. "I can see why he feels the same about you, Mistress Radley. But must marriage and the playhouse be worlds apart? Why cannot Edmund enjoy both?"

"Because he has no wish to do so."

"Have you given him the choice?"

"That is a private matter."

"Not when it affects the lives of so many others, my husband among them."

"Master Firethorn has already made that point to me."

"It can bear repetition."

"I think not," said Avice. "It is good of you to call, but I have to say I think less of Master Firethorn for delegating this work to his wife. Because he failed to prevail upon me himself, he has sent you to approach me afresh."

"That is not the case at all," retorted Margery. "I come strictly of my own volition. Were Laurence to hear of this visit, he would be exceeding angry. I am not allowed to meddle in the affairs of Westfield's Men."

"Then why do you do so?"

"Because the quality of their work is at stake."

"There are other playwrights in London."

"None so fruitful as Edmund Hoode."

"What of young Lucius Kindell?" asked Avice. "Edmund speaks well of him."

"And so he should, Mistress Radley. They worked together on *The Insatiate Duke*, and Lucius has written two tragedies of his own. His time will surely come," said Margery, "but he is no substitute for the master himself."

"Other companies have no difficulty in finding plays. Look at Banbury's Men. They are always announcing the performance of a new work."

"Yes," argued Margery, "and as soon as they find a talented author, they bind him hand and foot with contracts so that he can write for nobody but them. Banbury's Men have tried to lure Edmund away time and again. Has he told you that?"

"Naturally. We have no secrets from each other."

"Then you will know how much joy and satisfaction he gets from his work."

"The joy has gone, Mistress Firethorn," said the other sadly, "and the satisfaction has fallen away. Edmund seeks new pleasures. I thank God that he has chosen to do so exclusively in my company."

Margery could see that she was making little impact. Avice Radley was not susceptible to any form of persuasion. There was a quiet certainty about her that was forbidding. Margery decided to change her tack.

"I must thank you for one thing," she said effusively.

"Thank me?"

"You have brought some happiness into Edmund's life at long last. He has been led on such a merry dance by Cupid in the past that we feared he might perish from unrequited love." She smiled benignly. "It is heartening to see that he has finally found someone who understands his true worth."

"I adore him," said Avice quietly. "He is a complete man to me."

"What first drew your attention to him?"

"His plays. When I saw *The Merchant of Calais*, I was captivated. It had such a keen understanding of human nature. And such sublime verse," she went on. "I went home that afternoon with my head spinning."

"What else have you seen of Edmund's?"

"Almost everything that he has written. I watched in wonder until I felt compelled to send him a letter of appreciation. From that single action, so foreign to my character, all else has flowed."

"When you enjoyed his work so much, why prevent others from like pleasure?"

"But that is not what I am doing," Avice reminded her. "Those same dramas that delighted me are the property of Westfield's Men. They can be performed whenever Master Firethorn chooses. Edmund bequeaths them with his blessing."

"And lays down his pen for good."

"No, Mistress Firethorn. He wishes to employ it in a worthier cause. Henceforth, he will devote himself to sonnets and shun the cruder arts of the playhouse."

"It was those cruder arts that enslaved *you*," said Margery pointedly.

Avice Radley acknowledged the fact with a smile. She admired Margery for what she was trying to do and was touched by her obvious fondness for Edmund Hoode. But that did not sway her in the least. She sought to give her visitor an explanation.

"When did you meet Laurence Firethorn?" she asked.

"Many years ago."

"Can you recall the moment when you first set eyes on him?"

"Vividly," said Margery with a nostalgic grin. "I watched a performance of *Pompey the Great*, and he was every inch the hero in the title. When he stepped out onstage, the hairs stood up on the back of my neck, and I feared that I would never stop trembling. And the beauty of it is," she confided, "there are still times when Laurence has the same effect on me. I married a titan of the stage."

"So will I," said Avice. "You found love at first sight, and I did likewise."

"Yes, but I did not try to tear my husband away from his work."

"There's no tearing with Edmund. He comes of his own free will."

"Leaving the company he serves in ruin."

"Come now," said Avice, clicking her tongue. "Do not be so disloyal to your husband. No troupe that is led by Laurence Firethorn will ever be in ruins. He can bring the meanest play to life. And he has such able men around him, attracted by his brilliance. The loss of Edmund will soon be repaired."

"I beg leave to doubt that. But it is not only Edmund's departure that is so disturbing," said Margery. "It is the nature of that departure. Laurence tells me that he means to cut himself off from Westfield's Men within a week."

"That is so."

"How can he be so callous?"

"Edmund's intention had been to remain until the end of September."

"What changed his mind, Mistress Radley?"

There was a pause. "I can see that your husband has omitted certain facts."

"Ah!" sighed Margery as she began to understand. "So *that* is what happened, was it? In the interests of his company, Laurence attempted to work on your emotions himself. Do not expect me to be shocked," she said, holding up a hand. "It is no more than he does every time he struts upon a stage. That, after all, is how he ambushed me, and I am sure that there were other young ladies in the audience who were equally entranced. I was fortunate to be chosen."

"So am I, Mistress Firethorn."

"Yet, by your own account, you did the choosing."

"Not entirely."

"Your wrote to Edmund. But for that, he would have been quite unaware of your existence. Let us be honest here, shall we? You were the huntress."

"We were drawn ineluctably together."

"*After* he had read the contents of your letter."

"I had to declare myself by some means," said the other defensively. "Had I not reached out for Edmund, I would have remained a face in the crowd to him. Instead, he has turned my grief into ecstasy." He voice softened to a whisper. "Tell me, Mistress Firethorn. Have you ever mourned the death of someone close to you?"

"Many times," replied Margery. "I lost both parents, a brother and two sisters. My first child was stillborn. I, too, have been acquainted with grief."

"Then you will know the feeling of despair that grips you. When my husband died, he left me with nothing but dear memories. There were no children to help me bear the agony of his passing, no brothers or sisters on either side of the family to share my misery. I became a recluse," she confessed. "And I might still be locked away if a friend had not insisted that I visit the Queen's Head with her. No spectator ever went less willingly to a play, yet I left that innyard in high spirits. That was the effect that Edmund Hoode's play had on me. It brought me back to life."

"A play is only as good as the actors who perform it," said Margery, quoting one of her husband's favorite maxims. "What brought you back to life was the work of a whole company, not simply the genius of the author. You should be sufficiently grateful to Westfield's Men to let them keep their playwright."

"Edmund no longer wishes to stay."

"Thanks to your influence."

"Not at all. Were he so wedded to the notion, I'd live with him in London and let him stay at the Queen's Head. But he is adamant," said Avice with an invincible smile. "Edmund Hoode is determined to break off all ties with Westfield's Men. No power on earth can stop him."

Bartholomew Fair was at its height. The people of London and those from much farther afield came to buy, sell, haggle, steal, eat, drink, fight, frolic, be entertained, and generally enjoy the holiday atmosphere. The clamor was earsplitting, the colors dazzling, and the compound of smells so powerful that they reached out well beyond Smithfield. Peddlers and stall holders vied for the attention of the seething masses. Those enticed into various booths could see a cow with six legs, a dwarf with three eyes, a giant horse that seemed to talk, and sundry other freaks of Nature. A performing bear drew gasps of wonder from the onlookers. Drunken men sought the company of prostitutes; drunken women fell to brawling. Among the most popular characters at the fair were Luke Furness, the blacksmith, who took time off from shoeing horses to draw teeth with amazing dexterity; Ursula the Pig Woman, a vast, ugly, foul-tongued creature with a face that bore an amazing resemblance to that of the pig being roasted outside her booth; and Ned Pellow the Pie Man, massive, bearded, and obliging, renowned for the quality of his food and for the affability of his manner.

Nicholas Bracewell and Francis Quilter had to wait in the queue until they had a chance to speak to him. While the beaming Pellow was selling his pies, his hairy wife was bringing out fresh supplies from inside the booth. They gave off a tempting odor.

"Good day, my friends," said Pellow, recognizing them. "Can I offer you some of my pies to take away your hunger?"

"Another time, Ned," said Nicholas. "We are looking for Lightfoot."

"Then you must head for the ring. That is where he performs."

"The ring?"

"Follow the noise, sirs. It will lead you there."

They took his advice. Above the tumult was an occasional burst of cheering and applause. Nicholas and Quilter pushed their way through the crowd until they reached an open area between the stalls. A series of stakes had been driven into the ground in a rough circle so that a rope could be tied to them. The large crowd that pressed against the rope yelled and laughed as Puppy the Wrestler, a mountain of flesh with a bare chest, lifted his latest challenger high in the air before dashing him to the ground. While anxious friends tried to revive the fallen man, Puppy walked around the ring with an arrogant strut, hands held high in triumph, waiting for the next foolish hero to step over the rope and try his strength. Lightfoot did not hesitate. The brief time between wrestling bouts was his opportunity to earn money. He cartwheeled around the ring with such speed that he provoked spontaneous clapping. Concluding with a dozen somersaults, he landed on his feet, doffed his cap to take in the applause, and then used it to collect money from his audience. When he drew level with them, Nicholas dropped a coin into the hat and then indicated that he wished to speak to the tumbler. As soon as Puppy was grappling with his next victim, Lightfoot slipped out of the ring and took the newcomers aside.

"I hoped that you would come," he said.

"Do you have any news for us, Lightfoot?" asked Nicholas.

"I believe so, sir."

Quilter was eager. "Well? What have you discovered?"

"I spoke to Hermat."

"And what did he tell you?"

Lightfoot laughed. "*He* told me nothing, sir. Or rather, only half of what I heard came directly from him."

"Stop talking in riddles," complained Quilter.

"Lightfoot does not mean to confuse you, Frank," said Nicholas with a grin, "though I daresay that you would be confused if you met Hermat, for he and she are a study in confusion." Quilter looked bewildered. "You obviously did not read the sign as we passed it. Hermat is half-man and half-woman. A veritable hermaphrodite."

"That is so," said Lightfoot. "You can view him in his booth for a penny." He gave a chuckle. "If you offer him more, he will show you something in private that will amaze your eyes and make you marvel at the mystery of creation."

Quilter was impatient. "Another mystery has brought us here."

"I know, sir."

"My father was executed less than fifty yards from where we stand."

"Moll met her death even closer to us than that," said Lightfoot solemnly. "I am sorry to jest. It is not really a cause for laughter. Thus it stands," he said, pausing as another roar went up from Puppy's admirers. "Two nights ago, when it was dark enough to venture out, Hermat decided to take a walk. Night is his friend. It is the only time when nobody stares at him."

"Go on," said Nicholas.

"He swears that he saw a figure lurking outside Ned Pellow's booth. A tall, thin man, who scurried away when Hermat approached."

"What time would this be, Lightfoot?"

"Around midnight," replied the tumbler. "Hermat thought no more of it. A fair such as this is always haunted by strangers. The man could easily have been a scavenger, looking for scraps from the pie man. Hermat would probably have forgotten all about it."

"What jogged his memory?"

"He saw the fellow again, sir, later on."

"In the same place?"

"No, some way distant," said Lightfoot. "He was hurrying off with his head down as if leaving Smithfield altogether. Whether he sees like a man or like a woman, I do not know, but Hermat has sharp eyes. Even in the gloom, he knew that it was the same man. There was only one difference."

"What was that?" asked Nicholas.

"He was no longer carrying anything. When Hermat first spied him, he says that the man was holding something close to his chest." Lightfoot demonstrated with his hands. "Something big enough to be noticed. Yet it was gone when they next met."

"A blanket!"

"That was my thinking," said Lightfoot. "The murder weapon."

Cyril Paramore was so distressed by the news that his lower lip began to twitch violently.

"These are fearful tidings for all of us, Sir Eliard," he said.

"That is why we must work together."

"How did they know that you were implicated?"

"They picked up my scent," said Sir Eliard rancorously, "and they must be shaken off. I thought at first that Adam Haygarth might unwittingly have provided them with a clue, but he denies it hotly."

"He is in this as deep as any of us."

"I reminded him of that, Cyril."

"Does Bevis know what has transpired?"

"He galloped over here on receipt of my letter. Bevis was even more upset than you, especially when I explained what must have happened."

"And what was that, Sir Eliard?"

They were in the parlor at the house in Bishopsgate. Paramore was white with fear. That fear was in no way allayed when Sir Eliard told him about the celebratory supper at the Golden Fleece and the interruption by a stranger who sought to speak with Bevis Milburne. Paramore reached the same conclusion.

"It was this fellow, Nicholas Bracewell!"

"He saw us crowing over the execution of Gerard Quilter."

"Thank heaven that *I* was not at the table!"

"Stop thinking of yourself, Cyril," ordered Sir Eliard. "If one of us is arraigned, the other three will not escape. I did not summon you here to listen to your selfishness. I had enough vain bleating from Bevis. You are here for a purpose."

"And what is that?"

"Find out all you can about Westfield's Men."

"The troupe at the Queen's Head?"

"Francis Quilter acts with the company, and Nicholas Bracewell is its book holder. See what standing they have among their fellows. Investigate the company itself."

"I have already done that, Sir Eliard," said Paramore. "I know that you abjure the playhouse, but we admire the troupe. My wife and I have been privileged to watch them perform on three or four occasions."

Sir Eliard turned on him. "There's no privilege in watching two of their number perform," he snarled. "They will get no applause from me for their antics. What I need to know is how Gerard Quilter's son and his friend can find the time to bother us. Are they working alone, or do they have assistance from their fellows? Be careful," he advised. "Move with stealth. But find out everything there is to know about Westfield's Men."

"We already know the worst thing about them."

"Do we?"

"They employ this cunning fellow called Nicholas Bracewell."

"At the moment," said Sir Eliard with a sly grin. "But his contract may soon be terminated. By tomorrow, Westfield's Men will be looking for a new book holder."

Nicholas Bracewell approached Turnmill Street with a caution born of experience. It was at the heart of a district that was notorious for brothels, gaming houses, violence, danger, squalor, and abiding degradation. Bankside, too, had a reputation for drunkenness and debauchery but the inhabitants of Turnmill Street and its adjacent lanes, yards, and alleys were even more mired in corruption, crime, and licentiousness. Thieves, ruffians, pickpockets, forgers, prostitutes, gamblers, vagabonds, masterless men, discharged soldiers without pensions to sustain them, boisterous sailors, and all kinds of other unseemly individuals congregated in the area. The fact that Vincent Webbe's widow now lived there showed how desperate her condition must be. Nicholas felt a surge of sympathy for the woman. At one time, when her husband was in partnership with Gerard Quilter, they must have lived in style at a prestigious address. Now, widowed and poverty-stricken, she was reduced to renting a room in one of the vilest parts of London.

Striding up the main street, Nicholas passed Jacob's Well Court, Bowling Alley, Hercules Yard, and Cock Alley, home of the infamous Cock Tavern, where vices of every description could be purchased by customers who later found that they had also bought disease in the wake of pleasure. Beggars and ragged children lurked on every corner. Drunken men lurched out of taverns to relieve themselves against the nearest wall or to spew up the contents of their stomachs on ground that was already covered with excrement and refuse. The stench was revolting; the sense of depravity was oppressive. Nicholas walked on until he reached Slaughterhouse Yard, a place that advertised its presence by the most noisome reek of all. Holding his breath, he sought out the address he had been given. He knocked on the door and waited. A woman's head appeared through the shutters above.

"What do you want?" she croaked.

"I am looking for Elizabeth Webbe."

"Why?"

"I was a friend of her husband, Vincent," said Nicholas politely. "I came to pay my respects to his widow. Is she within?"

"I am Bess Webbe," she admitted. "Wait there, sir."

She withdrew from the window, and Nicholas heard her descending the stairs. When the door opened a few inches, she examined him with suspicion. Her face was gaunt, her eyes large and staring. Elizabeth Webbe was still in her forties, but time had dealt harshly with her appearance. Her hair was white, her skin like parchment.

"My name is Nicholas Bracewell," he said. "You will not know the name because it is some years since Vincent and I met. I have recently returned to London and was horrified to learn what happened to him."

"Cruel murder, sir," she moaned. "Cruel murder."

"I am anxious to know more. A lawyer gave me your address."

He looked up at the hovel. "I am sorry to find you in such a mean dwelling. You deserve better."

"We *had* better, sir."

"I know. Vincent was a prosperous man."

"It was Master Quilter who brought him down."

"Gerard Quilter?" asked Nicholas, feigning surprise.

"Brought him down then stabbed him to death."

It took him a few minutes to convince her that he had come in good faith. She invited him in, embarrassed by the state of her lodging and making continual apologies as they ascended the stairs. The room in which she lived with her two daughters was small, dark, and evil-smelling. It contained little beyond a few sticks of furniture and the bed in which all three of them obviously slept. She indicated a stool and he sat down.

"My girls are both out," she explained. "They are too young to work, but they pick up what they can from kind strangers. We have such limited means, sir."

"Then I hope you will accept a gift from me," he said, putting some money into her hand out of genuine concern for her, but also in order to win her confidence. "Vincent would have done the same for my wife had he found her in the same distress."

"Thank you, Master Bracewell. You are very generous."

"All that I have heard is that your husband was killed. You tell me that Gerard Quilter was the murderer. That astonishes me for he was such a gentle soul."

"He was not gentle when he turned Vincent out!" she protested.

"When did that happen?"

Elizabeth Webbe was an embittered woman who told her story with her eyes flashing angrily. It was evident from the start that she had accepted her husband's version of events without reservation. There was no mention of the embezzlement that had led to the dissolution of the partnership with Gerard Quilter. In her opinion, the latter was wholly to blame. Nor did she refer to Vincent Webbe's drinking habits. All that she would admit was that he became truculent at times, but even that she managed to excuse. Her account of the murder was substantially that which had been given in court.

"Two witnesses saw him thrust his dagger into my husband," she said.

"When was this?"

"On the night that he went to the Mercers' Hall."

"Why did he go there when he was no longer a member of the guild?"

"It was at the suggestion of someone else, sir."

"Who?" pressed Nicholas.

"He was a man who lent Vincent some money."

"Sir Eliard Slaney, perhaps?"

"Yes, yes," she said, searching her memory, "that could be the name. Vincent could not repay him, so he was advised to ask his old partner for funds. Master Quilter was ever a softhearted man, and Vincent felt that he was owed money for the sake of past favors. But he was spurned, sir," she cried. "Master Quilter not only cursed him, he set about Vincent with his cane."

"There was a brawl, then?"

"Several people saw it."

"And your husband was stabbed in the course of the fight?"

"No," she said. "It must have been later. Master Quilter was too cunning to do it with so many people nearby. He bided his time and killed Vincent in a yard behind the Mercers' Hall. Two men chanced to pass," she continued, tears welling up in her eyes. "They thought they had merely seen an affray. It was only when the body was discovered the next day that they knew they had witnessed a murder."

"When did you first learn of the crime?" asked Nicholas.

"The day after Vincent left for the Mercers' Hall."

"Were you not worried when he failed to return for the night?"

She shook her head. "It was not unusual for him to be away for a couple of days at a time," she confessed. "We sometimes did not see him for a week. Vincent was always looking for ways to get established again. He had to search for opportunities."

"What happened when you learned of his death?"

"I was distraught, sir. So were our daughters. We cried and cried."

"And you are certain that Gerard Quilter was the culprit?"

"Who else could it have been?" she said sharply. "The crime was witnessed by two honest, upright men. Master Quilter admitted there had been a brawl with my husband. What he did not admit was that he later took his revenge." She let out a hoarse cackle. "But we had

[176]

our own revenge on him this week," she sneered. "All three of us went to Smithfield to watch him being hanged for his crime."

Nicholas glanced around. "Were you living here at the time of the murder?"

"No, sir. We had our own house then, but it was taken away when Vincent died. I was turned out with my daughters, and we had to fend for ourselves."

"Who could have been so cruel as to do that?"

"The moneylender, Sir Eliard Slaney."

"Did you ever meet the man?"

"No," she replied, "but I saw his bailiffs. They threw us out without mercy. I had no idea that Vincent had borrowed so much money. It was a grievous shock."

"Yet you had heard Sir Eliard's name before?"

"Oh, yes."

"How did your husband speak it?"

"As if it were a foul disease," she said. "Vincent wished that he had never met the fellow. He feared that Sir Eliard would be the ruin of him. He was so angered by the demands for money that he went to Sir Eliard's house and caused a commotion. My husband had a temper when he was roused."

"Could no lawyer save your house from being possessed?"

"Lawyers cost money, sir, and we were left penniless."

Nicholas felt sorry for the woman but he was glad that he had made the effort to see her. She would never have divulged the same information to Francis Quilter. Nicholas believed that she might have given him the explanation that he needed. Thanking her for what she had told him, Nicholas took his leave and stepped out into the yard in time to see some frightened sheep being herded into the slaughterhouse. The scene was emblematic of the whole area. Turnmill Street was a slaughterhouse in itself, butchering the lives, reputations, and self-respect of all who came there. Elizabeth Webbe had once been the wife of a prosperous mercer with an assured place in society. She was now one more terrified animal, penned up in readiness for destruction.

Brooding on what he had heard, Nicholas headed back in the direction of Cow Cross. His instincts remained alert, however. When he walked past Fleur de Luce Yard, he caught a hint of sudden movement out of the corner of his eye. Nicholas turned just in time. A tall, slim, sinewy man came out of the shadows to lunge at him with a dagger. Nicholas caught his wrist and twisted the weapon away, using his other hand to get a grip on the man's throat. A fierce struggle ensued. His assailant was young and strong, but he had met his match in Nicholas. Instead of taking his victim by surprise, he found himself rammed so hard against a wall that all the breath was knocked out of him. The dagger fell to the ground and Nicholas kicked it away. He then snatched off the man's hat to reveal a thin, swarthy face that was half-covered with a straggly beard.

"Who *are* you?" demanded Nicholas.

By way of reply, the man spat in his eyes to blind him temporarily. Bringing up a knee into his captor's groin, he pushed Nicholas away as the latter doubled up in pain. Without pausing to pick up his dagger, the man fled. It had all happened so quickly that Nicholas was still bewildered. By the time he recovered enough to go in pursuit, the man was mounting the horse he had tethered in the adjoining lane. He kicked the animal into a canter and rode off. He would never be caught now. Nicholas walked back to retrieve the dagger and the abandoned hat. He chided himself for letting his attacker escape. One thought was uppermost in his mind. The man was free to strike again.

[CHAPTER NINE]

Francis Quilter was deeply upset by news of the attempt on his friend's life. It was one more dreadful setback for them. When he talked to Nicholas Bracewell that evening, he was overcome with guilt.

"You should have let me go with you, Nick," he said.

"I survived."

"But you could just as easily have been stabbed to death."

"Not if I remain alert, Frank. I have been to Turnmill Street before and know its dangers well. It's a place where you need eyes in the back of your head." He held up the hat and the dagger that he had collected. "In any case, I got the better of the encounter. My attacker had to run away, unarmed and bare-headed. I fancy that he took away a few bruises, as well."

"My concern is solely for you, Nick. I put you in jeopardy."

"Not with intention."

"It matters not," said Quilter. "Simply by helping me you have become a marked man. Moll Comfrey has already perished in my name. Now they have turned their attention to you. Consider your own safety and let me deal with this business on my own forthwith."

"That is the last thing I will do."

"I have a family interest here. You do not."

Nicholas was insistent. "The call of friendship brought me to your side, and there I'll stay. It is not only you that I help, remember. When we clear your father's name, the company will also profit. They will regain a fine actor called Frank Quilter, and their book holder's mind will not stray from his duties."

"Westfield's Men will not profit if their book holder is murdered."

"Then I'll ensure that it will not happen," said Nicholas with a confident smile.

"Take me with you wherever you go."

"It is you who may need a bodyguard, Frank. I do not expect another attack on me. My assailant has more sense than to risk his neck again. No," he went on, frowning with concern, "he may come in search of you next time. This, after all, is an investigation set in motion by you. If they kill Frank Quilter, they will hope to prevent any further inquiry into the trial and conviction of your father."

"I go abroad armed," said Quilter, indicating his sword and dagger.

"A companion is the best defense."

"I might say the same to you, Nick."

They were in Quilter's lodging. While the actor had remained at Bartholomew Fair to confirm certain facts, Nicholas had gone to Turnmill Street for his meeting with Mrs. Webbe. As arranged, they met up to discuss what each had learned. A thought occurred to Quilter.

"Can we be certain that the man *was* hired by Sir Eliard Slaney?" he asked.

"I believe so."

"Could he not as easily have been some thief in search of your purse?"

"He would not need to kill me in order to get that," reasoned Nicholas. "A thief would be more likely to cudgel me to the ground so that he could grab what he wanted. My attacker escaped on his horse, Frank. How many thieves in Turnmill Street own more than the clothes they stand up in? No doubt can exist," he emphasized. "I was followed there by an assassin who bided his time until he saw his opportunity to strike. He may well be the same man who trailed me to Bankside last night and who had earlier kept watch on Anne's house."

"Would you know him again, Nick?"

"I could recognize that mean face in a crowd. Do not look so worried," he said, with a reassuring hand on his friend's arm. "The attack was foiled because it was not unexpected. I take it to be an encouraging sign."

Quilter gaped. "Where's the encouragement in an attempt on your life?"

"It shows how worried they are, Frank. We have made more progress than we know. Sir Eliard Slaney must be fearful if he needs to order another death. His spy has put Anne and me under the same roof, so he will know that I must have asked her to find out what she could from Lady Slaney."

"It grieves me that I've put Anne's life in danger, as well."

"I do not think that you have," said Nicholas. "What advantage would they gain by her death? You and I are the targets here. Besides, Anne is well protected by those who work for her. Have no fears for her safety. And sit down," he advised, "so that I might tell you what I learned from Vincent Webbe's widow."

Quilter sat in the chair while Nicholas perched on the edge of the table. The actor listened attentively as his friend gave him a detailed account of the conversation in Slaughterhouse Yard. He seized on the name of Sir Eliard Slaney.

"So it was *he* who told Vincent Webbe to approach my father that night."

"Yes," said Nicholas. "Secure in the knowledge that your father would turn down his old partner's plea for a loan. Sir Eliard could also be certain that Vincent Webbe would lose his temper and become truculent. I daresay he also took care to see that Master Webbe had been drinking heavily before he accosted your father outside the Mercers' Hall. Hot words were followed by a brawl."

"My father would never have provoked it."

"He did not need to, Frank. Imagine the situation," suggested Nicholas. "Vincent Webbe is an indigent man who has lost his standing in the world. He sees your father about to attend a banquet at the Mercers' Hall because he is a respected member of the guild. His old partner must have been green with envy. When your father refused to lend him money, Vincent Webbe became choleric and struck out."

"With many witnesses nearby."

"Your father defended himself as best he could; then Master Webbe skulked off. From all that I've heard about him," decided Nicholas, "I'd say that he sought solace in the nearest tavern. The next day he was stabbed to death in an alley near Mercers' Hall, and the blame was laid on your father."

"You have still not explained why Vincent Webbe had to be killed."

"His widow did that for me," said Nicholas. "She told me that her husband borrowed a great deal of money from Sir Eliard and was hounded for repayment. He grew belligerent and offered violence to the usurer. Sir Eliard would not endure that. Since there were two men whom he had reason to hate, he devised a plan to get rid of both in the most brutal way. Your father was falsely accused of the murder of his old partner, thereby removing both of Sir Eliard's enemies at a stroke."

"Now I see it, Nick," said Quilter. "He has hit two marks with one shot."

"Or two birds with one stone."

"You were so wise to make a visit to Vincent's Webbe's widow."

"She is a good woman," recalled Nicholas, "still loyal to her husband, even though his dissipation brought about their downfall. I heard no word of reproach against him. I think that Vincent Webbe was loved far better than he deserved."

"So it seems."

"But what of you, Frank? How did you fare after my departure?"

"Lightfoot took me to meet Hermat," said Quilter. "I wanted to hear his evidence from his own lips. Or *her* lips, as the case may be. What a strange creature Hermat was! Neither man nor woman, yet possessing the features of both. I tell you, Nick, I would not like to have been left alone with Hermat."

Nicholas laughed. "Did you think your virtue would be in danger?"

"I simply did not know where to look."

"What did you learn?"

"Exactly what Lightfoot had told us," explained Quilter. "Hermat saw the man around midnight, close by the pie man's booth. But he remembered one new detail. When he noticed the fellow later, making off, they were close by a fire that had been lighted. Hermat was able to see him more clearly, albeit for a fleeting moment."

"What did he remember?"

"The hat, Nick. The man was wearing a big hat with a tall feather in it."

Nicholas held up the hat that he had taken from his attacker. "Like this one?"

Turmoil was Laurence Firethorn's natural element. True art, in his view, could not arise of itself without effort. It grew out of strife and conflict. Only when he had argued with his playwright, bullied his actors, and suffered doubts about a performance could he produce the magnificent portrayals for which he was renowned. Since crises were a necessary precursor of his work, he usually took them in his stride, knowing that they would only increase his concentration and redouble his commitment to the play in hand. But the latest emergency could not be dismissed as a positive stage in the creative process. It cast a blight over the whole future of Westfield's Men. When he returned home to Shoreditch that evening, he was in a pessimistic vein.

"We are done for, Margery!" he announced. "Dissolution is at our shoulder."

"Is Edmund still resolved?"

"Yes, my love. He quits the company within a week."

"Can his contract not keep him tied to Westfield's Men?" she asked.

"Our lawyer has waved that at him but to no avail. Edmund snapped his fingers and dared us to sue him. Even if we win the case," said Firethorn disconsolately, "all that we will get is money that Avice Radley will cheerfully pay. The court cannot restore our playwright. He is lost forever."

"Can nobody persuade him to stay?"

"We have been debating that very point at the Queen's Head this evening. Owen Elias offered to knock some sense into Edmund's head, but violence is not the remedy." Tossing his hat on to the table, he slumped in a chair. "Nor is Barnaby's suggestion that we increase the fee that he earns with a new play. Money can no longer tempt Edmund. His beloved has wealth enough for both of them."

"I still say that Nicholas is your best interlocutor."

Firethorn groaned. "He is too busy helping Frank Quilter wield the sword of justice. Besides, my love, even Nick is powerless here. When he talked to Edmund earlier, his sage counsel went unheard. *She* is the cunning viper here!" he said with sudden anger. "Avice Radley has bewitched Edmund."

"What sort of woman is she, Laurence?" asked Margery artlessly.

"The worst kind, my love. The kind that thrive on power over their victims."

"Did you find her attractive?"

"No, no," he said, curling a lip in disgust. "Mistress Radley is an ugly, misshapen, ill-favored creature. She would never appeal to me, that I can swear."

"What means did you use when you called at her house?"

"Means?"

"Yes," said Margery sweetly. "Did you persuade, threaten, or cajole her?"

"I used simple reason and nothing more."

"Did you not trade on your charm?"

"It never crossed my mind to do so. I was there on behalf of the company."

"Then you would surely resort to anything at your disposal."

"No," he said with righteous indignation. "You slander me. I used the arts of persuasion to convince her of our need to retain our playwright. I was a shrewd advocate, but it was a futile visit."

"I wonder about the cause of that futility," she said. "When you called at her house, you had Edmund Hoode in your service for at least another month. Yet, when he accosted you later at the Queen's Head, that month had shrunk to a week. Why?" she pressed. "What made him reach such a cruel decision?"

"Spite."

"That is not in Edmund's character."

"Avice Radley is consumed with it."

"I doubt that a spiteful woman could capture his heart," she said. "I am inclined to believe that Edmund's change of mind was prompted by something that happened when you chose to call on Mistress Radley behind his back."

"All that I did was to plead our case."

"That is not what the lady herself would say."

"What do you mean?"

"According to her," said Margery, fixing him with her eye, "reason soon gave way to a more intimate form of persuasion. In my opinion, Mistress Avice Radley is not in the least degree ugly, misshapen, and ill-favored. She is a handsome woman who could attract any man."

Firethorn gulped. "You have *seen* the lady?"

"I called on her myself to see if womanly argument could make her bend."

"Then it was wrong of you to do so," he protested, rising to his feet with an attempt at anger. "How many times have I told you, Margery? You must not meddle in the affairs of Westfield's Men?"

"Even if I am able to save them from a terrible loss?"

His face ignited. "Is that what you did?" he asked hopefully.

"Alas, no."

"Then you have only made the situation worse."

"It was your clumsy wooing that did that, Laurence," she said with vehemence. "Did you really imagine that you could charm the lady into bed? She is in love with Edmund and he with her. That bond will not be broken because Laurence Firethorn deigns to lift an eyebrow at her. Instead of seducing Avice Radley, you simply managed to turn a month of Edmund's time into a bare week. I'm surprised that he granted you that in the circumstances."

"You misunderstand what happened, my love."

"I understand it only too well," she returned. "When you see a pretty face, you forget all about your wife and children and think yourself a carefree gallant. Mistress Radley's is but the latest name that I could cite." She jabbed a finger at his chest. "You betrayed us all, Laurence. And the worst of it is that you betrayed yourself, as well."

"But I only did it to save the company," he said, conjuring up a look of injured innocence. "Show some faith in me, Margery. I did not go to the house to try her virtue. I was there to test the strength of her love for Edmund."

"It is the strength of your lust for her that worries me."

He reached out for her. "My love!"

"Stand off, sir!" she cried, beating him away.

"Truly, I found the lady lacking all attraction."

"I have *seen* her, Laurence. Do not lie to me."

"What else was I to do?"

"Send Nicholas in your stead," she replied. "He would have had the sense to get Edmund's permission to meet Mistress Radley; then everything would have been open and friendly. Nicholas would never have descended to your crude harassment of her."

"I was led simply by my desire to save Westfield's Men."

Margery was scornful. "You were led, as ever, by your pizzle."

Firethorn writhed in discomfort under her searching gaze. The fact that she had also visited Avice Radley took away all possibility of being able to manipulate the truth to his advantage. Only one avenue of reconciliation remained open to him.

"Let us discuss this in the bedchamber, my love," he whispered.

"Is that what you said to Mistress Radley?" she retorted.

Storming off to the kitchen, she slammed the door meaningfully behind her.

"She never gave me the chance," he sighed wistfully.

Sunday morning found the inhabitants of Bankside scurrying to the various parish churches south of the river. Nicholas Bracewell was among them, escorting Anne Hendrik and her two servants to matins while making sure that they were neither being watched nor followed. It was on their return to the house that Anne expressed her worries. She pointed to the dagger that lay on her table.

"That might so easily have ended up in your back, Nick," she said.

"I long ago learned how to protect it."

"What if the man tries again?"

"He knows the folly of doing so," said Nicholas, slipping the dagger into his belt. "Should he cross my path again, of course, I'll have the pleasure of giving him back his weapon. I fancy that it might be between his ribs."

"I fear for you."

"Without cause, Anne. Remember what I told you. He'll attack elsewhere now."

"Is Frank Quilter in danger, then?"

"Not if he stays on guard. He is an able fellow, skilled in the use of dagger and sword upon a stage. He'll be a worthy opponent for anyone who dares to try him. We are both prepared, Anne," he said, kissing her on the cheek. "Still your fears."

"Where are you going now?"

"Back to Smithfield. I want to see if a certain person recognizes this," he said, picking up the hat he brought back from Turnmill Street. "You tell me that it is like the one you saw, but I would value a second opinion."

"I only glimpsed the man," she explained. "Long enough to see that he wore a hat and cloak, but too briefly for me to be certain that it was this particular hat." She examined it again. "It does, however, look very familiar."

"Your experience as a milliner would make you note someone's hat."

"Who else may have seen him wearing it?"

"Hermat."

"A foreign name."

"Hermat is a foreign being. According to Frank Quilter, who has seen the sight, Hermat has no equal on earth. Frank thought him the weirdest creature who lived."

"Is he an animal, then?"

"No, Anne," he said. "Hermat is an hermaphrodite, half-man, half-woman, but so cleverly contrived that it is impossible to see where one leaves off and the other starts. Bartholomew Fair is filled with freaks, but Hermat takes the crown." He lifted the hat. "And, I hope, remembers this less exalted headgear."

After a fond farewell, Nicholas went to the stable and saddled the horse. It made a great difference, not only speeding up his journey but also allowing him a view from an elevated position. Even in thick crowds, he could see exactly where he was going. There was no performance at the Queen's Head, so he had a whole day in which to continue his investigations. Before meeting up with Quilter again, he wanted to visit the fair on his own. Smithfield was busier and noisier than ever. A sea of humanity rippled across the entire fair. Money was changing hands on every side, and the pandemonium continued. It did not take Nicholas long to find Lightfoot. Back in the ring, the tumbler was showing off his skills between wrestling bouts. Coins aplenty were being dropped into Lightfoot's hat. When he saw Nicholas, he hopped over the rope and pushed his way across to him.

"Good day, sir!" he welcomed.

"You are doing brisk business, Lightfoot."

"It is Puppy who brings in the crowds. I merely entertain them while he catches his breath between challengers. Do you have any news, sir?"

"I do," said Nicholas.

"Then let me hear it."

Nicholas dismounted to tell him of the visit to Turnmill Street. When he described the attack that was made on him, he saw the tumbler's face pucker with dismay before reddening with anger. Hands on hips, Lightfoot inflated his chest.

"You should have let me go with you, sir," he said.

"Had you been there, the villain would never have tried to kill me."

"That is my argument."

"But we would never have known how frightened they are, Lightfoot," said Nicholas. "We have learned things that they hoped to keep secret, so they needed to stop us. The simplest way of doing that, they thought, was to murder me. But I am not ready to meet my Maker yet. I dispatched their assassin without his hat or his dagger."

"Let me travel with you," pleaded Lightfoot. "As you say, it may well have been the same man who smothered poor Moll to death. I long to meet the rogue. Puppy has taught me all of a wrestler's tricks, sir. Even without a weapon, I'll get the better of him."

"I yearn for a second encounter with him myself."

"Let's go abroad together, sir."

"No," said Nicholas. "Your place is here, earning your living. It may be months before you find crowds as large as this. I promise to call on you when we need you."

"But there must be *something* I can do."

"There is, Lightfoot. Take me to Hermat. We'll try his memory with this hat."

The tumbler led the way through the press to a large booth. Hanging outside was a sign announcing that Hermat was the MOST AMAZING SIGHT EVER SEEN ON EARTH, a claim that was supported by some crude but vivid drawings. Further temptation was offered by the stentorian voice of a tall figure in a red uniform who stood on a box outside the booth and urged people to view Nature's Greatest Outrage with their own eyes. A small queue had formed outside. The man in red was relieving them of a penny before allowing them into the booth. Lightfoot went across to speak to him. When the situation was explained to him, the man told those in the queue that there would be a short break before anyone else was admitted; then he took Nicholas and his companion to the rear of the booth so that they could enter through a flap.

"Wait here," said the man. "I'll fetch Hermat."

He disappeared and left them standing in the area where Hermat and his manager obviously slept. Two truckle beds lay on the ground. A rope had been stretched between two poles so that series of garish costumes could be hung to it. When he saw the way that the garments had been cut, Nicholas wondered what sort of human being could actually get into them. The answer came in the form of Hermat, who stepped in to join them from the main part of the booth. Lightfoot greeted the newcomer as a friend, but it took Nicholas a moment to adjust to Hermat's appearance. It was truly startling. The face was essentially that of a woman, oval-shaped, smooth-skinned, and strikingly beautiful, yet the chin had a pointed beard whose raven color matched the luxuriant hair. The shoulders had a man's muscularity, yet the one large breast, half-exposed on the left side of the chest, was palpably a female organ. From top to toe, Hermat's body was a confused mixture of male and female, a fact that was cleverly accentuated by the spectacular costume that was worn.

Nicholas cleared his throat, introduced himself, and then explained the purpose of his visit. He offered the hat that he had retrieved in Turnmill Street. Hermat took it from him and held it between long tapering fingers whose nails had been painted with a purple dye. The voice that came was deep and gruff.

"It could be the same one, my friend," said Hermat.

"How close were you to the man?" asked Nicholas.

"Almost close enough to touch him. The shape of the hat is the same, but I cannot be sure of its color. Yet it had a feather, just like this. I remember that."

"Was the fellow moving swiftly?"

"Yes," said Hermat. "He was young and lithe. He was leaving

Smithfield as if he wanted to get away as quickly as possible."

"Did he see you?"

"I doubt it, sir. Look at me. When you spend your life being stared at in the way that I am, you do not stir abroad often. When you do go out, it is usually at night, and you keep to the darkest shadows. But I saw the fellow clearly," insisted Hermat, "even though it was only for a few seconds. He was tall, slim, wearing a hat and cloak. When I first noticed him, he was carrying a bundle to his chest."

"We think it may have been a blanket," said Nicholas.

"It was used to smother Moll Comfrey," added Lightfoot.

"Yes, I was sorry to hear about your friend," said Hermat softly. "Though I talk like a man, I weep like a woman. I cried for an hour when they told me that the poor girl was murdered. Is there any hope of catching the rogue?"

Nicholas gave a confident nod. "We believe so."

"Your evidence has been very helpful, Hermat," said Lightfoot.

"It is little enough." A look of fear came into the green eyes. "I'll not have to appear in court, will I? Spare me that, Lightfoot. It would be cruel." He indicated his body. "I cannot speak in public like *this*."

"Nor will it be necessary," Nicholas assured him. "We merely wanted you to inspect the man's hat, that is all. And to ask if you recall any other details, however small, from that night."

"No, sir. I've told you everything."

"Think, Hermat," urged Lightfoot. "Use your brains."

Hermat gave a mirthless laugh. "I sometimes wonder if I *have* any brains. When I was born, as you see, God could not decide what to make of me. I am partly a man, yet I am unable to attest my manhood in the most obvious way. I am partly a woman, yet I never dare to look in a mirror as women are supposed to do. What am I to be called?"

"A friend," said Nicholas, "with valuable evidence."

"Thank you, sir."

"And there is nothing awry with your faculties."

Hermat fell silent as a memory rustled. A deal of concentration was needed before the memory finally took on shape. Nicholas observed how feminine the face looked in repose. The man's voice destroyed the illusion.

"Did I mention the smell?" asked Hermat.

"Smell?" repeated Lightfoot.

"Yes. When I saw him the second time, there was this sweet smell."

Expecting reassuring news, Bevis Millburne was shocked by what he heard. He flew into a panic and strode up and down the room like an animal in a cage.

"You told me that we would be safe, Sir Eliard," he cried.

"We shall be, Bevis."

"Then how has it come about that this Nicholas Bracewell still lives?"

"He is more able than we thought."

"Able to put us all in prison."

"No!"

"That is what it is beginning to feel like, Sir Eliard."

"Be quiet."

"He and Francis Quilter get closer and closer."

"Quiet!" howled Sir Eliard, tiring of his friend's wild alarm. "Sit down and listen, man. For you have nothing to say that has the slightest use to us." Millburne lowered himself on to a chair. "That is better," continued the other in a quieter voice. "Remember this, Bevis. There is more than one way to bring the business to a satisfactory end. When one means fails, we simply try another."

"Gerard Quilter's son is the one to fear. He is driven by revenge."

"Nicholas Bracewell is the more dangerous man."

"Have them both killed."

"It is not as easy as that," said Sir Eliard. "They have been forewarned and are on their guard. My man was lucky to escape in Turnmill Street. He has no wish to take on Nicholas Bracewell again."

"Then let him relieve us of Francis Quilter."

"No, Bevis. We disable him in another way."

"How?"

"By taking away his lieutenant."

"We tried to do that with a dagger."

"There's a different means," said Sir Eliard. "Both men are contracted to Westfield's Men, a company that performs at the Queen's Head in Gracechurch Street. Their makeshift playhouse is not far from my house, yet I have never been there. Antics on a stage have always offended me. Cyril Paramore, however, admires the troupe."

"So?"

"I set him on to find out what he could about them."

"Will this help our cause, Sir Eliard?"

"It already has. Cyril has discovered the most important fact of all. I'll let him tell you about it when he comes. Meanwhile," he said, crossing to a table, "I suggest that you enjoy a glass of Canary wine and stop worrying."

"I am bound to worry," said Millburne. "I perjured myself for you."

"And were well rewarded for your assistance."

"No amount of money can buy peace of mind."

Sir Eliard smiled. "As a matter of fact, it can," he said complacently. He poured two glasses of wine and then handed one to his visitor. "Be patient. Cyril will be here at any moment, and he will bring glad tidings."

"They have been in short supply of late."

Sir Eliard Slaney ignored him and sipped his wine. They were in the parlor of the house in Bishopsgate. Millburne glanced enviously around, knowing that he could never afford the expensive plate that was on display or the items of furniture that had been commissioned from famous craftsmen. The room could have graced a palace. Envy slowly turned to solace. The house was a glowing tribute to Sir Eliard's success. Whatever his friend touched, Millburne knew, seemed to turn to gold. It was foolish to doubt his host. A man who could acquire such wealth and wield such power was beyond the reach of the law. They had nothing to fear. Once he had accepted that fact, Millburne began to enjoy his drink.

Cyril Paramore soon joined them. When he was admitted to the house, he made his way to the parlor and exchanged greetings with his friends. Sir Eliard poured the newcomer some wine and then invited him to sit down. Paramore was beaming.

"I hear that you have good news, Cyril," said Millburne.

"Excellent news," replied Paramore.

"Tell him," instructed Sir Eliard. "Put a smile back on his face."

Paramore set his drink aside to reach inside his doublet. Drawing out a document, he scanned it through before speaking. Millburne tapped a foot impatiently.

"Well, well?" he demanded.

"What do you know of Lord Westfield?" asked Paramore.

"Nothing beyond the fact that he is the patron of a theater company."

"It is only one of his indulgences."

"Indulgences, Cyril?"

"Yes," said Paramore. "Lord Westfield is a sybarite. He adores fine things. He likes fine food, fine wine, fine clothes, fine women. Fine everything, in fact. Westfield's Men are merely another suit of gorgeous clothing for him to wear in public. He uses them to dazzle the eye. There is one problem, however."

"What is that?"

"Fine things come at fine prices," said Sir Eliard.

"And that disgusting old epicurean does not have the money to pay for them," resumed Paramore. "He is in debt up to his neck. Yet the more he owes, the more he goes on spending. The fellow lives entirely on credit."

"Why are you telling me this?" asked Millburne peevishly. "Most of the nobility are short of money. They borrow to survive. Lord Westfield's problems are his own concern. They hardly serve our purpose."

"But they do, Bevis."

"Oh, yes," insisted Sir Eliard, raising his glass. "They most certainly do."

Millburne was baffled. "How?"

"Observe, my friend. I will give you a lesson in the art of destruction."

When he called at the house late that afternoon, Nicholas Bracewell was surprised and pleased to see that Francis Quilter had a visitor. Owen Elias was ensconced in the one comfortable chair in the room. The Welshman got up to greet the newcomer warmly.

"What are you doing here, Owen?" asked Nicholas.

"I came to offer my help," replied Elias. "When we first heard about what happened to Frank's father, I was among those who felt that the name of Quilter might tarnish the name of the company. I am heartily ashamed of such thoughts now."

"What changed your mind?"

"You did, Nick. You were so convinced of the innocence of Gerard Quilter that I began to entertain doubts. Frank has been telling me just how much evidence the pair of you have gathered. It is damning," said Elias. "Let me fight alongside you under your banner. One more pair of hands can surely be put to some use."

"And one more pair of eyes," said Quilter. "I am very grateful, Owen."

"Employ me as you will."

"Then first know what I have learned today at Smithfield," said Nicholas.

Quilter was eager for news. "Did you show him the hat, Nick?"

"Yes, and Hermat thinks it may well be the one."

"Hermat?" echoed Elias. "Is that the hermaphrodite that Frank mentioned?"

"It is. Hermat is a curious individual," recalled Nicholas, "though it will cost you a penny to enter the booth if you wish to judge for yourself. He, or she, not only saw the murderer on the night that Moll Comfrey was killed, but he, or she, may also have recognized the hat. One thing more emerged from my visit."

"What was that?" asked Quilter.

"Hermat remembered a smell, Frank. When the man flitted past him that night, there was a sweet odor that he had never sniffed before. Bartholomew Fair is known for smells of a very different kind, none of them pleasing to the nostrils. This one was rather special."

"Why?"

"Hermat did not expect to find it on a man."

Elias was intrigued. "A woman's perfume?"

"It was something rather similar," said Nicholas. "When he realized what it might have been, Lightfoot ran to fetch it from Moll's basket, and Hermat agreed that that was what he had smelled."

"What was it, Nick?"

"A piece of soap that gave off a powerful scent. It was like a keepsake to her. The one thing she owned that Moll would never have sold. According to Lightfoot, she always slept with it gripped tight in her hand. It sweetened the air for her. During the struggle, the assassin must have rubbed up against it and gathered some of its odor on his clothing."

Quilter was dubious. "Enough for someone to detect the aroma?"

"Not any of us, Frank," admitted Nicholas, "especially when the encounter was so brief. But Hermat is not like any ordinary human being, as you can bear witness. Many things may be lacking or deformed in that weird body, but Hermat's senses are far keener than ours. That delicate nose picked up a scent that none of us would even have known was there."

"Then it is proof positive that the man he saw was indeed the killer."

"Yes," agreed Elias. "And he may well have been the same villain who tried to stab Nick in Turnmill Street. You should have taken me there with you," he chided, turning to Nicholas. "I know every inch of that place." He gave a coarse chuckle. "And one or two beauties in that street know every inch of Owen Elias."

"I'll wager that he *was* the same man," decided Nicholas. "Since he disposed of Moll with such ease, he would surely have been hired again by Sir Eliard Slaney." He gave a wry smile. "A bawdy basket, a tumbler, and an hermaphrodite. It is a peculiar chain that leads to Sir Eliard."

"Do not forget the blacksmith," said Quilter.

"Luke Furness?"

"He identified Justice Haygarth for us."

"I remember him well," said Nicholas. "And I recall those huge muscles of his. I'd sooner have the blacksmith shoe my horse than pull out my teeth. There'll be a lot of sore mouths in London when Luke Furness rides away."

"Sore ears are what we endure at the Queen's Head," complained Elias with a grimace. "Laurence has been yelling at us all. This threat of Edmund's has made him even testier than he usually is. Laurence will deafen the whole lot of us."

"We will be gravely weakened if Edmund Hoode leaves us," said Quilter sadly. "It is so unlike him to take such precipitate action. What moved him to do so?"

"Laurence paid a visit to Edmund's beloved in order to use his charms on her."

"In vain," said Nicholas. "It was a ruinous course of action, and the company is suffering as a consequence. Edmund will not even speak to him now."

"He should have sent *me* to woo the lady."

"No, Owen. Nobody should have gone. It was a cruel undertaking."

"Anything is worth trying, if it keeps Edmund by our side."

"I disagree," said Nicholas sternly. "We have no right to besiege Mistress Radley."

Quilter heaved a sigh. "I know that my name has embarrassed the company in recent days," he said, "but at least I am innocent of one charge. Edmund's departure is entirely his own decision."

"He must be stopped," asserted Elias.

Nicholas was precise. "Only by fair means, Owen, not by foul."

"You are the one person who might win him back, Nick," said Quilter, "but all of your spare time is taken up with my family troubles."

"Yours is the greater need, Frank. If your father's name is not cleared of shame, you face a whole life in disgrace. It is true that I've neglected Edmund," he said with regret, "and I feel the pangs of guilt. It spurs me on to complete our investigation as soon as we can so that I may turn my attention to Edmund."

Elias thumped his chest. "I offer my heart, my hand, and my sword."

"All three are welcome."

"What is the next move?"

Nicholas pursed his lips and stroked his beard meditatively.

"I fancy that may come from Sir Eliard Slaney," he said at length.

Barnaby Gill was not pleased to be called to the Queen's Head that evening. He had intended to seek pleasures in a tavern that was more to his taste, but the summons had an urgency that could not be ignored. Dressed in his finery, he arrived to find Laurence Firethorn brooding alone at a table in the corner. Gill sauntered across to him.

"All that I can give you is five minutes," he declared loftily.

"You'll stay five hours when you hear what I have to say, Barnaby."

"I have business elsewhere."

"Let the boy drop his breeches for someone else tonight."

"That is a disgusting remark!"

"Mend your ways," said Firethorn, "and I'll not be able to make it." He grabbed Gill by the wrist before the latter could flounce off. "Sit down, Barnaby. This is no time for us to fall out. With all your faults, you love Westfield's Men as much as any of us and will do anything to secure its future. That is why I called you here."

"What has happened, Laurence?"

"Something so dreadful that I can scarce name it."

Gill let out a gasp. "Edmund is dead?"

"No," growled Firethorn, "he is very much alive, worshiping at the altar of Mistress Avice Radley. Our one hope is that this will bring him to his senses."

"What will?"

"I sent a message to his lodging. If Edmund has one ounce of loyalty to the company that made him famous, he will surely come. Nick, too, should be here."

"You have summoned Nicholas, as well?"

"George Dart went off to fetch them both as fast as his legs could carry him. We need their counsel. You, Edmund, and I can determine the policy of Westfield's Men, but we are now menaced by something that only Nick Bracewell can help us to beat off."

"And what is that, Laurence?"

Firethorn handed him a letter. "Prepare yourself, Barnaby. Before you read it, pray to God that it is all a foolish mistake."

"Why?" He glanced at the missive. "Lord Westfield's hand."

"It was delivered to my house earlier."

"Can its contents really be so abhorrent?"

"I'll let you decide that."

Gill opened the letter to read it. Almost immediately, his face went white, and his eyes bulged in disbelief. He began to froth at the mouth. With a cry of despair, he dropped the letter as if it were red hot. Before he could make any comment to Firethorn, a shadow fell across the table. They looked up to see Nicholas Bracewell. Standing behind him, sweating from his exertions, was George Dart. Firethorn jumped up gratefully to enfold Nicholas in his arms.

"Nick, dear heart!" he exclaimed. "You were never more welcome."

"George said that I had to come as quickly as possible."

"You and Edmund, both." Firethorn glared at Dart. "Well, where is he?"

"Master Hoode declined your invitation, I fear," said Dart.

Firethorn was aghast. "What did you say?"

"He refused to come, Master Firethorn."

"Did you tell him how important this meeting was?"

"Repeatedly, sir."

"I ordered you to bring him here, George."

"He would not budge."

"You failed me," said Firethorn, raising a hand to strike.

"Do not blame the messenger," said Nicholas, intervening to save Dart from a blow. "George went first to Edmund's lodging but was given short shrift. You or I or Master Gill might have met with the same response. It is not George's fault."

Reining in his anger, Firethorn sat down again and dismissed the cowering Dart with a wave of his hand. The assistant stagekeeper shot Nicholas a look of gratitude before scampering away. Firethorn and Gill said nothing, but their expressions were eloquent. Nicholas sat down and looked from one to the other.

"What ails you both?" he asked.

"The death of a beautiful dream," said Firethorn sadly.

"Worse than that, Laurence," said Gill. "It is the end of my rule upon the stage."

"Thus it stands, Nick. Or, rather, thus it falls." He indicated the letter, and Nicholas took it up. "Lord Westfield has received notice that a certain moneylender is to pay off all his debts so that he is our patron's sole creditor. The miscreant is not named in the letter, as you see, but he gives Lord Westfield a bare month to settle the debt or he'll drive him to bankruptcy."

"There is no way that Lord Westfield can meet this demand," wailed Gill. "He owes thousands of pounds. His property and all his assets will be seized forthwith. It is only a matter of time before Westfield's Men cease to exist."

"Now do you see why I sent for you?" asked Firethorn.

Gill was morose. "Not that Nicholas can do much for us. He has no fortune to bail out our wayward patron. Nor have we, alas."

"What I can do is to provide the missing name," said Nicholas, returning the letter to Firethorn. "I know who the man is and what prompted this vicious action."

"We are facing oblivion!"

"Be silent, Barnaby," scolded Firethorn. "Listen to Nick."

Nicholas took a deep breath before delivering the bad news.

"The moneylender in question is Sir Eliard Slaney," he said.

Firethorn erupted. "Hell and damnation!"

"Who is the fellow?" asked Gill.

"The biggest bloodsucker in London."

"How can Nicholas be so sure that he is the man?"

"It can be none other," replied Nicholas. "Sir Eliard Slaney is the person whom Frank Quilter and I have been stalking these past few days. We believe that he was responsible for the false accusations that led to the execution of Frank's father."

"In other words," said Firethorn, rounding on him, "you and Frank have so annoyed Sir Eliard that he is venting his fury on the company."

"It is further proof of guilt," argued Nicholas. "Do you not see that?"

"All I see," sneered Gill, "is a deadly poison by the name of Quilter. We should have expelled Frank the moment that we realized that his father was a killer."

"Gerard Quilter was innocent."

"He is guilty of killing Westfield's Men, I know that."

"Barnaby is right," said Firethorn. "Frank has brought this down on us. I should have revoked his contract when I had the chance. I rue the day that you talked me into giving him leave of absence, Nick. We shall *all* have leave of absence now," he added, pounding the table with a fist. "Westfield's Men will vanish into thin air."

"Perhaps not," said Nicholas.

"Even you cannot get us out of this quicksand."

"Hear my advice."

"We've heard it once too often," said Gill spitefully.

"Sir Eliard Slaney has shown his hand."

"Yes," agreed Firethorn, "before he crushes us to death with it. We are to lose Edmund within a week, then crumble into dust at the end of a month. I was a fool to listen to you, Nick." He picked up the letter. "When I saw the mention of a grasping moneylender, I should have guessed that it was none other than Sir Eliard. You had warned me that he was your quarry."

Gill was indignant. "You *knew* about this man, Laurence?"

"Only what Nick had told me."

"Why did you not warn us about him?"

"I did not see any need for caution. Nick and Frank were sniffing at his heels. That is all I was given to understand. It never crossed my mind that they would put us in jeopardy by their pursuit of this moneylender."

"You are as much at fault as they," accused Gill.

"Their cause was a worthy one, Barnaby. I tried to support them."

"And brought about the collapse of all our hopes in the process."

"No," said Nicholas. "That is not true."

"It is, Nick," said Firethorn. "This moneylender will buy us out of business."

Gill pointed a finger at him. "Much of the blame must rest on your shoulders."

"I did what I felt to be right and honest."

"Is it right and honest to steal my occupation from me?"

"Stop bickering!" yelled Firethorn.

"You have betrayed us all, Laurence."

Nicholas slammed an object down on the table to bring their argument to an end. Both men fell silent and stared down at the dagger that gleamed before them.

"What is that?" asked Gill.

"The weapon that was meant to kill me yesterday," explained Nicholas coolly. "You talk of losing your occupation, Master Gill, but I came close to losing my life. And I have Sir Eliard Slaney to thank for it."

Firethorn was alarmed. "Can this be true, Nick?"

Nicholas told them about the attack, omitting the reason that had taken him to Turnmill Street but telling them enough to convince them that the moneylender had ordered his death. Firethorn was full of sympathy for his friend, but Gill saw it only from his own viewpoint.

"Are we all to be hunted down by hired assassins?" he cried.

"You are quite safe, Master Gill," said Nicholas. "Sir Eliard has found a way to stab us by legal means. He knows that Frank and I are involved with Westfield's Men. A strike at the company is a broadside against us."

Gill leapt up. "Then there's the remedy, Laurence," he urged. "Evict both Frank Quilter and Nicholas from our midst, and we are saved. Sir Eliard will not need to destroy us then. Let him know that we have got rid of the troublemakers."

"Sit down, Barnaby," ordered Firethorn.

"My plan solves everything."

"Sit down!" He reached out to pull Gill back on to his seat. "Even for you, that is a shameful suggestion. At the very moment when we should pull together, you want to cast two of our number adrift."

"But they are the ones dragging us down into the water."

"We are not," said Nicholas firmly. "Apply a little thought to the situation, and you will see that it may not be so gloomy as it appears."

"What do you mean?" asked Firethorn.

"Firstly, there is the question of time. Westfield's Men will not expire at the end of the month. If our patron cannot repay his debts," Nicholas pointed out, "that is when he may be taken to court. But the law's delay will add valuable time to our life."

"That's like saying we'll twitch a little longer at the end of the hangman's rope."

"It was Gerard Quilter who was executed. Unjustly, in our view. We have already gathered some evidence to exonerate him. Once our investigation is complete," promised Nicholas, "we will be in a position to confront Sir Eliard Slaney with his villainy and free Westfield's Men from the threat of dissolution."

"True," said Firethorn, scratching his beard. "Sir Eliard cannot enforce payment of the debts if he is languishing in prison."

Gill was skeptical. "You are assuming that he is guilty."

"He is!" attested Nicholas.

"How do we know that it can be proved?"

"Put your trust in us, Master Gill."

"We did that before," retorted Gill, "and look where it has got us!"

"Sir Eliard is far too slippery to be caught," said Firethorn.

Nicholas shook his head. "We believe otherwise."

"He is, Nick. If your guess is correct, he has manipulated the law in the most blatant way. Sir Eliard could only have done that if he had powerful friends. We have none of equal merit," he said wearily. "Except our patron, that is, but be has turned out to be our worst liability." He picked up the dagger. "Sir Eliard will stop at nothing to get his way. He now intends to push this between the shoulders of the whole company."

"That is why we must fight back."

"How?"

"It is impossible," said Gill.

"Would you rather lie down and let him trample over us?" said Nicholas, trying to shame them. "Will you admit defeat without even lifting a hand to save Westfield's Men? Yes, I know that Sir Eliard Slaney is a dangerous enemy. The speed with which he has moved shows that. One of his creatures must have looked into our affairs," he concluded. "I'll wager that he goes by the name of Cyril Paramore. It is the kind of work that gentleman would do swiftly and well. No matter who it was, Sir Eliard had enough information at his fingertips today to threaten Lord Westfield with extinction."

"When our patron falls," said Gill, "then we fall with him."

"Not if Sir Eliard Slaney falls first."

"How can we ensure that, Nick?" asked Firethorn.

"I have a plan."

"If it involves Frank Quilter," said Gill, "I'll hear none of it."

"Nor will I," agreed Firethorn.

"It involves all of us," said Nicholas quietly. "The axe is hanging over Westfield's Men. If we are to avoid its keen edge, we must fight as a company. It is the only way to stave off Sir Eliard Slaney."

"Tell us how, Nick."

"Let me speak to Edmund first."

"Edmund?" repeated Firethorn. "He does not care if we sink or swim."

"I'll play on his loyalty."

"He *has* no loyalty," declared Gill.

Firethorn was dejected. "If we are to rely on Edmund Hoode, we may as well start to dig our graves now. He'll not lift a finger to help us. A pox on it!" he exclaimed. "I do believe that this is the worst day of my life. I am spurned by our playwright, abandoned by our patron, and brought down by a foul toad of a moneylender. As for Margery, I fear that she may bar the door of our bedchamber against me." Looking up, he raised both hands to the heavens. "What further torment do you have in store for me?"

It was at that moment that Alexander Marwood appeared, hobbling across to them on a stick. His face had a deathly pallor, but there was a sharp crackle of life in his voice.

"There you are, Master Firethorn," said the landlord. "Now that I am recovered, I have some complaints to make against your company. When I needed sleep, the thunder of your performances kept me awake for hours. I demand recompense, sir."

Firethorn sagged. "Why did I have to tempt Providence?" he said.

[CHAPTER TEN]

Edmund Hoode was enjoying a contentment that he had never known before. Events had moved so swiftly that he was in a state of pleasant bewilderment. A short while ago, he had never even heard of Avice Radley, yet now he could not imagine life without her. To his glazed and adoring eyes, she was the epitome of beauty, a woman who possessed all of the female virtues yet who was, miraculously, within reach of his undeserving hands. During their brief romance, he had moved through every stage of infatuation until he had attained the deep joy of lasting togetherness. Alone of all the women in his past, she loved him in the way that he wanted to be loved, admiring him for himself as well as for his talents and intent of creating a protected world in which they could grow even closer. Hoode put something of his devotion to her in the first sonnet that he had produced. Gazing soulfully at her, he recited the closing couplet.

"And yet, I own, I think my love so pure/In thy sweet arms, I stand at heaven's door."

Avice Radley was enthralled. She gave him a kiss of gratitude on the cheek.

"Thank you, Edmund," she said. "The sonnet was beautiful."

"It needs more work on it yet."

"I would not change a single syllable."

"It is too rough-hewn."

"Not to my way of thinking."

"I had thought to weave your name into the sonnet," he confessed, "but neither Avice nor Radley lend themselves to pretty rhymes. *Sadly* and *badly* have no place in any poem that celebrates you."

She smiled. "You may find room for *madly* on another occasion."

"That word rhymes with Edmund Hoode," he declared, "for I have been in the grip of a divine madness ever since we met."

"It was so with me. When I wrote that letter to you, I gave way to a madness."

"Then we are both happy lunatics, shut away in a private Bedlam."

"Throw away the key," she said, "for I can think of no finer place to be."

They were sitting beside each other in the parlor of Avice Radley's house. Hoode's cheek was still glowing warmly from the kiss that she had bestowed upon it. Wanting to place his lips on her own cheek, he lacked the courage to lean impulsively forward, so he kissed her hand instead. She stroked his arm with her fingertips until he was tingling all over. Sufficiently emboldened, Hoode was about to embrace her when there was a knock at the front door. He moved back guiltily.

"Are you expecting a visitor?" he asked.

"No, Edmund. I want nobody to disturb us."

His voice hardened. "I hope that it is not Laurence Firethorn again."

"If it is, he will not be admitted across the threshold."

"He will try anything to lure me back again."

"You are mine now," she avowed.

There was a tap on the door; then it opened to reveal the maidservant.

"A gentleman is asking for Master Hoode," she said.

"Tell him I am not here," he replied.

"No," said Avice, overruling him. "Let us at least hear his name."

"It is Nicholas Bracewell," said the maidservant, "and he sends his apologies for disturbing you at this hour."

Avice saw the indecision in Hoode's face. She suspected that he would refuse to see anyone else from Westfield's Men, but he had spoken so warmly of its book holder that she sensed a close friendship between them. The visitor could represent no danger to her. From what she heard of him, Nicholas Bracewell would hardly seek to pay his attentions to her as Laurence Firethorn had tried to do, nor could he divert Hoode from his chosen path while she was beside him. Though she was annoyed by the intrusion, she was also curious to meet a man of whom she had heard so much praise.

"Show him in," she said to the maidservant.

Seconds later, Nicholas entered the room. After introductions had been made, he reiterated his apologies for disturbing them. Avice Radley was very impressed by his appearance and by his manner. Hoode, however, was extremely wary.

"How did you know where to find me?" he asked.

"Laurence Firethorn gave me this address," replied Nicholas. "I went first to your lodging and, since you were not there, hoped that I might track you down here."

"You have come on a fruitless errand, Nick. My answer remains the same as the one I gave to George Dart earlier. I am no longer at Laurence's beck and call."

"I understand that, Edmund."

"Then take the message back to him."

"But I have not come at his behest," said Nicholas. "Had it been left to him, I would not be here at all, for he assured me that it would be a waste of time. I like to think that I know you rather better than he."

Hoode raised a warning hand. "I'll not be persuaded, Nick."

"Our decision is inviolable," said Avice. "Nothing can change it."

"I respect your decision, Mistress Radley," said Nicholas politely. "I am not here in the vain hope of retaining Edmund's services for Westfield's Men. Mine is a much simpler request."

"In that case," decided Hoode, "speak on."

"You did promise to stay with us until the end of the month."

"That is so."

"While you are there, we still have a right to call on you."

"That was the undertaking I gave to Laurence. I'll play the parts assigned to me and do so to the best of my ability. It is the least I can offer to the company."

"Do you know what we perform on Tuesday, Edmund?"

"*The Merchant of Calais.*"

"My choice of all his plays," said Avice, clapping her hands together. She appraised Nicholas. "And I believe that *you* had a hand in its invention."

Nicholas was modest. "Edmund is the sole author, I assure you."

"Come, Nick," said the playwright graciously. "You were my inspiration."

"Providing inspiration is not the same as writing the piece."

"Writing is impossible without a creative spark, and it was you who gave me that."

"Perhaps," agreed Nicholas, pleased to hear the warmth in his friend's voice. "It is also my favorite of your plays, Edmund, because it carries so many echoes of my own family. I am glad that you think I have some claim to its authorship because that is what has brought me here today."

"What exactly do you wish Edmund to do?" asked Avice.

"Honor his contract with the company."

"In what way?"

"He is not only obliged to take part in whatever we perform," said Nicholas, "he is also required to improve or make alterations to existing plays. That's my embassy. I want some important changes made in *The Merchant of Calais*."

"But why, Nick?" wondered Hoode.

"Because it may be the one way to rescue the company from extinction."

"You see how easily it is done, Adam?" he asked. "So much for the power of money."

"Or *lack* of money, Sir Eliard."

"Those who live on credit must face a day of reckoning."

Haygarth gave a brittle laugh. "It is now at hand for Lord Westfield."

They were in the upstairs room that Sir Eliard Slaney used as his counting house. The oak shelves that lined the walls were filled with ledgers and piles of documents. More tomes and sheaves of paper lay on the table. Sir Eliard was sitting in his high-backed chair while his visitor remained standing. Though he was pleased to hear the news, Justice Haygarth was not entirely persuaded that it would solve their problem.

"Will this cunning device work, Sir Eliard?"

"It has already worked, Adam," replied the moneylender. "Once I learned that Lord Westfield was heavily in debt, I saw the way to bring his company down. Nicholas Bracewell will have no time to bother us while he is fighting to save his beloved company."

"What of Francis Quilter?"

"He is no threat to us on his own. Besides, he has a contract with the troupe, as well. If they call on all their reserves, they may summon him back to their bosom."

"But what happens then?"

"They struggle in vain to survive," said Sir Eliard, gloating happily. "When I bring their patron down, they will fall apart. Nicholas Bracewell will have been taught the consequences of meddling with me. He'll not trouble us further."

"I fear that he might."

"He'll be too busy trying to find employment elsewhere."

"He'll want revenge. So will Francis Quilter."

"They've no means to achieve it, Adam."

"They have great determination."

"That will be taken up with the battle to keep Westfield's Men in existence. By the time that is over," said Sir Eliard airily, "they'll have no stomach left to measure their strength against me. In any case, the trail will have gone cold. I'll make sure of that."

Haygarth grinned. "You have thought of everything, Sir Eliard."

"That is a precept of mine."

"I would never have believed that you could bring the company to its knees."

"We have Cyril to applaud there. The irony is that he admires Westfield's Men and would rather see them flourish than decline. He and his wife have watched them perform at the Queen's Head. But he appreciates the need for our safety."

"It is paramount," said Haygarth.

"That is why he gathered the necessary facts so quickly." Sir Eliard leafed through some of the papers on his table. "Here they are. Outstanding bills that show the full extent of Lord Westfield's debts. He has borrowed from almost every moneylender in the city apart from me." He cackled dryly. "I have the sense to charge higher interest than they do. I also make sure that I lend only to people who can be made to pay. That is the beauty of these transactions, Adam. I made a profit before I even started."

"How, Sir Eliard?"

"By offering to settle a debt while paying only half of the principal. They could not wait to take my money. Cash in hand is better than the promise of twice that amount if you know that the promise will never be honored." He squinted up at his visitor. "We are in twin professions, Adam. The law and the lending of money have a kinship. In order to get the best results, we have to be merciless. Lord West-field is like so many of his kind. He is an extravagant man without the money to sustain that extravagance. As long as there are enough fools to supply him with credit, he'll continue his prodigal ways."

"Not anymore, it seems."

"No, Adam. Even as we speak, Cyril is still calling on some of his creditors. Well," he said, spreading his arms. "It is Sunday, is it not? Are we not enjoined to *give* on the Sabbath? I have been more than liberal in the way I have dispersed my funds."

"Only to gain a higher return, Sir Eliard."

"Usury is an art."

"Nobody practices it with such consummate skill."

"That is what Nicholas Bracewell and his company will find out. They will be wiped from the face of London. Their patron will be disgraced and forced to surrender much of his property to me." He cackled again. "Is this not cleverly done, Adam?"

"It has the luster of brilliance."

Sir Eliard preened himself. "What a joyous time it is proving to be!" he said. "I send a hated enemy to the gallows at Smithfield and then, when his son has the gall to pursue me in the name of justice, I destroy the company he belongs to and make a handsome profit into the bargain."

"There have been moments of apprehension," Haygarth reminded him.

"Trivialities that were brushed aside."

"Moll Comfrey was more than a triviality, Sir Eliard."

"She was a bawdy basket of no account."

"Her evidence could have put us all behind bars."

"Only if it had been heard and believed."

"She was a serious threat to us."

"That is why I had her silenced."

"You swore that you'd have Nicholas Bracewell silenced, as well."

"He deserved the same fate."

"What went wrong?"

"He was not such easy game as the girl," admitted Sir Eliard. "But he will be utterly silenced now. We'll hear no more from him while his company is in peril."

"Is he aware of what you have done?"

"He will be very soon, Adam." He held up the sheaf of papers. "When I had enough power in my grasp, I sent Lord Westfield a courteous letter, warning him that I would need repayment of all outstanding debts within a month. It was such a pleasure to ruin his Sunday for him," he added with a grin. "I daresay that he will have passed on the tidings to Westfield's Men by now."

"What will they do, Sir Eliard?"

"The only thing they can do."

"And what is that?"

"Shake in their shoes as Armageddon approaches."

Nicholas Bracewell was succinct. He gave them a concise but lucid description of the fate that confronted Westfield's Men. He also explained why he believed that Gerard Quilter had been the victim of a cruel miscarriage of justice. Nicholas awaited their reaction. There was a guarded sympathy in Avice Radley's face, but Edmund Hoode was frankly outraged.

"God's mercy!" he cried. "This knavish moneylender would destroy us?"

"Yes," replied Nicholas. "If we do not stop him, Sir Eliard Slaney will demolish all that Westfield's Men stand for, including the excellence of Edmund Hoode's plays."

"This is brutal vengeance, indeed."

"That is why it must be resisted."

"I agree, Nick. We should fight to the death."

"But it is no longer your battle, Edmund," said Avice, putting a hand on his arm. "I am truly sorry to learn that the company may disappear. It has given me so much pleasure and, in bringing you into my life, it has earned my undying thanks. But you are bidding the company farewell."

"Not until the end of the month, Avice."

"That's but a matter of days."

"Those few days may yet redeem the situation," argued Nicholas. "If Edmund follows my advice, we may still pluck ourselves from this disaster."

"Teach me how, Nick," said Hoode.

"There is no point," challenged Avice.

"Yes, there is."

"Let them manage on their own."

"They will do that when the month is up, Avice, Until then, it is only fair that I should do all that I can to help my fellows."

"Thank you, Edmund," said Nicholas. "All that I request is the use of your time."

Avice grew prickly. "Edmund's time is devoted to me, sir."

"And rightly so, Mistress Radley. But did you not claim earlier that *The Merchant of Calais* was your choice of all his plays?"

"I did. Its theme touches my heart."

"Would you not be proud, then, if that play—the one you most admire—were the means by which Westfield's Men remained upon the stage to perform the rest of Edmund Hoode's work? Think on it," said Nicholas. "Two hours upon the boards next Tuesday could decide our whole future."

"I fail to see how," she said.

"Nor I, Nick," added Hoode.

"Then let me explain," said Nicholas. "In the past few days I have learned a great deal about Sir Eliard Slaney. He is a callous, unscrupulous, vindictive man who has forced many people into ruin and reveled in their plight. But he is also jealous of his reputation. He'll not have his name besmirched. Many people hate him, but they are too frightened to put that hatred into words. Gerard Quilter had the courage to stand up to him in court and draw some blood from Sir Eliard. He paid dearly for that."

"So it appears," said Hoode.

Avice nudged him. "Do not get involved in this, Edmund."

"These are my fellows, Avice."

"You are taking leave of them to be with me."

"I know, I know," said Hoode, "and I do so without regret. But I cannot desert them until this ogre has been vanquished. Go on, Nick," he urged. "Instruct me."

"Think of the characters in *The Merchant of Calais*," said Nicholas. "Is there not one who reminds you, if only slightly, of Sir Eliard Slaney?"

"There is Pierre Lefeaux, who supplies the loans to the merchants."

"Exactly!"

"But he is French and nowhere near as rapacious as this money-lender of ours."

"That is why I need to call on your pen," said Nicholas. "We change his nation from France to England; then we alter his name from Pierre Lefeaux to something more akin to that of our man."

"Sir Peter Lefoe, perhaps?"

"We can be more precise than that, Edmund. And more insulting. Our audience will contain many people who know Sir Eliard by repute, and some who may have suffered at his hands. They will long to see him pilloried on stage."

"What name would you suggest?"

"Sir Eliard Slimy."

Hoode laughed. "You have it, Nick! I'll play the part myself."

"Then you must look and dress the way that he does, Edmund. I can help you there, for I have seen the fellow. And the character must become more gross and disgusting," he insisted, "so that they are watching the real Sir Eliard upon stage."

"He'll sue you for libel," protested Avice.

"That is our intent," replied Nicholas. "But before he can do that, he has to see and hear what *The Merchant of Calais* contains. If we let it be known that Sir Eliard is to be mocked and vilified at the Queen's Head on Tuesday, the one person who will certainly be in the gallery is the moneylender himself."

"What will be achieved by that?"

"His disgrace, Avice," said Hoode. "I'll paint such a hideous portrait of him on stage that he'll be ridiculed by all that see it."

"To what end?" she asked sharply. "As the author of the piece, it is you who'll be arraigned, Edmund. Bear that in mind. When we live together in the country, my wealth is at your disposal, but I'll not pay any damages imposed upon you in court."

Hoode was shocked. "Avice! You promised that we would share everything."

"Within certain limits."

"There was no talk of limits earlier."

"There was no possibility that you would go to prison then," she pointed out. "And that could easily happen if you write defamatory speeches about this man. What use are you to me if you are incarcerated in a cell?"

"I looked for more understanding from you than this," said Hoode.

"Edmund will not be taken to court," said Nicholas. "The changes to his play are but a device to ensure that Sir Eliard is out of his house on Tuesday afternoon. That is where the real evidence lies," he went on. "Locked away in his counting house. While he is enduring the gibes and the raillery at the Queen's Head, we will be gathering the information that will send him and his confederates where they belong. In short, Edmund will have helped to lift the dire threat that hangs over the company."

"By heaven, I'll do it, Nick!" exclaimed Hoode.

"Wait," said Avice. "I am not sure that I agree."

"It is my bounden duty to help."

"Not when it may land you into trouble with the law."

"That will not happen, Avice. You heard what Nick said."

"I heard what he proposed," she replied, "but I am not convinced that you will meet with success. What if the evidence that is sought is not inside Sir Eliard's house? The whole project then collapses around your ears. And there's another point," she stressed. "You cannot solve one crime by committing another. Break into someone's property, and you break the law."

"It is a justified breach, Mistress Radley," said Nicholas.

"No judge will view it that way."

"It is to expose a corrupt judge that we must do it."

"I'll not condone a criminal act."

"I do not ask you to do so," said Nicholas, trying to mollify her. "This is a matter between Edmund and us. It need not concern you."

She became proprietary. "Everything about Edmund concerns me."

"Then please support him in a worthy cause."

"Nick is right," said Hoode, excited by the notion. "This way answers all. We not only expose Sir Eliard Slaney on stage for the avaricious snake that he is, but we also clear the name of a man who was unjustly executed."

"I do not accept that he was."

"Avice!"

"It is all guesswork and hearsay."

"There was no guesswork involved when they tried to kill me," said Nicholas bluntly. "Why did Sir Eliard order my death if he had nothing to hide? Here is the dagger that was commissioned for the purpose," he said, pulling it from his belt. "Sir Eliard already has to answer for the murders of Vincent Webbe and Moll Comfrey. My name came close to being added to the list of his victims."

"The evidence is overwhelming," pleaded Hoode. "You must accept it, Avice."

"All I accept is the promise you made in your sonnet."

"Nothing will change that."

"It will, if you ignore my counsel."

"What counsel?"

"Keep clear of this whole business, Edmund," she decreed. "There are too many hidden dangers. I'll not have you putting yourself at risk like this."

"Would you prefer me to let Westfield's Men perish?"

"Dismiss them from your mind."

"That's heartless!"

"It is politic," she said coldly. "Let me put it more plainly. A decision confronts you, and you must think hard before you make it."

"Loyalty requires that I go to their aid."

"I demand that you do not."

Hoode was upset. "You would make such an unjust demand of me?"

"You swore to be mine and mine alone," she insisted. "All that I do is test the strength of that vow. Choose between Westfield's Men and me. You cannot have both."

* * *

[214]

Laurence Firethorn was still in a somnolent mood when he arrived home that evening. He felt like a condemned man awaiting execution. Lord Westfield was on the verge of bankruptcy, the company that bore his name was facing destruction, and, during its final days, it would be hounded by the disagreeable landlord who had risen from his sickbed at the Queen's Head. Of more immediate significance for Firethorn was the fact that his wife was in a state of hostility, brought on by his bungled attempt to entice Avice Radley. Professional ruin was allied to marital strife. When he reached Shoreditch, he went into the house with foreboding.

Alone in the parlor, Margery gave him a frosty reception.

"So, sir," she said through gritted teeth, "you have dared to show yourself again."

"Do not chastise me further, my love. I have enough to bear, as it is."

"Why? Have you been repulsed again by Mistress Radley?"

"That harpy is the least of my worries," he moaned.

"You did not think her a harpy when you tried to board her."

He held up a hand. "Please, Margery. Spare me more pain."

"You spared me none when you called upon the lady," she said. "How did you think I felt when I learned that my husband cared so little for his marriage vows that he sought to prey on someone whom he had never even met before?"

"Circumstance forced me to act as I did."

"The presence of a beautiful woman is all the circumstance you need."

He attempted gallantry. "None is more beautiful than the one who stands before me now," he said with a tired smile.

"Leave off, Laurence. I'll have none of your false compliments."

"They come from the heart."

"What of the compliments you paid to Mistress Radley?"

"Forget the woman."

"All that your wooing did was to turn her more strongly against the company."

"There *is* no company," he cried. "Westfield's Men live on borrowed time. And not because of anything that Mistress Radley has done. She is irrelevant now. It is our patron who will bring us crashing down."

"Lord Westfield? What's amiss with him?"

"Had you been speaking to me earlier, I might have told you. Our patron sent a letter that made all our other troubles seem slight. That is why I fled the house so swiftly," he explained. "I needed to share the misery with my fellows."

Margery was disturbed. "What misery? Why this talk of borrowed time?"

"My words were chosen with care, Margery. It is borrowed time because borrowing lies at the base of it. In brief, my love, Lord West-field has borrowed us out of existence. The company will suffocate under the weight of his debts."

Firethorn told her about the threat from Sir Eliard Slaney but said nothing about the evidence that Nicholas Bracewell had been helping to gather about the moneylender. He saw no point in confusing his wife with unnecessary detail or in relating a tale of injustice that he did not fully understand himself. What concerned Margery was the future of Westfield's Men because it would have a direct impact on her family. She listened with growing horror, her antagonism chang-ing slowly to sympathy.

"So that is why you quit the house so speedily," she said. "I thought that you simply wanted to get away from your wife."

"No, my love. I longed to stay here and be reconciled."

"I nourished that same hope."

"Then you kept it well concealed."

"Why did you not tell me that the letter was from Lord West-field?"

"Conversation with you was fraught with much pain. Besides," he said, "I had to see Barnaby and the others as soon as possible. There was no time for delay."

"Who is this moneylender?" she asked. "And why does he treat Lord Westfield so ruthlessly? Is some personal grudge involved here?"

"It matters not, Margery. The simple truth is that our patron is called upon to pay money that he does not possess."

"Could he not borrow it from elsewhere?"

"Nobody else will advance him credit," said Firethorn. "He has exhausted the purses of his friends and the patience of every usurer in London. The one sensible thing that Lord Westfield did in the past was to avoid Sir Eliard Slaney, because he is the most egregious member of his trade. Now—God save him!—he's been delivered up to the rogue, and Sir Eliard means to destroy him."

"Can nothing be done to fend this man off?"

"Nothing short of running him through with a sword."

"What did the others suggest?"

"Barnaby merely wrung his hands in despair."

"And Edmund?"

"He refused even to meet with us."

"Refused?" she said in amazement. "When the company is about to disappear?"

"At the end of the month, *he* is about to disappear from the company. Edmund feels that he no longer has a stake in our future."

"That is monstrous!"

"Behold the work of Mistress Radley!"

"Is Edmund so utterly under her spell that he has no speck of loyalty? What did Nicholas make of this tragedy?" she asked. "If anyone can find a remedy, it will be him."

Firethorn shook his head. "Even he is bereft of a solution this time, my love. Nick has a plan, but it requires the help of Edmund Hoode. That traitor has already shunned us. My guess is that he'll not even open the door to Nick Bracewell."

"But he must, Laurence. They are dear friends."

"Not since Mistress Radley showed her evil face," he said bitterly. "All friendship ended there. *She* is his only friend now. We have been discarded. Nick will try his best to reason with Edmund, but his visit will be futile. Truly, we are lost."

Anne Hendrik was frankly appalled. Having waited up for Nicholas, she was shocked by his description of the meeting at Avice Radley's house. Nicholas sank down into a chair with a sigh of resignation. He was deeply wounded by what he saw as the sudden end of his friendship with Edmund Hoode.

"What has *happened* to Edmund?" she asked.

"He is in love, Anne."

"Can love cause such pain to those who were closest to him?"

"Mistress Radley is a potent lady," said Nicholas. "And there is no denying that she has great charms. She is also a person of some wealth. If he marries her, Edmund will never have to work for a living again."

"Would he let her buy him so easily?"

"She, too, acts out of love. It may be a possessive love, but there's no doubting the strength of it. In her own way," he said defensively, "Mistress Radley thinks that she is protecting Edmund from trouble. My plan, I must admit, involves a risk, but it is one that Edmund would cheerfully have taken in the past."

"Yet now he will not even listen to you."

"Oh, he listened, Anne. He even agreed to help. Then a choice was imposed upon him and his resolve crumbled. When the final decision was made, Westfield's Men were outweighed in the balance by Mistress Radley."

"What will you do, Nick?"

"Look for some other means to achieve my end."

"Sir Eliard so rarely leaves his house," she said anxiously. "His wife tells me that he spends every day in his counting house, working to increase his wealth and extend his power. Master Paramore is often there with him."

"We must find some other way to lure them out."

"That still leaves the problem of how you gain entry."

"I was hoping that you might be able to help me there, Anne."

"Me?"

"Who better?" he said. "You've been to the house a number of times. And though your dealings were with Lady Slaney, you must have seen the other occupants of the house. How many servants do they keep?"

"Six. Two men and four women."

"One of those men must drive Sir Eliard's coach. Get his master out of the house, and we lose him, as well. That means we only have one man to contend with."

"He is the cook and stays in the kitchen."

"That's cheering news. How much of the house have you seen?"

"The better part of it, Nick," she said. "Lady Slaney could not resist showing it off to me. I have even been into their bedchamber."

"What about the counting house?"

"That has always been closed to me."

"But you know exactly where it is?"

"Yes, it is upstairs."

"Could you draw me a plan of the house?" he asked. "I know how deftly you hold a pen while you design a hat for your customers. Will you put it to some other use?"

"Gladly, if it will help."

"It may be our salvation."

"Before I do so, Nick, there is something that you should know."

"Go on."

"Sir Eliard is a cautious man," she explained. "Having made so much money, he makes sure that he keeps it. Whenever he is away from his counting house, the room is kept locked. Lady Slaney made a point of telling me that."

"I expected no less, Anne. It is a problem, but we'll surmount it somehow."

She was about to move off. "I'll fetch pen and paper."

"Thank you," he said, rising to kiss her. "Edmund might let me down, but you are always there to offer support. Would that he had your constancy!"

"Is there no hope that he may change his mind?"

"None, alas."

"Petition him when he is alone, Nick."

"That will not serve our turn," he said. "Edmund is never on his own. Even when he is apart from her, Mistress Radley occupies his mind. She has given her orders, and he has obeyed them. There's no more to be said. Edmund, alas, is gone."

Crouched over the table in his lodging, Edmund Hoode worked by the light of a candle. Though it was well past midnight, he was determined not to give up until he had written another sonnet to Avice Radley. It would be filled with love and tinged with contrition, fourteen closely woven lines that embodied everything he felt about her and regretted the upset he had caused by offering to go to the aid of Westfield's Men. He told himself that she was right. If a break with his past had to be made, it should be complete. Hoode had worn himself out in the service of the company. It was unfair of them to expect any more from him. As he read through the halting lines on the page, he knew that this was the direction in which he would turn his talents. Mellifluous poetry was of more account than the verse drama that he habitually produced. A sonnet to Avice Radley was worth more than a five-act play that appealed to more vulgar palates.

Yet his brain deceived him. Knowing full well what he wanted to say, he could not find the words that expressed his desire or the rhymes and rhythms that gave the poem its shape. Six pages, covered in abandoned attempts, had already been cast aside. When he scanned the seventh, it, too, failed to inspire him. The sonnet was dull and insipid. Instead of praising his beloved, it demeaned her with its blatant inadequacy. Tossing the parchment aside, he found a fresh piece so that he could start anew, intending to celebrate his love in high-flown language that would melt her heart. But something else appeared on the blank page before him. It was the face of Nicholas Bracewell, hurt, sad, and uncomprehending. Behind him were the others with whom he had shared such joy and success in the past. Laurence Firethorn looked deeply wounded, Barnaby Gill was overcome with grief, Owen Elias was pulsing with anger, James Ingram was puzzled, and all the other members of Westfield's Men—down to the hapless George Dart—wore expressions that ranged from fury to utter astonishment.

Hoode had betrayed them in the most signal way. It was one thing to resign his place in the company. To walk away when he was in a position to secure their continued existence was quite another. Avice Radley might admire from the gallery what she had seen of Westfield's Men, but she knew nothing of the inner working of a theater company. During the rehearsal and performance of a play, hearts were bonded and minds were linked in perpetuity. The playhouse bred a comradeship that was unlike any other. A week earlier, he would have died for men like Nicholas Bracewell and Laurence Firethorn, knowing that they would willingly have made the supreme sacrifice for him. Yet he could not even bring himself to make a few changes to a play that might never have been finished had it not been for the help of the book holder. Hoode writhed with guilt.

When his thoughts turned to Avice Radley again, the remorse faded. In pursuit of her, he believed, everything was permissible. A new and better life beckoned. The sooner he shuffled off the old one, the better. He decided to say as much in the opening line of the sonnet. Dipping his quill into the ink, he wrote the first thing that sprang to mind and then paused to admire it. Hoode could not believe his eyes. Having thought of nothing but his beloved, he had somehow committed to paper four words that had no bearing on her.

The Merchant of Calais.

"This must be some mistake, Cyril," he said angrily. "They would not dare to attack me."

"I heard it voiced abroad this very morning, Sir Eliard."

"There is to be a satire on *me*?"

"Westfield's Men are striking back at you."

"I'll take out an action for libel."

"You may still be held up to ridicule," said Cyril Paramore. "Laughter is a cruel weapon. It leaves wounds that last a long time."

Paramore had called at the house in Bishopsgate to report what he had heard. He found his master in his counting house, estimating how much he had gained from his latest seizure of property. The smile of satisfaction was soon rubbed from Sir Eliard's face. He smacked the table with a palm.

"This must be stopped!"

"On what grounds, Sir Eliard?"

"The ones that you have just given me. I am to be held up for mockery."

"So it is rumored," said Paramore, "but we have no proof."

"Go to the Queen's Head and secure it. Then we'll prevent this scurrilous play from ever being presented."

"But it is not scurrilous, Sir Eliard. *The Merchant of Calais* has been licensed by the Master of the Revels and performed with success before. I have seen the piece and could recommend it warmly."

Sir Eliard glared at him. "You'd recommend a play that attacks your employer?"

"No, no. That is not what I said."

"Then what do you say?"

"We can only be sure that libel takes place if we see the performance tomorrow."

"Am I to sit there and suffer the gibes of the audience?"

"Send me on your behalf, Sir Eliard."

"But you have already seen the play."

"I am given to understand that parts of it have been rewritten," said Paramore, "so there will be enough novelty to retain my interest."

"Is that all this defamation of me will do?" asked Sir Eliard, eyes aflame. "Retain your interest? You should be as outraged as I. Nobody works as closely with me as you, Cyril. An assault on my reputation is an assault on you, as well."

"I know that, Sir Eliard. And I apologize."

"Tell me about this play."

"It concerns an English merchant, late of Calais."

"Is there a moneylender in the story?"

"Why, yes," said Paramore, searching his memory. "I believe there is, but his part in the action is quite small. He is a villainous Frenchman."

"Is this the character who will counterfeit me?"

Paramore shrugged. "There is only one way to find out, Sir Eliard. Shall I go to the Queen's Head tomorrow? I'll give you a full account of what happens."

Sir Eliard Slaney pondered, his ire mingling with a strange curiosity.

"We'll go together in disguise," he decided. "I want to see this play for myself. If they have the audacity to put me on the stage, Westfield's Men will turn to dust sooner than they imagine."

On the third day, Bartholomew Fair was as vibrant as ever. Additional visitors poured into London from the surrounding areas, and those who had already tasted the delights of Smithfield returned there once more. There was always something new to buy or see. Horse trading was especially busy, but no part of the fair lacked its surging crowd. The performing bear was at his best, the Strongest Man in England did feats of wonder before his paying audience, and the extraordinary Hermat drew the longest queues of all. Nicholas Bracewell and Francis Quilter were among the mass of visitors late that afternoon. Dodging some scavenging dogs, they made their way to the ring and singled out Lightfoot for a quiet word.

"Your time has come," Nicholas told him.

"You need my help?" asked the tumbler eagerly.

"Your help and your agility."

"Take me with you, sir."

"Tomorrow afternoon is when I'll call on you, Lightfoot."

"You'll find me waiting."

"Let me go with you, Nick," urged Quilter. "It was I who set you out on this trail and I who should be there at the finish."

"We are well short of any finish, Frank," said Nicholas. "If I am to be absent, you are needed at the Queen's Head to do my office. Though your face may be recognized onstage, none but the players will see you behind the scenes."

"I'm no book holder."

"I'm no thief, but necessity compels me to take up that occupation."

"Thievery?" said Lightfoot. "Is that what we are about?"

"Do you have any objection?"

The tumbler chortled. "None at all, sir. You've come to the right person. If I did not have a quick hand, I'd long ago have starved."

"We will not so much steal as borrow," explained Nicholas.

"That's the excuse I always give myself, sir."

"Do not forget the lock," prompted Quilter. "That is highly important."

Nicholas gave a nod. "I know. It stands between us and success." He turned to Lightfoot. "Do you have any skill in picking locks, my friend?"

"No, sir," said the tumbler. "I never mastered that art."

"Do you know anyone who has?"

"Yes, sir. And so do you."

"Do we?"

"Luke Furness the blacksmith is your man," replied Lightfoot. "He makes locks, keys, bolts, and other means of safeguarding property. If you pay him enough," he said in a conspiratorial whisper, "he'll give you a key that will open almost any door."

"We'll pay him *anything*," announced Quilter. "Let's to him straight."

* * *

[223]

There was a buzz of expectation in the yard at the Queen's Head. It was a long time since *The Merchant of Calais* had been performed there, and its reputation drew a large audience. Many who stood in the pit had never heard of Sir Eliard Slaney, but it was a name that most people in the galleries knew and, in some cases, had learned to dread. The rumor that the moneylender was about to be ridiculed onstage had spread quickly, adding a spice and promise to the occasion. Moneylenders were universally loathed, none more so than Sir Eliard. Usury was forbidden by law under a statute that had been in existence for over twenty years, because the profession was declared to be against Christian precepts. Notwithstanding this, loans were still made openly with a maximum of ten percent interest permitted. Sir Eliard Slaney was known to charge much more.

Dressed in the unfamiliar garb of a country gentleman, the moneylender was there to watch the play with Cyril Paramore, also in a disguise that hid his identity. When they took their seats in the gallery, they were unsettled to hear the name of Sir Eliard Slaney from so many sides. The rumors were true. Mockery was at hand. Their gaze was fixed so completely on the stage below that they did not notice the handsome woman who sat two rows in front of them. Avice Radley was there to enjoy her favorite play. It would be the last time that she would ever see it, and she was going to savor every moment. When the moneylender's name drifted into her ears, she did not take it seriously. Edmund Hoode had left his play untouched. Forced to make a critical choice, he had obeyed her instructions. She saw it as symbolic of a happy life together.

As the yard filled and the time of performance neared, a ripple of anticipatory delight went around the galleries. Avice Radley could not understand it, but Sir Eliard and his companion feared that they did. They began to wish they were not there, but they were trapped in the middle of a row and were compelled to remain. It was not long before the entertainment started. A fanfare rang out to silence the throng, a flag was raised above the inn, and Owen Elias stepped out in a black cloak to deliver the Prologue. His lilting Welsh voice reached every part of the yard with ease:

> *Good friends, for none but friends are gathered here,*
> *Ours is a tale of villainy and fear,*

Of foul corruption, usury and deceit.
We give to you a liar, rogue, and cheat,
Who lends out money to bring men to shame
And ruin. Sir Eliard Slimy is his name. . . .

Nicholas Bracewell heard the first appreciative roar of laughter from the audience as he and Anne Hendrik approached the house. Sir Eliard Slaney had been unmasked. Nicholas went first to the quiet lane at the rear of the property to make sure that Lightfoot was in position below the designated window. Leaning idly against a wall with a rope over his shoulder, the tumbler gave him a signal to indicate that his task would not be difficult. Nicholas rejoined Anne at the front door. He, too, was in disguise, wearing the hat and sober garments of one of her Dutch employees and composing his features into an expression of timidity worthy of Preben van Loew. When a maidservant answered her knock, Anne first asked to see Sir Eliard in order to establish that he was not on the premises. Unable to speak to the master of the house, she then requested a meeting with Lady Slaney. The visitors were invited inside.

Hearing of their arrival, Lady Slaney came bustling out of the parlor in a green velvet gown. She was torn between surprise and embarrassment.

"I did not expect to see you here again," she said.

"I felt that I had to give you an explanation, Lady Slaney," said Anne. She indicated Nicholas. "This is Jan, who works for me. I needed his protection on the journey here."

"You could have used his protection on your last visit, I fancy. My husband all but threw you from the house. I still do not understand why."

"That is why I am here."

"Sir Eliard tells me that I must find another milliner."

"May we discuss this in private, Lady Slaney?" asked Anne.

"Yes, yes. Come in."

Anne turned to Nicholas. "Wait here, Jan. I'll not be long."

Lady Slaney led the way into the parlor and shut the door. Nicholas moved swiftly, knowing that Anne would not be able to distract her former client indefinitely. Making sure that he was unseen, he crossed to the stairs and went swiftly up them. Anne's plan of the house had been accurate. He found the counting house at once and tried the door. It was locked. From inside he could hear banging noises that alarmed him. If they continued, they would certainly rouse one of the servants. But the banging suddenly stopped and was replaced by the sound of a key in the lock. There was a delay of almost a minute as it was jiggled to and fro. Nicholas began to fear that the blacksmith's skill had let them down. If he could not get into the counting house, their hopes foundered. The illiterate tumbler would certainly not be able to find on his own the evidence that they required. To Nicholas's relief, the lock then clicked back. When the door opened, Lightfoot was grinning in triumph.

"Come in, sir," he whispered.

"What was that noise?" asked Nicholas, stepping inside and closing the door behind him. "I heard banging."

"The shutters were securely bolted. I had to force my way in."

"Did anyone below see you?"

"No, sir," said Lightfoot. "I brought a rope to help me climb up and dropped it out of sight when I was in. I can get down again without it."

"Then do so at once. When I find what I want, I'll drop it down to you."

"I'll be ready."

Lightfoot went back to the open shutters, peered down into the lane, and then stood back as two people walked past. When their footsteps died away, he checked that the lane was empty and then lowered himself out the window before dropping to the ground below. Nicholas, meanwhile, was searching quickly through the documents and ledgers on the table. As he leafed through some pages, his eye fell on the name of Lord Westfield, and he glanced with misgiving at a list of the patron's outstanding debts. The extent of Lord Westfield's profligacy made his stomach lurch. But it was the biggest of the ledgers that really aroused his interest. It contained details of every penny that Sir Eliard Slaney made or spent in that year, neatly arranged in parallel columns. Nicholas flicked through the volume. As soon as he saw a record of substantial payments made to Bevis Millburne, Cyril Paramore, and Adam Haygarth, he felt a surge of pleasure. Patently, they were bribes. The ledger would provide the incontrovertible evidence that they needed.

He crossed to the window, saw Lightfoot waiting below, and then dropped the ledger into his arms. A wave of the hand sent the tumbler scurrying off down the lane to the place where they had arranged to meet up again. Nicholas closed the shutters quietly, crossed to the door and removed the key from the lock so that he could use it from outside. But there was an unforeseen hazard. When he opened the door to leave, he was confronted by a tall, slim figure who barred his way. It was the man who had tried to kill him in Turnmill Street. He was brandishing another dagger. Nicholas backed into the counting house. Looking for the chance to strike, the man went after him.

"We've met before," he sneered.

"Yes," replied Nicholas. "You crawled out of the slime in Turnmill Street."

"What are you doing in Sir Eliard's house?"

"That's my business."

"You won't leave it alive, my friend. I can promise you that."

Nicholas looked into the cold, hard, unforgiving eyes of the assassin.

"You've killed before, I fancy," he said.

"It's my trade."

"Stabbing a drunken man in an alley? Squeezing the life out of a defenseless girl like Moll Comfrey? Can you take pride from such work?"

"I do what I'm paid to do."

"How many other people has Sir Eliard asked you to kill?"

"Enough."

"And was Vincent Webbe the first?"

"I know who will be the next," said the man, lunging with the knife. "You."

Nicholas jumped back just in time, but the confined space worked in his attacker's favor. There was no means of escape. Out of the corner of his eye, Nicholas saw a pile of documents on a shelf. As the man took a menacing step closer, Nicholas reached up to sweep the documents from the shelf, sending so many pieces of paper flapping in the air that the room seemed to be filled momentarily with a flock of birds. Taking advantage of the distraction, Nicholas snatched off his hat and flung it into the man's face before diving at him. They fell to the floor. The dagger flashed at him, but Nicholas managed to grab the man's arm and turn the point of the weapon away. They grappled fiercely. With his free hand, the man punched Nicholas hard on the side of the head and wriggled violently until he threw him off.

Still clinging to his arm, Nicholas unleashed punches of his own, working to the body and drawing gasps of pain from his adversary. They rolled over on the floor, struggling wildly and scattering the documents that lay there. The man punched, kicked, gouged, and spat in a bid to subdue his opponent. It was when he tried to sink his teeth into Nicholas's face that the latter found an extra reserve of energy. Flinging the man on to his back, Nicholas sat astride him and banged his hand repeatedly on the floor until he dropped the dagger. He then pounded his face with some fearsome blows, sending blood spurting from his nose.

The man seemed to lose consciousness. Breathing heavily, Nicholas rose to his feet and looked down at him with disgust. He then bent over to pick up the dagger. Before he could do so, however, the man came back to life, grabbed the weapon, and thrust at Nicholas's stomach with vicious power. Reacting with instinct, Nicholas caught the man's wrist and twisted it so that the point of the dagger went harmlessly past his thigh. The man did not give up, striving hard to inflict a wound so that he could regain the advantage.

But Nicholas had the superior strength. As the dagger flailed around in the air, he bent the man's wrist over and then pushed down with sudden force. The blade was long and sharp. It went straight through the man's chest and into his heart. All resistance ceased. Nicholas stood up and tried to catch his breath. Having come in search of evidence, he had been forced to kill the would-be assassin in self-defense. Nicholas was content. The ledger had been purloined and the murder of Moll Comfrey had been avenged.

"Two birds," he murmured.

[CHAPTER ELEVEN]

Anne Hendrik was very conscious of how much time had passed. As she sat in the parlor with Lady Slaney, she was rapidly running out of ways to divert her. She had told the other woman how sorry she was to have offended Sir Eliard, but she did not explain why the situation had occurred, pretending instead to be baffled by his outburst. She did not appeal against his judgment in any way. Anne accepted that her relationship with Lady Slaney would have to end but hoped that they could at least part as friends.

"I have no reason to fall out with you," said Lady Slaney magnanimously.

"Nor I with you, Lady Slaney. You have ever been my best customer."

"I would have been happy to go on being so."

"Perhaps you still can be in some small measure," said Anne, taking out a scroll of parchment. "This is the design that we discussed when I called here last time. I would like to offer it to you as a parting gift."

"That is very kind of you."

"Perchance, another milliner may make the hat."

"But the design is your own."

"It grew out of your instruction, Lady Slaney. I feel that it belongs with you."

"That is some compensation," said the other, taking the design from her to examine it. When she lifted her head, she gave Anne a curious look. "My husband said that you had been spying on him. Is that true?"

"Why on earth should I do that?" asked Anne, feigning innocence.

"That is what I said to him."

"What was his reply?"

"He told me that it was none of my business and scolded me for speaking so openly to you. I've never seen him in such a violent rage. He tossed my new hat across the bedchamber, and he knew how much I cherished it. Why did he do that?" she said. "There must be *some* reason for his anger."

"He misunderstood what I was doing, Lady Slaney."

"And what was that?"

Anne shifted uneasily in her seat. Lady Slaney was a vain, limited, and self-absorbed woman, but she was not unintelligent. There was more than a hint of suspicion in the older woman's eye. She glanced towards the door.

"Why did you come today, Mistress Hendrik?" she asked.

"To offer my apology."

"You could have sent that by means of a letter."

"I wanted to give you the design on which we worked."

"That, too, could have been sent by a messenger." Lady Slaney rose to her feet and pointed at the door. "Why did you bring that fellow with you?"

"London is never safe for a woman on her own."

"Yes, but why choose that particular escort?"

"Preben van Loew was unable to come. Jan took his place."

"Not quite," said Lady Slaney. "When you brought that other Dutchman with you, he came in here with us and took part in our debate. He was the man who would have made this," she went on, waving the design under Anne's nose. "And he made all the other hats I bought from you."

"Preben is sorry to lose your custom."

"This other fellow also works for you?"

"Yes, Lady Slaney."

"Why did you leave him outside?"

"So that we could speak alone," said Anne. "The subject we discussed has been very delicate. Had Jan been present, I would have been too embarrassed to raise it."

"Yet he must know the reason that you came here."

"Up to a point, Lady Slaney."

"And he has he probably been listening outside the door."

"I think not."

"Call him in."

Anne gulped. "What?"

"Call the fellow in," repeated Lady Slaney. "I wish to know what he is doing."

"Jan is waiting for me, that is all."

"Let us see, shall we?"

She marched purposefully towards the door. Anne was dismayed, not knowing whether Nicholas would even be there and fearing the consequences if he had not yet finished his search of the counting house. She wondered how she could explain his disappearance. Lady Slaney opened the door with a flourish. Standing in the hall with his back to her was Nicholas Bracewell. Hat in hand, he turned to give her a polite smile. He looked so meek and inoffensive that nobody would have guessed that he had just been involved in a fight for his life. Having spent so much time with Anne's employees, Nicholas even managed a passable imitation of a Dutch accent.

"Vot ken I do for you, Laty Sliney?" he asked.

Edmund Hoode had never achieved so great an impact on stage in such a relatively small part. Dressed in the garb similar to that worn by Sir Eliard Slaney, he had been instructed by Nicholas Bracewell in how the moneylender looked and moved. The moment he appeared, there was a delighted cry of recognition from dozens of people in the gallery. Though the changes he had made to his play were relatively slight, the effects were far-reaching. A new prologue, singling out the villainy of Sir Eliard Slimy, had been learned that morning with relish by Owen Elias, but the playwright reserved the best lines for himself. Since *The Merchant of Calais* was a study of love and marriage as financial transactions, the role of the moneylender was critical. Playing the title role with his accustomed vigor, Laurence Firethorn chose love in place of monetary gain, spurning the blandishments of the unctuous creature who offered to make him rich by investing in his ventures. Slimy was not easily shaken off. He lapsed into persuasive prose:

> *"Borrow to prosper, good sir, borrow to prosper. Marry your purse to mine, and I'll create a fortune for you. Wealth is power, and power the greatest wealth of all. On my behalf, you'll scour each country of the world until you are a Croesus among merchants. Learn to bribe, my friend, for that's the way to rise, as I know full well. I am quite beyond the reach of the law since I keep a handful of justices in funds. Bribe a man's belly, and you will surely command his mind. I made myself rich by frighting men out of their estates. We two shall stretch my empire into foreign lands till both of us can eat, drink, touch, taste, smell, and even fornicate gold! Partners let us be!"*

The honest merchant replied with the back of his hand, knocking the moneylender to the floor and earning a burst of applause from the audience. Cursing and spitting, Sir Eliard Slimy crept away. Avice Radley did not join in the clapping. She was too shocked by what she saw as an act of defiance against her. *The Merchant of Calais* was not the play that she remembered so fondly. In emphasizing the role of the moneylender, Hoode had sharpened its edge but lost some of its romantic magic. What outraged her was the fact that he had disobeyed her. Having agreed to abide by her wishes, he had done the very thing that she had forbidden. Hoode had chosen Westfield's Men instead of her, and that rankled. A wedge had been driven between them.

Seated behind her, Sir Eliard Slaney was throbbing with fury. The portrait of him on stage was so accurate and unflattering that he winced every time the moneylender came out onstage. Until that afternoon, he had never understood the extent of his unpopularity. Sections of the audience bayed with joy at his humiliation. Cyril Paramore was highly embarrassed by the attack on his master, fearing that someone might recognize them at any moment and turn the scorn of the spectators directly at them.

Behind his hand, Sir Eliard hissed a question at his companion. "Who wrote this play, Cyril?"

"His name is Edmund Hoode," said Paramore. "Insult is added to injury because he acts the part of the moneylender himself. Sue him for libel, Sir Eliard."

"The law is too tardy a revenger. I'll set Martin on to him."

"You'll have him *killed?*"

"This calumny deserves no less," said Sir Eliard. "This cunning playwright will not live to throw his taunts at me again. I'll have Martin stab him to death and make him die slowly and in agony."

"Shall I fetch Martin for you?"

"There is no need. He stays at my house. I like him there when I am away for any length of time. Martin and his dagger are a better guard than any dog." He gave a grim chuckle. "We'll see how well this Edmund Hoode can mock me with his tongue cut out."

It was only when they were clear of the house that Anne Hendrik noticed the blood on his sleeve. She became alarmed. Nicholas Bracewell gave her a reassuring smile.

"It does not belong to me, Anne," he said.

"Then how is it spattered on your arm?"

"Let's meet with Lightfoot; then I'll tell you both."

The tumbler was waiting for them in an alley off Gracechurch Street. Nicholas introduced him to Anne. Lightfoot was polite and deferential. As he handed over the ledger, his sharp eyes caught sight of the blood, as well.

"You injured yourself, sir," he said.

"I collected a few bruises," said Nicholas, "but I shed no blood. After you left the counting house, I was cornered by the man who ambushed me in Turnmill Street."

He told them what had happened, giving few details of the fight itself but explaining that the only way to escape alive was to kill his attacker. Anne was horrified that he might have been stabbed to death while she was talking downstairs to Lady Slaney. Lightfoot was pleased yet envious.

"If only he had come in when *I* was there," he said wistfully. "I'd have strangled the life out of him. He was the villain who smothered poor Moll."

"He also confessed to the murder of Vincent Webbe," said Nicholas.

Anne shuddered. "And the attempted murder of Nicholas Bracewell."

"He'll do no more mischief with his dagger, Anne."

"But what of the consequences? They'll come looking for you, Nick."

"I killed in self-defense."

"How will you prove it? Your word may not save you from arrest."

"There'll be no pursuit of me," he said confidently, tapping the ledger. "The only arrests will be caused by this. There's evidence in this book to bring Sir Eliard and his confederates to justice. One of them has already met his fate."

"What will they do when the body is discovered?" asked Lightfoot.

"That will not happen for a little while. I fancy that Sir Eliard is still at the Queen's Head with at least another hour of the play to watch. It will take him a while to make his way out through that crowd," decided Nicholas. "By the time he unlocks his counting house, I will already have set the wheels of the law in motion."

"Shall I come with you, sir?"

"No, Lightfoot. I have another task for you."

The tumbler grinned. "Will I have the chance to fight?"

"Yes," replied Nicholas. "You'll have to push your way through the crush on London Bridge as you escort Mistress Hendrik to her house in Bankside." Lightfoot was disappointed. "Anne did valuable work this afternoon. But for her, we would never have got into the house and seized this ledger. About it straight. I'll take this evidence to the lawyer. We can then finish the work that *The Merchant of Calais* has started."

The applause that filled the yard at the Queen's Head was long and loud. For once in their lives, neither Laurence Firethorn nor Barnaby Gill minded that someone in a lesser role collected the biggest cheer. Edmund Hoode's performance as Sir Eliard Slimy had been comically sinister to those who did not know the real moneylender, and hilarious to those who did. When he came out to take his bow, he was acclaimed. His had been a sublime exercise in theatrical assassination, and the galleries reveled in it. Of the other actors, only Firethorn and Gill knew the significance of Hoode's work. At the suggestion of Nicholas Bracewell, the precarious situation of Westfield's Men was kept from the rest of the company lest it breed gloom and listlessness. Nicholas's own absence was explained away in terms of sickness, and Francis Quilter proved a highly competent deputy for him. There was a buoyant atmosphere among the players, and it was translated to the stage. *The Merchant of Calais* had never been performed with such zest.

During his first and last visit to the Queen's Head, Sir Eliard Slaney had been stretched repeatedly on the rack of satire. He had not realized the sheer power of the theater to rouse an audience to such a pitch. All around him, spectators were quoting some of the choicer lines about the moneylender. Sir Eliard had never been the object of such scorn and derision before. As he and Cyril Paramore sidled towards the stairs, they kept their heads down in shame. It was only when they reached the waiting coach that Sir Eliard was able to show his fury.

"Why did they *do* this to me?" he snarled.

"I fear that you provoked them, Sir Eliard," said Paramore.

"Oh, I'll provoke them, mark my words. I'll provoke them out of existence. I'll have the company sued for libel and the playwright sliced to bits in front of me. Sir Eliard Slimy, indeed!" he said. "Edmund Hoode will pay for that."

Paramore knew better than to interrupt his master. He let him rant wildly all the way back to the house in Bishopsgate. When they entered the house, Sir Eliard was still fuming. His wife came out of the parlor to greet him and saw him for the first time in disguise. She was puzzled.

"Why do you wear that attire, Eliard?" she wondered.

"Do not bother me, Rebecca," he replied. "Keep out of my way."

"Have I displeased you?"

"You displease me now by badgering me."

"I only sought to welcome my husband to his home."

"Where's Martin?" he demanded.

"I've not seen him all afternoon."

"He must still be here. Martin! Martin!" he yelled, walking around the ground floor of the house. "Where are you, man? Martin!"

"Shall I look for him?" she asked obligingly.

"Out of my way, Rebecca." He pushed her aside and ascended the stairs with Paramore at his heels. "Martin! Martin, are you here? I've work for you." When he came to the counting house, he took out a key and inserted it into the lock. "I ordered him to stay here. Where is the fellow?"

As he opened the door, he almost tripped over the dead man. Sir Eliard gaped, and Paramore gave a yell of surprise. It was obvious that Martin would never be able to serve his master again. Sir Eliard was the first to recover. Stepping over the corpse, he went to the table and scrabbled among his papers. He let out a cry of pain.

"My ledger!" he exclaimed. "Someone has taken my ledger!"

Henry Cleaton chortled his way through the ledger like a man who has just stumbled on a treasure chest. Names that meant nothing to Nicholas Bracewell drew a chuckle of recognition from the lawyer. He pointed with a stubby finger.

"This name may be the most damning indictment of all," he said.

Nicholas read it out. "Archibald Froggatt? I do not know the man."

"Count yourself lucky, then. Justice Froggatt was one of the most bloodthirsty judges ever to preside at a trial. He was the man who sent Gerard Quilter to his death. That is why this payment from Sir Eliard Slaney is so revealing."

"Five hundred pounds!"

"To abuse the law costs a high price," said Cleaton, "and Justice Froggatt abused it mightily. He not only sent an innocent man to the gallows, but he added more agony by having him hanged at Smithfield in the company of a witch, as well. I'll wager that it was Adam Haygarth who was the interlocutor here. He dangled the money before the judge." He indicated another amount on the page. "Justice Haygarth was well rewarded for his work, as you see." Cleaton slapped the ledger. "By all, this is wonderful! We've evidence enough to put a dozen men behind bars. How did you come by the book?"

"Let us just say that it fell into my hands," said Nicholas discreetly.

"Frank Quilter will be overjoyed at this."

"He never believed that his father could be guilty."

"No more did I," said Cleaton. "This ledger vindicates him completely."

They were in the lawyer's office. Cleaton had examined the entries in the ledger with painstaking care. It was a written confession of the sins and stratagems of Sir Eliard Slaney. The evidence that the lawyer himself had gathered was given full confirmation. Picking up the ledger, he rose to his feet.

"I need to show this to someone else," he said.

"Make sure that he is not one of Sir Eliard's creatures."

"This ledger will go to a higher authority than anyone listed here. Even the bribes of Sir Eliard could not corrupt this man. When the evidence is scrutinized, there'll be sudden justice. I would expect arrests to be made within days."

"I'll not wait until that long," said Nicholas. "Nor will Frank. He'll meet me as soon as the performance is over. We mean to call the first of the villains to account this very afternoon. We'll attack Sir Eliard at his weakest point."

"And where is that?"

"Bevis Millburne."

Edmund Hoode was in a state of ambivalence. Exhilarated by the performance that afternoon, he was having regrets about the way that he had altered his play. There was no doubting its success. Time and again, the target had been hit with unerring accuracy. If his contribution helped to salvage the future of Westfield's Men, he would be happy. Yet an act of betrayal was involved, and that left him feeling pangs of guilt. In order to aid his fellows, he had disobeyed Avice Radley's decree and done so without forewarning her. It was a double blow for her since she would have been there to watch her favorite play. Expecting to take pleasure in it, she would have been jolted by the changes made and shocked to see Hoode impersonating a man whom she had expressly banned from appearing as a character in the play. Conflicting emotions troubled Hoode as he arrived at her house. When he knocked the door, it was with great trepidation.

The maidservant invited him in and conducted him to the parlor. Avice Radley was seated at the table, composing a letter. She did not even look up as he entered. Hoode studied her in profile, admiring once again the sculptured beauty and the natural poise. He was over-whelmed with remorse at having upset her and wanted to fling him-self abjectly at her feet. But something held him back. When he cleared his throat, she put her quill aside and turned to look at him.

"So, Edmund," she said, her voice icily calm. "It is you."

"I told you that I would come as soon as I could."

"The wonder is that you dared to come at all."

"Avice!" he protested. "You promised that I could treat this house as my own."

"I am glad that you raise the subject of promises," she rejoined. "Was it not in this very room that you promised to abide by my wishes? I asked you to let Westfield's Men fight their own battles; you agreed. You gave me your solemn word."

"I know."

"Yet the promise carried no weight."

"It did, it did."

"I see none."

"Permit me to explain," he begged.

"I saw your explanation at the Queen's Head this afternoon," she said. "You dragged me there to enforce my discomfiture."

"No, Avice!"

"It was degrading. You did not even have the courtesy to warn me in advance."

"Had I done that, you would have talked me out of it."

"I thought that I already had done so, Edmund."

"So did I," he admitted.

"What, then, changed your mind?"

"I do not know."

"Was it sheer malice? Or rebellion against me?"

"Neither of those things, Avice."

"Were you telling me that your love had gone away?" she pressed. "Is that the reason you turned on me so? I did not think you could be so fickle, Edmund."

"But I am not fickle. I remain as constant as ever."

She raised an eyebrow. "As constant as you were this afternoon?"

"Forgive me. It was not intended as an insult to you."

"That is how it was received."

"I shower you with my apologies, Avice," he said effusively, "and I will do anything to get myself into your good graces again."

"Then do so by leaving me."

He shuddered. "Leaving you? Am I to be given no right of appeal?"

"You gave me none, Edmund. Had I known what mischief you planned upon that stage today, I would have appealed with all my might. I did not take you for a vengeful man, but I see that I was mistook."

"The only vengeance was directed at Sir Eliard Slaney."

"It is time to bid farewell," she said levelly.

"No," he cried, moving across to her. "You do not understand. At least, let me tell you how it came about. For the sake of the love you once bore me, hear me out."

She took a deep breath. "Very well, sir. Be brief."

"I did bow to your wishes, Avice, it is true. When I saw your strength of purpose, I sent Nick Bracewell away from here with a cracked heart. He, of all men, had the right to call on my friendship, yet I turned my back on him. It made me sad to do so."

"There was no sadness when you consented to quit the company."

"No, there was only joy and relief."

"Did it so quickly vanish?"

"It is still there," he insisted. "My feelings for you have not altered in any degree. But you must allow for other claims upon my time. Westfield's Men nurtured me, taught me, made me what I am. Those long years could not so easily be forgotten, Avice. When I left here on Sunday, I was fired with the notion of penning another sonnet in praise of you. My mind was filled with sweet phrases and pretty conceits."

"I heard neither at the Queen's Head today."

"That is because an older loyalty dictated my hand," he said. "I tried to write for you but found myself composing a new Prologue to *The Merchant of Calais*. 'Tis all done now, Avice. My debt to the company has been discharged. I am yours alone."

"For how long, Edmund?"

"For all eternity."

"And how long will that last?" she asked scornfully. "Until the company next call upon you? Until you feel the need again to disregard my orders? You swore to love and honor me for all eternity once before. Its span was a matter of days."

"Only because of circumstance."

"I fondly imagined that *I* was the only circumstance in your life."

"You were, you are, and ever more will be."

"Leave off your protestations, sir. They are too hollow."

"I acted with the best of intentions, Avice."

"Yet you achieved the worst of results," she said coldly. "You rebuffed me, treated my wishes with open contempt, and showed yourself unworthy of my love."

"Is there no way that I can earn it back again?" he pleaded.

"None, sir."

"Avice!"

"The damage is done, Edmund. It cannot be repaired."

"Would you rather I had let Westfield's Men fade out of existence?"

"Yes," she said angrily. "The first time I made trial of your love, it failed. And there is nothing I abhor so much as failure, unless it be rank disobedience. You were guilty of both, Edmund, and are no longer welcome in my house."

Hoode's dreams suddenly went up in smoke, and all that he was left with was an acrid smell in his nostrils. Still mouthing his apologies, he backed his way out and opened the front door. He walked away from Avice Radley in a daze. Hoode did not blame her for what she had done. He had brought her ire down on himself. When he was offered the one chance of marital bliss that he was ever likely to get, he had deliberately cast it away. Westfield's Men had been given priority—if only fleetingly—over Avice Radley, and she would not endure it. Love had cooled, vows of fidelity were discarded. He was completely numbed by the interview with her. It was several minutes before he realized that his feet were taking him towards the Queen's Head. One love had perished, but another remained. Rejected by Avice Radley, he would be given a hero's welcome by Laurence Firethorn and Barnaby Gill. They did not expect perfection. They and the others loved him for his weaknesses as much as for his strengths. He began to smile. There was a world elsewhere, and it was one in which he could be himself.

* * *

When Nicholas Bracewell met up with his friend, Francis Quilter had a familiar figure with him. Armed and eager, Owen Elias did not wish to miss out on what he suspected would be some violent action.

"Something is afoot, Nick," he said. "Do not deny it. There has to be a reason why Edmund hurled those thunderbolts at Sir Eliard Slaney today. When I saw Frank sneaking away, I went after him."

"I could not shake him off," said Quilter.

Nicholas smiled. "We may have employment for him."

"Sword or dagger?" asked Elias.

"Wait and see."

"And why are you dressed like a Dutch hatmaker? Do you work for Anne now?"

"I did this afternoon, Owen."

Nicholas fell in beside them and explained what had transpired. Quilter was thrilled that the crucial evidence had been obtained and that the would-be assassin had been killed with his own dagger. Though he regretted he had not been there to help Nicholas, the Welshman was fascinated by all that he heard and understood why *The Merchant of Calais* had been slanted in a particular direction that afternoon. The fact that Sir Eliard had bought up all of their patron's debts made him seethe with rage.

"Destroy us out of spite?" he roared. "Let me get my hands on the rogue."

"The law will do that," said Nicholas.

"He deserves to be hanged from the nearest tree. When they learn what he tried to do, the whole company will dance around him with glee."

"Let us confront him, Nick," said Quilter.

"No," replied Nicholas. "We will save him until the last. I think we should strike at one of his lieutenants first. A confession from him will speed up retribution."

"From whom?"

"You will soon guess when we pass the Golden Fleece."

"Bevis Millburne?"

"Yes, Frank. One of the men who sent your father to his grave and who now enjoys the proceeds of that crime. He is a liar and a

[241]

knave. I talked to the man. I do not take him to be brave and steadfast under questioning."

"I'll question the rogue with the point of my dagger," said Elias.

"It may not come to that, Owen."

When they reached the house, Nicholas sent the Welshman around to the rear before he and Quilter went up to the front door. Their knock brought a manservant to the threshold. He refused to admit them until he had gained permission from his master. Quilter was too impatient to wait. Shoving the man aside, he stepped into the hall and yelled at the top of his voice.

"Bevis Millburne! The son of Gerard Quilter would have words with you!"

The anxious face of Millburne appeared at the door of the parlor, took one look at the two visitors, and then vanished. They heard a key turning in the lock. When Quilter put his shoulder to the door, he could not budge it.

"Come, Frank," said Nicholas. "Let's see what fish Owen has caught."

They left by the front door and walked to the back of the property. Elias was as good as his word. Eyes popping and chest heaving, Millburne was pinned against a wall with a dagger at his throat. When his friends approached, the Welshmen pricked his captive's skin enough to draw blood. Millburne yelped.

"You chose the right man, Nick," said Elias genially. "Master Millburne could not be more obliging. When I offered to trim his beard for him, he promised to tell us all that we wished to know."

"Did you give false evidence against my father?" demanded Quilter.

Millburne looked hunted. Elias flicked the knife to open another small cut.

"Give the gentleman his answer, Master Millburne," he said.

"We have Sir Eliard's ledger in our possession," said Nicholas. "There is a record of payments to you and all the others involved in the conspiracy. Admit your crime now, and it might buy you some leniency."

"Yes," added Elias. "I'll only cut off *one* of your ears."

"Did you lie at my father's trial?" said Quilter, inches from Millburne's face.

The captive's resolution crumbled. Surrounded by three strong men, faced with the information that Sir Eliard's payment to him could be verified, and realizing that the forces of law and order would descend on them all with a vengeance, he did what he always did in a crisis and tried to blame others.

"I did perjure myself, sirs," he admitted, "but only under duress. Sir Eliard forced me to do it even though my senses rebelled against the notion. He and Cyril Paramore are the real culprits. Believe me, sirs, they worked on me until I consented."

Nicholas was satisfied. "Let's take him before a magistrate," he said.

"Which one?" asked Quilter with a grim chuckle. "Justice Haygarth?"

"Yes," said Nicholas. "We need to collect him on the way."

Laurence Firethorn and Barnaby Gill rarely spent much time alone. While they worked together with surpassing brilliance onstage, they were less than friendly towards each other when they left it. The mutual antagonism went deeper than professional envy. Their private lives occupied such different worlds and their attitudes towards their fellow men were at such variance that they could find nothing to share with pleasure. It was all the more surprising, then, that the two of them sat apart from the rest of the company, deep in conversation and, apparently, in close agreement for once. Everyone else contributed to the boisterous atmosphere in the taproom, but the two principal actors were solemn. Over a cup apiece of Canary wine, they brooded on their future.

"When will you tell them, Laurence?" asked Gill.

"I hope that we may never have to do so."

"The other sharers deserve to know the truth."

"They have known the truth about Lord Westfield for long enough," said Firethorn. "Our patron is a pleasure-seeker, a man so riddled with bad debts that, were he a vessel, he'd have sunk to the bed of the ocean by now."

"The likelihood is that he will take the rest of us with him."

"Not if Nick Bracewell's plan has worked."

"It is too risky."

"We did our share, Barnaby. We traduced that despicable moneylender, as we were bid. If the fellow was in the gallery, his ears would have been burned off with shame. Edmund was a most slimy Sir Eliard."

"And that's the other thing, Laurence."

"What is?"

"Nicholas may save us from bankruptcy, but even he cannot keep Edmund."

"No," sighed Firethorn. "We must resign ourselves to his loss."

Gill pulled a face. "Then we head for the wilderness."

Alexander Marwood emerged from the crowd to push his emaciated face at them. Pallid and wasted, he looked as if he had risen from his deathbed to haunt them. He wagged a skeletal finger with indignation.

"You'll bring the law down around my ears," he complained.

"Then sell finer wine and better ale," said Firethorn.

"I speak of your play, sir. It was an outrage."

"Did you see it?"

"No, Master Firethorn. I never watch your performances. Plays are an abomination. When I lay sick in bed, I was forced to listen to some of them, and that was enough of an ordeal. Now you inflict this new threat on me."

"What threat?" asked Gill.

"Prosecution."

Firethorn snorted. "You should have been prosecuted for ugliness years ago."

"Everyone is talking of the way that you mocked Sir Eliard Slaney today."

"It was no more than the rogue deserved."

"That's as may be," said Marwood, "but he is a powerful man. Nobody with any sense dares to cross Sir Eliard or they will suffer for it. When he hears what you've done, he'll bring an action against the company for libel. Since you perform in my yard, papers will be served on me, as well."

"Prison is the best place for you."

"Do not sneer, Master Firethorn. I'll demand restitution."

"Demand all you will," said Firethorn. "You'll not get a penny from us."

"The Queen's Head must not suffer."

"It has been suffering since the day you became its landlord."

"Bah!"

Marwood turned on his heel and scuttled off, muttering loudly. Firethorn and Hoode were even more subdued now. Threatened by the loss of their playwright and the disappearance of their patron, they had Marwood's unending laments to cope with, as well. They were just about to sink into a deeper misery when Edmund Hoode arrived.

"What?" he said affably. "Sitting apart from your fellows?"

"Barnaby and I had business to discuss," said Firethorn.

"Is there room at your table for me?"

"For the few days that you are here," said Gill maliciously. "Though I am not sure that I wish to drink with a man who has treated us so harshly."

"Did I treat you harshly on that stage today?" asked Hoode.

Gill was honest. "No, you did not, Edmund. You were supreme."

"You are honored," said Firethorn. "Barnaby would never confess that of me."

"I never have good cause to admit your superiority."

"You have it every time we tread the boards together."

"Then why have I never noticed it, Laurence?"

Hoode laughed. "Shame on the pair of you! I am back with you for two seconds and you fall to quarreling. I swear I've never heard you agree about anything."

"We agree about your betrayal," retorted Gill.

"Barnaby is right," said Firethorn seriously. "We are of the same mind there."

"And would this unprecedented harmony remain if I came back?" said Hoode.

"Do not tease us, Edmund. You've made your decision clear."

"It has been changed."

Firethorn was startled. "By whom?"

"By me, Laurence."

"Not by Mistress Radley?"

"No," said Hoode. "I thought that Avice was responsible until I saw that I had decided for myself. I provoked her. In making those alterations to *The Merchant of Calais,* I so offended her that she dismissed me from her house. I am rejected."

"So you come crawling back to us, do you?" said Gill.

"I never really left you, Barnaby. Do you not see? When the company's future was in the balance, what did I choose? A life of idle luxury in the country or the exigencies of the playhouse? Without knowing it," he explained, "I put the company first. In doing what I did this afternoon, I knew that I would estrange a woman whom I loved. It was almost as if I willingly divorced Avice from my heart."

"Do you really wish to stay with us, Edmund?" asked a delighted Firethorn.

"If you will have me."

"Only if you bind yourself to us more firmly this time," warned Gill.

"Impose no conditions on him, Barnaby," said Firethorn, rising to embrace the playwright. "Edmund has come home. This is the best news we've had since the landlord was taken sick. Our playwright is not only back, but he has been also rejected by a woman yet again. In short, he is the Edmund Hoode that we know and love."

"Rejected I may be," said Hoode, "but not abashed. That is the wonder of it. Lesser women have thrown me aside and left me in the pit of despondency. But this repulse brings nothing but relief. Avice sought a perfection that I could never attain, and who would share his days with a wife who will always be disappointed in him? This is my true home," he went on, gazing around the taproom. "I am never happier than when I am with my fellows. In the name of Lord Westfield, I vow to march on."

Gill was pessimistic. "If, that is, we are allowed to march anywhere."

"True," said Firethorn. "Our future is still in doubt."

"Is there no hope of redemption?" asked Hoode.

"Yes, Edmund. His name is Nick Bracewell."

The capitulation of Bevis Millburne made things much easier for them. When they dragged him in front of Justice Haygarth, the magistrate could only splutter impotently. He was questioned relentlessly by Nicholas Bracewell, threatened by a bellicose Owen Elias, and forced to defend his actions in front of the man whose father he had conspired to send to his death. With a gibbering Millburne before him, Haygarth soon gave up all pretense of being able to defend his actions. He admitted that he had suborned Justice Froggatt with money given to him by Sir Eliard Slaney and furnished them with fresh details of the moneylender's villainy. Nicholas and his friends took the two men before a trustworthy magistrate, and both culprits made full statements about their part in the conspiracy. Grateful to the self-appointed constables, the magistrate was especially pleased to be able to dispatch Adam Haygarth into custody, telling him that those who manipulated the law for their own selfish ends deserved to suffer its worst torments.

"Where now, Nick?" asked Elias, keen for more action.

"I think we shall pay a visit to Master Paramore," said Nicholas.

"Will he confess as easily as the others?"

"No, Owen. He's made a sterner stuff. He'll deny everything."

"Good," said Elias. "I'll have the pleasure of jogging his memory."

"So will I," added Quilter.

They hurried through the streets towards Paramore's house, suffused with joy at the notion of being able to expose such a gross miscarriage of justice. It looked as if the stigma would be at last lifted from the name of Quilter. Enthusiasm lent wings to their heels. However, they met with resistance this time. Millburne and Haygarth had been caught off guard and compelled to admit everything. That was not the case with Cyril Paramore. Having witnessed the grisly scene at the house in Bishopsgate, he knew the danger he was in and was taking steps to avoid it. When the three friends arrived at the house, Paramore was mounting his horse to flee the city.

"There he is!" shouted Quilter, breaking into a run. "Stop him!"

"Leave him to me," said Elias, drawing his sword.

But neither of them was able to stop the horseman. As they ran towards him. Paramore kicked his mount into a canter. Quilter was pushed back and Elias was buffeted to the ground by the animal's flank. Nicholas stood his ground in the middle of the street. Whisking off his hat, he waved it violently to and fro in front of the horse's face. It gave a loud neigh, skidded to a halt, and then rose up crazily on its back legs. Nicholas dodged its flailing hooves and pulled Paramore from the saddle. Quilter and Elias rushed up to grab the man between them and drag him roughly to his feet. Holding the bridle, Nicholas calmed the horse with soothing words.

"Who are you?" demanded Paramore. "Unhand me, sirs."

"Not until we've talked to you," said Elias. He indicated his companion. "This is Frank Quilter. I believe that you knew his father."

"I knew him well enough to send him to the gallows. He was a murderer."

"My father was an innocent man," asserted Quilter.

"Completely innocent," said Nicholas, still holding the horse. "We already have the testimony of Bevis Millburne and Justice Haygarth. Both named you as their accomplice, Master Paramore."

"Then they are liars."

"Liars and rogues," said Quilter. "Just like you."

Paramore was defiant. "You have no proof."

"We have Sir Eliard's ledger in our possession," said Nicholas, "and that proves everything. Your name appears in it alongside those of the others who took part in the conspiracy. Justice Froggatt received the largest bribe, I see."

Paramore studied him with a mixture of disgust and apprehension. Remembering the corpse he had seen at Sir Eliard's house, he began to understand what might have happened. His lip curled in a sneer.

"You must be Nicholas Bracewell," he decided.

"The very same, sir."

"Martin should have killed you in Turnmill Street."

"He tried once too often to stab me with his dagger," said Nicholas. "I was obliged to take it off him."

"You murdered him! I saw the body for myself."

"I killed in self-defense. He was armed and I was not."

"You're a thief," said Paramore, struggling vainly to shake off the two men. "You broke into Sir Eliard's house and stole his property."

"Lady Slaney invited me in," explained Nicholas. "I merely took advantage of my presence in the house to borrow the ledger and settle an old score with a hired assassin."

Elias was impatient. "Shall I knock the truth out of him, Nick?"

"I admit nothing," said Paramore boldly.

"Then you need some encouragement, my friend."

"Leave him, Owen," ordered Nicholas. "We'll return his horse to the stable then take him before the magistrate. He can join his friends in prison."

"Yes," said Elias, pinching the man's sleeve. "He wears fine clothes now, but they'll be soiled after a night or two in a filthy cell. Take a last look at the daylight, Master Paramore. You'll not be seeing it again for a long time."

"We've caught the underlings, Nick," said Quilter. "What about the man who paid them all? When do we collect him?"

"As soon as we've bestowed this fellow where he belongs," said Nicholas. "Do not worry, Frank. Sir Eliard will not get away."

Cyril Paramore's harsh laughter echoed down the street.

The quick brain that had helped Sir Eliard Slaney to amass his wealth did not let him down. When his wife told him of her visitors that afternoon, he guessed immediately that Anne Hendrik had brought Nicholas Bracewell into the house. It was the only way to explain the death of Martin and the theft of the incriminating ledger. Sir Eliard's reaction was swift. Within ten minutes, he and his wife were climbing into their coach with a number of hastily assembled belongings around them. Lady Slaney complained bitterly that she had had to leave most of her precious hats behind. Clutching his strongbox, her husband ordered her to be quiet.

"You have done enough damage already, Rebecca," he said ruefully.

His wife was bewildered. "What is going on?" she asked.

"We are quitting the house for good."

"But why?"

"I'll explain in due course."

"Where are we going, Eliard?"

"Far away," he said. "To the one place they would not think of finding us."

Henry Cleaton had underestimated the power of his own profession to move speedily. No sooner had the Lord Chief Justice heard the lawyer's tale and seen the evidence in the ledger than he dispatched mounted officers to arrest Sir Eliard Slaney. They arrived too late. Perplexed servants told them how their master had fled the house with everything that he could grab. The officers were still pressing for details as Nicholas Bracewell and the others arrived. When they heard what had happened, the newcomers understood the meaning of Cyril Paramore's laughter. He knew of Sir Eliard's flight.

"I blame myself," said Nicholas bitterly. "We gave him too much time."

Quilter sighed. "That's what I feared, Nick."

"I thought we needed to round up the others first. Their confessions rip away any hope Sir Eliard has of defense. When we caught them, we tightened the noose around his neck. That was my reasoning."

"No matter. We simply run him to ground."

Elias turned to one of the officers. "Where has he gone?"

"To Oxford, it seems," replied the man. "The servants told us he has a house there. Sir Eliard and his wife travel by coach. That means they'll leave by Ludgate. We'll after them and try to catch them up."

"Wait!" advised Nicholas. "First, search the house."

"Yes," said Quilter. "That way you may be sure the bird has flown. You do not wish to gallop off on the road to Oxford if Sir Eliard and his wife are hiding here."

"That is not the only reason to go inside, Frank." Nicholas spoke to the officer. "Look in the counting house, my friend. You'll find a body there. I can shed light on how the man came to die."

"Thank you, sir," said the officer.

He led his companions into the house to begin the search.

"Why did you tell him that, Nick?" asked Quilter. "It will only delay us."

"Come," urged Elias. "Let's borrow horses and ride after the coach. We'll find it long before these fellows."

"I'm sure that we would, Owen," said Nicholas, "but to no advantage. I do not believe that Sir Eliard and his wife are inside it."

"Why not?"

"Because he is too guileful to be caught like that. If he told the servants that he was heading for Oxford, that is the one place he will avoid. I'll wager that he sent his coach through Ludgate to decoy us."

"He will surely need it himself," said Quilter.

"I think not."

"How else could he and his wife travel?"

Nicholas pondered. He recalled the boasts that Anne Hendrik had endured from Lady Slaney. Her customer talked in fulsome terms about her husband's properties. He owned a number of houses. To which of his expensive rabbit holes would Sir Eliard run? Nicholas clicked his fingers.

"Owen," he said.

"Yes, Nick," replied the Welshman.

"I must stay here to speak with the officers. A dead body must be explained. I've nothing to fear if I tell the truth. You must go to the quayside."

"Why?"

"Find out which ships sail this evening."

"Is *that* how the devil is escaping?"

"I believe that it may be," said Nicholas. "Hurry—and wait for us there."

Elias nodded and set off down the street at a brisk pace. Quilter was mystified.

"Are they fleeing the country, then?" he asked in alarm.

"It's possible."

"Then that black-hearted rogue will outrun justice."

"No, Frank. We'll catch him yet, I promise you."

"Will we?"

"If the company will release us both for long enough."

"I'll chase Sir Eliard to the ends of the earth."

"We'll not need to go quite that far," said Nicholas with a smile. "There is one question I must ask, however. How good a sailor are you?"

Lord Westfield was in great pain. His head was pounding, his stomach aching, and his gout at its most agonizing. Alone in the parlor of his London house, he sat in a chair with his foot propped up on a stool. Ordinarily, he saw himself as a leader of fashion, but he was not wearing any of his ostentatious apparel today. He had chosen a long gown for comfort and had taken off the shoe from his throbbing foot. A cup of wine stood within reach on the table. His physician had forbidden him to drink any more alcohol, but it was the only thing that gave him any relief from the pain. Nothing, however, could still the turbulence in his mind. Whenever he contemplated the future, a rush of panic overtook him. It was the end. After years of unbridled extravagance, he was finally confronted with the reckoning. He could no longer borrow from one person in order to pay off another and gain a temporary respite. All his debts were in the hands of one man, and they were being called in. Lord Westfield was compelled to face the truth. During his long years of overindulgence, he had been committing financial suicide.

A manservant knocked before entering the room with a tentative step.

"You have a visitor, my lord," he said.

"Send him away," replied the old man irritably. "I'll receive nobody today."

"The gentleman was most insistent."

"I, too, am insistent. Whose house is this? His or mine?"

Another spasm of pain shot through him as he realized the truthful answer to the question. The house, like everything in it, was not his at all. It had been borrowed from a friend to whom he had promised to pay a rent that never actually appeared. The servant was still hovering. Lord Westfield glared at him.

"Yes, my lord," he said with a token bow. "I'll send Master Firethorn away."

Interest was sparked. "Master Firethorn? You say that Laurence Firethorn is here? Why did you not tell me so, man?"

"Is he to come or go, my lord?"

"Send him in, but warn him of my condition."

"I will."

The man gave another token bow and withdrew. Lord Westfield sat up in his chair and tried to adjust his gown. When his visitor was shown in, the old man even contrived a weary smile of welcome. Firethorn practiced his most obsequious bow.

"My lord," he said.

"You find me in torment, Master Firethorn."

"Is there anything that I may do to relieve it?"

"Nothing, sir. If my foot does not hurt, my stomach does. When that pain abates, my head begins to split. Mostly, however, all three afflictions plague me at once." He peered at his visitor. "I am a poor host."

"Not at all, my lord."

"And an even poorer patron. Poverty-stricken, in fact."

"That is what I have come to discuss," said Firethorn.

"Has the company been informed?"

"Not yet, my lord. I have only confided in certain of the sharers. Tidings like that would dampen the most ardent spirits. I spared my fellows the shock."

"The longer it is delayed, the worse it will be."

"That is one way of looking at it."

"It is the only way, Master Firethorn." He shook his head in disbelief. "No more of Westfield's Men? That's like saying there's to be no more fine wine or pretty ladies. A precious adornment is about to vanish, and my name will vanish with it." He gave a wry smile. "Do you know *why* I wanted my own theater company?"

"You've told me many times," said Firethorn tactfully.

"It can bear repetition," said the other. "I wanted to bring some harmless pleasure to the capital. I wanted Westfield's Men to be a cipher for joyous entertainment."

"And so it has been, my lord."

"Until now. All that will go. And I'll be quite forgotten as a patron."

"Never," said Firethorn. "You'll live on forever in our hearts."

"Hearts, alas, cannot contrive to pay bills."

"They can if they are stout enough." Firethorn beamed. "Let me explain, my lord. I'm no physician, but I may at least be able to medicine your mind. Your plight is not so desperate as you fear."

"But it is," croaked the old man. "Sir Eliard Slaney demands a settlement of all my debts within a calendar month. If he gave me a decade, I could not settle them. Not without borrowing heavily from someone else."

"That loan is forthcoming."

"How? The players could never raise such a sum."

"It will not have to be raised. Thus it stands."

Firethorn gave him a summary of recent events surrounding the company. When he explained why the moneylender has turned with such venom on them, he gave his patron an insight into just how corrupt and vindictive the man was. Lord Westfield was entranced. The pain in his foot gradually eased, the ache in his stomach faded away, and the pounding in his head became a gentle throb. Firethorn's news lifted his spirits completely. He smacked his palms together in appreciation.

"Heaven forbid! This book holder of yours is a hero."

"Nick Bracewell sets a high value on friendship, my lord," said Firethorn. "That is why he risked his life to help Frank Quilter in his extremity. Their efforts have been richly rewarded—and you will reap some of those rewards."

"Is it true? Sir Eliard Slaney put to flight?"

"Ignominiously."

"What of his loans?"

"He is in no position to call them in."

"This grows better and better."

"His papers have been confiscated by order of the Lord Chief Justice and all his dealings suspended. In short, my lord," continued Firethorn, rubbing his hands, "you are released from your debts, and Westfield's Men are reprieved from their death sentence."

"These are wondrous tidings," shouted the patron, unwisely trying to stand on his tender foot. He winced at the pain and then shrugged it off. "Sir Eliard routed and his vile confederates jailed? I could not have wished for more."

"Nor I, my lord."

"Except, of course, the capture of the rogue himself."

"That will soon take place."

"But you told me that he had sailed out of the country."

Firethorn grinned. "Nick Bracewell has gone after him," he said.

"What—across the *sea?*"

"Nick is something of a sailor himself. They have hired a boat. He and Frank Quilter will not let Sir Eliard get away."

Lady Rebecca Slaney was unrecognizable from the woman who had presided over the splendid house in Bishopsgate. Deprived of her wardrobe, separated from her collection of hats, hustled out of her home and forced to run like a fugitive, she had endured a testing voyage to France. Three lonely days on the coast had followed while they waited for a vessel to take them to their destination. The strain of it all transformed her appearance. Her attire was stained by travel, her hair disheveled, and her face lined with with fatigue. No matter how much she pleaded with her husband, she was given only a partial explanation of why they had had to leave London so suddenly. When they finally secured a passage from France, she tried to question him once more. They were standing on deck as the ship scudded across a calm sea. Lady Slaney was dispirited.

"Are we never to go back to England?" she said with consternation.

"It was time for us to leave, Rebecca."

"What of the property that we left behind?"

"Think no more of that," he said. "It belongs to another life."

She was desolate. "Have I lost *everything*?"

"Be brave, my love. We have more than enough." He patted the strongbox that had never left his side. "This will buy us contentment for the rest of our lives."

"But contentment comes from our position in society, and we have none. A week ago, you promised me that we would be presented at Court. Yet now we arc hiding like wanted felons."

"That's not true, Rebecca," he rejoined. "Wait until we get to the house. It was ever your favorite of all the properties we owned."

"Only because we could come and go as we pleased," she argued. "This time, it seems, we come to stay with no prospect of escape."

"Bear with me."

"How can I when you will not be honest with your wife?"

"Look," said Sir Eliard, pointing. "There is a sight to gladden your heart."

But it failed to arouse any gladness in his jaded companion. As a rule, Lady Slaney was thrilled when she got her first glimpse of Jersey. It was a place that always inspired her. This time, however, she barely gave it a glance. Instead of gazing with pleasure at the magnificent Elizabeth castle that dominated the bay of St. Helier from its high eminence, she averted her eyes. The beautiful island with its mild climate and its rich soil had lost its appeal for her. Their house was no longer one of her prized possessions. It was a place of refuge. In England, they had lived in exquisite style. On Jersey, they would be in exile.

Rocks, reefs, and currents made navigation difficult around the island. It seemed an age before the helmsman steered them safely into the harbor. Further humiliation awaited Lady Slaney. When she disembarked in London, a coach would be waiting to take them home. Here, because no letter of warning had been sent ahead, there was nobody to welcome them or to drive them in comfort to their house. They had to make do with a horse and cart that rattled noisily along and seemed intent on exploring the deepest potholes on the road. The passengers were bounced and bumped for almost a mile until they turned into the drive of their splendid residence. Sheltered by trees, the house was set at the heart of an estate of thirty acres. It was an imposing mansion with a superfluity of glass that made it dazzle in the sunlight. Sir Eliard emitted a laugh of relief, and his wife rallied for the first time.

Spotting them through the window, the steward came rushing out to greet them.

"Your rooms will soon be ready, Sir Eliard," he said.

The moneylender was puzzled. "But you were not expecting us."

"Not until a short while ago."

"You had wind of our arrival?"

"Yes, Sir Eliard," said the man. "The visitors told us that you had landed."

"Visitors?"

"They came a short while ago. That is why we had no time to harness the horses. You arrived before I could dispatch the coachman."

"Who are these visitors?"

"They gave no names, Sir Eliard."

"Where are they now?"

"Waiting for you inside."

Nicholas Bracewell and Francis Quilter stood at one of the windows and watched them approach. They felt sorry for Lady Slaney when they saw the look of dismay on her face, but they had no sympathy for her husband. Angered by the news that his whereabouts were known, Sir Eliard came striding towards the house with his cane in his hand. The visitors drew back from the window and returned to their seats. Above their heads were matching portraits of the owners of the house. Lady Slaney's haughty expression was complemented by the arrogant pose of Sir Eliard. Judging by their appearance, they might have been the rulers of the island.

When he burst into the parlor, Sir Eliard had regained his imperious tone. "Who, in God's name, are you, sirs!" he demanded.

He paled as he recognized the features of Gerard Quilter in the latter's son. When his eyes flicked to the other visitor, he guessed that it must be Nicholas Bracewell. He needed a few moments to recover his composure.

"You are trespassing on my property," he said.

"That is open to debate, Sir Eliard," returned Nicholas. "As a result of information that we placed in the hands of a lawyer, all your property has been sequestered."

"Nobody can touch me here."

"We can," said Quilter, standing up. "Do you know who I am?"

"I believe so."

"Then you will realize why I am here."

"You and Nicholas Bracewell," said Sir Eliard with measured contempt. He looked at Nicholas. "Have you come to Jersey in flight from the law?"

Nicholas rose to his feet. "That was your prerogative, Sir Eliard."

"You are a murderer and a thief. You got into my house under false pretenses and broke into my counting house by force."

"A key was used to open the door."

"However you gained access, you violated the law."

"So did your assassin when he tried to kill me," said Nicholas. "Do not dare to stand upon legality, Sir Eliard. We know that you corrupted Justice Froggatt at the trial."

"Yes," said Quilter with bitterness. "It was not enough for you to pay two of your friends to bear false witness against my father, you made that weasel of a magistrate, Adam Haygarth, bribe the judge with five hundred pounds. Justice Haygarth swore as much on the Bible when we dragged him before an honest member of his profession."

Sir Eliard became sullen. "How did you know where to find me?"

"Your wife is too free with her boasts," said Nicholas. "She told her milliner a dozen times how much she treasured this house on Jersey. I guessed that you'd be here."

"No other ship was due for France for days."

"That's why we came in our own vessel. We arrived yesterday. Hearing that no ships had come, we bided our time at the harbor. When we saw you leaving the vessel today, we came on ahead to warn your servants."

"Nick sailed with Drake," explained Quilter proudly. "A voyage to Jersey was no test of seamanship for a man who has circumnavigated the globe. We hired a fishing boat, Sir Eliard. Its stink was vile but no worse than the one inside this house."

Tired and flustered, Lady Slaney came into the room and saw the visitors. Though Nicholas was now in his more usual garb, she recognized him at once as the man who had called on her in the company of Anne Hendrik.

"That was him, Eliard," she said, pointing. "The Dutchman of whom I spoke."

"He is no more a Dutchman than you or I, Rebecca," said her husband.

"Who is he, and what is he doing in our house?"

"Leave this to me."

"I do not trust the fellow."

"Step outside a moment."

He ushered her out of the room and spoke in an undertone to his steward. The man nodded and then escorted Lady Slaney away. Servants were unloading the luggage from the cart. When one of them carried in the strongbox, Sir Eliard took it from him and brought it into the parlor. He set it down on the table.

"I am sorry that your visit is so brief," said Nicholas. "Lady Slaney may stay here, but you will have to come back with us to England."

"No less a person than the Lord Chief Justice wishes to see you," said Quilter. "He does not look kindly on those who spread corruption in the courts. You will have to bid farewell to your wife."

"Need it come to this?" asked Sir Eliard with a sly smile. "I understand your resentment, Master Quilter, and I can see that you have your father's resolve. He and I fell out, alas. He was like a burr that stuck to me wherever I went. I had to brush him off." He took out a key. "There is no way that I can bring your father back, but I can offer recompense for his loss." He unlocked the strongbox and opened the lid. "I can make you rich, Master Quilter, richer than you ever imagined."

"Keep your money!" retorted Quilter.

"Let me go, and both of you can live in luxury hereafter."

"No," said Nicholas. "Ten times the amount in your strongbox would not tempt us. Besides, Sir Eliard, the money is no longer yours to give. Your property is confiscate. Officers will soon arrive from England to take this house and all its contents into the possession of the Crown. Your strongbox will sail back with them."

"Would you take me by force?" asked Sir Eliard.

Quilter drew his sword. "Gladly. Give me the excuse to do so."

"You are foolish men. You turned down the chance to gain from this enterprise."

"Your arrest is the only gain that I seek."

"It will not be effected by you, Master Quilter."

Sir Eliard snapped his fingers, and the steward reappeared with one of the manservants. Both were armed with muskets and looked as if they knew how to use the weapons. They moved swiftly into position to cover the visitors.

Sir Eliard smirked. "Be so kind as to lay down your swords, gentlemen," he said. "And your daggers, while you are at it."

Quilter turned to Nicholas for guidance. The latter gave a nod, and then both put their weapons on the floor. Sir Eliard waved them back a few steps so that he could pick up one of the swords. He brandished it with a malicious gleam in his eye.

"Your boldness is your undoing," he told them. "Had you waited, you might have sailed from England with the officers and looked to take me in irons. As it is, you came too quick and unprepared." He indicated the other men. "It is a rule of mine that I always have someone at my back. That is why I have prospered so."

"Your prosperity is at an end, Sir Eliard," said Nicholas.

"Is it? I think not. Your warning has been timely. If others are to come in search of me, they'll not find me on the island. Lady Slaney and I will be long gone." He gave a cackle. "We'll stay, however, to ensure that you have a decent burial. Take them out!"

His men obeyed. With a musket prodding their backs, Nicholas and Quilter were forced out of the room and along a passageway to the rear of the house. They went out into a formal garden that was neatly divided by a series of hedges and trees. Still carrying the sword, Sir Eliard led the way until he came to a secluded bower. He turned to face the prisoners, irritated that they showed no fear. He waved the sword at Nicholas.

"I've half a mind to kill you myself," he said. "But for you, we'd never have been caught. My only regret is that the interfering milliner is not here to die with you. Say your prayers, sir, for you will never see the lady again."

Nicholas had, however, seen someone over the man's shoulder. He alerted Quilter with a nudge and then took a step towards Sir Eliard. His voice was calm.

"You wrong us, Sir Eliard," he said. "We have learned from your example. We, too, have someone at our back. Here he comes."

Sir Eliard and his men turned their heads to see an extraordinary sight. Hurtling towards them out of the bushes was a man who was executing a series of such rapid somersaults that it was impossible to separate his head from his feet. The prisoners took full advantage of the diversion. Nicholas quickly disarmed one of the men and then felled him with a blow from the musket. Quilter wrestled with the other man until the weapon discharged its ball harmlessly into the air. Lightfoot, meanwhile, completed his performance with the most effective trick of all. When he reached the group, he put extra spring into a final somersault and kicked Sir Eliard full in the face, splitting open his nose and knocking him backwards. Nicholas was on the moneylender in a flash to snatch the sword from his hand and hold it to his throat. Having subdued the servant, Quilter recovered the loaded musket to point it at the moneylender. The long and destructive career of Sir Eliard Slaney was finally at an end. Dazed and bloodied, he could do nothing but groan with pain.

Lightfoot spread his arms to bask in applause that did not come.

"What is wrong?" he asked in disappointment. "Did nobody enjoy my tumbling?"

"*I* enjoyed it, Lightfoot," said Quilter.

"Yes," said Nicholas. "So did I. And I can promise you one thing. Sir Eliard will remember it for the rest of his days."

Lightfoot gave his audience a mock bow.

* * *

A new play by Edmund Hoode was always an occasion of note, but the premiere of *The Duke of Verona* gave particular cause for celebration. The fear of extinction had been lifted from Westfield's Men, enabling a revivified Laurence Firethorn to blossom in the title role and encouraging Barnaby Gill and Owen Elias to shine brilliantly in supporting parts. United once more with his fellows, the playwright himself caught the eye in the small but telling role of a Turkish ambassador. Another deserter had returned. Now that his father had been exonerated and given a posthumous pardon, Francis Quilter was restored to the company and acted with a new passion. The rest of the actors were unaware of how close they had come to disaster, but they followed where the leading players led. Nicholas Bracewell controlled everything with unhurried ease.

The Duke of Verona might not be a masterpiece, but it was a stirring drama, containing moments of high tragedy that were offset by scenes of comic genius, and touching on themes of loyalty and betrayal. The audience at the Queen's Head was spellbound for two hours in the afternoon sun. Anne Hendrik and Preben van Loew watched in wonderment. Lightfoot was an even more delighted spectator. Avice Radley was a wistful onlooker, admiring the quality of the play yet having grave reservations about its author. But the person who enjoyed the performance most was Lord Westfield himself, resplendent in a new suit and surrounded by an entourage that was even larger and more decadent than usual. Lord Westfield was back in his element. The closing lines of the play had a special significance for him.

All troubles now are gone, all dangers fled,
The noble Duke with bravery has led
The fight against his foes without surcease,
To triumph as the patron saint of peace.

Spurred on by the words in the Epilogue, he was at his most saintly and patronizing when he welcomed the members of the company to a feast in a private room at the Queen's Head. It was a rare treat for Westfield's Men. Their patron supported his troupe from his habitual seat in the gallery, but he never mingled with them, still less did he offer them a treat of any kind. They fell on the banquet with relish. As he bit into a leg of chicken, Firethorn turned to his book holder.

"This is all your doing, Nick," he said gratefully.

"Frank Quilter started it all," replied Nicholas. "Had it not been for his burning faith in his father, I would never have ventured on this business."

"I am glad that you did. But you must take all the credit for Edmund's return. Your appeal not only rescued him from Mistress Radley," Firethorn pointed out, "it also gave Edmund the urge to finish the new play. You saw the result this afternoon."

"Another success for Westfield's Men."

"Our patron revels in it. And there's more bounty yet."

"Is there?"

"Yes," said Firethorn, sipping his wine. "We actually coaxed a smile out of that ghoulish landlord. When I told him that Lord Westfield would be gracing us with his presence at a feast, Alexander Marwood all but kissed me."

"I am not surprised," said Nicholas, looking along a table that was laden with delicious food and expensive drink. "This celebration of ours will put a lot of money into the landlord's purse."

"That is the only thing that worries me, Nick."

"What is?"

Firethorn waved an arm. "How on earth can Lord Westfield pay for all of this?"

"With ease," said Nicholas. "Our patron will borrow the money."

They joined in the general laughter.

DEMCO